WHITHER THOU GOEST

REDMOND CIVIL WAR ERA ROMANCE SERIES
BOOK 6

T. NOVAN
TAYLOR RICKARD

AUSXIP PUBLISHING

Whither Thou Goest

Edited by Rosa Alonso
Cover Design by Mary D. Brooks
Cover Illustration by Lucia Nobrega
Interior Design by AUSXIP Publishing

ISBN: 9780648966784

Published by AUSXIP Publishing
www.ausxippublishing.com

DEDICATION

Dedicated to the brave and determined critical workers, whether they be doctors, nurses, first responders, grocery workers, druggists, truck drivers, and all the others who have kept life going during this horrific pandemic that has taken so many lives. Without them, we could not go on.

—T. Novan and Taylor Rickard
December 2020

HISTORICAL NOTES

This series of books started as a pair of short stories, but over time, it grew first into a book and then into an historical saga that explores the economic and social evolution of one family that, when completed, will reflect the times and stresses of the past hundred and fifty years of American history.

The Redmond family was founded by Charlie Redmond, a transgendered woman who ran from an abusive father, took the identity of a man, and rose through the ranks of the United States army to become a well-respected officer and achieve the rank of brigadier general by the end of the Civil War.

In actuality, there were a number of women who served in both the Union and the Confederate armies. The highest rank that a woman rose to, at least that we know of, was a major under the command of Philip Sheridan.

Wintering over in Culpeper, Virginia, a community that saw both southern and northern troops sweep through its lands repeatedly during the war, Charlie met Rebecca Gaines, a southern war widow and owner of what had once been one of the finest horse farms in Virginia.

These two survivors met, fell in love, and adopted a small horde of war orphans to begin what would become a strong family with a tradition of care and support for the community that would help Culpeper return to the successful farming area it once was.

But the trip to prosperity was not an easy one. The years immediately following the war were particularly hard in the southern states. There had been so much damage done to the land, especially in Virginia and Tennessee, where many of the major battles had been fought, that recovery was difficult. Labor resources were scarce, as many of the men had been killed in the war, and many of the Negro families had fled to the north after the war looking for work.

At the same time, the returning southern soldiers were still angry and resentful. For these men, the war had destroyed their way of life, their heritage, and their culture. The concept of freed blacks was alien, and the fact that colored men would work for a lesser wage, taking away jobs from poor white men, was a scourge. Yankees (carpetbaggers) and southern unionists (scallywags) were equally reviled. To add insult to injury, the southern states were not immediately reinstated to the union. Instead, they were under military control, with the criminal courts, law enforcement and many other governmental functions under the control of the military or the Freedman's Bureau, which was established to help the blacks acclimate to their new status as free citizens.

It is from this roiling cauldron of resentment and anger that the Ku Klux Klan in Tennessee, the Crimson Shirts in South Carolina, and similar organizations around the south arose. The behaviors of some of the characters in this story are modeled on actual events across the south in the years after the war.

After his second term as president, Grant and his wife Julia did indeed take a world tour. While the years immediately following the Civil War saw the rise of the robber barons, the 1880s were really the height of the Gilded Age. The robber barons were living the high life and building magnificent residences; they were also building public monuments to themselves in the form of magnificent theaters (Carnegie Hall), museums (Peabody Museum); endowments to universities, and other very public endowments. The working class were also doing well, once the labor unions established a foothold. At the national level, things were fairly quiet, as it was the era of the "forgettable presidents" and "do-nothing" politics. The trains opened the nation and it was a period of great growth, economically, culturally, and socially.

The role of women in society was also changing, though more slowly. More women were attending universities, and during this period, women slowly became accepted into the more advanced realms of academia. The first woman to officially be awarded a scientific Ph.D. was Winifred Edgerton Merrill, who received her degree from Columbia University in Mathematics in 1886.

The Homestead at Warm Springs has been and continues to be a place of healing, spa, and resort of one sort or another for hundreds of years. It was a place of healing for the American Indians, a resort as early at the early 1800s when Thomas Jefferson visited, a European style spa since the 1840s and continues to be a major spa and resort in western Virginia.

While many of the major players in this book are fictional, we have based a number of the secondary characters on real historical figures and on our beliefs on how they would present themselves based on our careful research about them.

As ever, we have tried to represent the historical context accurately and realistically, drawing on a wide range of research resources. And if you are curious, yes, General Grant's return to the United States after his world tour did include a massive parade through Chicago and a reunion dinner party that lasted into the small hours of the morning, with Samuel Clemens (aka Mark Twain) delivering the final speech of the evening.

Taylor Rickard, December 2020

UNITED STATES

The Redmond Household

Major General Charles "Charlie" Huger Redmond, US Army
Rebecca Anne Randolph Gaines Redmond, his wife
Prince and Dr. Tongzhi Xiang (Rex), member of Chinese Royal
Family, family friend and physician

Their children:
Darby Sweet Redmond
Stella Lord Redmond, Darby's wife
Jerome Huger (LJ) Redmond, Darby and Stella's son
Rachel Amelia Redmond, Darby and Stella's first daughter
Ruth Charlotte Redmond, Darby and Stella's second daughter
Suzanne Sweet Redmond Nailer
Jeremiah Carter, Samantha Nailer's son, a leather worker,
Suzanne's husband
Baby Andy Nailer, Suzanne and Jeremiah's adopted son, fathered
by Andy Redmond
Emily (Em, Squeak, Imp) Adams Redmond
Charles "Buddy" Huger Redmond II
Andrew (Andy) Richard Adams Redmond
Eliza Whitehead Redmond, Andy's wife

Their Staff and Household
Albert Randolph, Rebecca's cousin and Redmond Stables' buyer
Robert Brooks, barn manager

Otis Washington, the butler and major domo
Sarah Coleman, the senior cook (emeritus)
CeCe Coleman, the head cook
Beulah Jones, the senior housekeeper (emeritus)
Tess Jones, the head housekeeper
Louis, Charlie's valet
Lizbet Coleman, Rebecca's lady's maid, Tomas's wife
Bridget O'Connor, Roselle Jackson's cousin and Rebecca's lady's maid after Lizbet and Tomas moved to Washington.
Tomas Coleman, Charlie's old valet, now a Physician in Culpeper, moving to teach at Howard University
Alfred, the coachman
Seth Jones, footman and later Buddy's batman
Sammy, runner at Mountain View
Harriet Jones, Baby Andrew's nursemaid
Jack, Charlie's Horse

Residents of Culpeper:
Lt. Colonel Richard Polk
Dr. Elizabeth Walker, his wife

Their Children
Richard "Dickon" Polk II
Arial Polk
Esther White Jackson, his wife and tea room owner
Roselle "Ro" Jackson, his niece
Miss Mary Allison Simms, Ro's companion
Little John Jackson, Ro and Allison's son
Duncan Nailer, carpenter and cabinet maker
Samantha Carter Nailer, his wife and Jeremiah's mother
Samuel "Sam" Duncan Nailer, their son
John Foxworth, family tutor and headmaster of Culpeper School

Annabelle Calver Foxworth, his wife and school teacher
Jamie Benson, bar manager for Esther White at Jocko's Bar
Frank Granville, local blacksmith
Frank Halliburton, banker
Eloise Langley Halliburton, Charlie's secretary
Jimmy, black teamster
George, black teamster
Mrs. Allen, owner of a local tavern
Elmer Whitehead, farmer, father of Eliza Whitehead Redmond
Brenda Whitehead, his wife

Washington DC Residents:
Jerome Lord, attorney
Amelia Lord, his wife
General Ulysses S. Grant, President of the United States
Lieutenant General Philip Sheridan

Other Characters (in Charleston, Boston, New York, West Point, Warm Springs)
Joshua, boy that Charlie saved from his father's wrath in Charleston years ago
Fitzroy Lee, Virginia politician
Carolyn, Em's lady's maid
Mrs. Afton, Em's landlady
Dr. Frederic Ward Putnam, Em's advisor at Harvard
Erminnie Smith, Ethnologist, friend of Putnam's
General John Schofield, commandant, West Point
William Jacob Baer, Cartographer, Anthropology student (became miniature artist)
Horatio Hale, ethnologist, Anthropology student
Mr. Braxton, Manager of Kentucky farm
Thomas Goode, Inn keeper, The Homestead

M.E. Ingalls, with Chesapeake and Ohio Railroad
Louisa Ingalls, his wife
John Pierpont Morgan, Banker
Frances Morgan, his wife
Anthony Drexel, banker
Ellen Drexel, his wife

PROLOGUE

IN THE FINAL days of the American Civil War, two very unique people came together to establish what will become a southern dynasty. Colonel Charles Huger Redmond brought his cavalry regiment, the 13th Pennsylvania, to the formerly bustling town of Culpeper, Virginia to establish winter headquarters that would allow for the protection of critical rail lines. In order to support his men and horses until the upcoming spring campaign, their winter encampment also required the taking over of lands owned by Confederate widow Rebecca Gaines.

Charlie not only took over Rebecca's lands for the winter, but he took over her heart as well. For his part, Charlie was alarmed to realize he had become romantically involved with the lovely southerner, for he hides a secret that, if discovered, would mean social disgrace and the end of a distinguished military career. Under the carefully crafted and protected military façade, Charlie is a woman.

Before Charlie, who had now been elevated to the rank of brigadier general, and the 13th Pennsylvania were ordered back into the field of battle, they were married, in part so that Charlie could continue to protect and provide for Rebecca and for the two orphaned children, Emily and Andrew, they had taken in and planned to adopt.

During the final months of the war, Rebecca took in waves of refugees; women and children who had been made homeless by the ravages of the war. One of these included the infant son of a notorious Washington prostitute and one of the conspirators who orchestrated President Lincoln's assassination, whom she adopted.

Charlie and his troops saw battle after battle, from Petersburg to Appomattox, where Charlie was terribly wounded and the Army of Virginia was forced to surrender.

With the support of Dr. Elizabeth Walker, his regiment's physician, and his batman Jocko Jackson, Charlie's life was saved, but he was badly injured and permanently scarred.

The town of Culpeper began to recover after the end of the war, and several of Charlie's companions from the 13th Pennsylvania chose to join their leader and settle in the shattered town. With the end of the war, men and families were slowly returning to their homes or what was left of them, and with the support of the handful of Unionists, began the slow process of rebuilding. Elizabeth Walker, who married Charlie's second in command Richard Polk, settled in to be the town's only physician.

There were a few people in Culpeper who supported the Unionists; others were still angry and resentful. The reconstruction of the south had begun, and for Charlie, Rebecca and the residents of Culpeper, the next years were an uphill battle.

Much of the south was still under military rule, and even those who were committed to restoring the economic and social well-being of their communities were faced with many challenges. These years also saw the creation of the Ku Klux Klan and organizations like them, who tried to repress the Negro community from finding a new place in the economy and political environments through threats and even violence. Charlie, Rebecca and their family and friends faced many challenges, both personal and political, as Culpeper struggled to find its place in the post-war world.

In this morass of emotional, political and economic turmoil, Charlie was charged with the murder of the leader of the local, and very resentful, anti-abolitionist after months of his family and friends being harassed by these angry men. It was only through a last-minute chance of luck that his innocence was demonstrated and Charlie was vindicated.

In a rather abrupt about face, the town elected Charlie as their mayor, and he was left to lead Culpeper, and Virginia, to reinstatement within the Union. At least he and the family managed to escape from being called on by President Grant to serve in his administration.

After four years of hard work and long hours as mayor, guiding Culpeper and by extension Virginia back to economic stability and to statehood, Charlie was ready to retire and help his wife run their horse farm, raise his children, and lead the life of a private citizen.

But Grant had been elected to a second term, and this time, Charlie and Rebecca had no excuse to avoid being drawn into international politics.

Grant's administration faced scandal after scandal – some because of Grant's less than honorable family members, others because of the power and opportunities available as gold and silver were found in the American west, and global trade was burgeoning with the control of the British East India Company.

Grant thrust Charlie and Rebecca into this maelstrom of international trade and politics, as they are the only people Grant will trust with reaffirming the delicate relationship with the powerful British empire and the sometimes-demanding queen who controls it all. Charlie and Rebecca walked the path of politics and power in the great city of London. They had only begun to realize what pitfalls lie ahead.

As Queen Victoria started to dismantle the incredibly powerful East India Company, key stockholders were fighting to maintain their dominance in world trade. They did not appreciate the independence that traders from the United States tried to maintain and resorted to every strategy they could devise to hold on to their trade advantages – and their incomes. When normal negotiations did not get them the results they wanted, they resorted to every dirty trick they could dream up. The clever and business savvy American ambassador was a thorn in their side, so while the previous ambassador was easily discredited, Charles Redmond became a major threat. After battling off multiple attacks on Rebecca's and his own integrity, Charlie managed to maintain America's trade advantages and make some very beneficial deals in the process.

The family settled into life in England after the challenges of dealing with the now dissolved East India Company. Darby, while still at university, married his beloved Stella and welcomed their first child, Little Jerome, or L.J., into the world. Em found a Stone-Age trading site, and even at her early age, coupled with meeting with Charles Darwin, Thomas and Thomas Henry Huxley, began what would become her life's work under the supervision of Augustus Henry Lane-Fox Pitt Rivers, one of the world's leading archeologists. Sue anticipated returning to Culpeper to marry Jeremiah Carter, her childhood love, while taking a world of new knowledge about breeding thoroughbred horses. And the boys, Buddy and Andy, were boys – full of curiosity about the world and the audacity of youth.

All was well, until a telegram arrived from Washington ordering Charlie home immediately. Vice President Henry Wilson had died suddenly of a stroke and Grant needed someone he trusted to take his place. Leaving the children behind with Rex to shepherd them home, Charlie and Rebecca returned to Washington to face whatever was next. It was not to be as anyone expected.

CHAPTER 1

TUESDAY, SEPTEMBER 30, 1879

A DEEPLY DRAWN and leisurely exhaled breath signaled the fact that one of the two occupants of the bed was beginning the process of waking.

Rebecca stretched and then stretched again, very slowly. Her entire body flexed against the form next to hers in a way that was so familiar after more than a decade, it was difficult for Rebecca to tell where she ended and Charlie began. She smiled even before opening her eyes and placed a tender kiss on his exposed neck, drawing another deep breath slowly through her nostrils as she did.

There was just something about his scent first thing in the morning; she loved it. She always had. Rebecca had absolutely no intention of waking him. Though if she stayed next to him another minute she would want to do so, desperately.

However, today was Charlie's fiftieth birthday and she intended to let him sleep until he chose to get out of bed. As a matter of fact, she intended to do her best to spoil him all day long.

As she lay there next to him, her mind wandered to that very dark place four years ago. It had been the most terrifying time of her life and if it had not been for her dear husband's love, commitment, and determination, she knew she would not have come through it as well as she had.

She remembered the day it happened like it was yesterday, even though memories caught in the after-effects were still fleeting at best.

Charlie had been sworn in as Vice President of the United States. Morrison Waite had done the honors in the Oval Office as soon as they had returned from London.

She could recall standing there, holding the Bible and smiling. His eyes never left hers as he recited the oath. He looked so handsome, so dignified. She was so proud of him. The culmination of a lifetime of work had actually placed him where he should be, the second most powerful man in America. She remembered thinking he would be a magnificent Vice President for U.S. Grant's second administration.

She could even recall an admittedly unchristian moment of wondering what the citizens of Culpeper would think when they heard this news. She remembered inwardly chuckling at the idea of the crow and bitterness that would be eaten for weeks to come.

As they were making their way back to the Willard to get ready for a small reception President Grant had arranged, her world went sideways and then upside-down.

She remembered getting dizzy and feeling like she was falling, or that the earth was rapidly falling away from her. Then, there was the blinding white flash of light and pain in her head. She thought she called out to Charlie, but she could not be sure.

Darkness and confusion engulfed her, holding her in their

terrifying embrace, the results of which had kept her mind and body prisoner for nearly two years.

The doctors had called it an apoplectic seizure.

They had told Charlie that blockage of the carotid artery in her neck had caused her to pass out, that her brain was being deprived of blood. They had told him she needed immediate surgery or she would die. Even with it, he should expect her to be permanently disabled, both mentally and physically.

Her medical team in Washington recommended to Charlie that he consider sending her to the Ladies Lying-in Hospital, where she could be properly cared for during the remainder of her life.

It had been the first in a long line of heart wrenching choices he had to make during that first seventy-two hours of the crisis. He had also become the shortest serving Vice President in American history, giving notice just twelve hours after having been sworn in. His status had not even been recorded in the Congressional Record before he resigned.

Her illness had cost him the appointment of a lifetime. He had given it up without a second thought or hesitation. Her life and wellbeing were far more important to him.

Charlie made it clear to everyone around him, there was no way he was going to send his beloved Rebecca away. Nor would he leave her side. No matter what they might be facing, they would face it together.

She had been in and out of fleeting consciousness for nearly two weeks. When she finally awoke, the very first thing she felt were her fingers tangled in Charlie's hair as he lay sleeping as near to her as he could get. His head was resting on her stomach, his left arm thrown across her waist, while his body was slumped in a chair at her bedside.

Elizabeth had told her many months later, when Rebecca

could finally comprehend again, that Charlie never left her side, not even for a moment. He had read to her. Talked to her. Played guitar and sang to her. He prayed for her. He even staged chess games that she always won. But most of all, he just begged her to live.

The doctor had related her own moment of fighting tears as she watched her friend, crying while holding his cherished wife's hand and begging her to come back to him; pleading for her to live, to simply open her eyes.

Then there had been the early months of intensive therapy and relearning so much. The seizure had affected her right side, leaving her mostly paralyzed. She had to learn to walk again. She had to learn how to hold a cup and pen again. Nearly a year was spent simply helping her understand those around her.

She had been subject to periodic speech problems, with both speaking, and comprehending what was being said to her. Bouts of confusion had been normal for months on end, resulting in her being frightened and angry some of the time. She still had some trouble reading, but luckily there were more than enough people around willing to help her with that.

When Charlie sent to England for the children to return home, Rex had returned to the States with them. Between the two dedicated men, they had spent every single day, for nearly two and a half years making her whole again.

She gave his neck, one last tiny kiss, and gently extracted herself from their bed. Charlie mumbled her name, grumbling a bit as Rebecca placed her pillow in his arms, but then he cuddled the offering.

Her pillow was still warm and held her scent. With a sweet smile on his face, never even opening his eyes, he began the gentle snore that she knew meant he was still sound asleep.

She carefully moved to their washroom, closing the bedroom

door quietly. Ringing for Lizbet, she made her way to her dressing table and began the process of laying out her brush and hairpins.

Her lady's maid entered with a bright smile, and her mistress's clothes for the day. A simple burgundy day dress that was one of Charlie's favorites had been chosen the night before as was now their custom. "Good morning, Miss Rebecca. How are you feeling this morning?"

"I am fine, Lizbet. Excited for the general's birthday celebrations this week."

Lizbet smiled and nodded as she began brushing the nearly waist-length hair that she knew better than her own after tending it for so many years. "Another big party, I expect."

"Are there any other kind in this house?" Rebecca laughed.

"No, ma'am, there sure isn't." The faithful servant chuckled as well. "Fifty is a big number, too, especially for a man like the general."

This caused Rebecca to pause and glance back. "Like Charlie? How?"

"You know? No disrespect intended, Miss Rebecca, but men who aren't as healthy as they could be. I mean, he has had some serious colds and fevers. He hasn't ever been quite right since the fire, and then there is the damage to his body from the war that he has lived with for so long. I've known men who came home with far less troubles and already died. The general is just a strong fellow."

Rebecca nodded, sighing as she did, giving proper thanks to her deity. "Thank God."

"We do every day, Miss Rebecca. For him and you both."

"So," Rebecca looked to her faithful servant through the reflection in her mirror, "Are you and Tomas ready to make the big move?"

Lizbet's hands were still as she looked to her employer and friend. "Yes, ma'am, very nearly. Having the fall and winter to prepare has truly been wonderful."

"If there is anything I may do to help, you only need ask. I am very sorry to lose you, Lizbet, but I am thrilled for Dr. Coleman. A position as prestigious as this for a man so young is impressive. I know you will do well in Washington."

"It never would have been possible without Dr. Walker. That paper she insisted they write together about General Charlie and his injuries and recovery from the war was the thing that caught the attention of the Howard administration."

"And what, Mrs. Coleman, will you do with yourself? As the wife of a professor and physician, your social status has changed considerably."

Lizbet sighed, placing the brush on the table before taking her seat on the stool next to Rebecca's chair. She reached out and they clasped hands, something they had clearly done before. This was not the first time Lizbet had sat down with Rebecca.

"I don't know exactly," she admitted with a laugh. "I'm scared, Rebecca." She laughed nervously, doubling over into the elder woman's lap. Rebecca settled her free hand on Lizbet's back, rubbing in the soothing fashion she had used her entire life whenever someone she cared about was in distress.

"I will not try to tell you not to be." Rebecca soothed as she continued rubbing Lizbet's back. "You have every right to be nervous, but I also know that you will do very well. I am sure you will be invited into every fashionable organization for physicians' wives in the city."

"How is a girl from the country going to manage?" Lizbet asked as she pulled herself together and stood to resume her ministrations to her mistress's hair. "I haven't ever done anything but be your lady's maid."

"Says the woman who has travelled to England, Scotland, and France. Not to mention a number of our very own United States. You, Mrs. Coleman, are better traveled than your husband." Rebecca turned in her chair and looked up at her friend. "Says the woman who reads and writes in two languages and is almost as good at chess as I am. Please. I expect you will be leading society for negro ladies in Washington in no time."

"I have had a very good teacher." Lizbet smiled as she gently pulled the brush through Rebecca's locks.

"I will miss you terribly, you know," Rebecca said as they watched each other in the mirror. "I think of you as a dear friend and my life is always lessened when a dear friend departs."

"I will miss you, too."

"Of course, when the general and I are in Washington we will now have another friend to call on. So, there is that bright side."

Rebecca made her way to the breakfast room. There she found Rex reading the paper and drinking a cup of coffee. She went to the table, stopping to give him a peck on the top of the head. "Good morning, dear man. How are you this morning?"

"I'm fine. How are you, my dearest Rebecca?"

"Up, walking around, and on the correct side of the dirt." She shrugged as she took her seat, allowing him to pour her a cup of coffee as he chuckled at her joke.

"Where's the birthday boy?"

She pulled a large cloth napkin from a sterling silver ring and spread it over her lap. "Sleeping. If you cannot sleep in on your fiftieth birthday, it is not worth the effort to live that long."

After a young footman provided Rebecca with a plate from

the buffet along the wall, the pair sat together, enjoying their breakfast while Rex read the important issues from the paper.

"There was apparently a huge fire in South Dakota, says here, in a place called Deadwood. It has left more than two thousand people homeless and destroyed about three hundred buildings."

Rebecca was shocked, remembering what the Culpeper area looked like during the war with the troops of both armies traveling back and forth. "Oh, dear! Those poor people! We should see if there is anything we can do for them. I will have Charlie check in the morning. His reach with former colleagues will be much longer than ours in this situation."

Rex nodded his agreement and continued reading the paper. "Looks as if Mr. Edison in New Jersey is about to make a major breakthrough in electric lights."

Rebecca's head dropped and there was a deep groan from her chest. "Please, do not tell my husband. Next thing I know, he will be wanting to put electric lights into Mountain View. From what I know, electricity is just damn dangerous. I do not want it around the children and grandchildren. It was bad enough when he had that blasted elevator installed. Do you remember what a mess that was? Six months of non-stop pounding and sawing, the workmen traipsing in and out." She shook her head with disgust. "Had to replace two rugs and the runner for the stairs."

Rex could only chuckle inwardly. Even though many thought Rebecca was not, or could not, be aware during her recovery, he knew she had been conscious all along and her regular tirades about the improvements Charlie had made to Mountain View during that time proved it. "Yes, but you would have been trapped upstairs if he had not done so, dear lady. The elevator was crucial when we depended on your wheelchair." The Asian man shrugged. "Charlie is a futurist. He will find out about Edison's advances sooner than later, and you have seen the benefits of electricity on the ships to and from England. I believe he and Darby have both invested in Mr. Edison's business. Electricity will be coming to Mountain View."

"Yes, but we do not need to lead him down the garden path to do so."

"Yes, dear."

They both snickered at the response. Charlie had told Rex early on during Rebecca's recovery 'the phrase' was the easiest way to stop her before she really got going, and both men used it to their best advantage.

As the footman poured Rebecca her second cup of coffee, the door to the breakfast room swung open, and she fully expected to see Charlie. Instead, she was delighted to see her eldest son with her first grandchild.

"Good morning, Darby, darling. Happy birthday!" She smiled at her son as she opened her arms, gesturing for her five-year-old grandson to climb into her lap.

"Thank you, Mama." Darby nodded as he prodded L.J. to join his grandmother. "We thought we would come by for a bite of breakfast this morning. Jane is a bit under the weather and Stella is in no mood to cook, nor was she amused by the thought of my cooking. Apparently, I do not do it correctly."

Rebecca settled and then resettled Little Jerome as he made himself comfortable in her lap after a few exploratory wriggles. He looked to her and gestured frantically with his left hand. She smiled, nodded, and made a responsive gesture to the boy, letting him know it was alright for him to have a bite of her biscuit with Sarah's blueberry jam he loved so much. He smiled a slightly toothless grin (he was missing two), which was normal for a boy his age, as he dove into the sweet treats on Grandma's plate.

It had been a bad fever when he was about three that had robbed Little Jerome of his hearing. His mother had immediately taken up the mantle of learning sign language and teaching the rest of the family. Grandma and Grandpa Redmond were having the most issues learning the new way of speaking. Between Rebecca's ability being slowed because of her illness, and Charlie's missing fingers, they were both concerned the boy would not be able to understand them.

Darby and Stella had taken time and much patience with his parents to help them learn what they needed to know to communicate with their first grandchild. Darby took extra time with Charlie to reassure him that the boy would be able to understand him, that they would find their own special way of communicating. Even after her stroke, Rebecca was a loving and dedicated grandmother. Stella was convinced that having all the children around and learning sign language had been very good for Rebecca's recovery efforts.

Little Jerome had started to form and understand the meaning of different words before his fever, so he was a bit better off than some children who were born completely deaf. He could and would make certain spoken words for himself that the family had come to understand as his own special type of speech. The most amusing of these was what he chose to call Charlie. 'PaePoo' was the boy's moniker for his paternal grandfather. Rebecca had been graced with the grandmotherly title of 'MaBeh.'

"And where are my lovely daughter-in-law and sweet little granddaughter this morning?" Rebecca asked as she handed Jerome another piece of blueberry laden biscuit.

"Rachel is cutting her back teeth. She is in a right proper mood for a two-year-old, screaming and crying. Stella thought perhaps since it's Papa's birthday, you should be spared the fits of conniption. The only reason L.J. and I were allowed to escape is because it's my birthday as well," Darby opined as he poured a much need cup of coffee.

"So," his mother turned an annoyed eye on her eldest son, "You left my pregnant daughter-in-law home with a grumpy two-year-old, instead of bringing them here, where she might receive assistance?

Darby dropped his chin to his chest and sighed. "Yes, Mama. I am clearly a terrible husband, and father, and a complete failure as a son," he teased and he did not bother to remind his mother that they had a nanny, so Stella was not quite alone with the toddler.

Rex chuckled as he turned the page of his paper.

As Darby took his place and settled down for breakfast, Little Jerome took great delight in playing with MaBeh. Between stealing bites from her plate, they played a simple game of patty cake that was his favorite. The little boy delighted in the smile on his grandmother's face and did his best to make sure he kept it there, even gracing her with kisses to her nose in between rounds of the game.

They were in a particularly difficult round when Paepoo decided to make his entrance. With an easy smile that was reserved only for his first grandson, Charlie approached the table and leaned into Little Jerome's line of vision, gesturing in sign, "Good morning, little man," as he did.

"PAEPOO!" The boy literally leapt from his grandmother's lap to wrap his arms around Charlie's neck as he thrust himself into his grandfather's arms, wrapping his legs tightly around the man's waist.

Rebecca could only smile at the bond between grandfather and grandson. Rex, Darby and Stella had brought the family home from England at the beginning of her illness, and Charlie had bonded deeply with the boy. It was the consensus of the family that it was L.J. who helped keep Charlie grounded during the early stages of Rebecca's recovery when no one was sure how well she would do in that process.

Their bond was palpable; it was made even clearer by the way Charlie held the boy in his arms. He was not a tiny child, and his grandfather had no business trying to hold him while standing up, but he did anyway.

"Where are Rachel and Stella?" Charlie glanced about, looking for the rest of his family.

"They are at home, Papa. Rachel is not in the best of moods this morning."

"They will be here for the party tonight?"

"Of course," the younger Redmond nodded. "You could not keep Stella away. Especially since her parents will be here this afternoon."

Charlie grinned as he made his way to his seat at the table, L.J. still in his arms. His and Darby's private birthday celebration with family would be held in the evening. The formal party for friends and business associates would be the following Saturday. It was going to be a huge party as it was his fiftieth and Darby's twenty-fifth; probably the largest Mountain View had ever seen. Rebecca had taken every opportunity to tease him over the fact he felt the need to celebrate for a week.

L.J. gave Charlie a kiss on the cheek and then scrambled back to Grandma's lap because she still had the biscuits and jam he craved. Grandpa nodded his thanks to the young man who placed a cup of coffee in front of him, and then to Rex, who passed him the financial section of the morning paper.

They ate and read their papers in companionable silence until Andy and Buddy came running in, skidding to a halt as they entered the breakfast room and saw the annoyed look on their mama's face. The last thing they wanted to do was irritate Mama right now. They were hoping to be allowed to go off camping on the other side of the property for a few days, but they needed her permission first.

The boys explained what it was they wanted as they fixed themselves heaping plates of food from the buffet. Charlie just shook his head and made a mental note to order more meat from the butcher.

Feeding two rapidly growing fourteen-year-old boys was not cheap nor easy. Even with the food the farm provided, Charlie had to augment Sarah and Cece's stocks by at least an extra hundred pounds of various foods and basic supplies every month. They had nearly doubled their flour use because of the way the boys put away bread and biscuits. It was no wonder the kitchen budget had to be increased by a hundred dollars a year.

"I think that is an excellent idea!" their father agreed with a nod. "Take your fishing gear and bring home a few stringers. Or perhaps take a rifle and see what you can get. Your recent contributions to the family table have been few and far between, gentlemen, yet I still feed you."

"Yes, sir!" They agreed in unison, with smiles for their father. Then the smiles faded and their heads swung in Rebecca's direction.

"Mama? It is all right with you?" Andy asked with a devastatingly charming grin that went all the way to his eyes. He had practiced on many girls and a few grown women; it usually worked. Then he began shoveling in eggs and bacon.

Rebecca looked to Charlie, who just smiled and shrugged. He had given the boys their marching orders, if the real commander of the family decided to let them deploy. "What about school? Your lessons?"

"Well, Mama," Buddy chimed in because Andy's mouth was full of eggs. "There is not a lot going on at school in town right now. Most of the kids are helping bring in or put up crops. Miss

19

Calvert says we won't be starting back up until after the first or second Monday in October, maybe later. Depends on the farms. Mr. John always makes us give him some sort of report on what we did when we go off for a few days. Usually in natural sciences."

She nodded, satisfied. "You may go. Tomorrow, after your father and brother's birthday celebration, and you will be back on Saturday for the party. You will be here, cleaned up and properly dressed as gentlemen of this family to support your father in front of his business associates and political colleagues."

"Yes, Mama." Charles Huger Redmond the Second nodded solemnly. One thing this young man was beginning to understand about his family was that they were always a united front, no matter the occasion, and they were always united behind the family patriarch. Mama would tolerate nothing less.

JUST AFTER LUNCH, SUE ESCORTED REBECCA DOWN TO THE barns so she could inspect two new mares that had arrived that morning.

During Rebecca's recovery, Sue, at the tender age of fourteen, had taken over the daily running of the breeding program and the stables, supported by Robert Brooks and Cousin Albert, but she always enjoyed it when Rebecca visited the stables herself to see the outcome of their plans.

As they entered the largest stable complex, there were dozens of people moving about the big building. Stable hands mucked stalls. Exercise riders and trainers moved animals in and out to perform their respective tasks. Carpenters were always on hand repairing or expanding the facilities.

At the far end of the building, they found Charlie and Jack.

The big old war horse was doing his best to slobber down the back of his human's shirt while Charlie tried to clean his stall. He was busy trying to get a full fork to a wheel barrow, when a large, long black head dropped down next to his.

"Would you move!" Charlie tapped the horse on the nose, causing Jack to snort and pull his head back. "You can be the most annoying damn boy."

Rebecca and Sue stopped and watched. With his back to them, Charlie had no clue they were there. Jack's long broad neck craned around toward them, and she was not certain, but Rebecca could almost swear the horse winked at her. Then he took his nose and gave Charlie a gentle shove, sending his master head first into the water bucket hanging on the wall.

The women roared with laughter as Charlie stood, spitting and sputtering. Jack shook his head and danced in his stall, and his tail lashed about as his mane swished around Charlie's soaked head. The horse was very proud of himself.

His antics only made Rebecca laugh harder while Charlie brushed the water from his face and hair as he swung around. He lifted his finger, clearly ready to give his horse a soldier's dressing down, foul language included at no extra charge, until he saw them.

"Yes. Please. Encourage him." He pulled his handkerchief from his pocket and tried to dry his neck and ears with it.

"Tell me, General Redmond," Rebecca asked in her best newspaper reporter voice. "What exactly is it you are doing? It is your birthday. This is an odd way to celebrate."

"What does it look like I am doing?" He grinned as he leaned on his manure fork after stuffing the handkerchief in his pocket. "Occasionally, I like to shovel actual horse shit and not the figurative manure my business associates are so fond of."

This made his wife snort, while Sue excused herself to meet

with Mr. Brooks and Cousin Albert and keep from laughing outright at her father.

"We do have stable hands that can do this for you." Rebecca gestured to the stall.

"I know that, but you know me, darling. Jack is my horse and I would never ask anyone to do anything I would not do myself."

"You have always led by example."

"I try."

She drew a deep breath and stepped into the stall with the man and his horse. She ran her index finger down his sleeve from his shoulder to his elbow. "I should be looking at mares, but I cannot help myself. Care to lead me somewhere?"

"I...I..." he nodded, wide eyed, "would love to." He loved his wife and would jump on that particular train any time it decided to make a stop in his neck of the woods.

He tossed the fork in the barrow and rolled it out, closing the door behind them. Jack snorted his displeasure at their abrupt departure. Charlie threw a young lad mucking stalls a nickel to dump the mess from the barrow and bring Jack an apple.

Then he took Rebecca gently by the elbow and leaned and whispered, "Where?"

"I have no clue. You are supposed to be leading me, remember?"

AMELIA AND JEROME LORD ARRIVED THAT AFTERNOON, MEETING the carriage Charlie had sent for them but going directly to Darby and Stella's home to see their daughter and grandchildren. While Stella and Darby had taught Charlie and Rebecca how to sign with L.J., the Lord's had attended classes at the Columbia Institution for the Instruction of the Deaf and Dumb. They studied under Edward Miner Gallaudet, whose father had brought sign language to the United States from the original French developers.

As they walked into the house, young L.J. burst out of the back parlor. "JPAH!!! AMMA!!!" He flung himself into his grandmother's arms. Jerome came in and put his arms around his first-born grandson and his wife.

A rather harried looking Stella followed her son into the hall. "Hello, Mother, Father."

Rachel whimpered from behind her mother's skirts.

Amelia looked at her obviously tired daughter and asked with one raised eyebrow, "Teething?"

"Oh, yes. And miserable. Even the paregoric syrup is not helping her."

"Where is the bourbon?" Grandma Lord asked as she handed L.J. off to his grandfather and scooped her granddaughter up on her hip.

"What?" Stella asked as they all moved into the back parlor.

"The bourbon, dear. Where is it?"

Stella sighed and pointed to the tantalus at one side of the fireplace. "Over there. Why?" Suddenly a look of comprehension came over the tired mother's face. "Oh, why did I not think of that!"

"Exhausted mothers rarely remember everything." Amelia pulled her handkerchief out of her reticule, dampened it with bourbon, and carefully wiped the child's gums with the alcohol.

Rachel chewed on the piece of linen in her mouth, made a face, made another face, and promptly fell asleep against Grandma's shoulder.

"Oh, thank God!" Stella could not keep the exclamation from her lips. "She has not slept in two days. And if she does not sleep, neither do I! Even with Edith's help, it has been a nightmare."

"Well, daughter, why not go up and nap? We will put her down and we can entertain L.J. for the afternoon. You want to be at least somewhat fresh for the party this evening."

"I will, Mother. Thank you. I think if I were not pregnant again, this would not be so difficult, but…"

She did not get any further. "You are pregnant again? We are to be grandparents again? That is WONDERFUL, darling."

Jerome just stood there and grinned stupidly.

CHARLIE STOOD UNDER THE WARM WATER OF THE SHOWER, allowing it to run over his neck and back as he leaned on the specially installed railing along the top of the tub that had been put in place for Rebecca during her recovery. It might have been for her, but he found it quite useful too, especially when he wanted a nice long, hot shower.

He still had a couple of hours before the evening birthday celebration with the family. Having the opportunity to shower beforehand was a blessing. Jack had indeed managed to get an impressive amount of hay down his back, and even with Rebecca's careful removal of it and everything else he had been wearing, it still made his back itch.

He knew he should shut off the water and get out, but it felt good and was very relaxing. He closed his eyes and leaned heavily on the railing.

"Well," he heard Rebecca purr and he smiled, never moving or opening his eyes. "Look at this, the birthday boy in his birthday suit."

Her hands slid around his waist and he felt her press her body against his. Twice in one day, that had not happened in years; it had to be because it was his birthday. He felt her lay her head on his back as she hugged him close.

"I am going to say something to you and then we are never going to discuss it again. I just want you to listen," she offered, increasing her hold on him.

He nodded, resisting the urge to turn and face her.

She continued, in a rather small voice, "I know I am no longer the woman you married. I know that you have needs I am no longer fulfilling regularly. I want you to know that if you feel…"

He started to turn, but she stopped him.

"No, Charlie, let me get this out. I do not want you to suffer because I am no longer regularly capable. So, if you need or," she paused and he could hear her choke on the next words, "want to go elsewhere, I do understand. I will not begrudge you something so important."

Charlie took a deep, calming breath, forcing the tears from his eyes as he slowly turned and wrapped his arms around Rebecca as the water ran over them. He rested his chin on the top of her head as he offered gently, "Thank you for that, but there is no other woman in my life and never will be. I love only you. You are the only one I desire in that way or any way. The life we have together is more than satisfying."

Without a word, she nodded against his chest, thankful for him once again. So many others would have already strayed or worse.

Not her Charlie.

It was not even the fact that it was Charlie; she had lived long enough now and met enough people to know he would have no trouble finding companionship with another woman. She had not been his first, but he certainly made her believe she would be his last.

"Water is getting cold," he mumbled against the top of her head.

"Just another minute." Her arms tightened across his back as a flood of relief washed over her like the water they stood under.

～

THE ENTIRE FAMILY WAS GATHERED FOR THE CELEBRATORY supper. Charlie and Rebecca hosted all the regular suspects, including Richard and Elizabeth, Ro and Allison, Missy Frazier, Edward and Grace Cooper, Rex, all the children, and Jerome and Amelia.

As they were enjoying a drink before going in for supper, one of George Randall's messenger boys delivered a rather thick telegraph envelop to Charlie. "Oh, my! It is from Em! She obviously decided a long and expensive telegram was much more valuable than a real letter."

All of the people in the room knew Em and her peculiarities. A round of laughter went through the room, coupled with multiple requests of "Open it," and "Read it!"

Charlie reached into his pocket and retrieved his pen knife to slice the envelope. He pulled the yellow piece of paper out and unfolded it. After plucking his glasses from his pocket and placing the stems over his ears, he read the missive.

DEAR PAPA STOP

HAPPY BIRTHDAY TO YOU AND DARBY STOP

SORRY AM NOT THERE STOP

PROF LANE-FOX SAYS I GET MY DEGREE THIS SPRING THEN COMING HOME STOP

WILL BE THERE IN TIME FOR WEDDING STOP

THEN WANT MY DOCTORATE STOP

PROF PUTNAM, HARVARD IS BEST - PROF MARSH, YALE, - PROF FREDERICK, OBERLIN STOP

PAPA PLEASE USE YOUR CONTACTS TO SEE IF I CAN GET IN STOP

LOVE YOU STOP

MISS YOU STOP

AUNT LOTTIE JUST SHAKES HER HEAD UNCLE EDGAR SMILES STOP

CHILDREN ARE ALL GOOD HERE WISH YOU AND DARBY HAPPY BIRTHDAY STOP

The message was pure Em, abrupt, to the point, and, as ever, focused on her science. But that she remembered at all without the prompts of the surrounding family touched Charlie. She was always going to be his 'imp' and because of that, he would see what he could do to get her into an advanced program at one of the schools she mentioned.

The guests adjourned to the dining room where supper, cake and finally gifts where shared by the party amid much laughter, joking and admiration for the various gifts that Charlie and Darby received.

The meal had been outstanding, even though this particular feast was prepared by Sarah's daughter, CeCe, who was coming up as the logical and natural replacement for her aging mother. Sarah still supervised the kitchen and the staff. Rebecca even gifted the older woman her own custom desk and chair in the corner of the kitchen to work from. Most of the heavy work was now being left to the younger generation.

Just as they were getting ready to adjourn for after supper drinks, Jerome cleared his throat gently. "While we are all here and I have a captive audience, there is an announcement I would like to make."

"We already know. Stella is expecting. Again," Rebecca tormented.

"Be that as it may," Jerome winked at the blonde. Charlie growled. Even after all these years, they still played that game. "I would like to announce that my firm will be opening an office in Richmond next month."

Darby looked surprised; he had been commuting back and forth to Washington and had not heard a peep around his father in law's firm about an expansion. "When was this decided?"

"Last week," the older man grinned, "when we filed the paperwork to change the name of the firm to Lord, Lord, and Redmond. Congratulations, Darby. You will be opening the new office as a full partner."

"Thank you, sir." His grin lit the room as Stella hugged him and kissed him on the cheek.

Appropriate congratulations were offered to the young man as the occupants of the table adjourned to the parlor. Charlie and Rebecca brought up the rear. As they did, he leaned over and whispered to her, "All I got him was a watch."

"Well," she looped her arm through his, "Look at it this way; he will always be on time for his new position."

Charlie laughed. "Oh, I almost forgot. I got an invitation in the mail today for an event in Chicago in mid-November to honor General Grant. I have to go. It would look like an insult if I did not. Perhaps you could come with me?"

"I would love to, dear. Perhaps I can spend some time with Julia while you boys go off and retell old war stories, drink too much whiskey, and smoke too many stogies."

WEDNESDAY, OCTOBER 1, 1879

Andy looked over at his brother, who was lying on a bedroll, his' head resting on a small log. Buddy was reading a military history book by the light of a lamp balanced on the log.

"Only you," Andy grumbled as he poked a stick into their little campfire.

"Only me, what?" His sibling asked without looking up from his text.

"You would bring a book to read. You must be the most boring human being on the planet."

"Well, what do you suggest?" Buddy set his book aside and sat up, giving his brother his full attention. "The fish are not biting. We have not seen a trace of any game. What else is there to do?"

"We could go into town."

"We're not supposed to go into town. We're supposed to be camping."

"And we are!" Andy gestured around them, "Tent, bedrolls, campfire. This is camping. And we'll come back here."

"Why do we need to go to town?"

"We don't **need** to go to town. I **want** to go to town."

"Why?"

"Why not?"

Buddy shook his head. "You're looking to get into a mess with Mama you'll never get out of if you go wandering off to town."

"Does that mean you won't go?"

"That is exactly what it means. You might not mind being on her last nerve, but I certainly do. You want to risk it, go on then, but you aren't going to get me involved."

"Who's going to tell her?"

"Everyone? Anyone who sees you? Your face is fairly well known in town. You don't think that Miss Ro or Mr. Cooper are not going to mention it if they see you skulking around in town after dark?"

Andy was properly insulted. "I do not skulk!"

"When you're talking about sneaking into town, you had better learn. Right quick. I know what you're going to do. You're going to go nosing around that Mrs. Allen's place, seeing what kind of trouble you can get into. There's a bunch of it there. It's been nice knowing you."

"What is that supposed to mean?"

"It means, brother dear, that when you get caught, and you **will** get caught, Mama will **kill** you!"

"Come on, Buddy! No one is going to die if we go to town."

"Yes, you will. We have no good reason to do it other than to be looking for trouble."

"Do you ever get tired?"

"Of what?"

"Towing the family line."

Shock clearly registered on Buddy's face as he stammered, "What?"

"Is there ever a time when you get tired of being a Redmond? We're all supposed to be so perfect. I'm a little tired of it."

"You're fourteen. You have not lived long enough to be tired of anything."

"Now you sound like Papa."

"There are worse things."

"Come on," Andy cajoled. "Let's go into town and see what Culpeper is like at night."

"Do you remember when we were little and we went exploring that house in England?"

"Yes."

"Do you remember how disappointing that was?"

Andy sighed, "Yes."

"Culpeper at night," Buddy offered reasonably.

"Like you would know."

Buddy nodded and retrieved his book, lying back against his log. "You're right, and I do not want to know. Go ahead, Big Man. Go flex those non-Redmond muscles and see how far it gets you."

"Fine! I will." Andy grabbed his jacket from the tent and began marching away from camp.

"Hey, Magellan!" Buddy called after him. When Andy turned, his bother pointed in the opposite direction. "Town is that way."

"I hate you!" Andy stomped off in the direction his brother indicated.

"You do not," Buddy mumbled quietly as he listened to his brother thrash through the woods going toward town and the worst punishment of his young life.

ANDY FINALLY MADE HIS WAY TO THE LITTLE DIRT ROAD THAT would take him to town. He was still mumbling to himself about his brother when his boots hit the cleared brown path. "Stupid..." he groused as he pulled his jacket on.

He had forgotten how chilly it could get at the end of September. Perhaps staying cuddled up to the campfire had been a better idea. He had not brought a book, but he did have a deck of cards.

"Go into town if I want..." He kicked a stone as he stuffed his hands into his pockets. "Stupid..."

From somewhere to his left he heard a snicker. He stopped

and tried peering into the woods through rapidly settling darkness. "Who's there?!"

Another snicker.

Andy was confident in his ability to take care of himself. He had spent years at Uncle Rex's side learning his methods of self-defense, so he took a step closer to the side of the road and yelled toward a copse of woods. "You may as well come out. I know you're in there! That's Redmond land you're on. You better come out and explain yourself. My mama doesn't care for horse thieves."

There was a bit of rustling and a moment later a young brunette woman, leading a cow, emerged from behind two of the larger trees. "I ain't no horse thief. I just had to get the cow."

"You're that Whitehead girl from up the road?"

"Yeah. Liza Whitehead. Who are you?"

"Andy Redmond."

"Is that supposed to mean something?"

"So they tell me. You're new around here, aren't you?"

She nodded as they began walking down the road at a cow's pace. "Moved here in September. My pa inherited his uncle's place."

"The old Crawford farm?"

"That's the one. How did you know?"

"My family knows everything that is going on with the land that is next to ours."

"Sounds mighty nosey to me."

"That's one way of putting it."

"So, your family is important around here?"

"My father was a general in the Union Army during the war, and Mayor of Culpeper a few years ago. And he was an Ambassador in England. My mama owns the finest horse farm in Virginia. Does that count?"

"That counts." She nodded as she gave the lead rope on the cow a tug. "I know why I'm out here. Do you always walk around your property at night?"

"No, I was going into town. I was going to see what might be happening this evening."

"Wednesday night? Church meetings. That's where my ma and pa are. Over at the Presbyterian church."

Andy stopped in his tracks.

His father, as a senior deacon in the Episcopal Church, would be at the meeting and then all the gentlemen would no doubt adjourn to Jocko's for further celebration of Charlie's birthday.

Andy hadn't thought of that.

He stopped and bowed just a bit at the waist. "May I walk you home?"

"What about town?"

"Well," he unleashed his most charming grin, "My mama would be very upset with a gentleman in our family if we didn't see a lady home." He took the rope from her hand and gripped it in his fist. "After you," he gestured and let her lead the way.

AN HOUR LATER, ANDY TROMPED BACK INTO CAMP WHERE Buddy sat by the fire, warming his hands. "So, Mister Whoever-You-Are. How was town?"

"Didn't make it. Found something better."

"Sure you did. Just admit it. You chickened out."

"Nope." Andy threw himself down on a blanket next to his brother and started tugging his boots off. "I found a damsel in distress."

"Uh huh…" Buddy nodded skeptically.

"I did. One Miss Liza Whitehead. Just moved here. Over at the …"

"Crawford place. Yeah, I know. So, what happened?"

"Her cow was loose."

"So," Buddy's head swung slowly sideways, "You saved her from a bovine? Big man. Bet it was a milk cow well past milking time." Buddy moved sidelong and grabbed his brother by the bicep of each arm, his eyes wide with fake alarm. "You could have been killed!"

Andy pulled away and grunted, "Shut up."

～

SATURDAY, OCTOBER 4, 1879

Mountain View was absolutely packed with people. It seemed as if the big old house had the entirety of the state of Virginia and several other locations under its roof.

Toasts had been offered before the participants in the party broke up into various groups talking business, politics or gossip. The politicians who were honoring Charlie's birthday all had much to say about how badly he was once again needed in state politics. Various gentlemen spent almost an hour – and a great deal of Charlie's champagne – acknowledging the role he played in post-war Virginia and trying to encourage him out of retirement. The state of Virginia needed him as governor.

Even though it was a chilly night, all the doors and windows had been opened to mitigate the heat of the bodies trying to move around.

Rebecca was fairly certain no one else in three states could possibly be having a party as everyone was at her place. She had not laid eyes on Charlie in over two hours, and sightings of her children were few and far between. She turned to find the one constant this evening; Rex, standing back and smiling gently as he always did.

Tired, she reached out and he was at her side in a second. "Rebecca?"

"Just stay with me," she pled as she clutched his arm.

"Of course. Should I find Charlie?"

"No." She shook her head as he led her to a relatively quiet corner and placed her in a chair. "He is busy entertaining God only knows who. I am fine, just a bit tired."

"It is to be expected in this heat. Would you like to go to your room?"

"No, no, really I am fine. I just needed a quiet moment. I do not want to be a burden to Charlie, you know that."

"You never could be."

"You are sweet, but you are a terrible liar. We both know that if half these people had a clue about the last four years of our lives, they would pass judgment on all of us."

"That, dear lady, is their fault, not ours. We do what is necessary for family above all else."

She patted the hand that rested so comfortably on her shoulder. "Indeed, we do."

She was grateful when he placed a glass of cool water in her hand. "Thank you. I am a bit overwhelmed this evening."

"The house is absolutely crammed with people. Body heat aside, the noise is deafening. I myself am a bit overcome. How about a stroll to the gazebo?"

"Oh, yes." She nodded. "Lovely. Perfect." She stood, taking his proffered arm. "Absolutely perfect."

Rex escorted her protectively as they made their way to the nearest egress. He grabbed a long cloak from a rack near the door, not knowing nor caring who it belonged to. They would not miss it for a half hour.

As they stepped out, Rebecca shivered and the purloined garment was gingerly placed over her shoulders. She took Rex's arm and he led her slowly toward the structure near the pond. Not a word was spoken between them as they made their way.

That is probably why Charlie did not hear them as they approached. He got a rather sheepish grin on his face as the burning end of a cigar lit his face.

"Oh." Rebecca laughed when he stood and offered her his hand, taking over from Rex. "This is where you have been hiding."

"I am afraid so." Charlie chuckled as he settled her with a lap rug. "It is just so damn noisy in there."

Rex moved to Charlie's right and poured Rebecca a hot mug of whatever Charlie had asked be delivered out to him as he hid from his guests. As he poured it, he could smell the chicory and prepared the coffee to her liking. Retaking his seat, he poured for himself and grabbed a blanket for his own shoulders from the stack on the bench.

Rebecca turned a loving smile on her spouse. "Charlie, darling, I think we are getting old. We are running from our own parties."

Both men laughed and agreed with a nod.

"Of course," Rex offered as he looked at the empty fire pit, "there has never been a party quite like this one."

"I did not want anyone to know I was here." Charlie lifted a finger indicating why there was no fire in the brazier. "But now that you are both here, we may as well have one."

He stood and collected wood from the box near the little fire pit. With the expert precision of a man who had made many fires in his life, it was constructed, lit and warming the trio in just a few minutes.

Rebecca smiled at him as he pushed himself up and back into his own seat. "Thank you, darling."

"Of course." He lifted her hand and kissed the back of it, tenderly. "I know I am being a terrible host tonight, but I needed a few minutes of fresh air."

"No one is going to fault you for that," Rex reassured. "Besides, Darby and Stella are being charming stand-ins. Suzanne and Jeremiah are also at the center of attention at the moment with the horse crowd. So, I think it is perfectly acceptable for the heads of the family to slip away for a few minutes. I came along as your physician," he added with a chuckle. "The noise was making me sick."

"Speaking of Sue and Jeremiah," Charlie looked sideways at his wife, "Are wedding plans being made now?"

"Not just yet. It is a bit early. The wedding is not until June. Real planning will begin in January." She patted his hand. "I will give you fair warning."

"Thank you."

"I still cannot believe they are getting married." Rebecca shook her head as she sipped her coffee. "I have asked Sue to be considering her dress; that will be the most time-consuming part of the process. As it is June, I have given her my advice on material and design. The rest is up to her."

"How many people?"

"We will discuss it when the memory of this party has faded."

"Oh, dear God," Charlie moaned, knowing as father of the bride, he was paying for the wedding.

"Your son cheated me out of my first wedding…"

"I know." He nodded sympathetically. When irritated with a

child, Rebecca always gave ownership to Charlie. Clearly, their indiscretions were all his fault.

"She is our eldest daughter."

"I know." He nodded again.

"It is going to be a beautiful wedding."

"I know." This time he laughed.

He knew Rebecca was really looking forward to the planning of this wedding. She enjoyed weddings and this was for her own child. He had no doubt that Sue would have the event of a lifetime if her mother had any say at all, which she did. Most of it actually. "I suspect we should be getting back. We will be missed eventually."

~

MONDAY, OCTOBER 6, 1879

Charlie was surprised to find a letter from Phil Sheridan in his morning mail. The writing was unmistakable – scratchy and blotted with ink splotches from Sheridan's uneven pressure on the pen. *Oh, hell, what does he want now?* Charlie thought.

Charlie opened the letter, squinted at the sprawling scrawl that passed for handwriting, and laid the letter on his desk. He pulled his glasses out and tried again.

Dear Charlie,

I have been told you are attending this event in Chicago for General Grant and the reunion of the Army of the Tennessee, as a speaker at the dinner. We also are planning a parade honoring the general, and I am planning to ride one of the old war horses since I am supposed to lead the troops. I hope your old boy Jack is still around, and if so, would you be willing to bring him and ride with me? I would like it and I'm sure the general would appreciate your presence in the parade.

Sincerely,
P. Sheridan

Charlie looked up at Rebecca, who was sitting across their partners desk, thumbing through her own mail. He flapped the letter in her direction to get her attention.

"What is it, dear?" Rebecca could tell from his expression that he was not happy.

"Phil wants me to bring Jack with us to Chicago. He is twenty-three years old! We do not have any appropriate transport for him."

Rebecca looked at her husband. Jack was as much a member of the family as the children. She sighed. "I can have a boxcar frame here within a day or two, with measurements available within a couple of hours. I think we can get Duncan to fit it out as a proper transport stall for Jack in a month."

Charlie stared at his very clever wife. Her relationship with George Pullman was a godsend.

CHAPTER 2

FRIDAY, OCTOBER 10, 1879

ANDREW RICHARD REDMOND dressed in his Sunday best, approached the gate of the little farm house, and took a moment to wipe sweaty palms on his trousers. He drew a long, deep breath and manfully opened the little gate, letting it swing closed with a click as he stepped through.

This alerted one of the biggest dogs outside of the family's own beloved wolfhounds Andy had ever seen. And a big difference between this dog and his, was that he was certain this monster mutt wanted to eat him. The only thing stopping the beast with gnashing teeth and globs of slobber leaving its vicious mouth was a thick rope that looked to be stretching to its intended limits.

Andy stood frozen, not daring to take another step forward, nor feeling like he could safely retreat over the closed gate. He took a deep breath and looked at the dog and directed gently, "Easy, boy."

The dog paused briefly then once again began its ferocious attempts at intimidation. Again, Andy stood his ground, but commanded, "Down! Sit! Stay!"

The big black dog immediately sat down and his tail began thumping against the ground. Slowly, the boy stepped forward, offering the dog his balled-up hand to sniff. With another tentative step forward and more soothing words, Andy felt a lick to his fist.

"That's right. We can be friends. I'm not here to hurt anyone."

"Well, I'll be damned!"

Andy's head swung around to find an older man wiping his hands on a rag as he rounded the corner of the farm house.

The man cocked his head and asked, "Who do we have here? That dog hates everyone."

"Andrew Richard Redmond, sir. I've come to speak with Mr. Whitehead, if you please," he offered as he patted the dog on the head.

"Is that so?"

"Yes, sir."

"And what business would you have with Mr. Whitehead?"

"With all due respect, that would be between me and Mr. Whitehead."

The man laughed at the boy's self-assured manner. "Well, I expect that's true. I'm Mr. Whitehead," he said as he stepped up on his porch and gestured for Andy to join him. "What can I do for you, Andrew Richard Redmond?"

"It's Andy actually, but Mama says a gentleman always gives his full name." He joined the man on the porch and offered his slightly sweaty hand. "It's a pleasure to meet you, Mr. Whitehead, sir."

The older man took the boy's hand, impressed with his grip

and the callouses he found there. He expected a Redmond to have hands like a lady. This boy worked, at least enough to cause callouses. "It's a pleasure to meet you, Andy. Now, what can I do for you?"

"Well, sir." He stood tall and looked at the man directly in the eye. "I've come to ask permission to court Miss Liza."

Suddenly the man straightened and crossed his arms over his chest and Andy was faced with a protective father. "Is that so?"

"Yes, sir." The young Redmond did not flinch.

"How old are you, boy?"

"Fourteen, sir. I'll be fifteen early next year, at the end of February."

"And your pa is Charles Redmond? Federal Army, General Redmond?"

"Yes, sir."

"And he knows you're coming here to ask to court my daughter?"

"Yes, sir." Andy nodded earnestly.

Papa did know. Andy had gone to him and asked his advice. This had been it. "Be a man and ask her father for permission to see her if you think she is right for you and someone you want to know". Well, Eliza Whitehead was someone he wanted to know better so he did what Papa said.

Mr. Whitehead scratched the whiskers on his chin as he regarded the boy. His family wasn't dirt-scrabble poor, but they certainly did not have the wealth of the Redmond's. Usually the wealthy folks tended to stay to themselves, arranging relationships and marriages for their children among their own, as it were.

"And your pa is all right with this? We ain't got money, son."

"I'm not interested in your money, sir. I like your daughter."

This made the man smile and he laughed as he nodded. "All right then, I will give you my permission, young Mr. Redmond, tentative on me and my wife meeting with your folks to make sure it's truly all right with them."

"I understand. Would you and your family like to join us for Sunday dinner after services? We usually have lots of folks out on Sundays. I'm sure my folks wouldn't mind a few more."

"Well now, Liza has three older brothers. They'd have to come, too."

"That'd be fine, sir. We always have plenty. Your family is more than welcome and you could talk to my folks."

"Then we'll see you on Sunday, after services."

"Yes, sir." Andy grinned and offered his hand again. "Thank you, sir."

Elmer Whitehead took the hand of the earnest young man in front of him and winked. "Liza is out in the chicken coop if you want to say hello."

OVER SUPPER THAT EVENING, ANDY EXPLAINED THAT HE HAD invited at least six more people to Sunday dinner. Charlie just grinned and tried to keep from laughing out loud at the look on Rebecca's face when she realized they were being introduced to the parents of her son's first serious crush on a young lady.

"It was all right to invite them? Right, Mama?"

She nodded with a sigh. "Yes, of course it was. I will make sure Sarah and CeCe are aware of the additions."

"Thank you, Mama. I think you will like Liza, and Mr. Whitehead seems like a nice man."

"Andy's got a girlfriend..." Buddy tormented in a sing-song

voice from his seat next to his brother, earning him a kick to the shin under the table.

"Boys…" Charlie warned as he tapped his fork on his plate to make sure he had their attention.

They settled down and the approaching battle was cut short by the commander at the head of the table. They both gave him a rather sheepish smile and returned to the consumption of their meal.

Charlie still smirked at the slightly flustered look on Rebecca's face. He knew some part of her could not wrap her head around the fact that ALL of her children were growing up, especially the two she had with her since they were infants.

She had a special bond with all the children, particularly her own brood, but these two boys were both the light in her life and the frustration in her soul. She had diligently cared for Andy's mother and was the first person to hold him after his rather unfortunate entrance into the world. And Buddy had been with her since before he was two months old. These were the two that were the closest thing she had to children borne of her own body. It would be exceptionally difficult for her to loosen those apron strings for these boys.

Charlie poured himself a glass of wine, considering his family as he did so. Rex had retired early to write a letter to Edgar and Lottie.

Sue was having supper with Jeremiah and his family. Darby and Stella were at home with their family, so it was now just down to the four of them.

He stood and moved to his sons, upturning their wine glasses as he did. He splashed a bit of water in the crystal goblets and then filled them about half way up with wine. "Go ahead. It is time you learned the finer arts of being gentlemen. This will be much more palatable than the brandy you have been snitching from my stocks in the office. Lesson one, when wine will do, do not waste good brandy."

That caused Rebecca to choke on her wine as she did her best to catch the majority in her napkin. She gave her husband a dirty smirk that made him blush as he retook his seat.

"Go ahead, gentlemen. Let me remind you, no proper gentleman is ever completely drunk," their father said sternly.

"Duncan says no proper gentleman is ever completely sober either," Andy offered with a shrug as he picked up the glass and sniffed the contents before giving it a taste.

"Duncan may be a bad influence on you," Charlie said, glancing sideways at his son.

"May want to reconsider letting his son marry into the family," Buddy teased as he swallowed the last of his milk, completely ignoring the wine before him.

This made both his parents laugh, to the point that they dismissed the boys from the table while they tried to recover.

"What are we going to do with them?" Rebecca was still chuckling as the boys retreated out the door leading to the farm and barns.

"Pray. A lot," Charlie replied quietly from behind his coffee cup.

~

SUNDAY, OCTOBER 26, 1879

Charlie shifted slightly in his chair and offered his cigar case to Elmer Whitehead. The warmer, clear day was well received by everyone. It had been rainy and chilly the previous week, so the opportunity to get out of the house after Sunday dinner was most welcomed. The men had decided to settle in the gazebo while the children played croquet around the pond and the ladies slowly toured the grounds. Rebecca was always ready to show off their beautiful home and farm to anyone who would tolerate it for more than five minutes. Mrs. Brenda Whitehead was enthralled that the wealthy woman would want to show her around. In the two weeks since they had first met, they had become fast friends, chatting about books they enjoyed as they headed for the stables.

Elmer grinned, nodded, and withdrew one of Charlie's fine cigars. Within a moment, Charlie offered his guest a lucifer and both men drew deeply on the slow-burning tobacco.

"So, Mr. Whitehead…" Charlie drew on his cigar again, allowing blue smoke to swirl around his head as he gestured to Andy and Liza walking hand in hand by the pond as Buddy played his turn at the croquet game. "As a father of daughters, one of whom is engaged, how do you handle Miss Liza walking out with my son?"

Elmer sat back and drew on the cigar before taking a sip of the bourbon in his glass. "I suppose Liza could do worse."

Charlie chuckled as he drained his own glass. "Andy is quite smitten with your daughter. Let me assure you, I have spoken with him about how a gentleman should treat a lady. He will be properly attentive and respectful."

"General Redmond, may I be honest with you?"

Charlie's brow arched slightly as he shifted his body toward the man seated next to him. "Of course, sir. Whatever is said between us here, is between gentlemen."

The farmer nodded and leaned forward, letting his elbows rest on his thighs as he contemplated what it was he wanted to say, exactly. "My Liza, she's a good girl. Dutiful to me and her ma. Goes to church like clockwork. Good with her brothers. Even when she wants to kill them," he finished with a chuckle before gesturing to the bottle of bourbon with his glass.

Charlie gladly provided a refill, which his guest half drained before continuing.

"But she's a bit of a flirt. She's been in situations with boys before that have been less than proper." He drained the last half of the glass and shook his head. "We had hoped our move here would be a fresh start and I don't want Liza's infatuation with your son to cause problems for my family."

The man raised his head and looked Charlie in the eye. "General Redmond, sir, my family can't afford problems with you or yours. I hope Liza doesn't cause an issue, but I know from experience it wouldn't have done a damn bit of good to tell them no; they would have snuck around to be together and that would have been far worse."

Charlie nodded and grinned in a self-depreciating manner as he nodded. "Sir, I suspect we have a case of young love and it will be over by spring, but if it is not, we shall take it as it comes and deal with it together. My boy Andy is not the saint I would like him to be either."

CHARLIE BANKED THE FIRE, THEN WITH A BIT OF A STRETCH, HE lifted one of his special blends from the humidor on the mantle. Glancing sideways as he lit the end of the stogie, he drew a deep breath and decided to wade in to his waist. He gently cleared his throat as he watched his beloved wife finishing her evening routine at her dressing table.

"So, what do you think of this situation with Andy and

Eliza?" He asked as he poured them both a nightcap, placing hers on the left corner of her dressing table.

She sighed and turned to him. "What am I supposed to think, Charlie? The children are growing up. All we can do is guide them into adulthood. They are young and I would prefer they always have a chaperone."

Charlie nodded, taking a seat on the couch next to her table. "I agree, especially after a conversation I had with Mr. Whitehead. Seems Eliza is a bit of a flirt."

Rebecca's chin dropped to her chest and she groaned. "Of course. We would have a girl like that interested in Andy the cad. We are in trouble here."

"Not if we are careful. As you say, darling, they should never be alone."

Rebecca stood, taking her drink from the table before settling down on Charlie's left and burrowing under his arm and into his side. He kissed the top of her head, inhaling the scent of the soap she had used to wash her hair that morning. Rose oil had most certainly been a key ingredient.

They sat like that for several minutes, quietly sipping their drinks and watching the fire as their individual thoughts once again managed to take verbal form as one concise declaration, they both made at the same time.

"It is impossible."

Charlie snorted in amusement and nodded. "You may be right, my dear, but we will do our best."

"Well, we had planned to send the boys to school in the spring. Hopefully their romance will have cooled by then." Rebecca rolled the stem of her glass between her fingers as she further considered the situation. "I had a suitor at their age. It did not last long."

"Was he handsome?"

"Face like a cheese grater." She shivered at the thought of her youthful infatuation. "Turned out he was mean as a rattlesnake, too. Papa did not allow him to remain around the house very long."

Charlie nodded, tenderly kissing the crown of Rebecca's head. He understood completely. With Sue engaged, he knew if Jeremiah did not have a good disposition, he never would have approved the match.

"How is it," he began gently, "that you ended up with Gaines? He certainly does not seem the type your father would have agreed to."

"Well now, circumstances change. At the time, the match with him was a good one."

"Good for your family, you mean."

She nodded. "Of course. It was the norm, Charlie. It still is. We are just fortunate we can allow some latitude."

"I could never allow Sue or Em to be with someone I did not think would treat them right. If I could not chase them off, I would have to bury them in the north pasture."

She smiled and patted his chest, feeling his heart rate increase as he spoke of protecting his daughters. "I know. You are a good father."

He pulled back just slightly so he could look at her. "Am I?"

The shock was clearly evident when she looked up at him. "What? Of course, you are! Why would you even ask that question?"

"Sometimes, even after all this time, I wonder if—"

She silenced him by placing two fingers over his lips. "Just stop." She sighed, a bit frustrated with him. "How can you be unsure of your ability as a father? My God, Charlie, the majority of our sons want nothing more than to be like you and our girls want to marry men just like you. You have set the standard, General Redmond, for which I am very grateful."

Leaning in, she kissed him tenderly on the lips, lingering a moment until she felt him smile. "I love you, Charlie."

"Love you too, 'Becca."

MONDAY, NOVEMBER 3, 1879

Eloise had sent over Charlie's business mail late that morning, with odd notes on the envelopes as to what he should address first. Right on top was a missive from his old friend and commander, General Grant.

Dear Charlie;

As you may already know, Julia and I have just returned from our world tour. It has been a wonderful experience, but I have to admit, exceptionally costly.

As you told me I would, I found Queen Victoria to be truly charming, and she spoke highly of your tenure as our ambassador. But after this trip with Julia, I see just what a sacrifice I asked of you and Rebecca. I cannot tell you how much I appreciate it and how grateful I am for your support.

My son has gone into business with a brilliant young financier, Ferdinand Ward, and opened Grant & Ward, a Wall Street brokerage house. I will be joining them and urge you to consider investing with us. As I said, Ferdinand is brilliant, and I feel confident he will extend his brilliance to make you more profitable than you already are.

I have been writing the odd article for various magazines to bring in more money. I do wish I were as good a business man as you have proven to be, but my little jottings, and the kindness of friends, have brought in enough to make our lives very comfortable.

I have high expectations for my interest in the Mexican Southern Railroad, and President Hayes has promised to support a free trade agreement with Mexico. I suspect Hayes will not enjoy a second term. Still, I am hopeful.

My old friend Roscoe Conkling is urging me to run for a third term as president. To be honest, I do not know if the voters will approve a third term, but I suspect I am best at being a general, and by now fairly skilled at being a president. I certainly do not have the skills of an outstanding businessman. We shall see next summer what the Republican convention in June will tolerate.

Ah, well, Charlie. We both grow older and hopefully wiser. Please give Rebecca my love and again, thank you both for your support and the sacrifices you made for me and for your country when I sent you to England.

Cordially,
U. S. Grant

Charlie pulled his glasses off his nose and stared into the fireplace. In the past few days, the weather had grown decidedly chilly. Winter was on its inevitable way, and he had asked for a small fire to be built in his office. He sighed, knowing in his heart that any investment in Grant's business interests was probably a loss, but the man was a former President, his old commander, and most importantly, his friend. He considered carefully and decided he could probably afford to lose a thousand dollars. He would discuss it with Rebecca and Rex that evening.

The family underwent the usual evening diaspora after supper.

John Foxworth had assigned the boys what Andy considered an onerous task, though Buddy was thoroughly enjoying it. The boys were reading Caesar's *Bellum Gallicum* in the original Latin, translating it, and cross referencing it with an English translation of the *Commentarii de Bello Gallico*. Buddy was fascinated by the detailed accounts by one of the great generals in history. Andy was convinced he had been sentenced to Latin purgatory.

Sue and Jeremiah had adjourned to the library before Jeremiah went home for the night. They were planning their new house. Darby was in Washington for the week and Stella, in the last three months of her pregnancy, chose to stay home and rest.

Charlie, Rex, and Rebecca retreated to the upstairs sitting room between Charlie and Rebecca's bedroom and Rex's own suite. They had cut a door into the old guest room that was now Rex's domain on the other side of the sitting room from their bedroom. They gathered there most evenings when there were no other members of the family or friends around. There they usually played either three-player whist or mah-jongg, or one of the three read aloud while the other two played chess.

Tonight, Charlie opted to read the monthly financial reports from the bank. Rex was trying to teach Rebecca how to play go, a Chinese predecessor to chess. The room was quiet for a while, with only the crackle of the fire and the periodic click of stones on the playing board or the rustle of Charlie's papers breaking the silence. Eventually, the sound of a snoring wolf hound could also be heard coming from Peri-Cu, the offspring of Charlie and

Rebecca's first wolf hounds, sleeping across Charlie's booted feet.

Finally, Charlie put his papers aside and cleared his throat to get his companions' attention. "I received a letter from General Grant today."

"Oh?" Rebecca growled, "What does he want from us now?"

Charlie blinked and looked aside for a moment. "Well, he wanted to thank us again for the sacrifices we made in going to England. The trip he took with Julia seems to have taught him a lesson or two about Americans going abroad." Charlie sipped from his tea cup to give himself a moment.

"Well, it is about time he acknowledged what we did for him!" Rebecca still had moments of being annoyed at Grant for what he had asked of her and her family and what his whims had cost them.

Rex put a finger to his lips. Knowing both Charlie and Grant, he knew something was coming. It was just a question of what.

"Grant made an interesting offer. His son has opened a brokerage in New York with someone Grant calls a brilliant young investor, Ferdinand Ward. I sent a telegram to Jerome and he confirmed Ward's reputation. Since I know that Grant is once again hurting for money, I thought I could invest with this new venture."

Rebecca snorted. "If you invest, you had best be prepared to lose whatever you put in, dear. Grant has never had a successful business venture, and I see no reason why things should change now."

Charlie nodded ruefully. "True, but we all know that it will give him some income without insulting him by making an outright gift. I was thinking that I would put in a thousand or maybe two. Enough to give him a decent start but not so much that we will be hurt if it does not work out."

Rex smiled gently and finally said, "I will match your gift, um, investment, Charlie. However bad he is as a businessman, he was a great general."

~

TUESDAY, NOVEMBER 4, 1879

As the Redmonds were preparing to leave, Charlie and Rex each wrote a thousand-dollar check to Grant & Ward. Rex handed his to Charlie, who put it into his wallet. "I will give these to him when I see him next week. You will watch the place while we are gone?"

Rex smiled and nodded, gesturing around at the big old house. "I will try to keep the boys from burning it down around our ears. You and Rebecca have a good time in Chicago."

"I am planning on making it a bit of a holiday for us as well," Charlie offered as he checked his pockets to make sure he had everything he needed. "During the Tennessee reunion, there will not be a lot that Rebecca will want to or be able to attend. So, I am planning to stay a few extra days. I have wanted to take her away for some time, but never had such an opportune moment."

"Where will you be staying?" Rex asked as he plucked Charlie's valise from a chair before the two started downstairs, where Rebecca was no doubt impatiently waiting.

"The Palmer House. Part of the event for President Grant is being held there, so it made perfect sense. The Grants are staying there are well, so it will be easy for our ladies to entertain each other while we attend the pomp and circumstance events."

"Are you happy with the car that was built for Jack?"

Charlie nodded enthusiastically as they began taking the steps down to the front door. "Oh, yes! Duncan did a beautiful job of framing it out and then Jeremiah did all the padding and detailing. It is as safe and comfortable as we can make it. It has a very nice area for his groom, too."

"At a cost of nearly two thousand dollars because of the rush job the boys had to do, and that was with a family discount. Your horse has the newest, safest, and most well-appointed train car in North America," Rebecca commented from the bottom of the steps as she pulled on her gloves. "It is about time, Charles. We are late."

"It is not as if the train will leave without us, my dear," Charlie offered, dropping a kiss to her cheek as he arrived at the bottom of the stairs.

"Then I shall make sure you get the bill for the crew standing around doing nothing while you take your time."

"Oh, good Lord, I am costing her money," Charlie quipped as he shrugged into his cloak. "I had better get going."

"You tend to cost me money more often than not," Rebecca said reasonably as she tugged the collar of his cloak into place. "I still love you."

"I am very glad to hear it, Mrs. Redmond," Charlie said playfully, as he gave her a quick kiss on the tip of her nose.

Rex chuckled at the pair. He loved the lady, but knew his place. He would continue to support their efforts as a good friend, dedicated physician, and personal companion in the unusual triumvirate. It was a role he had embraced a long time ago and knew well.

Rex handed Charlie his valise and leaned over to give Rebecca a peck on the cheek. "Enjoy yourselves. Chicago should be bright as a new penny. So many of the buildings are new since the rebuilding after the fire."

"I intend to make a very costly trip to Marshal Field's,"

Rebecca said as she patted the Asian man's lapel affectionately. "The house could use new drapes."

Charlie groaned. Rex was sure he heard the tall man's eyes roll back in his head as well.

Rebecca patted her husband's arm. "You will survive. I am certain you will be occupied with your old army comrades. While it may be bright as a new penny, I am well aware there is little to do in Chicago. I intend to shop. Do you need anything for your rooms?" she asked Rex as she tugged on Charlie's hand to move him toward the door.

"Anything you wish to bring home will be gratefully accepted my dear." Rex laughed as he did his part and poked Charlie in the back.

"Where are Louis and Lizbet?" Charlie inquired as the stepped on the porch to find Alfred waiting at his best enclosed carriage. He had been tempted to transport it to Chicago as well, but after the expense of the custom car for Jack, he decided not to push his luck with his wife.

"They left an hour ago to load our luggage. They went with Jack and his groom. I told you we were late!" Rebecca chastised as she accepted Alfred's hand to board the carriage.

"I still do not understand how we can be late if it is our train!" Charlie tormented as he stood outside the carriage and tugged his own gloves on, clearly taking his time.

Rex just bit his lip in an effort not to laugh out loud.

"I swear by all that is holy! Charles Huger Redmond, if you do not get in this damn carriage I will file for divorce! I have a son who is a lawyer! A woman should only have to take so much!"

"Yes, dear." Charlie laughed as he pulled himself into the carriage and the seat across from her.

Rex pushed the door closed, securing the latch as Alfred climbed up on top.

"Do have fun," he offered again. "Try not to irritate each other the entire time."

~

CHARLIE MADE SURE REBECCA WAS COMFORTABLE IN THEIR CAR with both Louis and Lizbet to tend her before he excused himself to make sure Jack was just as comfortable and well attended.

He was pleased to see that Josiah Wilson, Jack's groom, was offering the horse cool, fresh water and that fresh shavings had been piled deep in the custom stall.

"General Redmond, sir!" Joe tugged on the brim of his cap. "Our boy is happy and relaxed, sir. He's doing just fine."

Charlie lifted a finger in acknowledgment of the groom's words, even as he bent at the waist to inspect the wrappings around Jack's legs from the pastern, up the cannon bone to just below the horse's knee. "Did he accept the wraps okay?"

"Oh, yes, sir." The groom nodded as he leaned against the front of the padded stall. "The old man knows, sir. He knows this is an important trip."

Jack snorted and stomped just after Josiah's comment, forcing Charlie to straighten and abandon his inspection of the leg wraps.

"He has traveled by train before," Charlie said as he gave his wartime companion a pat on his broad neck. "But it has been a long time."

"He remembers, General. He is going to take this trip just fine, sir."

"Well, we have arranged for lay overs to allow him to off load for some exercise. He is nearly twenty-four years old and

58

has seen more than any living creature should. I do not want this trip to be a strain on him. I am not sure why I agreed to this."

"It won't be, sir." The young man grinned. "He's enjoying it. We have everything we need. And if you don't mind my saying, Mr. Jack here deserves the grand parade you plan to ride him in."

Charlie nodded, once again laying hands on his horse. "He does. He really does."

Josiah just leaned on the stall gate, allowing the general to be with his faithful mount.

Finally, Charlie looked up. "Are you going to be comfortable back here with him?"

"Oh, yes, sir!" The young man gestured to the far side of the car where a thick wall with a sliding door were the clear dividers of the room. "I have a small stove in there! With the venting system, we will even be warm with no risk of anything catching fire! I have the ability to make coffee, and there is a food pantry! There is fresh bread, ham, jerky, cheese and lots of apples and pears! No mold or rot to cut off or nothing! It's top notch, General. Many thanks."

Charlie smiled at the young man, who had been hired two years before when the old trooper named Franklin, who had retired with Jack, finally actually retired.

Mr. Brooks had recommended young Josiah, while explaining to Charlie that he thought a position on the Redmond staff would benefit the boy, who might otherwise have taken to running with less than desirable individuals prone to wearing hoods and carrying torches while burning crosses.

The young man had proven himself a valuable employee and a damn fine caretaker for the most important stud at Redmond Stables. Not only was he very good with the horse, but the horse actually loved and respected the human, too. And when it came to Jack, if he did not respect you, there was no working with him.

"Alright, Joe, I need to get back to Mrs. Redmond, but if you need me, you can access our car through that door." Charlie gestured to the opposite end of the car. "There will be a canvas barrier up between the cars while the train is moving. It is a chilly walk, but safe."

"I have a couple of good books. Jack has a basket of apples. I think we will be fine, sir."

"You have the route map, so you can keep an eye on when it might get rough?"

"Yes, sir, and I have double checked that the mechanism to slide the wall of the stall is working properly. If we need to tighten up his quarters, we can do so easily. The conductor has promised to keep me updated."

Charlie nodded, hesitant to leave his faithful mount, but knowing he was as safe and comfortable as any horse could possibly be. "Well, if you need me…"

~

REBECCA SMILED AS CHARLIE PULLED THE DOOR TO THEIR CAR closed. "Are Jack and Joe well settled?"

"Oh, yes." He nodded as he took off his hat, cloak and suitcoat, and then kicked off his boots. "The car is wonderful, darling. Thank you for taking such good care of him." Charlie laid the pile of clothes on a small bench, knowing that Louis would tend to them later.

"Not only," Rebecca began as she poured him a cup of tea from the service on the table at her side, "is Jack your horse, which is reason enough to keep him safe, but he still throws some of our best foals."

Charlie found his slippers and slid them on before taking his chair on the opposite of one of the two the small stoves that kept their car warm. He accepted the tea, setting it aside so he could unbutton his vest and undo his tie. Once his sleeves were rolled to the elbow, he was comfortable enough to reconsider the tea.

Rebecca smiled even as she sipped from her own cup. She liked traveling by train with Charlie because he was allowed to do something in the privacy of their car that he rarely had the opportunity to do—really relax.

Even after all these years, he still worked very hard to maintain a certain image at home and in his professional endeavors. She knew it cost him a great deal to maintain his image and that at times it was simply exhausting.

In the privacy of this train car, he could shed the clothes that helped him maintain that image. He always started the process by taking off the heavy layers first. As long as the car stayed warm, by tomorrow morning, he would not even bother to put on socks. He would spend most of the trip in linen trousers and his undershirt.

"Comfortable?" She winked at him.

"Almost." He winked back. "What about you?"

"Oh, I did not even bother with a corset this morning. Absolutely no reason to be miserable. It is just me under this dress." She lifted the hem of said dress to reveal that she had already traded her own boots for her slippers, too. "We are going to be on this train for five days with stops for Jack, so I told Lizbet to leave that evil thing in the trunk until we arrive in Chicago."

"I am not sure why you still subject yourself to it." Charlie shook his head thinking of that particular fashion item.

"Because, husband dear, that is the last symbol of being a young woman. We give them up very begrudgingly, even though we hate them."

"Rex says they are not good for the female form."

"Says the man from a country where they regularly bind the feet of girls to supposedly make them more attractive as women."

"He is against that practice, too, which is why I trust his opinion on corsets."

"What did you bring to read?" she asked, clearly closing the corset conversation.

"A couple of selections I do believe you will enjoy, *Anna Karenina* by Mr. Tolstoy, and *Tribulations of a Chinaman in China* by Mr. Verne. Rex enjoyed it a great deal. He says it is very funny, with topical commentary. It is in French. You always enjoy when I read in French."

"Sounds delightful. Perhaps after lunch we will curl up in the bed together and you can start one of them."

"If we curl up in the bed together, the chances of getting through a chapter are slim."

"You have never complained before."

"And I do not intend to do so now." Charlie grinned and sipped deeply from his cup.

CHARLIE AND REBECCA WERE STILL SLEEPING WHEN LIZBET entered the car in the early afternoon to check on them. She smiled when she saw the drapes drawn around their bed, and returned to the travel car she shared with Louis.

Louis was sitting at the table in the common parlor in the center of their car. He alternated between drinking a cup of coffee and polishing the general's riding boots.

"I doubt they will be needing anything for most of the day. They are sound asleep," Lizbet offered as she poured her own coffee from a pot on a small stove and joined him at the table.

"They are not hard to work for." Louis chuckled as he buffed the toe of the right boot. "Especially on a trip like this."

"I suspect we will be busy enough in Chicago for six servants." Lizbet sighed as she settled in and splashed a bit of cream into her coffee.

"I enjoy these events." Louis smiled brightly.

"Why in the name of the Good Lord would you do that? The hours for these things are horrible. We are expected to be on call twenty-four hours a day."

"Yes." Louis nodded. "I take it that none of Miss Rebecca's lady friends have tried to hire you away."

"What?"

"It's true!" Louis lifted his hand high, paying respect to his God. "I have been offered many jobs because of my position with General Charlie. Some of them at three times the money."

"Why have you never taken one!?" Lizbet was truly curious. General Charlie and Miss Rebecca paid a good and more than fair wage, even to the negros in their employ. If the man had gotten an offer for three times as much, he should have taken it.

"Because no one will treat me like the general does. He has never denied me a raise when I have asked for one. He has always made sure I had anything I needed. I may be his employee, but I am also his friend. You know that's true. You have the same relationship with Miss Rebecca. Would you leave her? Even for more money?"

Lizbet smiled, remembering a long time ago when General Charlie had come to her begging, yes, begging, her not to leave Rebecca while her own husband was in medical school.

"No." The woman smiled warmly, cradling her coffee cup between her hands as tears formed in the corner of her eyes. "I wouldn't. But with Tomas' new position, I'm going to have to."

"But it sure does feel good to be asked." Louis laughed as he dabbed more polish on the boot. "General Charlie and Miss Rebecca don't need to be worried about who is looking after their most personal things. They have trusted us for a long time. I would never betray that. They have made every effort to keep us safe. That is the least we can do for them. I hope you find someone Miss Rebecca can rely on, like she has relied on you."

∼

THURSDAY, NOVEMBER 6, 1879

Cincinnati was the last multi-hour stop for Jack's comfort. The two or three planned stops between Cincinnati and Chicago would be for less than two hours each. Just enough time to refuel the train or replenish the water stores and maybe give Jack a quick walk.

This stop allowed everyone to really stretch their legs. Charlie even decided to throw a blanket on Jack's back to ride him around the small paddock in the yard, near the train, that had been reserved for the important equine passenger.

Rebecca watched from the rear platform of their car as her husband made the horse do one or two walking loops around the small enclosure. She knew for certain that Charlie would not be long on the horse riding with only a blanket. He was a tough old goat, but bareback with two good cheeks was hard enough.

She knew he was simply seeking a few quiet minutes with the one soul he could always trust. For as self-assured and confident as Charles Redmond was, there was always a moment of insecurity before any big event in his life.

For Charlie, being invited to ride in this parade and serve as part of the escort and bodyguard detail for President Grant during the progression through the streets of Chicago was just as important as almost anything he had done before this, at least from a military perspective.

It was a reunion of the Army of the Tennessee to welcome President Grant home from his two-year world tour. Army comrades Charlie had not seen in some time would be there. Even though he was as accomplished as any well-learned man could be, his status and reputation in the army was the most important thing to him.

This would be the first time he and Jack had participated in anything like this since before the war ended. Rebecca understood why he wanted to make a good showing.

She was sipping coffee and did not notice when Lizbet joined her on the platform, quietly pulling the door to the car closed behind her.

"Miss Rebecca, the cook asked me to inquire about your luncheon. Would you and the general prefer chicken or beef? He says he has a couple of lovely steaks in the larder."

"Steaks will be fine. I am sure Charlie will be ravenous after his morning with Jack." Rebecca lifted her chin toward the man and his horse, her eyes never leaving them.

Lizbet chuckled when she saw Charlie running as quickly as he was able with Jack right behind him. They were playing. It looked like some sort of equine game of tag. When Charlie would slow the horse would give him a nudge to the shoulder and then run away, tail up, head held high.

Then Charlie would lure him back and the cycle would start all over again. It was endearing to see them together. The love and respect that passed between the general and his horse was almost tangible. You might not be able to touch it, but like a rainbow, you could definitely see it.

"Won him in a poker game, you know," Rebecca offered as she leaned on the rail.

"Really?" Lizbet asked with another laugh as the chase continued with Jack running tight circles around Charlie.

"When he was a major, stationed in Washington. He got into a high-stake poker game and a colonel who could not pay his losses at the table had to forfeit Jack to Charlie. He said it is the best pot he ever won."

"They sure do love each other."

"They do indeed. Jack is part of the reason Charlie is alive now. The day he was wounded, Jack was left behind because of a bruise, but when he was being exercised, Jack took off and ran to Charlie, carrying Jocko on his back. That horse knew his human was hurt and needed help."

"They know. I have an old dog that always knows when Tomas or I just aren't feeling right. He always lays his head right in my lap if he thinks something is wrong. Our animals know more than we think."

"And Charlie is a natural with animals. Does not matter the species, he is simply good with them. I think he was a dog in a previous life."

Lizbet burst out laughing before sliding the door to the train car open once again. "I'll go tell the cook to prepare the steaks."

"Thank you, Lizbet, and let us make sure we have a good strong drink ready for him as well. He is going to need it after this."

"It's a bit chilly. I'll have Louis make a fresh pot of coffee and get out the brandy."

"Perfect." Rebecca smiled at her maid. "Thank you. I am sure we will be in shortly. I cannot imagine he has much more left in him."

"The general or Jack?"

"Your pick."

Rebecca listened to Lizbet chortle as she disappeared through the door. Sipping her coffee, Rebecca was happy to finally see Charlie hand Jack off to the groom and start for the train.

He was limping more obviously than usual. She shook her head and sighed, knowing that by the time they reached Chicago, he would be far worse off. She was grateful that he would be using his special saddle for the parade. Riding bareback was simply ridiculous for a man with his limitations. She expected him to be nearly crippled on the trip home. Thankfully, Rex would be at home ready to snap all of Charlie's pieces back together.

CHAPTER 3

THEIR TRAIN ARRIVED in the city a few hours later than expected due to a couple of cow related incidents.

Knowing they were going to be delayed, they prepared to stay on the train for the night and be taken to the hotel the next morning rather than try to move everyone and everything through the streets in the cold and dark. Truth be told, if Rebecca had her way, they would remain on the train for the duration of their stay, but it would be easier on Charlie to be at the site of the event.

Rebecca was looking forward to seeing Julia Grant again. She liked the woman well enough, and they had similar common interests, though Mrs. Redmond was not impressed with Mrs. Grant's refusal to publicly support the suffrage movement. They tended to avoid that subject, staying with more socially acceptable topics like husbands and children.

Charlie was looking for his place in the book he was reading when Louis entered the car. "General, I have three uniforms for you; which one do you wish to wear tomorrow?"

"Just my regular day uniform will be fine for going into the city and getting settled. Dress uniform with riding boots for the day of the parade and evening dress for the evening events."

"Yes sir." The valet bowed slightly at the waist. "Will you or Mrs. Redmond require anything else this evening?"

Charlie looked to Rebecca, who gave a quick shake of her head, then to his servant. "I think we are fine, Louis, thank you. Have a good evening."

"We have an alarm set for six, sir."

"Yay," Charlie said dryly, causing both the valet and the wife to snicker.

"I will make sure not to keep him up too late." Rebecca winked at Louis as he bowed out of the car, turning through the entrance to his own quarters as the door slid closed on theirs.

"We are still three full days from any of the planned events. Why am I waking up at six in the morning?"

"I suspect it has more to do with us being disembarked from the train at a reasonable hour so the cars may be put in side yards for the duration. Even if we are up at six, we will not be ready to leave before nine."

"Ah, yes, of course." Charlie nodded as he found the page he was looking for. He gave the book a slight lift and wiggled his brows. "Shall we adjourn to the reading lounge?"

"Why yes, dear husband, I think we should."

Charlie rose and offered her his hand and a smile. "I like the way you think."

SUNDAY, NOVEMBER 10, 1879

Rebecca's breath caught hard in her chest and throat when she saw Charlie. It had been years since she had seen him in this simple uniform. It was his standard day uniform, the one he was wearing when he rode away from her to the end of the war. The last time she had seen him whole and healthy.

Tears pricked at her eyes and she forced them away as she did the same to bring the smile to her lips. Old, painful thoughts were pushed far away as she gestured to him and offered, "You look very handsome."

Charlie adjusted the glove that covered some of his scars, the latest prosthetic designed to give him the look of having a complete hand. "Do you think I can still pull it off?"

"Without a doubt, General Redmond." She approached and brushed nonexistent lint from the front of his jacket. "As always, you are the quite proper representation of a United States Army officer."

"I know I should not be nervous…"

"No, you should not. Charlie, you are as accomplished as any man out there and more so than the majority. I never understood why you doubt yourself like this in these circumstances."

Charlie's head shifted slightly as he bit his lip. His mouth moved, but at first there were no words. He was clearly looking for them.

Rebecca watched as a flurry of emotions crossed his face in rapid succession. She saw the tears form in his eyes and she immediately took his hand. "Charlie, what is it?"

"Sometimes," his voice was very small, "Sometimes I feel like I failed. Right at the very end, I failed. I lived when so many died."

"Failed?!" Rebecca's eyes were wide with astonishment as

she wondered what that admission had cost him. "You certainly did not fail. You and your men stopped that train. If you had not, the war would have gone on. You nearly died stopping the war."

She was almost undone herself when she saw his shoulders shake just a tiny bit. She wrapped her arms around him, pulling him down so his head was on her shoulder. "Oh, my darling," she soothed as best she could. "How you could think that you are anything other than the hero that you are is beyond me. And the one thing you certainly are not is a failure. Oh, Charlie."

She just held him there for several minutes, allowing him to find his composure. She gently stroked his back and scratched her fingers at the base of his neck. "I love you, Charlie Redmond. You are the best partner anyone could ever have asked for. I thank God every day that you are my husband and the papa to our children. I am so very proud of you, and that includes your army career. I am sorry I have not always been as supportive of that as I should have been."

He stood and pushed a tear from his eye with his thumb as he smiled down at his loving wife. "You are not required to like the army because I have a moment of self-doubt."

She palmed his cheek, smiling gently, making sure she had his full attention. "I understand that, but it is such a big part of who you are. I never meant to disparage that part of your life and I am sorry if I did not realize you were having doubts or that you felt like you could not talk to me about them. I will do better. I promise."

He took her hand and kissed her palm. "You have never made me feel that I could not talk to you. Sometimes these things sort of creep up on me and I am not even aware of them until they are right in front of me. I think about all the men and," he looked up as a single tear fell and his voice shook, "God, the boys who did not make it home. Soldiers who cannot be here to celebrate. I feel guilty that I am."

"Think of everything you have done because you did live. Look at our children and grandchildren, Charlie. Those children you raised with your sense of honor and duty. The children you raised to be kind and loving. The force you have sent forth toward the next century with their fierce determination and the intelligence to survive and make the world a better place. Do you remember what the old fortune teller said to me in New Orleans? That I would be the mother of leaders of men? I could not be their mother if you were not their father. Everything we have accomplished is because of your determination to survive and for us to thrive."

"You always seem to know exactly that to say." He kissed her lips tenderly. "Thank you."

"I only speak the truth. If you need to hear more of it regularly, I will be happy to tell you." She smiled and kissed him back. "Now, my darling, we do need to get going. Are you alright?"

"I am now," he assured her with a nod as he stood and plucked his hat from the hook where Louis had carefully placed it after brushing it clean. Once it was settled on his head, he took her overcoat from the next hook had held it open. "Shall we go see what wonders and excitement the reunion committee has managed to arrange? I very much want to get Jack settled at the hotel stables as well."

As Charlie and Rebecca stood outside of the transport car and waited for Joe to bring Jack off, a nervous young captain and a grizzled old sergeant major made their way through the mud of the railyard. Stopping a few feet away, the captain offered a crisp salute. The sergeant major gave one that was a little more relaxed, but still respectful.

"General Redmond, sir. Captain McGuire. Sergeant Major Edwards. It is our privilege and pleasure to escort you and Mrs. Redmond to The Palmer House for the Reunion of the Army of the Tennessee."

"Pleasure to meet you, Captain." Charlie shook the man's hand and nodded. Then he grinned at the man behind him. "Good to see you again, Edwards. I see you have earned a few up and down."

The non-commissioned officer smiled big and wide and extended his hand to his old commander, "Yes, sir, General. I decided to stay aboard for the full tour. I'm fifteen years in now. On the downhill slide."

"You were just a pup when we went to Appomattox Station. A fresh- as-Hell private."

"Yes, sir. I didn't get to ride with you for very long, but it was a learning experience."

"A good one, I hope." Charlie grinned.

"I'm still in the army, sir," the sergeant major offered in response.

"Good enough!" Charlie responded with a hearty laugh.

Joe brought Jack down the ramp. The horse snorted and stomped, demanding tribute from his favorite person. Charlie turned and pulled part of a breakfast apple from the pocket of his great coat.

"A bit spoiled, are you?" Charlie teased as he gave the apple to the horse.

Jack just nodded as he munched down the treat.

"General Redmond, sir," Captain McGuire said, "we really should be going. The reunion committee is waiting to receive you and the other guests at the hotel. General Sheridan arrived yesterday. I was given specific instructions to let him know when you had arrived, sir."

"Oh, it looks like we can expect to be spending some time with Philip this week." Rebecca smiled as she pulled on her gloves. "I have missed him."

Charlie leaned in and grinned. "You do realize he is the head of the snake that has caused all your consternation for the last fifteen years?"

TUESDAY, NOVEMBER 12, 1879

Louis was busy brushing all the lint from Charlie's dress uniform one last time. Charlie stood stock still as his valet used a combination of brushes to make sure his appearance was impeccable.

Rebecca looked out the windows of their room, not liking the growing dark clouds she was seeing take their ominous form over the city.

"Charlie, I think it is going to rain. Please make sure to wear your scarf."

"Yes, dear." He winked at Louis as the man brushed the arms of his coat. "I promise not to catch pneumonia today."

"You had better not," Rebecca chastised as she retreated from the window to sort her own things required to go out on a cold, dreary day. "Rex is not here to make you well. You will have to suffer all the way back to Culpeper."

"Duly noted." Charlie nodded as Louis lifted his greatcoat onto his shoulders. "Are you still going down?"

"I do not see how I can avoid it this late in the program. The parade starts in an hour and as the Grants have invited me to ride with them, it seems I am caught between a rock and a hard place."

"Darling, I can send your regrets to the Grants. They would understand completely if you did not want to risk catching cold."

"No, you are here to support your friend and I am here to support you. I do want to see you and Jack in the parade."

"You will have a good view. I will be riding Honor Guard next to the carriage." He leaned over and kissed her cheek. "I really must get down to the stables. I will see you just as soon as I am able after the parade. Sergeant Edwards will be up shortly to escort you to President and Mrs. Grant."

"I shall be ready. Lizbet is tightening a button on my cloak, but I will be properly presentable when the good sergeant arrives."

Charlie took his hat, gloves and sword from Louis, gave Rebecca another peck on the cheek, and was out the door.

"REBECCA, MY DEAR!" JULIA GRANT ENTHUSED AS THE WOMEN all met in a front parlor of the hotel, where they would have coffee or tea and await the carriage meant to carry them through the streets of Chicago. "Have you met Irene Sheridan? Since Phil is leading the parade, she will be joining us in the carriage as well."

Rebecca smiled big, extending both her hands to the women in the room. "No, I have not had the pleasure!" She grasped Irene's hand when it was offered. "It is a delight to meet the woman who could tame Philip. I was positive he was a confirmed bachelor."

"It is a pleasure to meet you, Mrs. Redmond. Phil speaks so highly of your husband!"

"Your husbands are two of the best friends and colleagues my husband could have ever hoped for. I am eternally grateful for their support. And for yours, as well." Julia gave Rebecca's hand a tight squeeze. "I know it has not always been easy."

In that moment of eye contact with Julia, all of Rebecca's animosity toward Ulysses melted away. What she saw was a grateful, but tired woman.

Not only had this world tour been physically and financially draining on the couple, but Rebecca understood in that moment the actual differences between them.

While Julia's husband was loved and well received wherever he went, he was still a poor businessman and their financial security was constantly in jeopardy. Rebecca realized how very fortunate she truly was.

Not only was Charlie an astute businessman who had made sure his wife and family would be well cared for after his passing, but he did not try to stop her own business ventures. He was always the first person she turned to for advice when undecided. He never tried to talk her out of anything, but he always made sure she understood the benefits and risks of any venture that she consulted him about.

She could not imagine Julia Grant having that kind of a relationship with her husband and that made her a little sad for her friend.

Rebecca understood that she had a truly unique and very special relationship. And she knew it was the man himself. If every woman could have a man like Charlie, there would be a lot less strife in the world. True gentlemen where becoming harder and harder to come by.

He respected her ideas and opinions. He readily bowed to her superior knowledge on a variety of subjects including horses, current literary offerings, and chess. And he was not afraid to engage her in debate on the subject of the day.

Rebecca smiled at both women and then leaned in to give Julia a kiss on the cheek. "I am delighted to be here to support our men!" She turned to the younger woman. "And it is indeed a true pleasure to meet you, Irene! Philip and President Grant have always been close to our hearts, and regularly in our thoughts and prayers."

They only had a few minutes before President Grant entered the room and announced the carriage had arrived to take them to the start of the route.

A canopy had been placed over the front entrance to shield the very important guests from the rain that was beginning to drizzle down. As Rebecca was escorted out by some young officer, she noticed the streets were becoming very congested with people on foot and horseback.

President Grant assisted his wife and Irene Sheridan into the carriage and then turned to Rebecca offering his hand. "It is lovely to see you again, my dear. I am very happy to see you looking so well."

"Thank you, Mr. President. You may add my good health to the list of miracles Charlie Redmond has performed."

Grant leaned over and said quietly, "He is very good at those. Clearly, Charlie is favored by God Almighty."

"I think you are right, sir." Rebecca even blushed a bit at the compliment paid to her husband as she took Grant's hand and used the other to pull herself into the carriage, taking the seat across from where the president would sit.

Once he was inside and settled, the door was secured and the carriage jerked into motion, carrying them to Park Row, where the parade would start.

It only took a few minutes to get the carriage into place.

Rebecca smiled when she saw that Charlie had been placed at the rear right side of the carriage; she would get to see Charlie ride in the parade.

She noticed his foot twitching a bit in the stirrup and immediately knew that meant he was fighting pain in his hips and knees. Fortunately, Jack, accustomed to his master's unusual seat, stood stock still, waiting to step off.

The rain continued to drizzle down and she hoped Charlie had remembered his scarf as she watched a stream of water run off the brim of his hat and down his cloak.

She knew that cloak would keep his body warm and dry, but she worried about his face being exposed to the cold and rain. She said a quick prayer to God to keep him safe and healthy.

They very briefly made eye contact and Charlie winked at her before becoming the properly stoic cavalry officer again.

A whistle signaled the start and the carriage set off at an easy pace. As soon as they made the turn onto Michigan Avenue, Rebecca's eyes were torn from her husband.

She had not been expecting the roar of the crowd. The din was deafening. She tore her eyes from her husband and took her first look at the citizens assembled to pay their respects to President Grant.

Even with the rain, people were six deep, standing shoulder to shoulder. They jostled each other, everyone straining to get the best glimpse possible of the returning American hero. Some people slipped in the mud, but rarely hit the ground because someone was right there to stop their fall.

She smiled when she noticed that the rain was letting up. That was a very good sign as far as she was concerned. She was very glad Charlie was no longer getting drenched. She glanced back to him and noticed how carefully Jack was moving. The old war horse was making his best parade showing, his head was high and he slowly moved it from side to side watching the crowd for himself.

He was doing what Rebecca had always called his parade walk. He was at a walking pace, but raising his feet just a bit higher than normal, giving him an appearance of a slow-paced prancing. It was one of the gaits Charlie had taught the horse. She had never known another horse to do it.

She had made him instruct Sue on how to teach the horses this particular move. Apparently, it was a normal and typical move for war horses and was not a technique regularly taught to domesticated horses.

The things Charlie had taught Sue had originally come from ancient Greece. He regularly mentioned Xenophon's writings on the subject as they worked together. The art of training horses in this manner had remained mostly within military organizations around the world, such as the Spanish Riding School in Vienna.

Rebecca was almost giddy at the idea of her horses knowing something that most farms and trainers could not teach. It gave them a large advantage in the market. There was no practical reason to own a horse that could do these things other than to show off, and she was happy to take the money of men that wanted to show off.

Sue and one of her trainers taught the buyer the basics of handling the horse. After that, they were welcome to figure it out for themselves or pay for further lessons. They usually hired Stephen Bradford, Sue's head trainer, for at least a month to teach them more of what their horses already knew.

Rebecca had actually thought the crowd would grow thinner as they progressed, but to her amazement, it did not. If anything, it grew thicker and louder.

Her gaze was once again taken from Charlie as she caught a glimpse of daring men and boys who had climbed the half-built structure of the courthouse on Clark Street as they tried to get the best view of the parade from fifty feet in the air.

The streets were so crowded with people that she could tell that the procession was moving through the streets just inches away from human bodies. If she had to guess, there was barely enough room for two carriages abreast to pass. The crowd most certainly slowed the progress of the entourage, but no one seemed to care. President Grant and Julia smiled and waved to the enthusiastic crowd, causing more of an uproar among the sea of spectators.

Rebecca's eyes slid back to Charlie and Jack. The big black stallion was having the time of his life. To the day she died, Rebecca would tell stories of that horse and how he smiled all through the parade in Chicago. She was convinced he thought the tens of thousands of people assembled were there just for him.

CHARLIE HAD BEEN MAKING THE ROUNDS OF THE ROOM AS ALL the speakers for President Grant's dinner waited for the event to begin. The Grand Dining Room of The Palmer House had been turned into a proper banquet hall and as the attendees were seated at their tables, the invited speakers waited in a parlor across the hall enjoying whiskey and cigars while making small talk in various knots of men.

Charlie had spent a few minutes trying to say hello to everyone. He and Phil Sheridan had been corralled by President Grant, who introduced them to Samuel Clemens. The four men had spent twenty minutes in a corner laughing and carrying on. Mr. Clemens took an opportunity to exchange cards with Charlie so they could stay in touch.

"He only wants to bring you over to his side of the argument that I should write a book," Grant groused as he pulled his cigar from his lips.

"I do not see why you should not do so, sir." Charlie nodded. "Based on the reception you have gotten here, I suspect a book detailing your life and career would be well received. I know I will buy a copy."

"Well said, General Redmond!" Clemens laughed as he patted Charlie on the back. "Does not look like I need to bring him to my side, Mr. President. He is already there!"

"I thought you were my friend, Charlie," Grant grumbled, making the other three men laugh heartily.

Charlie excused himself on the premise of refilling his drink. In reality, what he needed was a place to lean for about ten minutes. Riding in the parade in the morning and returning to his room just long enough to bathe and change into his day dress uniform before going back downstairs to mingle with the various attendees of the reunion had taken it out of him.

Then it was back to his room for a quick wash and another uniform change into his formal evening dress attire. He had ordered the grand uniform of the Ambassador, with all the embroidery, to be burned, but it was rescued by his wife and valet and carefully packed away in a trunk in the attic until this trip.

He still wore the trappings of his previous office, the blue and silver sash of his ambassadorship crossing from is right shoulder to his left hip. His Medal of Honor hung snuggly at his neck, just under the knot of his tie. Ribbons and local medals earned from various commanders over his career adorned his left breast.

Louis had carefully tied the gold cavalry sword sash around his waist and Charlie was lifting his sword belt into place around his waist when Rebecca entered the room.

He smiled when he recognized the look on her face. She stopped, took a deep breath, bit her lower lip, and patted her breast. Lust. That was what he saw. He hated having to leave their room.

As he made his way to the elevator, he made himself a promise to stay sober and have an early night.

He approached the bar, placing himself in a corner as he leaned the left side of his body against the structure. He put his glass down with his right hand and gestured to the young negro man tending bar. "Bourbon. Neat, please."

He needed to rest. He was tired. He was sore. He had seriously over estimated his stamina. He groaned, leaning harder on the bar as the young bartender placed a new drink in front of him.

"Are you alright, sir?" The barman quirked a brow as he searched Charlie's face.

"Just a tired old solider," Charlie offered as he lifted his glass and drained it in one swallow. "Keep those coming if you do not mind."

"Not at all, sir." The young man smiled before turning to pluck the bottle from the display behind him. He quickly and efficiently refilled Charlie's glass. Then he quietly placed the bottle on the bar. "If there is anything else you need, my name is Charlie."

"Well," the general laughed as he extended his hand over the bar, "I am a Charlie as well. Good to meet you, young man."

The bartender looked startled but took Charlie's hand, and as they shook, he began to smile. "Pleasure to meet you, sir."

As Charlie pulled back his hand, he lifted his chin to a small stool behind the bar that held a leather case with paper sticking out of it. "Are those yours?"

The young man glanced back, swallowing nervously before

turning back to the general. "Yes, sir. But I promise I was not ignoring my duty..."

Charlie drained his glass again before placing it back on the bar and pouring another. "I know. I saw you sketching earlier, before you relieved the previous bartender. May I see them?"

"Um." The man took a step backward and picked up his portfolio without looking back. "Yes, sir, of course, but please, sir, I can't afford to lose this job."

Charlie squared himself along the bar when the leather case was placed before him. "I have no intention of getting you in trouble, son. I wanted to see your sketches."

Charlie lifted the cover and began slowly paging through the sketches. There were a number of subjects, from wildlife to still-lives to portraits. There were two that caught Charlie's attention.

One had been done from a balcony or a window of the hotel earlier in the day. It clearly showed him astride Jack as the parade ended at The Palmer House with President Grant's coach. A figure that was obviously Rebecca could be seen in one of the windows of the carriage.

The second was a very nice, detailed sketch that had been done while Charlie was speaking with Grant, Sheridan, and Clemens. All the men were smiling; President Grant with his trademark cigar in the corner of his mouth; Sheridan resting a hand on Charlie's shoulder as the joke passed through the group; and Mr. Clemens, a cigar between his fingers, gesturing to make a point.

General Charlie looked to Charlie the bartender. "Are you interested in selling these?"

"Excuse me?" The surprise was evident on the young man's face. "General, if you like the sketches, I'd be happy for you to have them, sir. A gift."

"Oh, no." Charlie shook his head as he reached into his jacket for his wallet. "I am a firm believer in being a patron to the arts. You are very talented. My wife and I have some sketches by Monsieur Degas, and I am sure she would love to add these to that collection." He pulled a ten-dollar bill from his wallet. "I am afraid after the festivities of today, this is all I have at the moment. I am willing to make it double the amount if you will trust me until tomorrow."

The young man smiled and shook his head in disbelief. "No, sir. That is more than fine. This is the first time I have ever sold anything. Ten dollars is more than fair."

"And I doubt it will be the last. Could you do me a favor?"

"Yes, sir, anything."

"I am afraid I do not have time to deliver these to my room. Please hold on to them until tomorrow and bring them to room three oh four any time after," Charlie plucked his watch from his vest pocket and saw it was already quarter to seven, "Noon."

"I'd be happy to do that, sir. Thank you."

"You are very welcome, Charlie. You really are very talented. Do not let anyone convince you otherwise."

Before the young man could say anything, the manager of The Palmer House opened the parlor door and announced it was time to be seated for dinner.

Charlie drained the last of his whiskey and nodded to the bartender before turning to make his way to the dining room.

The artist fingered the ten-dollar bill as he watched the general limp away, a proud and satisfied smiled forming on his lips.

THE EARLY EVENING CHARLIE HAD HOPED FOR HAD NOT COME TO pass. He had been one of more than a dozen speakers both paying homage to and also managing a fair amount of teasing of the former chief executive.

President Grant had not moved a muscle through the entire event. Had not twitched a brow, winked an eye, or even hinted at cracking a smile. That was until Mr. Clemens, as the last speaker, offered up a speech that had all the attendees, including the stoic President Grant, laughing until they cried.

The dinner had gone on until after two in the morning and then there was the expected two or so hours of socializing among the men. Charlie had tried to escape several times, but kept getting caught by one fellow or another, pulled into another group and given another drink.

Charlie leaned against the wall of the elevator, managing to pull his watch from his pocket. With a little effort, he opened the cover and after refocusing his eyes several times he managed to make out it was about a quarter to five in the morning.

"Four forty-five, sir," the elevator operator offered quietly without even turning his head to look at Charlie.

"Thank you." The general slipped his watch back in his pocket and then unbuckled the belt holding his sword. He was damn tired of carrying the thing around. He blinked several times as he wrapped the belt around the scabbard to make it easier to carry. When the elevator stopped, it jostled his balance and sent him forward. The operator managed to catch him and help steady him on his feet.

"Are you alright, sir?"

"Fine, just a hair too much imbibing, I am afraid."

"Do you need help to your room, sir? I'd be happy to assist you."

"No, no," Charlie protested as he straightened and tried his best to appear more sober than he was. "I am fine. I can make it from here. Thank you."

The young man nodded and opened the gate for Charlie. Taking a deep breath, the general took his first steps, very slowly. Once he found his footing, he continued at a pace a snail might consider too slow, but it was sure and steady.

He made the short walk to the door that would let him into the sitting room of their suite. Charlie knew he had to change and make some effort to clean up before getting into bed with Rebecca. He had no desire to subject her to the smell of old whiskey and stale cigars.

He began patting pockets in search of the key. He could not for the life of him remember where he had put the little brass bastard. Pants pockets were checked first, causing his sword to drop from his hand and clatter against the door.

"Shit," Charlie mumbled as he leaned over to get the sword and banged his head on the door.

He was only stopped from falling into the room face first by Louis, who caught him as soon as the door opened.

"Whoa, there, General. Have a bit of head, do we, sir?"

"Not, not as bad as you would think." Charlie did hiccup as he stood upright, swaying just slightly. "I can still see and hear you."

"Then we will call that a win, sir." The valet chuckled as he guided his inebriated boss to the sofa.

"Thank you," Charlie groaned as he settled onto the soft surface.

"Miss Rebecca said you would come in boiled tighter than an owl," Louis told Charlie as he began tugging off the general's boots.

"She did, did she?"

"Yes, she did." Louis nodded as he tossed the footwear to the side. He stood and leaned over, removing Charlie's Medal of Honor from around his neck.

"I love her," Charlie commented with a silly grin.

"She loves you, too," Louis assured as he carefully placed the medal back in its storage box.

"I am a very lucky man."

"Yes, sir." The servant could not help but snort with amusement. It had been a while since he had seen his boss this deep in his cups.

Charlie stared at his valet through bleary eyes and gestured. "You are in your robe and night shirt."

"I often am at five in the morning, General."

"Oh, God," Charlie groaned as he shook his head. "I have to get cleaned up before I go to bed. General Sherman smokes the most disgusting cigar I have ever smelled. I am fairly certain it is horseshit wrapped in cow shit."

Louis just shook his head and proceed to peel off Charlie's sashes, coat, vest and tie in record time. They were all tossed into a pile near the boots. The general was correct; they were badly in need of laundering.

Charlie watched as Louis gathered a pitcher and bowl, several towels, and a bar of soap. The general unbuttoned his shirt and tugged it from his trousers.

"That will be easier to get off if you lower your suspenders," the valet commented as he placed a small table in front of Charlie and went on with preparing the water.

As Charlie dropped the suspenders, he watched Louis pour the water. "If I have not said so recently, thank you for taking such good care of me."

"You are very welcome, General. I enjoy my position with you. Not a lot of fellas like me get an opportunity like this. I make a good wage, have nice clothes, get to travel with you most of the time, and have a very nice home. There is nothing I would rather be doing."

"Even at five in the morning when I am half drunk?"

"Even then. You haven't done this in quite some time." Louis chuckled and dropped a cloth into the bowl as Charlie pulled his shirt over his head. "Given the event it was to be expected. Can you manage? I'll go fetch your nightclothes."

"Yes, I think I can take it from here."

By the time Louis returned Charlie had managed a decent job of washing up. The valet laid Charlie's fresh small clothes and robe on the sofa and went about collecting the soiled garments. Taking those from the room gave Charlie enough time to change into his fresh clothes. He was tying off the belt of his robe when Louis returned. He handed Charlie a bottle of Bay Rum. "You might want to put some of this in your hair."

"Good thinking." Charlie applied the cologne to his palms and rubbed his hands through his hair, combing it back into something that resembled place with his fingers.

Louis cleared the bowl, pitcher and towels. "Cup of tea before bed, sir?"

"Yes, please. Join me."

"Thank you."

Louis had the tea service ready long before Charlie had come in. It did not take him long to make two cups and rejoin Charlie on the sofa.

"What time did Rebecca go to bed?" Charlie asked before sipping his tea.

"A little before midnight, but she did not sleep well and was up and down until about two."

"Terrors?"

"I think so."

"You could have sent for me."

"She wouldn't let us. Lizbet and I both offered to go down

and find you. Lizbet sat with her until she fell asleep. It's too bad that Xie isn't here."

"I am glad our arrangement with him does not interfere with your relationship."

"Not at all. I know those nights spent with her are in the capacity of physician and caring friend."

"You are a good man, Louis. I am happy you and Rex have found something that makes you both content and happy. You are both invaluable to me."

"Thank you, Charlie."

"I had better get to bed before Rebecca wakes up." Charlie sighed, setting his cup to the side. As he stood, he looked down to his friend. "Thank you again. I will see you sometime later today."

"Good night, sir."

~

"I WILL ADMIT BEING A TAD JEALOUS, REBECCA! THESE ARE wonderful!" Irene Sheridan enthused over the drawings Charlie had purchased the night before.

Charlie was still sleeping when the artist arrived just after noon, but Rebecca was delighted to receive him, even unexpectedly.

He presented her with the now beautifully framed sketches, explaining that he had spent the evening making the frames so the sketches would travel home safely.

Rebecca was very impressed with his skill as both an artist and a craftsman. She assured him the sketches would no doubt hang in a place of prominence in their office back in Virginia.

Charlie was still sleeping, but now Rebecca was entertaining Philip and Irene Sheridan with a light tea. They had come by to invite Charlie and Rebecca to dinner that evening, but Rebecca graciously declined. She was positive Charlie would be too tired or too hung over, or both, to be social.

So, while Charlie slept on, the threesome sat in the parlor having a lovely visit and admiring the sketches.

"I do love this one of Phil and Charlie with Grant. Dear," she turned the frame so her husband could see it, "Who is the gentleman with the mustache?"

"Samuel Clemens. You might know him as Mark Twain."

"No! Really?" Rebecca chirped as she looked at the portrait again. "Oh, Darby is going to be green with envy. Mr. Twain, eh, Clemens is one of his favorite authors."

Charlie's voice was rough with sleep when he said, "I think he will forgive me. I managed to get him an autographed copy of Tom Sawyer."

"Well, good afternoon, my sleepy man!"

"I do apologize for my appearance," he offered to Phil and Irene as he tightened the sash of his robe. "I did not realize we had company."

"Charlie, do not be silly!" Irene laughed. "Phil was in much the same condition two hours ago."

WEDNESDAY, DECEMBER 17, 1879

Richard stood at the rail of the porch in front of the bar that the residents of Culpepper still called "Jocko's" even though the original owner had been dead for more than five years. Jamie Benson had made sure it continued to prosper for Jocko's widow, his savior and employer, Esther Jackson. Richard was waiting for Charlie. Every Wednesday, come rain or shine, they met at Jocko's for lunch unless one of them had to be out of town.

He saw Charlie coming up the street from the bank, so he tossed his cigar aside, brushed off some errant ashes, and strolled inside, where he took his usual seat at the end of the bar.

Jamie, having seen him coming, had a mug of coffee bolstered with a shot of brandy waiting for him. He dropped a second mug at the seat beside Richard and turned to go into the kitchen at the back of the building to get both gentlemen their lunch.

Richard did not bother to look up when Charlie came in the door. He simply called over his shoulder, "You are late. Lunch is on the way."

Charlie laughed as he pulled his bar stool out a little. "It is not as if you actually had to make an order, Richard. Do not be so dramatic." He climbed up and settled himself and took a significant slug of the coffee as Jamie returned and placed their smothered pork chops on the bar.

"So, how goes your day, now that you no longer have to patrol the streets of Culpeper?"

Richard had recently retired from his position as sheriff of Culpeper County. "Oh, I am looking into this and that. A little trading, a little land."

"Um," mumbled Charlie, who had just stuffed an enormous bite of the pork chop into his mouth. When he managed to swallow, he rejoined the conversation. "You know, Jerome has started going to these auctions the army has been holding to get rid of excess supplies, stock, and whatever other junk they no longer need. He says he found something I would like for not much money. It is supposed to be on the train this afternoon, so I've asked George and Jimmie to meet the shipment for me."

"And what did he buy you?"

"I honestly do not know. He just said he was sure I would like it."

"Hmmm." Richard chewed his food thoughtfully. "Maybe I will join you in discovering this find from Jerome."

"Well, you will have to come over later. I have a meeting at the bank after lunch and will not be heading home until after four. So, what do you think about collecting Elizabeth and joining us for supper?"

"Sounds like a pleasant evening. I always love watching Rebecca react to your little surprises."

"Then it is a shame you missed the best one. I had a crate of furs from Russia show up at the house in England one day. I did not know they were coming and could not warn her."

"Furs? What was her reaction?"

"Oh, well, she took the best ones and used them to have her dress maker trim her winter wardrobe with them." Richard did not need the details of how he and Rebecca had utilized the rest.

"Well, for your sake, I hope this surprise from Jerome is as, um, well-received."

Charlie grinned, remembering their little English hideaway. "So do I."

The sun was getting low in the sky when Charlie's coach pulled in front of Elizabeth and Richard's house. They came out promptly and joined their old friend. Charlie thumped on the roof as they settled in, and Alfred, his new coachman, set off at a brisk pace.

Otis met them at the front door, his facial expression conveying a warning to Charlie before he said a single word. "Miss Rebecca's in the back parlor, sir, and wants to see you as soon as you arrive. And a large number of crates were delivered. I had them put in the carriage house."

"Thank you, Otis. Could you show Colonel Polk and Dr. Walker to the smoking room and get them something to drink?"

Richard and Elizabeth both started laughing. Elizabeth spoke up. "Oh, no, Charlie. Whatever it is, you are **not** getting off that easily. We get to watch."

Charlie, Richard, and Elizabeth shed their coats and hats and then made their way to the back parlor to face the family virago. Otis hurried downstairs. As he burst into the kitchen, rather breathless, he announced to CeCe that Gen'l Charlie was about to have his head handed to him and Colonel Richard and Dr. Elizabeth were going to watch.

"Gently, Otis. Do what your father would have done. Take that tea tray up, move very quietly, and make sure the sherry and the brandy are handy." CeCe had learned well from her mother.

CHARLIE GENTLY OPENED THE DOOR TO THE PARLOR, IGNORING the prodding in his back from his ex-second in command. Rebecca was sitting by the fire and Rex was in his usual chair by the chessboard.

"Hello, sweetheart. How was your day?" Charlie entered the room carefully. He was perfectly aware that when truly irritated, Rebecca was not beneath heaving any convenient small object across the room. Her temper had gotten far touchier since her stroke, and it had never been the most mild-mannered. The only things that were sacrosanct were her collection of Fabergé hardstone sculptures.

He walked over to her and kissed her gently on the top of her head. She had yet to say a word. Charlie looked over to Rex with a bewildered look on his face, hoping for some sign. Rex nodded hello, but nothing else.

Richard and Elizabeth slipped into the room. Rebecca smiled at them and started to rise to greet her guests, but Elizabeth intervened. "No, dear. You need not get up for us. We are just part of the woodwork for now."

"Just flies on the wall," added Richard with a wink as he poured a cognac for himself and a dry sherry for Elizabeth from the tantalus.

"Flies who drink my best brandy," muttered Charlie under his breath. As he settled himself beside Rebecca, he continued. "So, dear. Anything interesting happen here today?"

"Nothing particular, except that load of crates and other cargo that George and Jimmie dumped in the carriage house. What damned thing have you gotten us into this time?" Rebecca was clearly not amused.

"Oh. That. Well, I do not really know, dear. Jerome had a chance to buy a lot of materials at one of the army's auctions and there was something in the lot, so he bought it and had it sent to us." He shrugged. "I really do not know. Maybe a carriage or something."

"A carriage. Another damned carriage? Charles Huger Redmond, you have twenty-five carriages, coaches, traps, buggies, and wagons in there now. We do not need another one!"

"I said maybe, dear. I did not do this. Jerome did it and told me about it after the sale so I could have someone meet the freight train."

Otis had slipped in during this exchange with a fresh tea tray. Rex smiled at him and quietly poured Rebecca a cup, and then reached over her shoulder to place it on the table beside her. She reached for it automatically and took a sip before she spoke again.

"So, this is as much a surprise to you as it is to me?" She paused and sipped again. "Except you, at least, knew something was coming or George and Jimmie would not have known to retrieve your crates. You could tell them, but not tell me?"

"Dear, I only found out this morning. There was a telegram waiting for me at the bank when I got there."

"And you could not find anyone to run a message out to me?"

"Um…" Charlie sighed, frustrated with her interrogation. There was no good or right answer that was going to placate his wife. He was mostly used to it, but sometimes he needed the patience of Job. He bit his bottom lip, drew a slow, deep breath and looked to the ceiling. Surely there would be Heavenly intervention.

Richard cleared his throat to remind Rebecca that he and Elizabeth were in the room. "So, what do you say to going over to the carriage house and find out what Jerome sent you?"

Charlie scrambled to drape Rebecca's shawl around her shoulders. "Shall we go?" she asked as she turned to Richard and Elizabeth. "I trust you two are enjoying yourselves. Are you playing Greek chorus or just audience today?"

"Oh, audience today. We got free tickets from Charlie for this performance." Elizabeth grinned evilly.

The five friends trooped down to the carriage house. No one said a word. Rebecca was exuding such an aura of stony silence no one had the gall to break it.

As they entered the shadow-filled carriage house, Charlie slipped around lighting the gas lamps. He had spent a small fortune installing gas lighting at Mountain View when they returned from England. While the improvement in lighting was, in his opinion, worth every dollar he had spent, Rebecca hated the gas lights, and used candles and oil lamps by preference, but here, and in their office, his preference prevailed. She had rather sullenly admitted that the gas lights were brighter.

There, piled in the middle of the floor, lay a heap of crates and parts of what looked like an old hard topped wagon.

Elizabeth gasped, "My God! It is an old ambulance!"

Charlie shook his head while Richard stepped behind his wife to support her.

"Elizabeth, are you sure?" Charlie was bewildered as to why Jerome would have sent such a thing to him.

"Charlie, I spent far too many hours of my life in one of those things! I swear, I would recognize it in pitch dark. It is an ambulance."

Charlie shook his head again, unable to comprehend why Jerome would have sent such a thing.

Rebecca started chuckling. "Jerome is as bad as you, Charlie. Perhaps he sent it so you could fix it up for Elizabeth's clinic to use."

"Wellll..." Elizabeth spoke slowly. "I suppose we could use it when there has been an accident on a farm or something. I can think of a lot of reasons why we could use an ambulance. Remember last year when the barn fire had that beam fall and trap the two Hansom boys? We had to use a couple of buckboards to transport them. A proper ambulance would have been a blessing."

Charlie stood there, still in disbelief, while Rex, who had not said a word until now, spoke up. "Elizabeth, we could rig it with the latest equipment and get a pair of fast horses... and have it re-sprung to cut down on the jostling."

Rebecca added, "I can help with the horses. I have a couple of excellent carriage horses for sale."

"Sell, darling? I would have thought you would donate them," Charlie questioned.

Her response was entirely sarcastic. "I have a business to run. I would be happy to sell them to you, dear husband, and you can donate them. Or perhaps I should send them to a warehouse in Washington, throw a tarp over them, and have Jerome buy them at auction for you."

Rex stepped in again. "Oh, no, Rebecca. You must sell them to me, as the ambulance is as much a service for me as for Elizabeth."

Rebecca took a deep breath. "You are right, Rex. And I am being a bit testy about this. I apologize. Shall we see what other wonders Jerome has sent us?"

Charlie called one of the stable hands in to pry open the crates. The first few had a goodly collection of tack – harness for carriages, blinders, driving reins, bridles and bits, and a couple of rather badly beaten up military saddles. The next had various bits of barn gear – buckets, leads, feed bags, hoof picks and other items.

While the rest of the group continued to look through the equine equipment, Richard went on to the other crates.

The last three were very different.

"What the heck is this? It looks like nothing more than a whole crate full of silk!" Richard was digging down into the crate and kept pulling out fold after fold of carefully stitched silk with ropes sewn into the seams.

"Old tents maybe?" Charlie looked over Richard's shoulder.

Richard shook his head. "Silk tents? Really, Charlie? What army were you in?"

The next crate held a large wicker basket with various metal fittings around the rim.

The third held something that looked rather like a very large oil burner – with a large copper container.

Richard dropped his chin to his chest. "Oh, dear Lord. Jerome lost his mind."

Charlie looked up, questioningly.

"Charlie, your idiot in-law has bought you a hot air balloon."

Supper that night was strained. Elizabeth and Rex sat together, with a pad of paper between them. They talked, made notes, drew sketches, and generally ignored everyone else at the table and mostly overlooked their supper. Richard, Charlie, and Rebecca ate silently. Neither man had the courage to break into Rebecca's stony silence over the hot air balloon. After one terse comment to Charlie about "not daring to risk your life in that damned thing," she had withdrawn into her best imitation of the Sphinx. They knew better than to interrupt her sulk.

THURSDAY DECEMBER 25, 1879

Christmas this year was somewhat more subdued than it had been on previous occasions. Stella was due any time, so she and Darby opted to celebrate Christmas morning rituals at their home. Charlie, Rebecca and Rex rose, had coffee and sweet rolls, presented the boys with their gifts, and drove into town for the Christmas morning service.

They arrived at Stella and Darby's just in time for luncheon. MaBeh and PaePoo were mobbed at the door by L.J., with two-year-old Rachel toddling at top speed behind her big brother. Buddy and Andy helped Louis haul in the pile of presents that the indulgent grandparents had acquired for the family. Jerome and Amelia appeared in the hall, with Darby bringing up the rear. Stella had struggled to haul her fecund self out of her chair in the parlor and failed.

Jane led her small kitchen staff, several of whom had been hired for the holidays, into the parlor, bringing dishes and plates that were laid out on every flat surface in the room. She proudly showed off her culinary skills, inherited from her mother Sarah, and expanded over the past few years in part through collaboration with her big sister CeCe. The two Redmond households were the envy of the valley when it came to the food coming out of their kitchens.

Rex quietly prepared a plate and a cup of tea for Rebecca, who had taken possession of a comfortable chair near the fire. L.J. was busy looking over the pile of presents that his uncles had deposited under the Christmas tree, but as soon as he noticed his grandmother had biscuits and jam on her plate, he made a bee line for his Mabeh's lap.

Charlie was occupied by his granddaughter, who had attached herself to his neck like a leech. "PaePoo bring pressies?" she whispered in a very earnest, childish lisp.

Charlie laughed. "Yes, child. PaePoo brought presents for you, your brother, your mother, your father, and your other grandparents. But you will have to wait until we eat our luncheon, little one."

The impatient, disappointed pout was epic.

Grandpa remained unpersuaded. This time.

As the adults ate and chatted about this and that, the children latched onto their uncles to examine the packages and sort them into piles based on the intended recipient. They paid no attention at all when Aunt Sue and Uncle Jeremiah arrived, having stopped at the Carters' briefly after church. That changed when Jeremiah came over to add to the piles of gifts sorted under the tree.

Finally, little Rachel could stand the suspense no longer. With her most winsome look, she approached her grandfather Charlie, the one adult she thought she could now wrap around her finger most easily, and lisped, "PaePoo, please. Pressies?"

Charlie, who in the end was always a sucker for pleading

little girls, folded like one of Rebecca's finest silk fans. "All right, little one." Addressing the assembly of adults, he added, "I think we have tormented the children long enough, folks. Shall we?"

The adults moved to seat themselves around the Christmas tree in the family parlor, with Stella taking the seat of honor near the fireplace, while Darby manned the tantalus in the corner. Jane sent a tea tray laden with small Christmas cookies and fruit cake up from the kitchen, and they all settled down to enjoy present opening.

Once again, Charlie had spent a small fortune with his old friend Frederick Schwarz, who had moved to New York and opened his own toy store, following the same pattern set by his brother in Baltimore, but expanding on it until he boasted it was the finest toy store in America. Schwarz privately told Charlie that his Christmas catalog, which he started publishing in '76, was all Charlie's fault – he needed to let his best customer know what he had available for the upcoming holiday and a catalog simply made sense.

Charlie had decided that five was a good age to start L.J. on the family tradition of toy soldiers and famous battlefields, and had gone a bit overboard to make sure his first grandson had enough of the small figures to play with properly. Uncle Buddy was more than happy to help L.J. lay out a plan of battle between the French and the Allied forces at Waterloo. Uncle Andy sat back and looked bored.

Dolls were the order of the day for two-year-old Rachel, and although Charlie had gotten her a beautiful doll with a hand painted porcelain face and real human hair, the winner and her absolute favorite was a stuffed horsey that Uncle Jeremiah had fashioned from leather scraps.

Each person had received a lovely collection of Christmas

presents, though most were predictable. Scarves, gloves, riding gear, and, for the ladies, jewelry was the order of the day, including a beautiful necklace that Charlie had commissioned for Rebecca that included all of her children and grandchildren's birthstones. Once all gifts had been opened, the family adjourned to Christmas dinner. Jane had worked hard to duplicate her mother's traditional Christmas dinner and set a very credible table that was properly consumed by the family. With Buddy and Andy at the table, the leftovers were few and far between.

~

FRIDAY DECEMBER 26, 1879

While the family Christmas had been relatively subdued compared to Christmases from previous years, the Redmond's had adopted a thoroughly British tradition during their sojourn in England, while as always, putting their own unique spin on any event. It was Boxing Day, and it was anything but subdued.

On this one day, the magnificent home known to employees as Mountain View, and to most of the residents of the area as Redmond Stables, was open to everyone who helped support the horse farm and estate throughout the year.

It was an open house; everyone was welcome and more importantly invited, to join the family for the huge community party hosted the day after Christmas. Anyone who chose to take part knew there would be no tolerance of discrimination. White men and women were not only expected to sit down to eat with negro men and women, but to be friendly, civil and make polite conversation. Anyone who could not adhere to the simple directive of Matthew 7:12 *"Therefore all things whatsoever ye would that men should do to you, do ye even so to them: for this is the law and the prophets"* was given a basket of food and a polite but firm escort to and out the front gates, usually by Mr. Brooks or General Charlie himself.

Over the course of the day, starting at around ten in the morning, they would begin serving what could end up being a couple hundred people if the need in the community and surrounding area was great. Everyone knew that if you were hungry, go to Mountain View; no one would be turned away, especially on Boxing Day.

It was a bright, clear, but chilly day. Even with temperatures in the mid-forties, there was still about an inch of slowly melting snow on the ground, but no one seemed to mind. There was a cacophony of voices, talking, laughing, and some of the children were singing as they played in a group.

CeCe and her staff had exceeded all expectations, setting a board for all of the residents of Mountain View and Redmond Grove, as well as for what looked like half the residents of Culpeper County.

In addition to the traditional turkeys and hams, the long tables in the covered passage between the house and the summer kitchen were heavily laid with roasted boar (complete with the head and an apple in its jaws), roasted beef, and a magnificent whole saddle of venison. There were multiple side dishes, including fresh green beans from the hot house, a wonderful sweet potato casserole, New Orleans style dirty rice, and all sorts of fresh winter squash, broccoli, cauliflower, roasted new potatoes, and gravies or sauces for each entrée. CeCe stood at the head of the buffet, grinning like Mr. Carroll's famous cat as Rex and the Redmond children stood behind the buffet tables ready to help serve any of their guests. Darby and Stella kept a watchful eye on their brothers, especially Andy, who kept trying to find a reason to excuse himself from serving duties to go mingle with the young women that were in the crowd.

Sue and Jeremiah retreated to Sue's office near the kitchen. There, she handed out end of the year bonus envelopes to every employee, both house and farm staff.

Seated in one of her most comfortable chairs purloined from the back parlor, with blankets tucked tightly around her legs and a shawl around her shoulders, Rebecca held court on the back porch just outside the kitchen door.

All the guests made sure to take a moment to make their way to the steps to say hello and pay proper respects to the matriarch of the Redmond family. She was gracious and open to each and every soul who approached her. Mrs. Redmond was quickly becoming a well-respected elder of not just Culpeper, but the entire Virginia Piedmont as well. Her opinion carried great weight with a number of people, not just in the surrounding communities, but the state.

Standing quietly behind her, Christiana Baldwin observed with a critical eye. Miss Chris, as the family had come to call her, was a nurse Rex had hired very early on during Rebecca's recovery. In the years that followed, the young woman had become a good friend to Rebecca and even though her medical skills were no longer required at home, Rex had plenty of work for her at the hospital when she was not serving as Rebecca's secretary and companion. She was still very aware that Rebecca could tire quickly, and was intent on seeing to it that her friend did not over-extend herself trying to be a gracious hostess to all of Culpeper.

Charlie was in the yard between the house and summer kitchen, waist deep in boys and girls of all colors, sizes and ages, each clamoring for one of the packages he would retrieve from three large piles on the long table behind him.

Rebecca watched indulgently as he laughed and played with the children as he gave them their little gifts. She would never begrudge him the Christmas season and the money he would spend on toys for all the children. It was not just his children and grandchildren who benefitted from the shipments from her husband's toy connection in New York. For many of the children gathered around him, Charlie's gifts were a bright spot in an otherwise gloomy and poverty-stricken life.

When she thought back to the things he had shared about his past, the fact that he never had toys as a child always stuck with her. She understood why he wanted to make sure the children around him were not deprived in the same way.

Charlie knew toys and books sparked the imagination in children and he always felt it was important for a child to have an active imagination. He said it made the difficult times more tolerable. She could not find fault with his logic and she enjoyed watching him with the little ones. They brought out a happy, childlike quality in the normally very self-contained and controlled general that she adored. Charlie's smile traveled all the way to his eyes when the children were near. Rebecca loved that smile.

Rebecca raised her hand, acknowledging her friend as she watched Ro Jackson walk toward the backyard party. Ro had her son, Jocko, and a young woman with brilliant red hair that the matriarch had never seen before in tow. She watched as Ro stopped and spoke with Charlie, depositing both Jocko and the young woman with the general, before making her way to Rebecca's side.

"Where is your lovely companion today?" Rebecca inquired as she took Ro's hand, welcoming her to the party.

"She is home baking bread. She decided it was the perfect

temperature outside to heat up the kitchen and fill up the cabinet."

"So, what brings you by today?"

"You mean other than Jocko knowing there would be more toys to be had from Uncle Charlie?" Ro laughed.

"Yes, other than that." Rebecca nodded with a chuckle of her own.

"Well, actually, I do have a favor to ask of you."

"Anything, you know that. Your family has always been here for mine; we can do no less. What is it you need?"

Ro gestured to the young lady, now smiling shyly as she and Jocko helped Charlie hand out the presents to the gaggle of children. "That young woman is Bridget, my first cousin on my mother's side. She arrived last month from New York. We, that is Allison and I, had hoped she would be able to help with our place. Sadly, she is not suited for working at a dog kennel. She's far more suited to being a house servant. Perhaps a parlor maid or a kitchen assistant."

"And you thought you would see if we had a position open here?"

"Indeed." Ro nodded. "She's a sweet girl, but too shy and timid to truly be useful for me. She also needs to be in a place with decent and patient people. Never mind the fact that she, like the rest of the family, is Catholic and there are a few around here who put that on the same par as being negro, but she is quiet and extremely reticent."

"I am sure that we can find a spot for her here." Rebecca smiled gently as she patted Ro's hand. "We will take good care of her."

"Thank you, Rebecca. That is a huge load off my mind. I promise you she will be an asset to your household."

"I know. If you did not believe that to be true, you never

would have even broached the subject. Have her come by next Friday, on the second. We will find something for her here. Will she need a room as well?"

"Oh, no! We are happy to have her living with us. She's wonderful with Jocko and helps as much as she can, but Allison is very set in her ways at home and Bridget tends to muck up the works. I have no desire to live in a home where Allison's systems are upset on the regular."

Rebecca burst out laughing so hard it caught the attention of the vast majority of the people present. She could only signal that she was fine as she continued to laugh, wondering how many times Charlie had said the same thing about living with her.

Rebecca watched the young woman. She could not tell if it was Charlie's ebullient imitation of Father Christmas or the large number of small children surrounding him, but she thought young Bridget was trying very hard to be invisible. Whatever she decided to do with the little Irish immigrant, she concluded that keeping her as far away from Andy as possible was an absolute necessity. This fragile little thing would collapse instantly in the face of her boy's salacious charms.

CHAPTER 4

FRIDAY, JANUARY 2, 1880

CAREFUL NOT TO SPILL HIS coffee, Charlie opened the door to the office he shared with Rebecca to find his wife and the young woman he knew only as Bridget from the Boxing Day party.

"Excuse me, darling." He smiled at his wife and nodded to her guest. "I did not mean to interrupt you."

"No, it is fine. Charlie, allow me to properly introduce Bridget O'Connor. As you know, she is Ro's cousin, recently arrived from New York. Ro asked me if perhaps we had a position for young Miss O'Connor within our household. I have employed her as a parlor maid."

Charlie smiled at the young woman, bowing slightly at the waist. "I do hope you are happy here, Miss O'Connor."

"I'm sure I will be, Mr. Redmond. I'm very grateful to your wife for giving me this opportunity. I promise to do my best."

"I am sure you will." Charlie smiled as he took his seat at his desk. "My wife has a knack for hiring the right people for the job."

Rebecca chuckled as she rose from her chair. "You are sweet. Clearly one of the reasons I married you."

"Clearly." Charlie nodded as he retrieved his ledgers from a drawer. "It could not have been my charming personality and boyish good looks."

Bridget could not help but giggle at the exchange. She tried valiantly to hide her grin, but to no avail.

"Your boyish good looks will only get you so far," Rebecca chastised playfully. "Bridget, come with me. I will introduce you to Beulah and she can get you started on your duties."

"Yes, ma'am." Bridget nodded as she rose from her chair to follow the lady of the house. "Have a good day, Mr. Redmond."

"Thank you, Bridget. Have a good day." Charlie nodded to her as he focused on his books.

As they left the office, Rebecca was careful to pull the door closed before they made their way down the hallway. Rebecca stopped and turned to the woman at her side. "For future reference, he is to be addressed as General Redmond. Once you get to know him, General Charlie is acceptable."

Bridget nodded earnestly. "Yes, ma'am. I did not mean to offend."

"I know. You had no way of knowing, but in this house, we take great pride in General Redmond's service during the most recent war. He is a hero and we respect that."

"Yes, ma'am. I understand. It shan't happen again." Bridget ducked her head timidly, feeling herself appropriately reprimanded and worried it came so soon after her hiring. Cousin Ro would stripe her six ways to Sunday if she were to cause problems in the Redmond household.

The ladies continued down the hall to the elevator. Rebecca

slid the gate back and gestured for Bridget to enter the little iron cage. She smiled at the young woman's hesitancy. "I promise you it is perfectly safe."

"If it is all the same to you, ma'am, I'll use the stairs."

Rebecca chuckled with a nod as she stepped into the elevator and slid the gate closed. "I understand completely. It took me quite a while to get used to it, too."

Bridget listened to the lift creak and clatter as she made her way to the bottom of the stairs, quite grateful she had not risked her life in the contraption. She hoped she would not be expected to use it to perform her duties.

Bridget followed Rebecca through the grand house, taking the opportunity to look at the hall furnishings, the carpets, and the things hanging on the walls. Ro had told her this was a home on a par with the finest homes in Europe. If General Redmond had served the Crown with as much distinction as he had during the War Between the States, he would have been granted a title and lands. She understood now that her cousin wasn't just talking up her friend's status. The family really was as important as Ro claimed.

Rebecca gestured to her left. "That is the gentlemen's smoking room and occasionally General Redmond's poker room. Beyond that is the formal dining room. The family breakfast room and the ball room are across the hall."

The lady of the house stopped at a set of double doors at the end of the hall. "This is the servants' hallway. It services every floor of the house and is actually the shortest, fastest route most of the time. It is not unusual for us to use it as well."

Bridget was careful to follow slowly down a set of stairs she was not familiar with. She had heard stories of ankles being broken because of a loose runner or poorly constructed step. She was surprised to find this passageway well lit, very clean, and properly maintained. The steps did not squeak or groan, and the banister was smooth and tight against the wall. The runner was tacked down securely and looked nearly new, still retaining both color in its design and knapping in the fibers.

They stepped down into the end of the basement hallway. Bridget followed Rebecca's hand as the older woman gestured to the left. "My daughter Sue's office. She runs our stables from here. The kitchen is right next door." She stopped at an open door just past the large kitchen and rapped on the doorframe, "This is the office of the major domo and the head housekeeper."

A tall, very dark-skinned man came to the door, smiling brightly when he saw Rebecca. He smoothed his already perfect vest front before clasping his hands in front of his stomach and bowing just slightly. "Good morning, Miz Rebecca. What can we do for you this morning?"

"Good morning, Otis." Rebecca made an introductory gesture toward the girl, who was still a step or two behind. "I was wondering if Beulah is at her desk yet. We have a new hire I need to introduce to her."

"Not just yet, ma'am, but she should be in any moment now. I can't imagine there is much more to be done in the kitchen this morning."

Rebecca nodded as she stepped past Otis to the servants' entry to the kitchen with Bridget right behind her. "I know what is going on in that kitchen."

"Yes, ma'am." Otis laughed as he watched them make their way. "You most certainly do. I think there are cinnamon rolls this morning."

"Is the coffee fresh?" Rebecca called as she pulled the door open.

The question was met with several different amused voices, all laughing and answering in the affirmative.

"Otis said something about cinnamon rolls," Rebecca teased as she made her way into the kitchen.

Bridget scooted in behind Rebecca, mousing up in the corner by the door and the end of the counter. She watched as one of the younger black women stood from her place at the kitchen table where three older black women sat with a full coffee service before them. The girl had never seen anything like it in her life. No house she knew of would ever tolerate servants acting as if they owned the place, let alone be so cavalier about it as to invite the lady of the house to join them.

"Otis was wrong," the apparent leader of the group offered. "It's blueberry muffins." The woman laughed and called to one of the younger women milling about. "Get Miz Rebecca a fresh cup of coffee and one of those muffins that just came out of the oven."

"Do not forget the butter," Rebecca called as she settled at the table with the other women. "What have I missed?"

"Oh, nothing worth repeating." Beulah reached out and patted Rebecca's arm. "What brings you down this morning? More than just gossip, I hope?"

"The gossip is just a fun benefit." Rebecca gestured to the wall where Bridget was trying to be as inconspicuous as possible. "That young miss there is the reason for my visit this morning. That is Bridget; she has been hired for the basement or first floor. Kitchen assistant or parlor maid. Wherever we might have a place."

"Wherever I can create a job that doesn't exist!" Beulah laughed. "Lord, Miz Rebecca, you're taking in the white waifs now, too!"

"Well," Rebecca smiled and nodded her thanks to the young kitchen girl who placed her coffee and muffin in front of her, "A favor was asked and it was in my power."

"You realize we have four maids more than we need now? And how many kitchen assistants do you have, CeCe?"

"Enough to staff three kitchens," CeCe said from behind her coffee cup.

"That's the way it has always been here," Sarah piped up, shaking a bony finger at her daughter, the cook. "That's how you got your job. You started over there peeling carrots and potatoes, along with three other girls. Did you really think we needed four of y'all peeling vegetables?"

"Caroline," Beulah called to one of the women on the far side of the kitchen, where a group were working at various tasks.

The middle aged woman nodded to Rebecca as she approached the table, but gave her full attention to the head housekeeper. "Yes, ma'am?"

"Caroline, that is Bridget. She will be floating between the kitchen and front parlors. Please, see to it that she is issued the appropriate uniforms. Show her around the house and introduce her to everyone else. Bring her to my office after lunch and I will get her in the register and on the schedule."

"Yes, ma'am." Caroline curtsied quickly before collecting Bridget and heading off to the servants' pantry.

Rebecca gave her faithful housekeeper and nod and a wink. "Thank you."

"It's your house, Miz Rebecca. As long as you want to pay them, I'll find something for them to do. It's one of the reasons you have the cleanest house in Culpeper county. Probably in the state of Virginia." The housekeeper laughed as she poured another cup of coffee.

"So?" Rebecca asked as she tore open her muffin. "What gossip did I miss?"

～

FRIDAY, JANUARY 16, 1880

Rebecca slipped into Beulah's office and waited quietly until her housekeeper completed what she was doing.

"So, Miz Rebecca," Beulah asked as she finished up the last of her notes. "What can I do for you this afternoon?"

"I thought I would ask after young Bridget. How is she coming along?"

Beulah smiled gently. "Oh, she will do all right if she can ever overcome her shyness. I think she is having some issues with being a white servant here as well. Where she comes from, I think white folk and colored folk don't mix much."

Rebecca nodded. "I am not surprised, but is she doing a good job?"

"Oh, yes. Very neat, orderly, and thorough. Although I suspect she would make a better lady's maid than a parlor maid. Perhaps you could ask Lizbet to train her?"

Rebecca tapped her lip. "Perhaps. We could certainly use another lady's maid for when Em is home or we have guests. Lizbet has been stretched more than a little thin on occasion. And with Lizbet's eventual departure, it might be the wisest thing to do, but I do not want to cause upset among anyone here who might have been hoping for the job."

"You let me handle that, Miz Rebecca. The girls understand you always have a reason. I think Lizbet is in the kitchen for the afternoon hen party. Let me go get her." Beulah hauled her bulk out of her desk chair and lumbered out the door, her slippers scrapping over the floor.

Rebecca smiled gently. *For a woman of her age and mass, Beulah can move at a right proper clip,* she thought.

Within moments, Beulah had returned with Lizbet in tow. The two women settled in and looked to Rebecca questioningly.

"Well, ladies, what would you think about training young Bridget as a lady's maid? She could spend half her time doing light housework and the rest of the time with you, Lizbet, if you would be willing to train her. I would even be willing to be your training model."

Lizbet looked at Beulah, who nodded slightly, then at her old friend and boss. Very softly, she asked, "What about General Charlie, Miss 'Becca?"

Rebecca smiled at her old friend. There were folks here at Mountain View who would protect Charlie from any risk. "I think we can be discrete."

~

SUNDAY, FEBRUARY 8, 1880

Charlie, Rebecca, and Rex, with Buddy and Andy in tow, arrived at St. Stephen's just as the bell was ringing to call worshipers to services. Smiling and murmuring quick greetings to various friends, the family made its way to their pew at the front of the church. As they settled, Rebecca looked at the blatantly empty pew behind theirs where Darby and Stella usually sat. She tugged on Charlie's sleeve.

"Charlie!" She was whispering, but the urgency in her voice was clear. "Do you think it is time?"

Her husband looked around, searching for any sign of his old friend, the doctor. Neither Elizabeth nor Richard were present. "Well, Elizabeth is missing in action too, so I would say we are headed for Darby and Stella's after church."

Rebecca nodded her agreement as the organist struck the opening chords of the first hymn and Reverend Addison motioned for the congregation to rise.

As the minister called for announcements from the community at the end of the service, Charlie stood, waiting patiently to be recognized. When he was, he spoke simply. "Friends, I know many of you were planning to join us for our regular Sunday dinner, but we believe there is another Redmond coming into the world as we speak, so I am afraid Rebecca and I will not be joining you. Feel free to avail yourselves of CeCe's wonderful offerings and we will keep you informed of the status of our ever-growing family."

There were a few snickers as the congregation realized it was Darby and Stella once again adding to the Redmond clan.

Charlie drew Buddy and Andy aside as they walked out of the church. "Gentlemen, you are going to have to stand in for your mother and me this afternoon. Be the best hosts you can be and let CeCe and Otis take care of most of it. We will let you know what is going on as soon as we can."

"Yes, sir." Buddy was just short of saluting. Andy was considering how much he could get away with since every young woman at the dinner was now fair game without Mama watching over him like a hawk. He knew that the Whiteheads would not be there, since yesterday when he called on Eliza, Mr. Whitehead had told him that his wife was unwell. Maybe that new maid would be working today. His thoughts ran rampant at the possibilities.

As Buddy and Andy caught a ride back to Mountain View with the servants, Charlie, Rebecca, and Rex headed to Darby and Stella's.

"So, do you know if they finally decided on names?" Charlie was hoping that Rebecca would be distracted enough to cease her fabric shredding or at least to keep it to the handkerchief she was rapidly reducing to small bandages.

"Well, I think that they were considering Ruth if it is a girl –

my mother's name, and I believe Amelia also had a well-loved aunt named Ruth. They agreed that they wanted Charlotte as a middle name."

Charlie suppressed a smirk. If only they knew the true lineage of that name. "And if they have a boy?"

"Oh, I think you will like their choice. They want to name a boy Edgar Xavier."

"Not John Xavier?"

"No. They did not want to give him the same name as Little Jocko, but wanted to remember the men who were like uncles to them."

"Well, we will find out soon enough who gets remembered."

They arrived at the house to find Jerome pacing on the front steps and puffing on a cigar, so he looked rather like a train engine moving up and down in a switching yard. He stopped to watch the carriage approach. As soon as Charlie opened the carriage door, Jerome strode up and snapped. "What the hell took you so long? I have been waiting here alone for what seems like hours."

Charlie snapped back as he climbed out, turning to offer Rebecca his hand. "What do you mean? We went to church and figured that since you all were not there, and Elizabeth and Richard were also missing, Stella must be having the baby."

"You are damned right she is having the baby. I sent a runner over to you at the same time I sent one to get Elizabeth this morning."

Charlie dropped the hand offered to his wife as he turned and half groused at his friend, "I am sorry, but we did not get the message."

The Redmond matriarch growled, "Oh, would you two stop this ridiculous bickering! Brothers you should be! Now Charlie, give me a hand out of this carriage so I can see to my daughter and grandchild." Rebecca was decidedly annoyed at both of them.

As the two grandfathers stood there squabbling, Rex quietly slipped into the house and up to Stella's laying in room. He nodded quietly to Darby, who was waiting nervously in a chair in the hall, then stepped into the room and stood silently by the door until he could catch Elizabeth's attention. "How is she?" he asked quietly.

Elizabeth stepped away from the sweat-drenched woman in the bed and grimaced. "As well as can be expected, given that she has been in labor for the last eight hours."

Rebecca entered the house with both men in tow. Jerome gestured upstairs. Charlie slipped his arm around her waist to support her, preventing his headstrong wife from rushing up the stairs like a mama bear charging to protect her young.

At the top, they could see Darby sitting outside the master bedroom door, hands between his knees, head down.

The two men joined the impending father; Rebecca entered the bedroom, where she found Elizabeth and Amelia on either side of the bed where Stella was propped up on pillows, drenched and looking drawn.

"Hello, Mama," Stella panted. "This one is being stubborn. Probably knows it's cold outside and wants to stay in the warmth."

All three women chuckled and the long process of waiting for childbirth to occur continued.

BUDDY AND ANDY TALKED WITH OTIS AND CECE AS THEY RODE home that morning, explaining the situation to them and asking for their help in hosting the Sunday dinner. They both agreed to serve as the boys' advisors and assured them that there would be no problems. Since both boys were to celebrate their fifteenth birthday the following Saturday, they were feeling like clearly mature gentlemen. Why, several of the farm boys they knew from school were already married and expecting their first children.

Since many of the normal guests for Sunday dinner came to Mountain View directly from church, it was only a matter of minutes before people were gathering in the front hall, shedding coats and wraps, and generally keeping the stable hands busy disposing of carriages and buggies and the footmen stashing outer garments as quickly as they arrived. Buddy and Andy stood in the hall, greeting guests and explaining that Mama and Papa had gone to Darby's to await the birth of their next grandchild.

The ladies gathered in the front parlor, where CeCe had already set a light tea and sent up hot water as soon as she hit the kitchen. Esther Jackson volunteered to serve as hostess in Rebecca's absence. The gentlemen clustered in the smoking room, where Otis presided over the table of drinks, serving hot milk punch to ward off the chill of the day.

While CeCe and her minions set the buffet in the formal dining room, Andy and Buddy separated to provide a Redmond presence for their groups of guests. Buddy headed for the smoking room; Andy, as could have been predicted, headed for the front parlor.

Entering the room, Andy's eyes scanned to see what ladies were present – especially lovely young ladies. But his propensity to target young women was cut short.

Esther looked up from her station behind the tea service, smiled a rather evil smile, and called to Andy. "Ah, Andrew. There you are. Come, sit by me, young sir, and be the host your mother expects you to be."

For the next hour, Andy was kept busy providing the married ladies with refreshments and the tea in their cups, bringing little plates with biscuits on them to elderly ladies, and generally being kept far away from the younger women in the room. He was incredibly relieved when Otis came to the door to announce that dinner was served, until he realized that it was his duty to escort the most elderly woman in the room. He took a deep breath and offered his arm to Missy Frazier.

As the ladies stepped into the hall, the gentlemen were waiting for them. Lead by Andy and Missy, the assembly trooped into the dining room, where Andy filled her plate and found a seat for her. He was trapped at a table filled with the senior members of Culpeper society, looking with envy at his brother, who was sitting at a table with the boys and girls from school.

Dinner was one of CeCe's works of culinary art, drawing on the various vegetables and fruits that she and her staff had canned that summer and fall, as well as on the hot house production to compliment the meats and fish that were the heart of any dinner. Dessert was a work of wonder, consisting of several Rousses – raspberry, lemon, strawberry, and chocolate set in her delicious lady fingers and Bavarian crème. It was not sufficient to make up for the torture that Andy's plans going awry inflicted on the young man's patience.

As the guests were finishing their last cups of coffee or tea or their last snifters of brandy, Charlie's coachman Alfred appeared at the dining room door, gesturing for the boys to come to him.

"Gentlemen, your father asked me to tell you that you are the proud uncles of a new baby girl named Ruth Charlotte. She and your sister-in-law are doing well. Your father said to not expect him and your mother back until later tonight or possibly even tomorrow."

Andy nodded, shaking the man's hand as he did. "Thank you,

Alfred. You should get back to our parents now. We will make the announcement."

Alfred tipped his black top hat and hurried back out to the coach.

Andy and Buddy turned to the guests, all of whom were looking at them expectantly.

Buddy, in his best formal voice, announced the arrival of another Redmond grandchild, which was well received by all in attendance.

The guests spent the next half hour driving the footmen and the stable hands insane as coats, cloaks, scarves, and muffs were retrieved and sorted among their owners, and carriages, buggies and wagons were brought around to carry people home.

As the last of the guests were escorted out the door, Buddy and Andy retreated to the private parlor at the back of the house, where they collapsed into chairs by the fire. Andy looked around for a moment and noticed that the tantalus was open, so he got up and poured himself and his brother small glasses of Papa's good brandy. Handing the glass to Buddy, he commented, "Now I know why Mama and Papa always end up back here for a glass or two after Sunday dinner!"

~

SATURDAY, FEBRUARY 14, 1880

The boys were not surprised to find both their parents and Uncle Rex waiting for them in the breakfast room that morning. After all, it was their birthday, and birthdays in the Redmond family were major events.

"Gentlemen, good morning and happy birthday. I cannot believe our boys are fifteen – why you are almost full-grown men!" Charlie was grinning. "So, I have gotten each of you a gift appropriate for full grown gentlemen." With a flourish, he produced two boxes from a well-known watch smith in Washington.

The boys eagerly opened their first gifts of the day, knowing full well there would be more as the day progressed. Inside, they each found a silver watch with a matching chain and fob, each emblazoned with their initials.

"Thank you, Papa." Andy grinned. "I suppose I need to wear a proper vest now to show it off."

Buddy, always quieter than his brother at these events, looked at the chain and fob across his father's stomach, looked at his own new watch and chain in his hands, and grinned. "Thank you, Dad. They are just like yours."

Rebecca smiled from her chair at the end of the table. "Well, since you two are getting to be proper full-grown young gentlemen, you need to look the part." She pulled two packages from her lap and handed them to the boys. "You do indeed need proper vests to sport your new jewelry on."

The boys ripped into the packages, producing two very similar and proper double-breasted vests. Andy's was red and silver, while Buddy's was blue and silver, though the paisley patterns were the same. Grinning, the boys stripped off their coats and donned the new finery, carefully arranging their watches across their waists. They pulled their coats back on and turned to their mother, modeling their mature looks and each thanking her whole-heartedly.

Rex just sat quietly smiling. He knew the coming evening celebrations would be outrageous, as family birthdays always were. Given that the boys were about ready to cross the threshold into adulthood, he knew what his gifts would mean to them. He had opened bank accounts for each of them to fund their out of pocket expenses without having to go to their parents or dip into their trust funds. It gave them a certain level of independence.

Rex cleared his throat and withdrew the two bankbooks from his breast pocket. "And since no gentleman is without funds, you now have your own accounts that are not linked to the Redmond family funds. You will have a monthly stipend deposited into your accounts to do with as you wish without having to ask your parents for mad money."

Both Buddy and Andy looked at Uncle Rex with surprise and gratitude. The little man somehow always seemed to know how to make them feel more mature than anyone else in the family.

"Thank you, Uncle Rex." Buddy was grinning. "I will use this to cover my out of pocket expenses at The Point."

"Good, good. You will no doubt be an honor to your father's name."

"Yes, Uncle Rex, thanks." Andy grinned. He had a stake for tomorrow night's poker game now.

As breakfast came to a close, Rebecca looked closely at her sons. "I know full well you two want to spend the day with your friends in town, but be sure to be back in plenty of time for supper. Darby and Stella are coming, as are Aunt Elizabeth and Uncle Richard, and Duncan and Samantha, with Sam and Jeremiah, so be home with enough time to get cleaned up and ready for a proper family gathering."

"Yes, Mama," the boys intoned in chorus.

As they walked out, Buddy told Andy, "I promised Miss Ro that I would help her with some new puppies she has. Want to come with me?"

"Spend my birthday with a bunch of grubby little dogs jumping up on me? I don't think so." I'm going to go see Liza and show her my new watch and vest."

"Fine. See you later then, brother."

The boys went their separate ways.

Ro gave Buddy a new puppy for his birthday.

In the hay loft of her family barn, Liza gave Andy a much more exciting gift, one that would stay in Andy's memory for the rest of his life.

SATURDAY, FEBRUARY 28, 1880

Rebecca sat patiently while Bridget carefully brushed her hair out and tried to duplicate the rather intricate array of waves and curls that Lizbet normally created when Rebecca was holding a formal event. The girl was concentrating hard, a frown furrowing her forehead, and the tip of her tongue was visible at the corner of her mouth. Rebecca's hair was almost perfectly straight, so implementing the tight curls and ringlets that were the fashion of the day was not a simple project. What is more, Bridget was terrified of scorching Rebecca's hair with overheated curling irons.

Finally, Rebecca could not stand the silence. Out of pure boredom, she asked, "So, Bridget, how do you like the idea of becoming a lady's maid?"

"I like it just fine, Miss Rebecca. Lizbet has been teaching me all sorts of things." The girl spoke softly – so softly that Rebecca had to strain to hear her.

"You can speak up, girl. I am not going to bite, you know." Rebecca chuckled to defuse the young woman's discomfort.

"Thank you, ma'am. I never thought to be able to come up in the world like this. A lady's maid is a wonderful opportunity."

Rebecca thought for a moment, then realized that most female Irish immigrants ended up with jobs at the bottom of the social ladder, as scullery maids, seamstresses in sweat shops working twelve to fifteen hours a day, six days a week for small change, or worse. "Well, my dear, you cousin Ro is a dear friend, and her uncle Jocko was General Charlie's batman and best friend. Of course, we want you to have the best opportunity we could offer you."

Bridget stiffened slightly. "Yes, ma'am. Ro and Allison have been very kind." Her voice was politely neutral.

Rebecca turned to look at the young woman, who was slowly flushing so that her face almost matched her hair. "I take it you have a problem," she said gently. "Is it the child? The dogs?"

"No, no, ma'am. Little Jocko is wonderful."

"Then what is it, child?"

Bridget looked down at the toes of her shoes, then mumbled, "I'd rather not say. I do na want to sound ungrateful, as they are surely good to me."

"Then what is it, Bridget?"

In a tiny voice, the young woman said, "It's them, ma'am. I'm just not comfortable with two women... with women... together like that. It's just not right, begging your pardon, ma'am." Bridget twisted her fingers together and shook her head, lost between the rigid morals of her upbringing and the kindness she had been shown without reservation.

Rebecca looked at the young woman, a hundred different things running through her mind all at once. *Damned self-righteous morons. And what if she finds out about Charlie, let alone what she knows about Ro and Allison?* Rebecca took a deep breath and closed her eyes for a moment, searching for what to say. Finally, she started, very gently and very softly, using her most persuasive motherly tones. "Bridget, you must know Ro and Allison are both very dear to me. They are sisters in my heart. So, I do not wish to hear ill of them. And to be honest, I do not think that the love between them, love that they share so generously with all, is a bad thing.

"You know what St. Paul told the Corinthians, dear. Love is patient, is kind: charity envieth not, dealeth not perversely; is not puffed up; is not ambitious, seeketh not her own, is not provoked to anger, thinketh no evil; rejoiceth not in iniquity, but rejoiceth with the truth; beareth all things, believeth all things, hopeth all things, endureth all things. And when all is said, what Ro and Allison have is love." Rebecca smiled gently at Bridget's reflection in the mirror.

"My dear, everyone deserves to have and share love. And in these years following the war, there are too few men, so some women have turned to one another, rather than suffer loneliness and lovelessness, but if living with them makes you uncomfortable, I am sure we can find a place for you upstairs."

"Thank you, ma'am. I truly appreciate your kind words and reminder of the Gospels, but that would be easier." She looked down, shaking her head. "For me at least."

"Then a room you shall have. It is not unusual for a lady's maid to live in residence. It will be an easy and covenant separation for you, but remember, should you cross their path…"

Bridget finally found a bit of a voice, "I will be able to show nothing but love and respect. Your kindness has made that possible, Miss Rebecca. Thank you."

TUESDAY, MARCH 9, 1880

Louis brought a thick stack of envelopes to Charlie and Rebecca's office. He placed about half the stack on Rebecca's side and the other on the corner of the desk at Charlie's elbow.

"Most important things are on top, General Charlie. Mrs. Haliburton sent a few things from the bank and there is a letter from West Point."

Taking the pile, quickly passing over the things from the bank, Charlie plucked the letter with the seal he knew so well. "Wonder what this is all about."

"Only one way to find out, sir." The valet smiled as he handed Charlie the letter opener from the desk set.

Carefully opening the letter, Charlie adjusted his glasses as he unfolded the document. After a few seconds he looked to his friend. "They want me to teach a class in cavalry tactics this fall."

The valet blanched. "Oh, Miss Rebecca is not going to like that."

Charlie nodded, dropping the letter to his desk. "Fall and the beginning of winter in New York, on the Hudson? Not sure I am going to like that."

"Does this mean we are going to New York, sir?"

"I do not see how I can decline. It is an honor to be asked."

"OH, CHARLIE!" REBECCA COMMENTED CHEERFULLY AS SHE SAT on the right side of their sofa knitting a new set of undergarments for him. "You should absolutely do it! What a compliment to you and your years in the army!"

Well, that was not the response he had been expecting and he had to blink several times to clear his head of every argument he had been prepared to make. "Umm, thank you, sweetheart. I suspect this is a reaction to the Chicago event. They are reaching out to some of the old dogs now, but I had hoped to go."

"Oh, yes, you should!" She nodded as she took out and

reknitted a stitch of her current project that she did not care for. Since her stroke, Chris had encouraged her to continue her handywork for Charlie, and now her knitting was almost as fast as it had been before the incident.

"Rebecca," Charlie took a seat next to her, pouring them both cups of tea from the service on the small table near their bedroom couch, "You do realize I would be gone for a few months? They want me to teach a full term. It is not like the lecture series I did before. Would you like to go with me?"

"Would I like to? Of course. Am I going to? No." She shook her head gently, smiling at him. "I love you, Charlie, and this is an honor, and important to you, and I absolutely think you should go, but I do not want to go with you. I have no desire to spend winter on the Hudson."

"Thank you for understanding." He leaned over and kissed her temple.

"You should take Buddy with you," she offered as she wrapped another stitch. "He would enjoy it immensely and then I will not have to worry about you. Or him."

With a nod, Charlie chuckled before sipping his tea. "Lovely idea. I will ask him tomorrow if he wants to go. I doubt Andy will have any interest."

"Andy has no interest in anything but Eliza right now. I am worried about those two."

Her husband nodded, knowing that their son was far more attached to the young woman than was good for him. It had infuriated Rebecca when he had chosen to spend his entire birthday with Eliza and her family a few weeks before.

MONDAY, MARCH 15, 1880

Rebecca settled herself in her chair beside the fireplace in the front parlor, arranging her skirts just so. She was prepared for the ladies of Culpepper to arrive to begin the final stages of planning for Sue's wedding.

Sue was less than happy since she had been called away from the stables for this meeting. One of her best mares was in foal and ready to deliver and she wanted to be at the barn, but Mama was insistent. It was her wedding; she had to be up at the house. Rebecca had managed to corral Chris Baldwin to bring a notepad and act as secretary for the afternoon. Jeremiah and Charlie had both managed to escape, one with the excuse of having to make a delivery to a client in Charlottesville, and the other by noting that there was a stockholders' meeting at the bank. Rex was at the hospital in town, consulting with Elizabeth and Tomas on a difficult case.

Right on time, Rebecca could see carriages and traps pulling up in front of the house. Otis started escorting ladies into the parlor, while his footmen and stable hands either directed the drivers to the stable yard or took the traps that some ladies drove for themselves around.

The turnout was excellent. Of course, the first to arrive was Samantha Nailer, Jeremiah's mother, accompanied by Esther Jackson. They had stopped to gather Allison Simms-Jackson on the way, although her partner Roselle had the same attitude toward planning weddings that Charlie did – something to be avoided like the plague. Annabelle Calvert Foxworth arrived next, followed by Reverend Addison's wife Ariel. The full complement of Rebecca's Culpepper allies soon joined the festivities, including Missy Frazier, Grace Cooper, and Penelope Armistead.

For the first two hours, the ladies did as was expected; they enjoyed coffee, tea, and CeCe's offering of fine finger foods including her special cucumber sandwiches. Suggestions were given, choices were made, and a list was compiled. Then the brandy, sherry, and ratafia started flowing. It did not take long for the respectable ladies of Culpeper society to become less than respectable – or at least less than sober.

Even Ariel Addison, the minister's usually proper and soft-spoken wife, was found to be tittering to herself after her second glass of ratafia. She knew she should not indulge, but it was good, sweet, fruity and packed a wallop. Being around the Redmond women always seemed to lead her to do things that required confession to her Church and the forgiveness of her husband. She watched as Rebecca handed Sue a lovely blue box with a yellow ribbon around it.

"I bought this," the elder Redmond began, "in Paris, but never had the opportunity to wear it. I thought you might enjoy having it. It will no doubt be useful."

Sue nodded her thanks to her mother and tugged on the ribbon. A moment later, removing the lid revealed a very, very sheer negligee with a matching, nearly as sheer robe.

"Mama!" Sue blushed as she doubled over into her own lap to both laugh and hide the naughty gift.

"What? I thought you would like it and I know Jeremiah will enjoy it."

"Mama!" Sue squealed again, causing every woman in the room to break out laughing. She looked around, shocked at their reactions. "What?"

"I take it, my dear," the mother of the groom inquired, "You have not yet sampled the goods?"

Sue looked as if she would pass out when the meaning of the

question hit home. "No! Mama Nailer, of course not! Jeremiah and I have been...been..."

"Good, dear? Is that the word you are looking for?" Grace Cooper asked as she poured another brandy.

"Yes." Sue nodded vehemently. "We have been good."

"Pity," Rebecca mumbled as she placed her glass on the table.

"Mother!" Now Sue was on the verge of being insulted, or fainting. She did not know which.

"Calm down." Rebecca patted the young woman's hand. "I am just having a bit of fun. It is perfectly all right that you and Jeremiah have maintained those boundaries. It is a lovely tradition for a first marriage."

Sue looked at her mother and, in that instant, she realized something she had rather not have known. Her eyes went wide, her mouth dropped open, and she sputtered, "You mean, you and Papa?" The young woman gestured aimlessly. "Before you were married?"

"If," Rebecca imitated Sue's gestures, "means we made love before we were married, then yes. Many times. One of the reasons I decided to marry him. He is very good."

Sue nearly fell off the sofa as the older women roared with laughter.

CHAPTER 5

CHARLIE AND REBECCA stood in the front hall greeting their guests for this particular gathering. It was going to be a small, intimate party in a house accustomed to hosting grand affairs. Darby and Stella, Sue and Jeremiah, Elizabeth and Richard, along with Edward and Grace Cooper were enjoying Rex's and Chris Baldwin's company and before supper drinks in the parlor while awaiting the guest of honor to join them.

"So, has Rebecca found a new lady's maid yet?" Grace inquired as Rex handed her another glass of wine.

"Yes, I think so. Lizbet has been training Ro's cousin Bridget and I think she will do fine."

Chris grinned cheerfully. "Thank God! I surely did NOT want to be cajoled into helping her. I have enough trouble doing my own hair."

Rex patted her on the shoulder. "We need you at the hospital, dear lady. I assure you, being a lady's maid was never in your future."

"Not at all, Chris. But I am not sure I want to be around Rebecca for any amount of time if she is unhappy with her new lady's maid." Elizabeth chuckled.

"Could not be any worse than you when you are expecting, dear," Rebecca offered as she swept through the door. She and Elizabeth gave each other playful looks having been caught teasing each other just as the final and most important guests had arrived for supper.

"Ladies and gentlemen," Charlie brought up the rear as he followed their guests in, "May I introduce the gentleman of the hour, Dr. Tomas Coleman, and his lovely wife, Mrs. Lizbet Coleman."

There was a polite round of polite applause from the gathering as the guests of honor made their way into the room. Tomas was quickly pulled into the knot of men, while Lizbet was settled with the ladies as libations were poured for the new arrivals.

Excited conversation was made in both groups, the men talking of Dr. Coleman's new position at Howard University College of Medicine while the ladies discussed the newly purchased townhome that would require staffing and furnishing.

Tomas leaned over to speak with Charlie privately. "I can never repay you."

"You already have, Tomas. You became exactly what we both knew you could be. I am very proud to have been a part of that. The world needs men who want to do good. It needs men like you. Howard could not have made a better choice."

"All because of that little piece of wood that decided to play hide and seek in your leg." Tomas shook his head as he sipped his whiskey.

"Well, that and you are an outstanding physician," Charlie offered sincerely.

"I am grateful that Dr. Walker insisted that we write the paper. I just never could imagine this would be the outcome."

Darby took the opportunity to slide across the room to where the ladies where seated. He leaned over and whispered in his mother's ear as he handed her a thick envelope.

"Thank you, my darling." Rebecca smiled up at him as she patted his cheek.

He leaned in and kissed her cheek before bowing and returning to the men.

Rebecca reached out and took Lizbet's hand as she offered the envelope. "This is my formal commitment to you. You will find a partnership agreement and a check for a thousand dollars. When you decide what it is you wish to do in Washington, I hope to be a part of it."

"Oh, Miss Rebecca, this is too much!"

"No, my dear, it is not. It is the least I can do for a woman who has been nothing but a good and faithful friend for so many years. I want you to have the best start possible. There should be more than enough there to help you get settled properly and have the time you need to decide what it is you will do with yourself."

Otis stepped into the parlor and cleared his throat ostentatiously to get the attention of the guests. "Ladies and gentlemen, supper is served in the breakfast room."

Smiling, Charlie offered his arm to Lizbet. "Madam, may I escort you to supper?"

She took his arm, blushing lightly. With her relatively light skin, it showed up charmingly.

Lizbet sat at Charlie's right, while Tomas was seated at Rebecca's right – the two seats of honor at any formal dinner party. Once all the guests were settled, Otis opened the door for the footmen to bring in the first course.

CeCe had outdone herself on the menu for this meal. She adored her cousin Lizbet, and the entire staff of Mountain View thought she and Dr. Tomas had shown what the negro community could produce if given the opportunity. They were so honored that Gen'l Charlie and Miss Rebecca agreed with them and had broken every rule of southern society in holding a formal dinner to honor these two. The staff was going to make sure that Lizbet and Tomas got the very best on this very special night.

Otis and his staff served the elegant dinner, beginning with consommé a la reine served with a very delicate, dry sherry. Once the soup was consumed, they brought in the so-called light fish course. This evening, it was truite au bleu with a beurre blanc sauce. The wine was a very dry grand cru Chablis, with an almost grassy, flinty nose to compliment the unique trout dish and cut the richness of the butter, cream, and shallot sauce. Course followed course, with pigeons stuffed with unsmoked bacon forcemeat, then sea bass poached in a rich white wine and lemon sauce. After an elegantly tart lemon sorbet to cleanse the palate, a full rack of venison garnished with red currants and currant jelly and accompanied with roasted tiny new potatoes in a parsley sauce was presented. A reasonable respite was allowed for the diners to recover somewhat before the next course was presented. It was a subtle meringue topped with a compote of berries, garnished with fresh versions of the same fruit, and served with an ice-cold flute of champagne. Finally came the cheese course, served with a fine cognac and elegant little demi tasse of rich dark roasted coffee.

Rebecca beckoned Otis to her and quietly asked him to bring CeCe up from the kitchen. When the cook entered, looking rather confused as she was rarely summoned to the dining room, Rebecca smiled reassuringly.

The hostess rose, lifting her snifter of cognac, an unusual act for any lady, but then Rebecca was not just any lady. "My dear friends, today we have had the opportunity to share with and honor our dear friends Tomas and Lizbet. But without our dear CeCe's magnificent contribution, this celebration would not have been so deliciously enjoyable." She turned to her cook and raised her glass. "To CeCe! Our deepest thanks."

Everyone else at the table rose, with a resounding, "Here, here!" accompanying the lifting of their glasses.

Throughout this gustatory fete, conversation had ranged over multiple topics, from what the hospital would do with Tomas's departure from the staff to housing in Washington to the latest in the presidential campaigns. With Rutherford Hayes having declared that he would not run for a second term, it was obvious that this would be an interesting election. The argument as to which candidate was less onerous, Garfield or Hancock, droned on. The ladies grew more and more bored. Finally, they escaped to the back parlor, leaving the gentlemen to their brandy, coffee, cigars, and talk of politics.

As the ladies discretely loosened the ties on their corsets and settled in for a soothing cup of mint infused tea, conversation turned to what Lizbet intended to do in Washington. "Ah, well, first I must get my house in order, but then I think I would like to do something for the community. After all, look at the examples I have in my life." She grinned at Rebeca, Elizabeth and the other ladies in turn. "You have all certainly given me a host of possibilities to consider."

~

THAT NIGHT AS CHARLIE AND REBECCA PREPARED FOR BED, Louis slipped in to bring their evening tea and collect Charlie's boots to be polished.

Rebecca called him aside. "Louis, I know I really do not need to ask this of you, but I wanted you to be aware that we will need to be particularly discrete around Bridget. Her upbringing and rather rigid morals would probably not allow her to be as accepting of our, um, situation as you are."

"I have been careful since the day she began her apprenticeship, ma'am." Louis smiled with a knowing look. "I rather suspect, ma'am, that she would not be terribly accepting of my relationship with the doctor, either."

As he turned away, taking the boots with him, Rebecca smiled at him fondly.

~

WEDNESDAY, MAY 12, 1880

Charlie and Rebecca stood on the platform waiting for the train that would bring Em home after four long years. Rebecca sighed impatiently as she continually craned her neck to look up the tracks. Charlie quietly chewed on a cigar, tapping his foot just as impatiently.

Rebecca was thrilled that all her children would once again be home and under her motherly supervision. Charlie was wondering how his Imp had grown in the last four years. He was afraid he might not recognize the young woman who was coming home in place of the girl they had left in England.

Foot tapping finally led to pacing, but only small steps that kept him close to Rebecca. She smiled as she tugged his sleeve. "Relax."

"Our baby is coming home, but she is not a baby anymore, is she?" he asked quietly as he took her hand. "They are growing up."

"You are just now figuring this out, General Redmond?" Rebecca teased gently. "You only notice them growing up when it is Emily?"

"She is the closest thing we have to a first born."

"And she has had you wrapped around her fingers since the day you met in the church." She gave his hand a playful pull. "Admit it; she is your baby and this is rattling your nerves."

"I admit it." He nodded, tossing his cigar away.

Five minutes later the train rumbled into the station, Charlie settled Rebecca on the bench by the station master's office and began pacing the length of the train, looking for his Imp.

"PAPA!" The cry was piercing, causing everyone in the immediate area to stop and look as a tall, dark haired young woman jumped from the landing of the second passenger car to run a short distance before colliding with her father, who immediately wrapped the young woman up in his arms, hugging her close even as the tears slid down his cheeks. "I've missed you!" she cried, her arms holding him just as tightly.

"And I have missed you, Imp." He hugged her once again, trying to staunch his tears. Wiping his face, he leaned over and kissed her cheek. "We are so glad you are home."

"Where's Mama?"

"Oh, I am over here!" Rebecca called with a wave. "Just waiting for the meeting of the Redmond Mutual Admiration Society to be over."

"Oh, Mama!" Em laughed, as she dashed over and knelt before her mother. "I love you. I've missed you so much!"

Charlie pulled a linen handkerchief from his pocket and handed it to Em. The young woman and her mother were well and truly embroiled in tears of happiness as they held each other close.

"You have grown up," Rebecca whispered as she slid her fingertip across her daughter's rosy cheek.

"That happens as we age, Mama." Em laughed as she stood and held her hand out to her papa. "I'm so happy to be home!"

"Then let us get you home!" Charlie waved his hand for Alfred to bring the carriage to the platform. "You have nieces and nephews you need to meet, and wait until you see your brothers! Built like brick sh—"

"Charles Redmond!" Rebecca shook her finger at him.

"Smoke, smoke house," he finished with an ornery grin as he offered his hand to his wife.

~

THE ENTIRE FAMILY GATHERED FOR SUPPER THAT EVENING TO welcome Em home. Greetings, hugs and laughter interrupted service of the supper that CeCe had been laboring over all day, preparing nothing but dishes her mother had said were Em's favorites.

There was so much excitement over the return of the prodigal daughter, no one really noticed how far CeCe had extended herself to provide an outstanding celebratory meal. No one except Em. Quietly, she slipped down to the kitchen after supper to thank CeCe for the meal that told her beyond doubt that she had come home.

As the various members of the family finally wandered off to their respective beds, Charlie, Rebecca, and Rex settled into the upstairs parlor for their last night cap and cup of tea and to discuss the day's events. A soft knock at the door preceded Em's intrusion into that almost sacred ritual.

"Mama, Papa, Uncle Rex? May I come in?" Em was a little startled to find that Rex had joined what had been a tradition between her parents, with no other participants. But she had not seen her parents since before Mama's stroke, and she knew from the many letters that had passed back and forth that things had changed because of that event.

Em looked around, found herself a seat and gratefully accepted a cup of tea from her mother. It gave her a few minutes to prepare to ask her parents to send her away again on the same evening she had arrived home after four and a half years of being separated.

"Mama, Papa," she started then added, "Uncle Rex. There is something I want to do and I will need your help to do it."

The three adults said nothing but waited for Em to go on. Rebecca's expression was encouraging, Uncle Rex's was neutral as he simply waited, and Charlie developed a distinct frown. He knew his daughter and knew damn well it was something they would not like, given her opening statement. They already knew she wanted to go on to another school, but to talk about it on the first night she was home seemed a bit much.

Em looked down at her teacup, took a deep breath and then started. "Professor Fox thinks I should go on to get my doctorate. He has written to a friend of his, Professor Putnam at Harvard, to get me into his graduate program. Could you help me get in?"

Rebecca gasped. She hoped that her daughter was coming home to live, and that she would have time to convince her to do so. It seemed that Em was viewing her trip home as just a waypoint between universities.

Charlie scowled.

Uncle Rex stroked his chin and said thoughtfully, "Putnam, you say. Hasn't he been working with Othniel Charles Marsh?

I've read about the competition with Dr. Cope, trying to find more and more species of dinosaur bones."

"Yes, Uncle Rex. That is the one. Professor Putnam is working on the Serpent Mound in Ohio and bringing archaeology and anthropology together in a fascinating way. Professor Fox and Professor Putnam have been communicating for years over their excavation and preservation techniques, and Professor Putnam's outstanding work at the Peabody Museum. Professor Fox thinks that Professor Putnam will be a wonderful advisor for me to obtain my doctorate."

The mention of Harvard University had gotten Rebecca's attention. "Harvard, hmmm? I believe Mr. Eliot, the president, started a women's program last year. I was so thrilled to see such a major university finally deciding that women deserved a proper education, I cannot express it."

"Yes, Mama. And they are supposed to start an official graduate school this fall, though they have not said specifically if they will allow women. I want to be part of that class. And with recommendations from Professor Fox, and Mr. Darwin and Mr. Huxley, I should be able to get into the graduate program . I have every reason to believe that by the time I finish my studies, they will have moved forward in granting doctorates to women."

Charlie interrupted this small celebration of women's rights. "So, you will want to go live in Boston, I assume."

"Actually Cambridge, Papa."

Rex had a thoughtful look on his face. Slowly, he joined the conversation. "I am acquainted with the dean of the medical school. I have found him to be a very kind and affable fellow, and think he might be willing to assist in finding an appropriate place for Em to live."

"Oh, Uncle Rex. That would be wonderful!"

Charlie looked from Rebecca to Rex. Both were looking

more thoughtful than distressed. "Well, I suppose you must go and be a real Yankee, Imp. But for now, let us enjoy the summer and your sister's wedding celebrations."

SUNDAY, MAY 16, 1880

Charlie was surprised to find Elmer Whitehead waiting beside the family carriage after Sunday services at the Episcopalian church, especially since the Whiteheads normally attended the Presbyterian church down the street.

"Mr. Whitehead, what can I do for you?"

"I am sorry to bother you on a Sunday morning, General Redmond, but could we have a word privately?"

"Certainly." Charlie turned to Rebecca. "Darling, please excuse me. I will be with you as soon as I can, but Mr. Whitehead needs me."

Rebecca smiled. "Of course, dear." She went back to herding their brood into the carriage.

Andy climbed up on top of the carriage wearing a concerned look on his face. *What did ol' man Whitehead want with Papa?*

Charlie drew Elmer Whitehead to a corner of the low fence around the churchyard. "How can I help you, sir?"

"Well, Gen'l, I am afeared we have a problem. You may remember that I warned you that my Eliza was, um, a bit more forward with boys than she should be? Well, it seems Eliza is expecting now, and she swears that the only boy she has been with is your Andy."

Charlie looked at the man, desperately searching for something appropriate to say. Finally, he cleared his throat. "Um, are you quite sure?"

"I am." He nodded. "Eliza has her faults, clearly, but she's never been a liar."

"Well, it will never be said that a Redmond did not live up to his responsibilities. My daughter Sue is getting married next month. Perhaps we can make it a double wedding?"

"That is more than I could hope for. I was only expecting that you would help with the medical bills and that we could put the issue up for adoption."

"No Redmond child will ever go for adoption if I, and especially Mrs. Redmond, have anything to say about it. Andy will marry her **if** she will have him, and as long as you and Mrs. Whitehead agree."

"Yes, sir. We do. Thank you, sir."

∼

CHARLIE RODE HOME WITH THE FAMILY IN STONY SILENCE. THE normal guests for Sunday dinner were arriving as they got home.

In one of the few private moments they had as they got into the house, Rebecca whispered to Charlie, "What did Whitehead want, dear?"

"Darling, please, give me a little time to digest what he said. I promise, as soon as I can, I will talk with you about it."

Rebecca looked at him, her eyes narrowing slightly. Then she glanced around, looking for Andy. He was lurking at the side of the hall, trying to be as inconspicuous as possible. Normally, he would place himself in the center of any gaggle of girls he could find. The doyenne of the house bit her lower lip and nodded to herself. She was fairly certain she knew what was coming.

∼

As THE LAST OF THE GUESTS LEFT, CHARLIE NODDED TO Rebecca and motioned to the upstairs parlor with his chin. "Shall we go talk, dear?"

Rex glanced over at the two of them and decided his presence was not needed. Instead, he retreated to the smoking room for a glass of brandy, the rare treat of a cigar, and an hour with a good book before he headed for bed.

They went up to the sitting room and settled in front of the unlit fireplace, face to face. Charlie drew a deep breath and told her what had transpired with Mr. Whitehead that morning.

Rebecca leaned back and sighed. "Given how you were acting, and more importantly, how Andy was acting, I suspected as much. But I do not want Andy's mistake to dilute the day for Sue. We can have Andy's wedding that day, but I would like to keep it small and private, either before or after Sue's nuptials."

"I rather suspect that will be easily arranged." He took a sip of the tea that had gone cold while he talked with her. "Shall we call the soon to be bridegroom in for a conversation?"

"I think that would be the best approach."

Charlie rang for a footman, and when one appeared promptly, asked him to bring Andy to them as soon as possible. Less than ten minutes later, there was a soft knock at the door.

"Enter," Charlie growled.

Andy slipped into the room, eyes down, and stood at semi-attention before his parents. He was fully aware that if a footman came to get him, he was in serious trouble.

"We asked you to come in so we could congratulate you on your upcoming wedding. You are going to be a husband and soon after that, a father." Rebecca was very matter of fact.

Andy's head came up with a jerk. His eyes were as big as tea saucers. His mouth was hanging open in shock. After a moment, he stuttered, "Marriage...**husband**...**FATHER?**"

"Of course," Charlie added. "Assuming Eliza will have you. Where would you like to live after the wedding?"

Andy just stood there, mouth hanging open.

"Oh, close your mouth, Andrew Richard. You will catch flies." Rebecca had no sympathy.

"Tomorrow you and I will ride over to the Whiteheads so you can make a proper proposal." Charlie was equally abrupt.

Andy blinked, groping for words. Finally, a very subdued, "Yes, sir," emerged from his mouth. He then tried to make a quick escape.

"Not so fast, young man." Rebecca's tone could have cut bone. "You have had intimate relations with a young woman without making any commitment to her. You have FAILED to act as a gentleman would or should. We did NOT raise you like this. And now, you WILL pay the price. You will make an honest woman of her and you will bring your child – our grandchild – into this family properly. Do I make myself clear?"

Andy examined the toes of his boots. "Yes, Mama."

Rebecca shook her head. "Andrew Richard Redmond, look at me!" She waited until he finally, reluctantly lifted his eyes to hers. "What do you have to say for yourself, young man?"

"I am sorry. She gave me a present for my birthday. I never expected it would end up like this. Honest, Mama. I didn't."

Charlie glowered at his son. "You will have to earn a living to take care of your family. Tomorrow, I will see if I can find an appropriate job for a man with your skills – or your lack of skills, as the case may be."

"Yes, Papa. Thank you."

MONDAY, MAY 17, 1880

After spending several hours talking with Rebecca into the middle of the night, they had concluded that the best opportunities available to Andy were working with horses.

However, Rebecca did not think working for her and Sue at Redmond Stables would serve anyone. She knew Andy and was sure he would try to use his position in the family to either avoid work or to get away with the easiest jobs, which would be unfair to the other members of the staff.

The very idea of him working at a bar sent shivers down both Charlie's and Rebecca's spines. They were perfectly aware that if Andy spent time at a bar, he would consume as much as he sold.

Yet, the thing that Andy knew the most about was horses – handling them, training them, working with them. So, there were only two available options. They could send him to work as a trainer at another farm, something that Sue would not appreciate as he would be taking Redmond Stables' training techniques to her competition. Alternatively, he could work with a blacksmith as a handler.

CHARLIE SPENT A LONG TIME THAT MORNING CAREFULLY composing a note to James Granville, the town's blacksmith.

Granville was the one man he had never felt comfortable with since the terrible events with Alex Raeburn being murdered by Edward Rainey and Charlie being accused of the murder. He was trying to tactfully explain the situation to Granville without making it look any worse than he had to. It was not easy.

He finished the note, sealed it and sent it into town with one of the younger boys hired to run such errands. There was always a small group of boys from Redmond Grove around the back-kitchen door looking for a handout from CeCe or a job from the general or Miss Rebecca. He had no trouble having one sent to his office. He placed a new penny in the hand of the lad, who was about eight or nine. "When you come back with a response from Mr. Granville, there is another penny for you."

"Yes, sir, Gen'l Charlie. Thank you!" The boy bounded out of the room.

Charlie stood up from his desk, straightened his vest and jacket, picked up the bouquet of flowers he had asked Otis to put together, walked down the hall to Andy's room, and knocked. When Andy came to the door, his father asked, "Are you ready?"

"Yes, sir," Andy croaked.

"Then let us go get this over with." Charlie slapped the flowers into Andy's chest. "You will need these. Do you have the ring?"

"Yes, sir." Andy patted the pocket of his coat, where a small ruby and diamond ring his mother had given him from her jewelry box was tucked securely away.

Charlie marched him downstairs, where the trap was waiting for them. The short drive over to the Whiteheads' farm was conducted in absolute silence.

When they arrived, Whitehead's big dog was tied to a tree. The dog recognized Andy, and immediately started alternately barking and whining, as he wiggled his butt and bowed down, wanting attention from his friend.

Charlie gestured to the beast. "Based on the dog's reaction, it is clear you are a regular visitor here, son. Even the dog thinks you come to visit him."

Andy did not respond. What could he say?

Elmer Whitehead stepped out onto the porch to meet them and escorted them into the front parlor.

It was about what Charlie expected; a horsehair stuffed chesterfield that was as stiff as a board and itchier than badly carded wool, several stiff ladder-back chairs, a rocking chair, and not much else.

Brenda Whitehead was sitting in the one comfortable chair in the room, the rocker set on one side of the hearth. Eliza was perched on the edge of one of the ladder-back chairs, looking miserable. Elmer took a position in front of the fireplace and stood with his arms crossed and his legs akimbo. Charlie bowed over Mrs. Whitehead's hand and then seated himself on one end of the chesterfield and motioned to Andy. "I think my son has something to say."

Andy stepped over to stand in front of Eliza. Handing Eliza the bouquet, he looked back over his shoulder at Charlie, who motioned to him to kneel, which he did – very slowly. He tried to speak, but nothing came out.

A second try resulted in a squeak, followed by a very shaky proposal. "Eliza, would you, um, consent to, er, marry me?" He fumbled in the pocket of his vest and pulled out the small ring his mother had given for the purpose of sealing his offer.

Before Eliza could respond, Mr. Whitehead took a step forward. "She would be happy to marry you Andy. Right, Eliza?"

"Yes, Father." The girl nodded to her papa and then turned to the father of her child. "Yes, Andy."

Andy shakily reached for Eliza's trembling hand and placed the ring on her finger.

Charlie cleared his throat.

All eyes turned to him.

"We are having a wedding for Sue and Jeremiah on June twenty-sixth. We could hold a small, private wedding that afternoon, and celebrate together, if you wish."

Brenda Whitehead finally said something. "That would be

perfectly lovely. Quiet, discrete, and yet with good food and drink to be shared. Thank you, General Redmond."

"Perhaps you can come over one afternoon next week to discuss details with my wife?"

The still distraught, but slightly relieved mother nodded, smiling gently. "Eliza and I would be happy to do so. Thank you again."

With that, Andy stumbled to his feet, Charlie rose, and they made their exit for another very silent drive home.

SATURDAY JUNE 19, 1880

Sue and Jeremiah had taken over the gazebo for the afternoon. From the stormy look on Sue's face, and the sullen one Jeremiah's, it was not a time to interrupt the two of them.

"So, you mean to keep working? I mean, with marriage and the possibility of children and taking care of the household..."

"Jeremiah Carter, my mother raised five children, runs this huge household and built the best horse farm in Virginia. And I am definitely my mother's daughter. I think I can handle being married and running the stable."

"But my mother..."

"Your mother made her decisions. My mother made her decisions. I damned well will make my own decisions! And who said we will have children immediately?"

"Well, I thought..."

"Jeremiah, I have to be honest. The thought of having children scares me. Mama and Papa have all the children they do because mothers die – childbirth is just plain dangerous. Maybe we should do what Mama and Papa did and adopt children."

"But, um, what about, um…"

"Making love? Aunt Elizabeth can help us deal with that until – and I mean if and when – we want children."

Jeremiah stood there with a stunned look on his face. "You mean when YOU want children. I am ready to be a father now."

Sue nodded, admitting, "All right. When I am ready for children."

Jeremiah could only shake his head. "Sue," he hesitated. "I thought you wanted what I want – a loving marriage, children, to build a home and family."

"I do want those things, but I also want to continue making Redmond Stables one of the best horse farms in the country. Just like you want to make Carter Leather one of the best."

The young man turned and walked to the edge of the gazebo, staring out over the pond. In a very dejected voice, he asked, "I don't know what you want from me. I thought you wanted a husband like Duncan is to my mother. But I just don't know now. I know I love you, but is it what you want?"

Sue looked at his very dejected back. She wrapped her hands around his arm. "Come with me and I'll show you."

They walked around the pond toward the little grove of oaks on the far side from the gazebo. Sue had seen her mother and father walk toward the grove earlier and she suspected they were still there, as they often were on particularly warm afternoons.

As they entered the grove, Sue held her finger to her lips and made a "shushing" sound. Very quietly, the two proceeded into the cool shade of the trees until they came to the edge of a small opening.

Strung between two large oaks was a hammock – a hammock for two, shaded by the tall trees surrounding it. Charlie lay with Rebecca next to him, her head resting in her regular spot on his left shoulder, his arms wrapped securely around her. Both were fast asleep.

Jeremiah looked to the pair. Even in his sleep, Charlie's chin rested gently on the crown of Rebecca's head, a satisfied smile on lips. The young man could see their chests rising and falling together, in perfect unison as they lay entwined in their hammock, slumbering peacefully. He nodded to Sue and smiled his understanding.

Sue and Jeremiah left as quietly as they came. They made the walk from the grove in complete silence. When they got back to the gazebo, Sue quietly said, "That is how I need you to love me."

Jeremiah sat her on one of the benches and sat down beside her. Leaning back against the railing, he put his arm around her shoulders and pulled her into his own side.

His mind wandered back to the angry ten-year-old boy he was that had first played checkers with the so called 'Yankee interloper'. He had been prepared to hate Colonel Charlie Redmond from the moment he met him and yet he had never been able to bring himself to do so. Now he was about to marry into the Redmond family. If it had not been for the things General Redmond and Duncan had taught him, it never would have been possible. Those two "Yankees" had made him a better man. He kissed the top of Sue's head saying quietly, "I can do that. We can work the rest out as we go."

∼

SATURDAY JUNE 26, 1880

The entire household had been a scene of turmoil and chaos for the past week. Meals coming out of the kitchen were meager on a good day, often just soup, salads, cold meats, cheese, and fruit from the garden or orchard. Charlie was heartily sick of ham biscuits, which with coffee and tea and some apples, was all that was available for his breakfast every morning that week.

Every bed in the house was filled, and not only was the garçonniere filled, so was every bed at Stella and Darby's house. And that included every trundle bed and cot that could be scrounged up.

He sighed as he flipped through the pile of bills on his desk. There were bills from every possible source. He figured that the fabric store on G Street in Washington had made their annual profit from him, as had the wine dealer that supplied his champagne, cognac, and other potables. He had also purchased various foodstuffs from the farms around Mountain View, as his own farms had not produced enough or enough variety to feed the incoming horde.

Then there was the matter of the bill from Charlie's tailor in Washington. Not only was he paying an arm and a leg for the new suits for the wedding for himself, Rex, Buddy, Andy, Jeremiah, and Darby, but he had also paid for the man to come down to Culpepper, stay for several days using the local dressmaker's facilities, and return to Washington – three times – to make sure the suits fit properly. The only other time he had spent this much time, energy, and money on clothing for himself was when he was presented to the Queen of England.

That bill was nothing when compared to the bill from the milliner and her small horde of assistants and cases of materials. Rebecca had sent to Washington for her favorite designer to provide hats for all of the women. The time and the bill for Rebecca, Sue, Em, Stella, Allison, Amelia, and Esther, *hell, practically every woman in Culpeper,* he thought, made the tailor's bill look like pocket change.

Jeremiah was paying for the honeymoon, a trip for the two of them to New Orleans. His ability to foot the bill was an indicator of how well his leather working business was doing. Charlie had purchased some land adjacent to the Mountain View property and Duncan was coordinating building a house for them on the property, including new workshops for Jeremiah's growing business. *It could have been worse,* thought Charlie.

He pulled his check book out of the desk drawer and patiently paid the stack of bills. When he was done, there was an impressive pile of envelopes on the corner of his desk to be mailed out on Monday. He looked at it and shook his head. *Oh, well, this will be over and done with tonight. Maybe Rebecca will have enough energy to spend a little time with me by Monday when she has had a chance to sleep.*

A soft knock on the door heralded Louis's entry into Charlie's office, followed by a footman with a loaded tray. Louis had Charlie's suit over one arm and his shaving kit in his hand. The footman set down the tray, which held a bowl, a jug of hot water, a pot of coffee, some cookies, and a bowl of fresh strawberries. "I know you didn't get much of a breakfast, Gen'l Charlie, so I thought a morning snack would be welcome. And the ladies have taken over the wash rooms, so I thought we would just lock the door and get on with it."

Charlie looked up at his valet, a grateful grin on his face. "And if you are in here with me, we both get to avoid the mayhem out there. Excellent idea, Louis. Excellent idea."

Louis did his most careful work to make Charlie the absolutely perfect image and presentation for father of the bride. His face was cleanly shaved, with nary a nick to mar the line of his chin, while his hair was carefully brushed. The black pants were absolutely flawless, without a hint of lint or a shadow of a crease. The black patent leather boots were so polished that, as was expected, one could see their face in them. The white linen shirt was perfectly pressed, and the black silk tie was carefully arranged so the folds were immaculate, and the pearl and silver pin was flawlessly centered. The silver silk brocade vest went over that, followed by the waist cut black coat with square short tails. Louis pinned on Charlie's red rose boutonnière, gave Charlie's black beaver top hat a final brush, and handed Charlie his hat and gloves. "You are ready, sir."

Charlie smiled at his valet. "Louis, if the ladies get half as much attention and care as you have given me, they will be stunning. Thank you."

Charlie made his way downstairs, where he was joined by Rex, Stella, Em, and the boys. They waited patiently. Finally, Sue emerged and progressed down the stairs like a great white swan, slender and stunningly graceful. Rebecca followed, dressed in a blue gown that took Charlie's breath away when he turned to look at her.

Charlie loaded up the carriages and the family made their way into town and to St. Stephens, where they were to meet the other members of the wedding party.

The church was filling with people when they arrived and hustled Sue into the coat room, where the wedding party had agreed to gather. Jeremiah and his brother Sam waited in the minister's office on the other side of the vestibule, where they were joined by the Darby, Buddy and Andy. Rex escorted Rebecca to the family pew at the front of the church, followed by Chris Baldwin, who was there to attend Rebecca during the events of the day. Behind them came Duncan and Samantha, who were given the seat across the aisle from Rebecca.

Darby, Buddy, and Andy as the ushers showed the many guests to their seats, working as quickly as possible to settle the crowd so the wedding could actually begin. Finally, it was time.

Sam, as best man, escorted Em up the aisle and they each took their positions on either side of the steps up to the chancel. They were followed by Darby escorting Stella, Buddy with Allison on his arm, and to the mild amusement of several parishioners, Andy escorting Esther. L.J. proudly walked up the aisle by himself, very carefully bearing a cushion with the rings. A rather nervous looking Jeremiah took his place beside Sam, who reached up and tweaked the white rose pinned to his lapel back into place. Then the first strains of the wedding march began.

Rebecca, who had been talking quietly with Chris while the various members of the wedding party progressed into the church, finally turned to watch her husband escort their oldest daughter to the altar.

In Rebecca's eyes, Charlie was the most dashingly handsome man she had ever seen. But then, she mused to herself, he was always the most dashingly handsome man she ever saw, with his gray-streaked black hair and his still flashing blue eyes. Beside him, Sue's strawberry blonde looks and slender athletic form looked like the perfect English maiden, an image they had intentionally emphasized in the design of her dress, hat, and flowers.

Reverend Addison stepped into place before the couple and in a rather sonorous voice called the first question of the wedding ceremony. "Who gives this woman to be married to this man?"

Rebecca stood and joined Charlie as they escorted Sue for the last step forward, and in clear voices, they responded, "We do."

A ripple of suppressed giggles went through the crowd. Those Redmond's could NOT keep to tradition. Women of the Redmond clan just had too much power in that family.

Charlie reached out for Jeremiah's hand, placing Sue's hand in his. Then he whispered in the young man's ear, "Take good care of her, son, or I will come whup your ass."

Jeremiah burst out laughing as he took Sue's hand and said, "Yes, sir." It was a much needed, though unexpected, release from the stress of the moment.

Elizabeth, who was sitting behind Duncan and Samantha, leaned over to Richard and whispered, "Jeremiah is about to become a Redmond, even if he doesn't take the name."

Duncan and Samantha heard her, even if no one else did, and joined Richard in snickering.

The wedding proceeded, drawing on the *Book of Common Prayer* as the guide for Reverend Addison's service. He got to the reading from the *King James Bible* on which he was basing his homily. It was from *Colossians, Chapter 3*, and included the verse that admonishes, "Wives, submit yourselves unto your own husbands, as it is fit in the Lord."

Elizabeth nearly choked herself trying to stifle her laugh. Richard pulled out his handkerchief and handed it to his wife, while gently patting her back. "Are you all right, dear?"

"I will be," Elizabeth gasped. "But the thought of Sue submitting herself to anyone was more than I could take."

Once the wedding was over, the party moved from the church to Mountain View. There, waiting for the wedding party, were the guests who had only been invited to the reception and enormous feast that CeCe and her assistants had prepared, since the church could not seat that many people. In addition to the food, the guests enjoyed the rich wines and spirits that had been pulled out of Charlie's cellar and the musicians who had been brought in for the day. As they became more relaxed, and the music became more festive, dancing and games, with the inevitable laughter and celebration, continued into the evening.

Rebecca had recently allowed CeCe to hire a new pastry chef, since the Redmonds' level of entertaining had escalated. Rebecca introduced some of the formal traditions she had learned in England and wanted to augment her table with more sophisticated delicacies. So, when CeCe had hired a man from one of the big hotels in Washington named Roberto, Rebecca turned over the recipes she had obtained from Jersey, their outstanding pastry chef in England.

Roberto had outdone himself in preparing the wedding cake, much to Rebecca's pleasure and Charlie's amazement. The wedding cake brought the entire party to a standstill as it was presented. Four feet tall, with multiple layers and tiers on white pillars, decorated with ornate marzipan doves and bells as well as red and white roses, it was to Charlie's eyes less a confection and more an architectural and engineering accomplishment. It seemed a desecration to cut into it, but that did not stop the party from consuming it down to the last crumb by the end of the day, except for the top tier that CeCe had salvaged for the newly married couple's consumption later that evening.

Once celebrations were in full swing, and the location of specific members of the Redmond family and their guests was no longer obvious, a small group, including Andy, supported by Buddy, Charlie and Rebecca and the Whitehead family quietly adjourned to the formal downstairs parlor. Reverend Addison and his wife were waiting for them, along with Rex. There were just enough people to properly witness the small, quiet second wedding of the day.

CHAPTER 6

REBECCA STARTED SNIFFLING as the trio headed downstairs. Charlie was on her left side, his right arm around her waist, his left hand holding hers as they descended. Rex was behind them. Em was waiting in the hall, eager to be on her way to Cambridge and her opportunity to become part of the first group of female graduate students at Harvard.

The four of them climbed into the carriage, which had already been loaded with Em's cases of clothing, books, equipment and artifacts. She was ready to establish her own home in Cambridge.

Rebecca was far more than teary by the time they arrived at the train station. "Why do you have to go now? You just came home. Why must you leave again so soon?"

Em tried not to sound as exasperated as she felt. In the few months she had been home, it had become clear to the young woman the time she had spent in England had changed her mother and she had to remind herself not to be cross. She was much clingier. "Mama, I've told you. This is what I need to do to be happy, to be the academic and scientist I want to be. There is a fascinating history of this country from before the white men came, and I want to be one of the people who discovers that history and shares it with others."

Charlie put his arm around Rebecca's shoulders, hugging her close. "Sweetheart, we raised our children to be free to make their own decisions, to do the things that make them happy. This has been Em's dream from that first day that she found a fossil and wanted to know 'why fishy in rock'. If we are going to be the parents we always wanted to be for our children, we have to let her go."

"I know," she nodded. "It is just so soon." Rebecca cried into Charlie's handkerchief, which she had already managed to soak with her tears.

"Without letting go of Rebecca, Charlie leaned forward and patted his daughter's hand. Looking deeply into Em's eyes, he added, "And our imp will be home as soon as she can."

"And when I finally come home for good, Mama, I will be Doctor or Professor Redmond. Won't that be wonderful?"

Even through her own desire to hold on to her child, Rebecca could not help but hear the eager hope and steely determination in her daughter's voice. She nodded. "Of course, it will. I am so proud of you, Em."

Charlie whispered in Rebecca's ear, "She sounds just like you did when you talked about saving the farm and building the best stables in Virginia when we first met, dear. You have raised her to be like you in so many ways."

Rex, who had been silent through all of this, finally spoke up.

"Rebecca dear, you know I will see to it that she is safely established. The place we have found for her is a house specifically dedicated to being a safe haven for scholarly women, supporting them, watching over them and caring for them in the best way possible. She will have her own bedroom and sitting room where she can study, and will be well fed and cared for. I have found a responsible woman to serve as her lady's maid who will live at the house with her and tend to her needs. She will be watched over by one of my oldest friends, Dr. Oliver Wendell Holmes, who lives just two blocks from where she will be staying. You have said you like his poetry. And you already know his son."

The distraught mother nodded. "I know you have done everything you could to make her safe, Rex. Thank you."

They parked at the station, where Rex and Em disembarked from the carriage. Rebecca chose to stay where she was. "I am a mess. I cannot let people see me like this. And I cannot watch my daughter leave so soon after she just got home."

"That's all right, Mama. I will write you often and let you know how things are going." Em leaned forward and kissed her mother's tear streaked cheek, then stepped out of the carriage.

Rex followed her, making room for Charlie to step down and embrace his daughter.

"Be careful, Imp. We love you. Go be the best scholar you can be."

"I will, Papa. Thank you."

Charlie climbed back into the carriage to be with Rebecca as Rex and Em went to board the train, while Alfred helped unload Em's cases and saw to it that they were properly stowed on the train.

Once the train pulled out of the station, Charlie signaled to

Alfred to take them home. Rebecca sniffled into her husband's lapel the entire way.

~

WEDNESDAY, AUGUST 25, 1880

Rebecca wandered around the house like a lost child. On Monday, she sent Em to Cambridge, with Rex as her escort. On Tuesday, Charlie and Buddy left for The Point. Sue and Jeremiah were getting ready to move into their new home on the far side of the big pasture. Andy was at work at Grenville's blacksmith shop, or so she assumed. Eliza was staying in their room as pregnancy was not agreeing with her. The whole house felt empty and silent. Her footsteps echoed in her ears wherever she went.

Finally, it was supper time. At least Sue, Jeremiah, Andy, and Eliza would be there. Rebecca was eager for the company of family – even if it was only a small portion of them. She took her seat at the table well before the others and fidgeted with the silverware and napkin as she waited.

Sue and Jeremiah came in, engrossed in a serious discussion of where they should put various possessions in the new house, and having problems coming to anything that vaguely resembled agreement. They barely acknowledged Rebecca's presence as they continued their conversation.

Jeremiah threw up his hands. "It's your house. Put the stuff wherever you want to. I'll learn to live with it."

"Thank you, I think." Sue was clearly not happy with the result.

Jeremiah sat in sullen silence.

Rebecca motioned the footman to serve the soup before it got cold. Jeremiah waited for Rebecca to start, then silently spooned soup into his mouth. Sue ignored it, staring icicles at her husband.

As the soup bowls were being removed, Andy finally showed up, still wearing the clothes he had worn at the forge, smelling of sweat, horses, and fire. "Sorry to be so late, Mama. We had a team of Percherons come in this afternoon for shoes and they were having none of it."

"That is all right, son. I hope you at least washed your hands. Where is Eliza?"

"I did, Mama. And Eliza is not feeling well at all. She's having soup up in our room."

"It seems to me that she is just not comfortable here and is using her pregnancy as a way to avoid the rest of the family."

"I wouldn't know about that, Mama. She's sick half the time and feeling miserable and crying the other half. Definitely not fun to be around."

Rebecca nodded. "I will look in on her after supper then. She needs to know that we care about her."

"Thank you, Mama." Andy spent a few minutes shoveling his roast beef into his mouth, then looked up and said, "Since you are going to look in on Eliza tonight, maybe you wouldn't mind keeping an eye on her if I started working evenings. What do you say?"

"What do you mean evenings?"

"I talked to Mrs. Allen at lunch today. She's getting older and, um…"

"We all are," mumbled Rebecca.

"Well, she needs a good fellow to help her out at night and I thought it would be a great job for me – and a whole lot cleaner!"

Rebecca took a deep breath. The last thing she wanted Andy doing was working at a bar. Finally, she said, "You know, Andy, your wife needs you. While an agreeable woman, I would much rather you did not work for Mrs. Allen."

"Well, Mother, I am going to, whether you like it or not. I am tired of being hot, sweaty, exhausted, and smelling like horse shit all the time. That is the sum of what working for Mr. Granville is about. I was not made to be a hostler or a blacksmith. Unlike most of the members of this family, I don't enjoy reeking of horse. I am much more suited to tending bar."

"Andrew Richard Adams Redmond, you are too young to be working in a common bar. I forbid this!"

"If I am old enough to be married and to be a father, I am old enough to work in Mrs. Allen's establishment, and you can't stop me." With that, Andy threw his napkin on the table, reached over and grabbed a couple of biscuits and an apple, and stomped out of the dining room.

Rebecca looked at his retreating form, then back at her very stony and silent daughter and son-in-law. She sighed, and asked, "Sue, did you hear your brother? What am I to do?"

"You know you have never been able to control Andy. No one has. That brat will do what he wants to do, and good luck trying to stop him."

Rebecca sighed and then excused herself. "I shall write your father. He will know what to do with Andy."

THURSDAY, AUGUST 26, 1880

Charlie could only smother a grin behind his hand as he brought his cigar to his lips. Watching Buddy try not to fidget on this last leg of travel to West Point was far more amusing than he had expected it to be. He had patiently answered every question about what it was like to be a cadet, to learn and live at the academy. Now, Buddy stared out the window of the train, apparently contemplating the answers he had been given as his fingers tapped rhythmically, but nervously against his knees.

"Is there anything else you want to know, son?" Charlie let the smoke filter slowly from his nose, spitting away an errant piece of tobacco from his bottom lip.

Buddy turned from the window and nodded slowly. "Was it hard?"

"Attending The Point?" Charlie nodded solemnly. "Yes, it was. It was one of the hardest things I have ever done."

"No, Dad. I know that would be hard." He turned watery eyes on his father. "Leaving your mama and papa. Was that hard?"

Charlie tried hard not to smile. Now was not the time for his son to think he thought the question funny. He considered what he wanted to tell the boy and with a bit of a sigh he offered, "My mother had passed by the time I left home and struck out on my own. My father was lost in his own grief and it was better for me to leave. I had already been in the army when I was selected to go. For me, attending The Point was actually a wonderful thing." He grinned and nudged the toe of Buddy's boot with his own. "It put me on the path that led me to your mama, you, and your brothers and sisters."

Buddy smiled and nodded, glancing out the window again. "Would you like me to go to West Point?"

"Buddy," Charlie leaned forward, touching the young man's leg, tapping it to make sure he had his son's full attention, "All your mother and I have ever wanted for you is for you to be happy. We are going to guide you and do what we think is best while you are under our care, but you are growing into a young man capable of making your own choices. If you want to go to The Point, I will do what I can to get you in. If you decide it is not for you and university elsewhere is what you need, then we will support that as well. I do not expect you to choose a military career just because you are my namesake."

"But would you like it if I did?"

"Charles Huger Redmond." Charlie grinned and winked. "It would make me very proud if you went to West Point." He settled back in his seat and gestured with his cigar. "It does not matter what you do or where you go. You are my son and I love you and I will be proud of you. Unless you vote Democrat. For that I would have to disown you."

Buddy outright laughed, having listened to many a ranting from his papa about the detriment of the Democratic party to the political landscape of the United States. "An officer and a gentleman, but never a Democrat!"

"Well said, son. Well said. Now, if you will excuse me for a few minutes," Charlie stood and stretched, groaning a bit as he did, his back protesting leaving the sitting position, "I have to change into my uniform."

~

FRIDAY, AUGUST 27, 1880

Upon their arrival at the academy, Charlie had to take a moment to place a steadying hand on his son's shoulder. Buddy was a barely contained ball of energy, wanting to see and experience everything all at once. Increasing his hold on the boy, Charlie leaned over and whispered, "Easy there; we are here for the next four months. There will be plenty of time to look around."

Buddy stiffened under his father's hand, watching as dozens of young men hustled across a large expanse to form in clusters under the orders of other higher-ranking cadets shouting commands and pointing as they found their final formations. Charlie recognized a small welcoming detail when he saw it; his son would pass out when he saw a full formation of the entire student body.

"Relax," Charlie whispered and patted Buddy's shoulder. "Just stay two paces behind me."

His son nodded nervously, licking his lips. "Yes, sir."

With a bob of his head, Charlie turned on his heel to face his old friend Lieutenant General John Schofield. Charlie snapped to attention and threw a crisp salute. "General Schofield, sir. Good to see you again."

The heavily bearded man smiled, glancing at the young man behind his colleague. Looking to Charlie and seeing absolute approval in his friend's blue eyes, Schofield sobered, saluted and said gruffly, "Good to see you again, Redmond. I see you have actually managed to make something of yourself."

Charlie nearly snorted his amusement, but did manage to quickly recover in order to maintain the commandant's authority in front of his son. "Yes, sir," he bellowed in his best camp voice. "I hope my time here will be beneficial to the cadets, sir."

Schofield just could not go on with the charade. He burst out laughing as he clasped his friend on the shoulder and shook his hand vigorously. "I know it will be, Charlie!"

Buddy felt like passing out. He had been so nervous and now his father and the commandant of West Point were laughing like they were old comrades. After a moment, Buddy realized – they were.

"Who is this very serious looking young man?" General Schofield asked with a bit of a grin.

"Sir," Charlie began solemnly, "this is my son, Charles Huger Redmond the Second."

Schofield nodded and took a step past Charlie to extend his hand. "Pleasure to meet you, Mr. Redmond. I hope you will enjoy your visit to The Point. Are you planning on enquiring about admission?"

"Sir," Buddy's posture suddenly improved. Charlie noted he would have to mention that to Rebecca in his first letter home. "I would be honored to attend The Point like my father before me."

The general nodded. "We shall see, Mr. Redmond, if you are Point worthy. We shall see."

Buddy glanced at his father, wide-eyed and swallowing hard before answering the commandant. "Yes, sir. I hope you will not find me lacking, sir."

The young man's eyes slid back to his father, who smiled and nodded.

~

SUNDAY, AUGUST 29, 1880

Rebecca stood at the door welcoming guests for the traditional Mountain View Sunday dinner. Even with Sue and Jeremiah standing with her, Rebecca felt very alone without either Charlie or Rex at her side, but the traditions that she and Charlie had established must go on.

Esther, Ro, and Allison appeared at the door with ten-year-old Jocko in tow, and Allison carrying a young child in her arms.

"Who is this precious girl?" Rebecca asked, rather surprised as she had heard nothing of a new child coming into Ro and Allison's lives. Since Katherine Reynolds had moved to Canada with Nicholas Galloway and taken little Esther Anne with her, they had been rather gun-shy about children, or so she thought.

"Well," Allison said, "we stepped out on the porch a few days ago and there she was, sitting on the front step holding a rag doll to her chest and crying her eyes out. There was a note pinned to her dress that said, *I am Eleanor, I am two years old, and I need a new mama.* We asked Richard to try and find out who she belonged to, but so far he has found nothing, so we have a new child in our family."

Ro simply stood behind her partner and grinned; a big, stupid, happy grin.

The dog trainer had been as heartbroken as her partner when little Esther Anne had been taken away by her birthmother; evidently, they were now ready to take on another child.

"Well, she is more than welcome here. You know that," Rebecca said as she drew her hand over the child's fair hair. She smiled and added, "Is Ginny thrilled to have another little one to care for?"

Ro answered, "Oh, yes. She is indeed, even at her age! She's been running after Little Jocko for ten years; a new child and a girl at that is just her cup of tea! She seems to be enjoying it immensely."

TUESDAY, AUGUST 31, 1880

Buddy was up well before reveille sounded.

In the four days he and Charlie had been at the academy, his body seemed to adjust naturally to the rhythms and systems of The Point. After getting dressed in his room, he grabbed his boots, planning on putting them on in the living room so that his departure from the house would not disturb his father or the servants.

Charlie had made it quite clear he still had two weeks before he was going to have to be up before the cadets to be ready for his classes and he intended to rest until then. He had gained permission from General Schofield and the first captain, the highest-ranking cadet, for Buddy to watch morning formations during the last part of summer encampment, so the younger Redmond was up and ready to head for the commons, where the tent city was set up. He would watch with great intensity every movement. He listened to every command and response.

He quietly made his way into the little living room, where he tried to settle on the end of the sofa to put on his boots. He jumped about three feet into the air when he heard his dad's voice grouse from the sofa, "That was my damn foot!"

Buddy nodded. In the barely lit room, he had not noticed him sleeping on the sofa. Then he realized Charlie could not hear his brains rattling. "I'm sorry, Dad. I didn't know you were there."

Charlie groaned, nodded and managed to sit up, swinging his legs over the edge of the couch, pulling the blanket around his legs. He patted the now empty space next to him. "It is all right. I am sorry. I just did not expect you to sit on me."

"To be fair, Dad," Buddy offered as he sat down next to his father and pulled on his boots, "I didn't expect you to be sleeping out here." He swung his head slowly to look at his father. "Why, by the way, are you sleeping on the davenport?"

With a sigh, Charlie adjusted the blanket over his legs and bare feet, tucking it tightly. "I do not sleep well in a bed without your mama. The sofa is easier. I do not toss and turn all night looking for her. This is more like an army cot. I am accustomed to sleeping alone on a cot."

The young man chuckled. "May I say, with all due respect, sir, that is just sad."

Charlie laughed as well, and nudged Buddy's shoulder as he nodded. "Yes, and one of these days, I hope you will be just as sad."

Buddy nodded, reaching out to pat his father's leg. "So do I."

"I will tell you the same thing I told the cadets last time I was here. Marry well. I never would have survived if it had not been for your mama. The right partner can mean the difference between life and death."

"When did you know you loved Mama?"

Charlie gave the question careful consideration. The moment he saw Rebecca, his soul cried out to her, but had he fallen in love at that moment?

No.

He smiled, gently shaking his head as he prepared to answer. "I was not at my best. Too many days in the saddle, with not enough time to rest and clean up. I was," Charlie shook his head and sniggered, "a nasty, dirty thing. Your mama made me take a bath. She noticed I had been injured and she tended my wound. That was when I fell in love with her. She was a southern widow; everything she knew had been taken by the war and yet, she was so kind and gentle with me. I was not a northern soldier to her. I was simply hurt and it was her natural response to take care of me. I needed that kindness in my life."

"Wait a minute." Buddy shook his head vigorously. "Mama saw you," he gestured frantically, "you know…"

"Naked?"

"Yeah!" The younger Redmond nodded "You let her see you that way?!"

"I did not have much choice; it was her bathtub and she insisted I take a bath."

"Dad!"

"Maybe she was just trying to see me naked," Charlie tormented the young man. "It had been a long time since she had seen a man." Papa grinned evilly. "It is not as if I did not have anything she had not seen before."

"Don't!" Buddy stood and placed his hands over his ears. "Just don't."

Charlie fell back into the sofa laughing as Buddy grabbed his jacket from the hook and pulled open the front door.

"I love you, son," the general called as he stretched his long frame back out on the sofa and plumped the pillow to his liking.

"Then don't do that again!" Buddy yelled before stomping out the door to watch morning formation.

Charlie continued to chortle as he rolled over and pulled the blanket over his shoulder to get another half hour of sleep.

~

SATURDAY, SEPTEMBER 4, 1880

It was a few minutes after nine o'clock in the evening when Richard slipped into Mrs. Allen's tavern through the back door. He stood in the shadow between the door and the window where Mrs. Allen handed out jugs of moonshine to customers who were just passing by, motioning to her to be quiet. He watched as Andy pulled glasses of beer from the big keg behind the small bar in the back corner of the room under the stairs and poured glasses of shine for other customers, taking a shot himself between filling orders.

Finally, he stirred himself and walked up to the bar. "Good evening, Andy. What are you doing here? You are supposed to be at home with your very pregnant wife."

"Uncle Richard!" Andy was startled. As far as he knew, Uncle Richard never came in here; he always went to Jocko's bar. "Um, what are you doing here, sir?"

"Checking up on you. Your mother told you not to work here. Your father telegraphed me and asked me to check on you. Make your apologies to Mrs. Allen and come with me." There was no arguing with Uncle Richard when he was in this mood.

Andy rolled his sleeves down, reached behind him for the jacket on a hook behind the bar, and said, "My horse is out back."

"Fine. I will come with you."

"Yes, sir."

Andy spoke with Mrs. Allen for a moment and then went out the back door to the small run-in shed to collect his horse. He saddled the horse and led him around out front where Uncle Richard's horse was tied.

Richard rode home with him, delivering a blistering lecture on the way. Andy never told anyone what Uncle Richard had said, but he was unnaturally quiet and compliant for several days thereafter. And the next morning, he went back to Mr. Granville to beg for his old job back.

THURSDAY, SEPTEMBER 16, 1880

As Buddy approached the cottage he and his father shared, he took a moment to appreciate the early fall weather. New York was very different from Virginia. Fall in Virginia had been known to be miserably hot straight into late October, but here, the difference was appreciable. Even early September in New York felt crisp and clean. There was a light and cool breeze.

Buddy had learned from his dad and others that the Hudson River provided regular cooling effects over the land The Point occupied. Taking a deep breath, he realized he liked it.

He could live in this place. He could be a good student here. He felt it in his heart. He could come here and not disappoint or embarrass his parents. He meandered slowly down the walk, contemplating how Mama would take the news. He chuckled to himself as he realized that all the Redmond men seemed to worry about what Mama would want and think. His dad was right—he wanted to be that kind of sad someday, too. But first, a career would be in order.

As he pondered his future, a noise began to invade his thoughts. Not quite a tapping. Though the actual sound could have been a tap, they were far too random to be any kind of a pattern. Not Morse code, he thought immediately. Stopping to listen, he waited for the next tap. When he heard it, he realized it was coming from the cottage.

Intrigued, he picked up the pace and took the small stoop in one long stride. Popping open the squeaky screen door, he stepped inside to find his father in the little dining room to the left of the entry hall.

Charlie was seated at the dining room table with a large black box of some sort on the table before him. As Buddy slowly entered the room, he noticed the look of absolute concentration on his dad's face as he stared at the machine, the index fingers of each hand poised over small black ovals. After a long moment, Charlie squinted and jabbed at one of the ovals, causing a reaction in the box that made the tapping noise.

"What the heck is that thing?" Buddy queried as he poured a cup of whatever his dad was drinking from the pot on the table.

"This is a typewriter," Charlie answered without ever looking away from the keyboard, his brows still pulled together.

"What does it do?"

"It is supposed to make my life easier, but somehow I am missing the point."

Buddy moved behind his dad to peer over his shoulder. Looking down at the paper scrolling around a roller he could see a few words had been embossed in black ink. "What are you trying to do?"

"I am not sure." Charlie shook his head and stood up from the table. He stretched, cracked his knuckles and then poured a cup of coffee. "I thought I was making lecture notes, but my inability to find the letters on the keyboard is a complete hindrance." He gestured at the typewriter. "I have managed to put down exactly three words."

Buddy nodded. "*Good morning, Gentlemen.* Nice start. Unless your class is in the afternoon. Why not just write them out?"

"Well, yeah." Charlie held his hands up for inspection. Buddy could see fifty years of hard work and dedication in those hands, especially the right one. His dad's knuckles were swollen and his fingers were starting to show a slight bend that was just not normal. "Arthritis. Flares up in colder, damp weather. Makes holding a pen a bit of a challenge. One of the other instructors suggested I try this and he loaned me his machine, but I am not so sure."

"So, hire a secretary. Like Miss Eloise," Buddy offered reasonably. "One who knows how to use it. She can typewrite while you tell her what to put down."

"It is just called typing," Charlie offered back just as reasonably. "And that is a grand idea, young man. Thank you."

"My pleasure." Buddy settled in a chair across the table, head down, cradling his coffee cup between his hands.

"Something wrong?" Charlie eyed his son with trepidation. If

Buddy had committed an offense at The Point, the only saving grace Charlie had was that he and Schofield were Brothers of the Class of 1853. That point alone might get him out of trouble.

"Oh, no, sir." Buddy looked up and smiled. "I have decided. I would very much like to attend The Point." He ducked his head and tried to be acquiescent in an appropriate manner. "And I would appreciate any help you could give me with admission."

Charlie could not help himself; he moved to his son and pulled him into a fierce hug, offering a solemn promise, "I will do what I can. You will be an asset to The Point and the army."

Buddy pulled back and grinned. "You HAVE to tell me how to get a donkey into the commandant's office."

FRIDAY, SEPTEMBER 17, 1880

Rebecca took the stack of mail from Otis when he presented it to her in the office first thing in the morning. She smiled when she saw a letter in Charlie's own distinctive script. She did not even bother with an opener; her nail ripped cleanly through the seal of the envelope. Pulling the pages from their confinement, she found she needed to take a deep breath and to swipe at a tear which had the bad form to appear in the corner of her eye.

She could not help it. She missed him so. They had not been apart for this long since that horrible March and April of 1865. Unfolding the letter, she smiled as she began reading.

My Dearest Becca,

I cannot begin to tell you how much I miss you. I feel half empty without you. I should not be this way. However, you are so ingrained in my heart that I should be able to manage a few weeks without you, but I find it a nearly unbearable strain.

My days are filled with energetic young men with unending questions and desirous for demonstrations of abilities that I still possess. However, showcasing them is now a bit more of a challenge. I need to spend more time on top a horse, and as I know the finest breeder in Virginia, could we perhaps take it out in trade?

My nights are long and lonely. I just cannot sleep in a bed without you by my side, your head resting on my shoulder, grounding me to that which is most important.

Much to Buddy's dismay, I have taken to sleeping on the sofa in the living room most nights. While it is for my peace of mind, it also cuts out his ability to sneak out and carouse with the older fellows he is so desperate to impress.

I have to tell you, with much amusement, he got out one night, had one too many contraband drinks, and had a head the size of Custer's ego the next day.

No Cure was offered. Made him suffer through his hangover. Runny eggs, greasy bacon, burnt toast, and cold coffee were offered to help him regain his sense of self. He did not speak to me for three days.

Even though we have several weeks to go, I am ready to be home with you now. I feel like a child denied my favorite toy. I simply want to be with you so badly I ache in every way.

I miss the scent of your hair, the smell of your skin, the sound of your heartbeat and the warmth of your beautiful body. Not to mention the touch of your lips and fingers on my skin.

Rebecca smiled and shook her head; all through the letter, he was still flirting with her. Thank God.

Even with the evening hijinks concerning the older cadets, Buddy is thriving in the academy environment. He adapted to it almost immediately. He has made several friends among the cadets, though I have had to caution him that some of the men may be trying to gain favor because he is my son. A good lesson for him to learn now, I think, if he truly wants to follow me to The Point. I think, my darling, you may have to resign yourself to having another soldier in the family.

Rebecca shook her head. She had known that when Buddy saw West Point, he would not want to come home. She could only hope Charlie would be able to drag him back to Virginia for the time being.

When I get home, let us go away for a short trip. Anywhere you like, my love. New York, Boston, New Orleans... You always enjoy New Orleans. Of course, we have never visited St. Louis. Does not matter to me where we go; only that we go together.

Now, for the fatherly, head of the family and household section of this missive, as for Andrew Richard, you, my dear, are not to worry about him. I have sent telegrams to Darby, Richard, and Rex. They will ride herd over our recalcitrant boy until I get home and then I shall thump some remembrance of respect and manners back into his hide.

He is trying my patience and good nature and even my skill as a father. I have advised his brother and Uncle Richard to relay that message. I shall assume he will behave appropriately until I return. If he does not, cable me immediately and I shall have Richard and Darby take him in hand.

You should only worry about yourself and our dear Eliza, who carries the next Redmond grandchild. Take good care of her. I know she needs your motherly love and concern. As much as I like and respect Elmer and Brenda for what they have accomplished, their reaction to their daughter's situation, even though she has been welcomed to our family, is less than delightful. While her condition is entirely her and Andy's fault, she still needs to know someone cares for her and I suspect Andy is rather lacking in that aspect of his life as well.

So, my darling, shepherd the Redmond women and the next generation as you always have, and I will see to kicking Andy's ass as soon as I return home.

All my love eternally,
Your Charlie

~

BUDDY TOOK THE STEPS OF THE COTTAGE IN TWO LONG STRIDES, pulling open the screen and pushing open the door in one fluid motion. As soon as he pushed the door closed, his attention was brought to the dining room, where the laughter of a woman echoed off the walls.

The young man sighed. Another evening with the new secretary, he suspected. Buddy gritted his teeth and forced a smile to his face before entering the room. Since her arrival three weeks ago, she had managed to ingratiate herself into their lives far more than he thought a secretary should.

She always seemed to be laughing at something Charlie said. She, as far as Buddy was concerned, stood too close to his dad, smiled too often at him, and Buddy was pretty sure he would slap her hand if he saw it on Charlie's arm one more time.

As he expected, she was seated to his dad's left at the dining room table, coffee cups and pastry dishes before them. The typewriter and a stack of papers were at the other end of the table. He nodded politely as he poured himself a cup of coffee from the service on the side table.

"Good evening, son!" Charlie gestured to a chair. "Did you enjoy the mounted drills?"

Buddy nodded. "I did. I'm hoping that my skills are up to snuff."

Charlie chuckled. "Buddy, you are one of the best young horsemen in Virginia. You are not going to have any problems with the riding lessons here. Trust me. It looks harder than it is. And I can give you pointers."

"May I bring Lucky?"

Charlie nodded. "Probably. The army is usually happy to have men bring their own horses. I would suggest bringing a backup as well. When I was in the army, I had Jack and Shannon. I am sure your mama and your sister would be happy to provide you with," he chuckled again, "at near cost, another fine horse."

Buddy laughed as he agreed, "They don't let family stand in the way of profit. So, what have you two been doing?"

"Well," Charlie sighed, "Up until about an hour ago, we were working on my lesson plan. Now," he gestured, "We are enjoying coffee and dessert. By the way, there is still soup on the stove if you are hungry. The servants have already retired, so you will have to serve yourself."

"The soup was very good," Sarah, the secretary, offered as she reached over and patted Charlie's hand.

Buddy managed not to growl. He stood and slowly turned to the kitchen, and as he disappeared through the doorway, he grumbled to himself and took a bowl from the counter and ladled in some soup. Grabbing a couple of rolls from a basket nearby, he returned to the dining room. He tried not to act as irritated as he felt when he took his seat. He glanced up at the pair and was relieved to see Sarah had retreated to her own space.

"Let me," Charlie stood and smiled at Sarah, "go find that book I promised to loan you."

"Oh, yes! Please. I am looking forward to reading it. I've always been fascinated with the subject."

"Then let me see if I can find it." Charlie bowed to the young woman and excused himself from the room.

"What book?" Buddy queried as he broke his roll into bits and dropped it in his soup.

"Oh, the new translation of Caesar's *Gaelic Wars;* I found trying to wade through the Latin to be too much, but I am fascinated with early British history," Sarah gushed.

"You should meet my sister Emily. She spent four years in England digging in Stone and Bronze Age sites. She knows far more about it than our father does."

"Oh, yes, your father speaks of her regularly. He's very proud of all of you."

"Does he speak of our mother?"

Sarah blinked, completely taken aback. "Yes, of course he does. Your mother, Rebecca, yes?"

Buddy looked up from his soup. His eyes did not reflect friendship. "She's in Virginia, waiting for him."

"I know; he's talked about how much he misses her."

"Good."

"Have I done something to offend you?"

He looked up from his soup again, then settled back in his chair staring directly at her. "You're flirting with him and I don't like it."

"I am doing no such thing."

"You are. You're always laughing at his jokes…"

"They're funny," she defended. "Your father is a funny, charming man."

"Funny, charming MARRIED man."

"You mentioned that." Sarah leaned forward, trying to make Buddy see her sincerity. "I promise you I am not trying to steal your father…"

"You couldn't if you wanted to; my parents adore each other. And keep your hands off of him," he warned with sincerity.

She nodded and smiled, rather amused and fascinated by this

young man's defense of his father. "After working with him for nearly a month, I am sure of that. I am sorry if I've upset you. I promise to do better in the future."

"Thank you."

CHAPTER 7

EM TRUDGED the three blocks from her office at the Peabody Museum to the women's boarding house that Uncle Rex and Dr. Holmes had found for her on Irving Terrace. She was lugging a carpet bag filled with books that Professor Putnam had suggested she read over the next month so that she could be working on a par with the other students who were studying under the noted biologist and archeologist.

Dr. Putnam was pursuing similar interests to those of his friend, Thomas Huxley. These men were creating and formalizing a new field of study – anthropology – that brought together elements of history, archeology, and culture using rigorous scientific methods.

Em staggered into her sitting room and dropped the bag beside her desk. She looked around the room, smiling to herself. Mrs. Afton, her landlady, had obviously been in. It was dusted, the windows had been washed, the room smelled of pine soap and lemon oil, and there were fresh flowers on the mantel.

She walked into her bedroom and opened the wardrobe to hang her raincoat on its hook. Clearly, Carolyn, her lady's maid, had also been busy while she was meeting with Dr. Putnam, as the clothes had been rearranged and the small mess that Em had left on the dresser had been cleaned up.

Slipping off her boots and into a comfortable pair of carpet slippers, Em wandered back into the sitting room. There was a fire laid in the hearth, and she struck a match to light it and to heat the kettle that was hanging on a hook beside the fireplace. It was a typical October day in Cambridge – neither hot nor cold, but cloudy, gray and damp. When she had left this morning for the museum, the sky had threatened rain, though it had yet to carry out its threat.

When the fire caught, she heated water and made herself a cup of tea, which she carefully set on her desk under the bay window that looked out over Irving Terrace. The trees were sporting autumn colors, the sky was still the color of gun metal, and there was no one in sight on the residential side-street in the usually busy community.

She pulled a sheet of paper from her desk drawer and started writing.

Dear Mama;

I find myself in a house full of intensely interesting women. Mrs. Afton has a personal library downstairs that has a better collection of history books than many schools have. She may even have a title or two that Papa is missing.

The woman with the suite at the back of the house, Laura Lakeworth, is studying American Literature. She is a pleasant young woman, but very given to keeping to herself. She asked, and received, permission to read at the breakfast table, though

Mrs. Afton forbids her to bring a book down to dinner or supper.

The two girls who live on the third floor are nursing students, and I see very little of them as they are either at the hospital or trying to catch up on their sleep. I do not think I could study any field of medicine – the hours are atrocious! Please ask Aunt Elizabeth how she managed?

I have to tell you; my childhood has followed me here. When I went in for my first interview with Professor Putnam, he had letters on his desk from Professor Lane-Fox, Mr. Huxley, and Mr. Darwin. Mr. Darwin's letter included the story of how we met and how he had enjoyed a lecture on fossilized shark teeth from eleven-year-old 'Squeak' Redmond. I have to admit, I was less than thrilled to have Dr. Putnam call me 'Squeak.' On the other hand, given his interest in fish, being knowledgeable on shark fossils was an advantage.

He is a fascinating man, with expertise in biology, archeology, and history, and, like Mr. Huxley, is an adherent of Mr. Darwin's evolutionary theories, and how they may apply to cultural as well as biological evolution. He is very encouraged by the work I did on Stone and Bronze Age cultures in England with Professor Lane-Fox and wants me to bring those skills to the work he is doing on the Great Serpent Mound in Ohio. He has blessed me with a PILE of books to read so that I can catch up with his other students, though I have not yet met them. Two gentlemen are still working in Ohio and are not expected back until next month. So, for the next few weeks, I will spend my days and evenings with my nose buried deep in a stack of books that would bore the average person. It is a very good thing you and Papa raised me not to be average.

When I have the opportunity to do some exploring in this community, I will write you about the amenities available to me *here. But first, I have plunged into the challenges that Professor Putnam and the University have for me.*

I will be spending Sunday afternoons at Professor Putnam's house. It seems that he and his family have the same kind of open house approach to Sunday afternoon that we do at Mountain View, and his students are expected to join them. Unfortunately, his wife passed last year, but his children support him and his friends turn out in force for the Sunday events.

With the other students returning in November, I do not think I will be able to come home for Thanksgiving, but will be home for Christmas and New Year's, as I promised.

My love to you, Papa, and the family.

Your loving daughter,
Em

She sealed the letter and set it to post on Monday. It was growing dark, even though the afternoon was still relatively young, so she lit the gaslight, made another cup of tea and settled in a comfortable chair in front of the fire to start her arduous reading assignment.

THURSDAY, OCTOBER 8, 1880

Rebecca eagerly opened the letter from Em. Her daughter's handwriting was distinctive; half proper long hand and half printed, but easy to read. With her damaged eyesight, partially from her stroke and partially from the simple reality of aging, Em's script was a blessing. She often had to have Chris or Rex read her correspondence to her, especially if the writer had particularly ornate or shaky handwriting, but she could always read Em's letters.

She lifted a small magnifying glass to her left eye and read through her daughter's letter, smiling and nodding until she got to the end, and realized that not only would Charlie and Buddy be absent for Thanksgiving, so would Em.

She stared at the letter, re-reading the paragraph about Thanksgiving. Rex came into the parlor as she was brooding over the news.

"Good afternoon, my dear." He leaned against the mantle. "What has you sitting there with such a melancholy expression?"

"Oh, I just got a letter from Em. It seems she will not be home for Thanksgiving. So, this year will not be much of a celebration. More a recounting of who is not home."

"Rebecca, please do not be such a Moping Maggie! We will have Andy, Sue, Jeremiah, Darby, Stella and the grandchildren – and there may well be another grandchild by then. There is much to be thankful for, my dear."

"I suppose you are right. Em has not been home for such a long time, I almost feel like I do not know her any more. When we left England, she was still a child. Now she is a woman grown and an outstanding academic. When I was her age, I had been married to Gaines for almost two years."

"She is still your Em, dear."

Rebecca smiled ruefully. "She has always been more Charlie's child than mine."

Rex looked at her and shook his head. "Rebecca Anne Redmond, she is very much your child! You have raised both of your daughters to be lovely, capable, intelligent women."

"They ARE good girls who work hard and tend to knock down obstacles that get in their way." Rebecca grinned. "And Em seems to have acquired a reputation and a moniker that may follow her through her career." She laughed at her own comment.

"Moniker?" Rex queried, confused by the reference.

"It seems that Mr. Darwin included the story of how he came to call her 'Squeak' in his letter of reference to Professor Putnam. Putnam was amused by it and I suspect will never let her live that one down."

"That could be amusing. Em may have to put up with being Professor 'Squeak' Redmond. Can you imagine what her students will do with that?"

Rex sat down in the chair across from her and a serious look came over his face. "I just came from checking on Eliza. I would like to have Elizabeth come out and take a look at her. She has not borne this pregnancy well and I am concerned that it is going to be a difficult birth."

"Difficult? How so?" Rebecca's face immediately reflected concern. She had been worried about Eliza for weeks, and Andy's inability to remain in the manse for more than five minutes with his pregnant wife was wearing very thin on his mama's nerves.

"She is just not faring well. I do not like her color, her energy or lack of energy, or her pulse. But since she feels awkward with me, I would like to ask Elizabeth to check on her. There may be something we can do."

"So, let us send for her. I would enjoy seeing her, too."

"I will do so in the morning when I go into the clinic."

"Lovely. I will ask CeCe to do something special for lunch."

~

FRIDAY, OCTOBER 9, 1880

Darby walked into Mrs. Allen's. He had been in Richmond that week and before he returned home, decided to check in on his wayward brother.

Andy was sitting in front of the small fire with a glass of beer beside him. He was flipping through a deck of cards, laying out assorted poker hands.

"Hello, little brother."

"What the hell are you doing here? You're always the good family man, not a moonshine mooch."

"Just checking on you. I was in Richmond and came in on the train. Figured I would come see my little brother on the way home. How is Eliza doing? She must be getting pretty close."

"Yeah, right. Just like Papa asked you to. If you want to know how Eliza is doing, ask Uncle Rex. He checks on her every day. I can barely stand to be in the same room with her. All she does is whine and moan and complain about the baby kicking her in the gut."

"Ah, you are finding out what it is to have a pregnant wife!"

"Yeah, well, I could do without the whining. She was a lot of fun when we met, but since the wedding, she's been nothing but sick and bitchy."

"What you get for getting her pregnant, brother."

"Gotta get myself some of those sheep skins. I do NOT want to go through this again."

"A thought, but you know they are not terribly reliable. Ruthie is a sheep skin baby."

"Great. Know anything that works better?"

"Abstinence is the usual answer for single men."

"Yes, well, that is not any fun."

"Not everything in life is fun, Andy."

"Speak for yourself, brother. I have a couple of friends coming in soon for some cards. Maybe I can make enough to get the hell out of here."

"Oh, so you are already tired of this job, too?

"Working is not for me. You can slave away all you want. I will find a way to make play pay."

"Good luck. I'm going home to my wife, children, and a good supper." Darby settled his hat on his head and stomped out to his carriage waiting to take him home. *Make play pay, huh,* he thought. *Wait until Papa hears this one. I think his head might explode.*

～

SUNDAY, OCTOBER 31, 1880

Em was rather overwhelmed by the collection of scholars wandering around Professor Putnam's house that day. There were botanists, historians, archeologists, and God only knew what other disciplines represented at the table. But the guest of honor was a friend of the Professor's from Washington. Erminnie Smith, an ethnologist from the Smithsonian Institute was visiting. She was working on a book that would be something of a breakthrough for those of Professor Putnam's students who were working on the Serpent Mound and similar Indian sites. Her research into the myths of the people of the Iroquois nations was revealing a whole world of Indian mythology, from creation to a pantheon of gods, to a world view that was dramatically different from the traditions of the Judeo-Christian world. Em was fascinated and felt like she was far out of her depth. As Mama had taught her, she listened intensely and spoke very little.

As the assembled people broke into small groups to visit and drink coffee or something harder after dinner, Professor Putnam waved Em over to meet his friend. "Em, I would like you to meet Erminnie Smith. She takes a fascinating approach to understanding cultures. We dig up their tools and leftovers. She digs up their stories. I've been thinking that somehow we need to merge these into a more comprehensive view of the cultures we study."

"Mrs. Smith. I am very pleased to meet you. Professor Putnam gave me some of your articles to read and your approach is fascinating."

"Professor Putnam was telling me about your work in England. It seems to me that you have brought some of the same discipline and ability to cross ethnology and archeology to your work that he and I are trying to bring to studies of the Iroquois Nation and those who preceded them."

"I am flattered, ma'am. I am doing my best to prepare to work on the Indian mounds in Ohio and Indiana within the year, and I believe that they are related to your Iroquois nations, from what I've learned so far."

Erminnie subtly led Em to the side as they talked, freeing the professor to visit with his other guests. "That is possible, but please be careful. I am not sure the imagery that we are finding in the Serpent Mound lines up with all of the stories we have collected."

"I certainly will. What I found in my work in England with Professor Lane Fox was that imagery depended on the date – as a culture evolved, so did the decorations and pottery styles. So perhaps the mythos evolves the same way – becoming more sophisticated and complex as the culture matures."

"A very valid point, Squeak."

Em turned a brilliant shade of red as Mrs. Smith chuckled. "Professor Putnam told me Mr. Darwin's story and somehow I could not resist, especially when you started delivering a small speech on cultural evolution."

Just then a tall young woman with dark hair, dark eyes and light-colored skin, wearing a beautifully beaded dress in the latest fashion came up quietly behind Mrs. Smith and stood waiting for an opportunity to speak. She leaned in to whisper to Erminnie, who smiled at her and responded just as quietly.

Mrs. Smith then turned to Emily, smiling. "Miss Redmond, let me introduce you to Camille Parker. Miss Parker is doing groundbreaking work in ethnology, working with the traditions of the Iroquois nations. I believe you and she have much in common, as Camille did her studies at the University of London. You may also have other commonalities. Her uncle Ely served under General Grant, along with your father. Camille, this is Emily Redmond, General Charles Redmond's daughter and, I understand, a protégé of Mr. Huxley."

As the two young women shook hands, Em smiled welcomely. "It is a pleasure to meet you, Miss Parker. I would enjoy talking with you about your research."

"Miss Redmond, I would be happy for an opportunity to chat. Unfortunately, Mrs. Smith and I are returning to Washington in the morning, but I expect I will be back in Cambridge off and on over the coming weeks and months. Perhaps we can meet then?"

Erminnie Smith interrupted the two young women. "Well, ladies, you can at least start talking now. Off with you, while Frederick and I plot out our next steps to upset the world of archaeology."

~

TUESDAY, NOVEMBER 9, 1880

A scream broke through the quiet in the middle of the night.

Rebecca awoke with a start, her heart pounding. She struggled to sit up on the edge of the bed, groped for a match on the table to light her lamp, and fumbled to find the lamp with her hands and slippers with her feet.

A moment later, Rex burst through her door. "Are you alright?"

"I am fine. What was that scream?"

As she asked, another one reverberated through the house.

Rex got the lamp lit, and together, the two of them opened the door into the hall, looking down the hall toward Andy and Eliza's room.

Chris Baldwin emerged from her room at the far end of the hall and immediately moved toward Eliza's room.

CeCe came running down the stairs from the servants' quarters. She was the only member of the staff who lived at the house; the rest lived in Redmond Grove, with several of the older children taking turns to stay in the kitchen and tend the fire overnight.

Another scream tore through the night air; the only one it could be coming from was Eliza.

Rex mumbled, "I will be right there," as he took off at a jog to his room, emerging again before Rebecca had gotten to Eliza and Andy's door carrying his medical bag. "CeCe, get me hot water and towels. Lots of towels. NOW!"

They burst into the room, stunned to find Eliza alone, doubled over on her knees beside the fireplace. She had obviously slipped off the chesterfield when the first contraction hit. Rebecca went around the room lighting lamps, while Rex went to the young woman's side. Chris went to her other side.

As the light grew, it was obvious that her water had broken, but it was also apparent that she was bleeding, and bleeding heavily.

CeCe bustled into the room with a pitcher of hot water and an arm full of towels. She dropped the towels in a chair, set the water beside the wash bowl on a side table, and went to turn the sheets back so Mr. Rex and Miz Chris could get Eliza to the bed.

"Gently, Chris. She is bleeding and she shouldn't be."

"I see, Dr. Rex. I had a cousin who went this way, too. It isn't a pretty sight."

Eliza moaned. "Andy. Where's Andy?"

The kitchen boy arrived with another load of towels. CeCe took him aside and told him to go to Redmond Grove and get the rest of the senior servants, then to town to find Dr. Elizabeth.

CeCe went down to the kitchen to get a pot of coffee going. Miss Rebecca, Dr. Rex, and Miss Chris were going to need it.

The first of the house servants to arrive was the head footman. CeCe sent him to get Dr. Elizabeth, have someone tell Mr. Darby and Miss Stella what was happening, alert the Whiteheads, and then to go find Mr. Andy.

It was a long night. Rebecca sat beside the bed, holding Eliza's hand and gently wiping the sweat from her face, trying to comfort the young woman as best as she could. Rex and Chris, joined by Elizabeth within the hour, worked over the woman, trying to encourage the baby and to staunch the hemorrhage. Rex and Elizabeth agreed; a caesarian section was necessary or Eliza would die from blood loss.

The thin light of pre-dawn was creeping in the window as Elizabeth lifted the child out of its mother's belly, tied off and snipped the umbilical cord, and coaxed the first cries from the little boy.

Rex continued to work over the mother's prone and limp

body. Elizabeth cleaned the infant, wrapped him and laid him at his mother's breast, hoping that the so critical first milk would still flow. As the first rays of the sun entered the room, Eliza breathed her last. Rex's and Elizabeth's efforts were in vain; she had lost too much blood.

Shortly after that, Eliza's parents finally arrived. They were too late to say goodbye.

By now, Darby and Stella had been notified. Stella stayed with the children; Darby arrived to support his mother and his brother. He was appalled that Andy was not home.

He immediately took Chris aside. "Can you take care of Mama for a while? I am going to get my damned brother."

"Go on, Mr. Darby. I will get her to bed."

"Thank you."

Darby slipped down the stairs and called to the boy who was taking his horse around to the stable to bring him back. He mounted up and headed to town.

There were two places his brother could be – a poker game at Mrs. Allen's or a small house on a side street where two women entertained gentlemen into the early hours of dawn.

All of the lights were off at Mrs. Allen's as Darby rode by. He turned his horse down the side street, tied the horse to one of the posts holding the roof of the front porch, and stomped into the house without knocking. Standing at the foot of the stairs, he roared, "Andrew Richard Adams Redmond. Get your sorry ass down here right now!"

Andy stuck his head out of a door at the top of the stairs. "What the hell? What happened?"

Darby continued to bellow, "Get your clothes on and come with me. Your son has been born, your wife has died in childbirth, and you, you worthless piece of shit, were here whoring while she was crying out for you."

~

WEDNESDAY, NOVEMBER 10, 1880

Tears pricked Charlie's eyes as he crumpled the telegram in his fist. His newest grandson had arrived, but at the cost of his mother's life. Shaking his head, Charlie knew what he needed to do. He needed to go home and be with his family.

Charlie was still seated by the fire, sipping a drink when Buddy came through the door with an arm load of books. Immediately noticing the look on his father's face, he put them down and crossed the room. "What's wrong?"

"News from home. Your nephew, Andrew Charles Redmond, was born yesterday."

"That's wonderful." Buddy smiled.

"But Eliza did not survive the birth and your brother is not living up to his responsibilities as a father."

"Oh, Dad, I'm sorry."

"So am I. We raised him better than that. I will never understand your brother."

"I don't think any of us understand Andy, Dad. All he wants to do is play cards, drink, and carouse with women."

"His carousing has already cost one woman her life and he is not even sixteen yet! Maybe your mother and I made a mistake making him get married."

"Dad, getting married or not getting married wouldn't have changed the outcome for Eliza."

Charlie nodded. "True. We need to make arrangements to go home. Your mother will need me right now."

"Yes, of course." Buddy nodded. He was certainly willing to do what his dad needed, but he hated the thought of leaving The Point.

"Well, go to your classes today, and get as much information as you can so you can study at home for the entrance exams. We will pack tonight and leave tomorrow. I will work with Sarah to make all the necessary arrangements."

BUDDY SLOGGED OFF TO CLASS, MOPING OVER HAVING TO LEAVE The Point, and angry with his brother for his careless behavior. The only good thing about this was it would get his dad away from that woman who kept flirting with him.

He walked into his first class and told the professor that he would be leaving because of a family emergency and that he hoped to be back next fall. After class, he got a list of books to read to prepare for the entrance exams. Walking to the next class, he told the friends he had made among the cadets the situation and they all commiserated with him. Each class proceeded the same way, with Buddy collecting a huge list of books to read before the fall. Fortunately, he had already read a number of them.

As he came out of his last class, General Schofield, the superintendent, was waiting for him. "I understand you are returning home with your father, Mr. Redmond. It seems to me that you would probably prefer to stay through the end of term. So, if you would like, I will ask your father to let you stay with me and my wife. I will make arrangements to send you home, if you stay."

"Oh, General Schofield, sir, that would be wonderful. Thank you so much. I want to be as well prepared as possible for the entrance exams and staying through the term would be very beneficial."

"Let me see what I can do, Mr. Redmond. Let me see what I can do."

Schofield walked home with Buddy and dismissed the boy to talk privately with his father. Within a matter of minutes, Charlie called Buddy back downstairs. "General Schofield has offered to keep you here until the end of term. However, you will be staying with the general, not with the cadets. I want him to keep an eye on you."

"Thank you so much, Dad, General Schofield. I truly appreciate it."

"Just so long as you do NOT bring a donkey into my office." Schofield laughed.

"John, can you take Buddy tonight? If you do, I can leave now, hire a boatman to take me down the Hudson and catch a late train out of New York."

"Certainly, Charlie. Go to your wife. I will see to the boy. After all, I have plenty of practice. There is a train out of Highland Falls at seven. It is faster than a boat."

∿

FRIDAY, NOVEMBER 12, 1880

Charlie's train arrived at a few minutes before two in the morning, having ridden the last leg of his trip attached to a freight train out of the train yard in Washington. Leaving his bags with the station master to send home in the morning, he and Louis walked up the street to Jocko's. Jamie Benson was just cleaning up after the last patron had finished his drink at the bar.

"Jamie, I need a horse. I have to get home tonight. Can I take yours if I send it back first thing in the morning?"

"General Charlie! Of course, you can. We thought you were going to be gone until Christmas."

"I came home because my family needs me. Do you know when the funeral is planned?"

"This afternoon out at Mountain View. Miss Esther is going."

"Thank God. I made it in time."

Jamie locked up, then escorted Charlie and Louis out to the shed behind the house. Together they quickly got Jamie's gelding saddled and bridled. Charlie and Louis, riding double, headed home.

He rode around to the kitchen door, knowing he could find someone to let him in. Louis went on and took Jamie's gelding to the stable. The fire boy was sitting in front of the stove, with a cup of coffee beside him and a dime novel open in his lap.

"Could I have a cup of that coffee?" Charlie startled the lad, who jumped up, dropped his book, and knocked his chair over. "Easy, Jerrod. I did not mean to surprise you."

"Oh, General Charlie. We did not expect you."

"I know. Now, how about that coffee?"

Jerrod got him a mug and poured him some rather thick coffee, handing it to him.

Charlie was tired. He had taken a local train from Highland Falls, got into New York at ten o'clock, managed to get a parlor car added to a freight train leaving at midnight, and had made connections to other freight trains in Baltimore and Washington to get home as quickly as possible. Now he trudged up the flight of narrow back stairs to the ground floor, kicked off his boots by the front door, and up the main stairs to the first floor. He slipped into his bedroom, expecting to find Rebecca asleep in their bed.

Their bed was empty.

Under the door to their private sitting room, he saw a thin glimmer of light. He opened the door and found his wife sleeping in a rocking chair beside the fireplace, where a small fire burned low. In her arms was a new born babe, and in her lap a half-consumed bottle of milk. Rex was curled on the settee.

He looked at the three of them and smiled. Rebecca was ever and always a mother to any child who came her way. Their newest grandson was no exception, obviously. *I guess we will be raising another generation.*

Charlie carefully lifted the baby boy out of Rebecca's arms and transferred him to the cradle that was sitting on the other side of the fireplace. The child slept on peacefully, his tiny lips moving as he dreamed of the bottle his grandmother had given him.

"Rebecca," Charlie whispered. "Sweetheart." He spoke a little louder as he stoked her hand.

Rebecca roused herself. "Oh, Charlie! What are you doing here?"

He smiled gently at her. "I could not let you go through this without me, dear."

She smiled, reaching out to cup his cheek, "How did you get home so fast?"

He kissed her palm, taking her hand to help her from the chair. "It is a long story. I will tell you at breakfast. Now we had best get some sleep. Rex needs to go to bed, too."

A sleepy voice came from the settee. "Thank you, Charlie. I am glad to see you and on my way to bed. Sleep well, you two."

Once the cradle was moved to their room and Rebecca has assured herself the baby was well, she and Charlie retired to their bed, both of them exhaling a sigh of relief and relaxation. As Rebecca settled into her usual place on Charlie's good shoulder, she whispered into his ear, "Darling, I am so glad you are home. I missed you something awful."

WITH THE NURSEMAID HAVING SLIPPED INTO THE ROOM JUST before dawn to fetch Baby Andy, his grandparents slept in that morning. They woke at a time that was not as late as most city dwellers but late for tried and true country folk. When they awoke, they spent nearly an hour just holding each other and talking quietly, happy to be reunited even under such somber circumstances.

When they finally rose, they dressed quickly and went down for breakfast. Rex was the only one sitting in the breakfast room, drinking tea and reading a paper. A footman poured coffee for Charlie and tea for Rebecca, setting the cups at their usual places.

"Good morning, sleepy heads. I assume you slept well." Rex was grinning at his two friends.

"Yes, old boy. I slept better than I have in weeks. It is good to be home." Charlie grinned back. "I assume Tess is taking care of Baby Andy?"

Rebecca smiled. "No, Tess has finally taken over the housekeeping from her sister. We retained another of Beulah's unending supply of family members, Harriet, to be the nurse maid. On another subject, I assume my son is still sleeping, given how late you both got in last night."

"Um, actually, he did not come with me. John Schofield agreed to keep him until the end of term next month and since he truly wants to attend The Point, I agreed."

"Oh." Rebecca's response was decidedly subdued. All of her children were growing up too quickly for her taste.

At that moment, Sue stomped into the breakfast room and looked twice when she saw her father at the table.

"Good morning, daughter," Charlie drawled. "What has you so annoyed?"

She did take the time to give her father a kiss on the cheek. "Good morning, Papa. It's good to have you home." She settled at the table and looked to her mother. "Brooks tells me that we have two horses missing from the stable. Andy's thoroughbred and one of my best standardbreds."

Rebecca looked up from the tea cup she had been staring at since Charlie told her that Buddy had not come home with him. "Andy's horse is gone?"

"Yes. And another one with it."

Rex stood up. "Let me go get Andy and find out what this is about."

Rebecca sat with a look of deep concentration on her face, worried about what her boy had done this time.

As they waited for Rex to return with the family reprobate, CeCe came in with a deeply worried look on her face. "Miss Rebecca, someone has been raiding the larder. I was checking my inventory this morning and we are missing some cheese, some jerky, apples, bread, a jar of mustard, and several of preserves."

Rebecca looked at her very worried cook. "Never mind, CeCe. I think one of our children may have been the culprit. Andy never likes confrontation and may have fixed himself a picnic to avoid the funeral today. So please know that I do not hold you or your staff responsible for this."

"Yes, ma'am. Thank you, ma'am." She left with a relieved look on her face.

Rex entered with a scowl on his face. "Well, he is not here, and his large saddle bags are gone as well. The room is a wreck, but it looks like he has taken some clothes, and favorite items like his cards, his dice, a couple of his dime novels, an extra pair of boots, and his blanket roll that he uses for camping."

Sue, who had been brooding over a cup of coffee, snarled, "Spoiled brat. Damned coward."

"Now, Sue, dear. Please do not say such things about your brother," Rebecca chided, though rather halfheartedly.

"Mama, Andy has spent his whole life trying to get out of work, blame, or anything that vaguely resembles responsibility. He has lied, cheated, and blamed others for his misdeeds for all of his life. Why should this be any different? I cannot count the number of times you punished one of us, and especially poor Buddy, for something Andy did. And as far as he is concerned, if something he wants is here on the farm, it is his to take. If I could get my hands on the little shit! I'd choke the life right out—"

Rebecca interrupted her. "Sue, please, stop. I am sorry that Andy has been the trouble you say, but he is still your brother, my son, and a member of this family. And no matter what, Redmonds stand together."

"Even if one of them is a good for nothing gambling, womanizing scoundrel, and damned horse thief?" With that, Sue stood and stomped out of the room.

Charlie watched his daughter storm out and then looked at his wife, whose face was a portrait of misery. He mumbled, "Remind me to write Sue a check for the horse."

As the day wore on, Otis reported several other conspicuously missing items from around the house; a pair of silver stirrup cups, some additional gear from the household tack room, a bottle of Charlie's best brandy, and every last penny from the petty cash reserve that Charlie gave Otis to pay delivery men and such.

The final straw was a note Charlie got that afternoon from Frank Halliburton. It seems that Andy was at the bank as soon as it opened that morning, and that he had cleaned out his bank account.

Charlie looked at Rebecca and Rex, both of whom were dressed and waiting for it to be time to go down to the funeral for Eliza. "Well, this makes it clear. Andy is on the run. All we can do now is wait to hear from him." Charlie shook his head, thinking, *we all thought it would be Buddy who was the reprobate and Andy would be the charmer. So much for that!*

SUE AND JEREMIAH WALKED TOWARD THE MAIN HOUSE FROM their new home on the far side of the horse pastures, across the creek and toward the family cemetery. As they walked, Sue gathered her courage and broached an incredibly sensitive subject.

"Dear husband, I know you want children, and that my problem with having them is an issue for us. You have been incredibly patient and understanding, but I know that it has left a hole in your heart. But you have to understand; I do not dislike the idea of children; I am terrified of childbirth. Too many women die in childbirth; women who are otherwise healthy, like Eliza, and like Andy and Em's birth mother. And it terrifies me. But now, with Baby Andy, you and I have a chance to do as my mother and father did, and as Duncan did for you, and make a home and family for this little boy. What do you think?" It all came out in one long, hard breath, rushed as if she wanted to get it all out while she still had the courage.

Jeremiah looked thoughtfully at his wife, who was marching along with a determined step. "And your mother and father are no longer in any condition to raise a newborn baby. Darby and Stella already have a house full of children as well. So yes, I think this may be a perfect solution for all of us, but can we call him Andy Carter? I want him to be my, no, **our** son."

Sue's face broke into an enormous grin. She let out a gust of air and her shoulders slumped in pure relief. She stopped and wrapped her arms around her husband's neck. "I do love you so, Jeremiah Carter."

Jeremiah chuckled, returned the embrace, and said, "I love you too, Mrs. Carter."

THE FUNERAL WAS SMALL AND PRIVATE. THE REDMONDS WERE IN attendance, along with Eliza's parents and her three brothers, Luke, Mark and Matthew. Richard and Elizabeth, with Esther, came in from town. Rebecca had asked the Presbyterian minister from Elmer and Brenda's church to perform the service. Ralph Hudnut had made a small, but tasteful headstone and the men of the Redmond staff had dug a grave in the corner near the memorial to Rebecca's brother. Duncan Nailer had provided a lovely mahogany casket with brass fittings, so the funeral had all of the trappings of a proper Redmond service.

As the service concluded, Elizabeth went to Brenda and Elmer. "I am so sorry. I assure you; we did our best to save her, but the hemorrhaging was too severe."

"Thank you, Doctor. I know that you and Dr. Rex tried to save her," Brenda spoke through her tears, trying to be as gracious as she could.

CeCe had laid a simple repast in the breakfast room, which was large enough to accommodate the small gathering, and Otis had set a simple collection of wines and brandy to go with the tea and coffee CeCe provided.

Harriet brought Baby Andy in to meet his maternal grandparents and uncles. The baby, who was clearly healthy and rosy, brought some cheer to an otherwise gloomy day. Brenda took her grandson into her arms, looking for her daughter's features in the little face. Elmer stood beside her with an arm around her shoulder, letting the little boy grasp his index finger.

Sue and Jeremiah looked at one another and nodded. If they were going to ask for this baby, now was the time.

Jeremiah stepped up to stand in front of the Whiteheads while Sue motioned for her parents to join them. Jeremiah cleared his throat, then spoke. "Mr. and Mrs. Whitehead, General Charlie, Mama Rebecca, Sue and I would like to adopt Baby Andy. We can give him a good home, lots of loving attention, and the education he will need to face the next century. The only thing we ask is that he be called Andrew Charles Carter. I want him to be my son in all ways." He lifted his hand to the Whiteheads. "Though he would always know you as his grandparents. We would never try to take him from your family."

All four grandparents looked startled, then somehow relieved. It would mean that Baby Andy would be well cared for, loved, and raised to be a good man. Elmer and Brenda looked into Jeremiah's eyes, then Sue's, then at one another. Rebecca and Charlie just smiled gently. Keeping the baby in the family and close to both sets of grandparents was a good thing.

Elmer cleared his throat, and said, "Let Mrs. Whitehead and I discuss this." Brenda handed the baby back to Harriet, and the two of them stepped aside to talk rather intensely in the corner.

Rebecca took her daughter and son-in-law by the elbows. "All right, you two. What has inspired this?"

Jeremiah smiled gently. "Why, Mama Rebecca, we are just following the example you and General Charlie and Papa Duncan set. Babies need parents, and here we are, ready, willing, and able."

Rebecca nodded and smiled gently. "Then I am glad we

could provide a good model for the two of you. You certainly have my blessing."

Charlie just stood behind her and smiled his paternal approval.

~

THURSDAY, NOVEMBER 18, 1880

Andy had ridden and camped for five long days, down through Charlottesville and on to the town of Big Lick on the Roanoke River. Big Lick was an important crossroads, with the Great Wagon Trail, the Carolina Road, and the Wilderness Road converging, making it a major trading town. To Andy's eyes, it was an ideal place to find a warm room at an inn, and a hot poker game to pad his wallet, and perhaps a soft woman to ease his mind.

He found an inn that clearly catered to the teamsters hauling loads south from Philadelphia to the Carolinas and west to Tennessee. A clean stable provided space for his horses, a large bunk room had a reasonably comfortable bed that he only had to share with one other boarder, and a good-sized bar provided a table with a felted top that was obviously ready for the transient card players. It was a perfect place for Andy to prove that he could make play pay.

Calling himself Andy Adams, he settled into his new base of operations. He spent his days either sleeping or researching opportunities on the famous Mississippi riverboats that had captured his imagination. He was planning to move west to the Mississippi when he had accumulated enough money to buy himself into a major stakes card game on one of those boats. He figured he could get a job with one of the wagon caravans going west on the Wilderness Trail to get himself to Memphis and the great Mississippi River with minimal risk.

As the bar began to fill that evening, Andy sat at the card table, waiting to see if anyone would join him for a game. He drank judiciously, sipping beer to keep his wits about him. He needed to get a feel for the competition.

As soon as the supper hour wound down, men began to file into the bar, breaking into groups that were drinking and talking, playing dice games in the corner, or settling into play some cards. Andy sat quietly, waiting for someone to start a game.

A burly teamster came up to the table and looked at the man-boy sitting there. "You're a little young to be hanging out for a card game, boy. Go home to your mama!"

Andy looked up at the man, a polite smile on his face. "Sir, I have broken green horses, worked a man's day on the farm, been a blacksmith, tended bar, gotten married, and fathered a child. I think I am old enough to play a hand or two of poker." To back up his statement, he dropped a handful of coins on the table, including several silver dollars. "Name your game, sir."

The man laughed and waved a couple of his friends over to the table. "Come on, fellows. Let's see if we can relieve this boy of some of his coins."

"Name your game, gentlemen." Andy was in his element.

The evening progressed with Andy betting cautiously as he got the feel for his opponents. He watched them closely, deciphering each player's tell. By the end of the evening, he had almost doubled his initial stake, and there were several teamsters who regarded him with new-found respect.

As he readied himself for bed, he thought, *Well, if I can keep this up, I'll be on the Mississippi in no time. Perhaps tomorrow, I can find myself a girl. Don't want to scare the teamsters off too quickly.*

THURSDAY, NOVEMBER 25, 1880, THANKSGIVING DAY

Em sat at her desk looking out over Irving Terrace. The weather outside was vile, cold, windy, and damp. The trees were bare, with moldering piles of wet leaves in every possible corner of buildings and fences.

The house was eerily quiet. Em had given Carolyn the day off to spend with her family, and the three other students that shared the lodgings with Em had all gone home for a long weekend. Mrs. Afton was downstairs somewhere, either in the kitchen or in the library. There were no signs of celebration for the traditional American holiday; no smells of good things cooking, no sounds of people chatting and laughing together. While Em had been in England since she was eleven and living with the Fox-Lane family since she was fourteen, she had always been in a house full of people, people who laughed and shared, and included her in everyday socialization, so she never felt either alone or lonely after her family had returned to Virginia.

Today, she felt very alone and very, very lonely.

She pulled out a sheet of paper, meaning to write Mama and Papa, then slowly put the paper back. With Eliza's death and Andy's disappearance, Em decided her loneliness was not something she wanted to burden her parents with today. She would write them tomorrow, when her own mood had improved.

Instead, she made herself a pot of tea, broke out a tin of sugar cookies, and smiled remembering Sarah's incredible butterscotch cookies. They had been her father's preferred form of bribery when she was little, and were still her favorites. In a moment of wistfulness, she hoped that CeCe had her mother's recipe and would make some for her over the Christmas holidays. She made a mental note to ask for them in her next letter home.

Picking up one of the many volumes of publications she was still trying to absorb on the aboriginal cultures in North America, Em found she could not concentrate. After she re-read the same page three times, she gave up. She wandered into the bedroom, looking for something to occupy her thoughts and failed to find anything of interest.

She wandered downstairs to the library, hoping to find something to read that would catch her attention. She found Mrs. Afton sitting in front of the fire, reading.

"Ah, come in, Miss Redmond. Have a seat. Would you like a cup of tea?"

Em smiled at the woman and settled in a wing back chair on the other side of the fireplace. "Good afternoon, Mrs. Afton. Please, call me Em; all my friends and family do. And yes, please, a cup of tea would be lovely. Thank you."

"Having a difficult day, Em?" Mrs. Afton's shrewd eye had seen the distracted look in the young woman's face as she came in the room.

"Yes, well, it is just so quiet. If I were home with my family, there would be people all over the place, and the family I lived with in England was large and, to be honest, often somewhat raucous."

Mrs. Afton had seen this before with students whose families were too far away to visit often. She knew exactly what to do. "So, tell me about your family. What was it like growing up with a war hero for a father?"

Em accepted the cup and saucer, making herself comfortable as she considered that question. "You know something? Until I became an adult, and a student and my peers mentioned him, I never really knew that about him. He was always just my papa. I actually had to do a bit of research to understand his importance in the grand scheme of things."

Mrs. Afton smiled, her eyes twinkling as she watched Em's face change entirely when she spoke of her father. "You love him a lot."

Em sipped her tea and nodded. "I do. He's always encouraged me. From the time I was so small." She raised her hand to about three feet above the floor. "He never told me that girls shouldn't dig in the dirt." She laughed, nearly spilling her cup. "He gave me my first little shovel and pick. Some rough set that he'd had a blacksmith friend of his make for my sixth birthday I think it was. They are far too crude and primitive for real work, but I still have them somewhere because they are physical proof of my papa's faith in me."

Shaking her head, she looked to the older woman, a few happy tears lying in her eyes. "He never told me I couldn't. He always made sure I knew I could. I have friends whose fathers are only worried about what the dowry is going to cost them. My papa has been paying my way for five years to make sure I can focus on my studies."

"And your mother?" The landlady was truly curious. She had housed a lot of young women over the years, but very few that were not studying to be either teachers or nurses. Mrs. Afton felt like Em Redmond was one of those 'hen's teeth' that people were always going on about.

"Oh, Mama!" Em's laughter was loud and contagious. "I really do hope you get to meet my mama someday. She is both the literal representation of propriety and the figurative representation of everything improper. She is the strongest woman I know. To have come through the war and one unhappy marriage before she met my papa..." Em shook her head and sighed. "She does not make apologies for the way her life has turned out. My parents have endured a lot by choosing to be together and adopting a bunch of war orphans."

"You're all adopted? I thought perhaps one of them was a natural parent to some of you."

"No. We are all adopted and we all know it. They knew there was no way to hide it. We all came to them so quickly at the end of the war; everyone knew we were all orphans. Mama and Papa knew it was just best to always let us know so no one could ever hurt us with it. Doesn't matter to us kids. They loved us, never once making us feel like we were anything but their own flesh and blood."

Em took a cookie from the tray and slipped it into her tea, breaking every rule her mother had ever taught her. But it was Thanksgiving and it was a relaxing afternoon. "Now my brother Buddy tries to make a case that he is actually Papa's son, but we, the other kids that is, don't think it's possible."

"Why not?"

"Because our papa is not the kind of man who would have gotten a woman in that condition and left her. He's not the type of man who is likely to have a dalliance."

For the rest of the afternoon, Em's life was laid out for Mrs. Afton's amusement. The two women laughed together over Em's collection of memories. They prepared a simple supper together of soup and sliced ham, cheese and bread, and continued talking until neither of them could keep their eyes open any longer.

"Thank you so much, Mrs. Afton. You have allowed me to remember all of the things I have to be thankful for today. And after all, isn't that the purpose of Thanksgiving?"

∾

JEREMIAH AND SUE USUALLY WALKED ACROSS THE PASTURES from their house to Mountain View, but today they rode in her father's closed carriage with Alfred driving them.

Not only was it Thanksgiving, a day that Mama always enjoyed as an assembly of her family, but it was also the day that they were going to take Baby Andy home with them. Exposing a two-week-old baby to the weather was not on Sue's agenda, so Papa had quickly offered his coach.

Alfred was happy to work for a few hours to drive the new family safely from point to point. He had been told by several staff members that a little extra effort for General Charlie would go a long way. For the coachman, it was not a bad way for a single man to spend the holiday. He was being paid extra. While the children visited, he would get to sit in the kitchen with a cup of hot coffee and access to all the food as it was being made. He even got to flirt with a couple of the kitchen assistants.

Sue and Jeremiah walked into the family sitting room to find Mama and Papa holding court, with Darby and Stella and their brood surrounding them. Little Jerome was pestering MaBeh for biscuits and jelly, Rachel was climbing on Paepoo's legs, and Stella had Ruthie, who was gnawing on a bourbon-soaked handkerchief. Rex was in his usual place to one side, watching the antics of the family with a benign smile on his face.

Charlie hailed the next wave of children with a grin, a wave, and a shrug.

Rebecca looked up and smiled. "So, are you two ready?"

Sue smiled. "Yes, Mama. The nursery is all set and properly stocked; Harriet has looked it over and it has met with her approval. So, when we leave today, we will take Baby Andy home." Of course, Sue and Jeremiah had been at the house every day for the past two weeks, spending time with the little boy, who was growing at an astounding rate. Rebecca was pleased to see that Jeremiah was the same kind of loving, doting papa Charlie was.

Darby strolled over from the side board where he had been collecting a cup of tea for Stella. He set the tea down and reached into his coat pocket. "If you are going to take the baby, you need these." He pulled out a sheaf of papers in a blue legal folder. "The official adoption papers. You two are Andy's legal parents now."

The smiles that lit Jeremiah's and Sue's faces were bright enough to illuminate the room.

Rebecca settled back into her chair, absentmindedly handing L.J. another piece of biscuit. "Well, it has been a hell of a year, but that alone is worthy of celebration. Happy Thanksgiving, family."

CHAPTER 8

MONDAY, NOVEMBER 29, 1880

GENERAL SCHOFIELD ORDERED Buddy up to his room that morning at breakfast. "Young man, you will write your mother and father a letter before you go to class. Be quick about it or you will not go to lessons!" General Schofield was used to being obeyed by his cadets and he made no exceptions for his young guest.

"Yes, sir." Buddy had learned to pay attention when addressed by the commandant.

He quickly folded his napkin, drained the last of the milk from his glass, excused himself to Mrs. Schofield with a polite bow, and hustled up to his room.

A piece of paper and a pencil were easy to find. Words for his parents were not so easy.

Dear Mama and Papa,

How are you? I am doing very well. General Schofield and

Mrs. Schofield are very nice. They are feeding me well, and I am working very hard.

General Schofield has put together a study plan for me so that I can prepare for the entrance examinations this spring. I hope Mr. John or you can help me with the engineering sections. It is really harder than I expected. He says that if I pass the entrance exam, he will make sure I get an appointment.

I will be getting out of here on December 17th, so maybe I can meet up with Em in New York and she and I can come home together. Papa, can you have Miss Eloise arrange for transportation?

I was sorry about Eliza's death, and glad Papa could get home. How is Baby Andy doing? Is Andy being a good papa?

Well, I need to get to class, so will be going. Love to all. Miss you all. See you soon.

Your Son
Buddy

He folded the letter, addressed it, and pulling on his jacket and grabbing his books, headed down the stairs, where he dropped it in the basket beside the door to be picked up by the post man later that day. Then he scurried off, running most of the way, to avoid being late. He was the last student to drop into his desk, huffing and panting as the clock ticked over to mark the start of the lecture.

EM DROPPED HER SATCHEL BESIDE HER DESK, SAT AND PULLED her boots off, stripped off her soaked hose, and slipped into a pair of slippers. The short walk back to her lodging from her office at the museum had been nothing short of miserable with the roads awash in a messy combination of mud, slushy ice, and water. Her boots were soaked and her toes were freezing. She went into her bedroom and rummaged in the dresser for a pair of her father's wooly boot socks she had absconded with while she was packing last summer. Going back into the sitting room, she built up the fire that had been smoldering in the fireplace while she was at work, and warmed the socks in front of the flames. Taking off her slippers, she pulled them on and sighed in glorious relief. Her feet were warming up.

She put the kettle on to boil. She needed warmth inside her as much as she needed hot socks on her feet. Fetching a notepad and pencil from her desk, she settled back in front of the fire to write home while she defrosted.

Dear Mama and Papa,

I hope you had a decent Thanksgiving, though with Eliza's recent passing, I suspect it was rather subdued. I spent the day with Mrs. Afton. We talked, laughed, scrounged a simple supper and had an absolutely lovely time.

One of the things we talked about was Sarah's wonderful butterscotch cookies. I am so hoping that CeCe got her mother's recipe for those marvelous little bribes. Has Papa taken to using them to bribe LJ and Rachel yet? If not, I am sure he will sooner or later.

The two gentlemen who have been working on the Serpent Mound are due back tomorrow. I hope I can keep up with them, but I have managed to wade through all of the books Professor Putnam assigned me, so I am as prepared as I can get. I will fill you in on what I learned when I come home.

About my coming home, my last day here before the winter break is the 16th, so I will be free to head home on the morning of the 17th. Perhaps you could ask Miss Eloise to make arrangements for me? If possible, I can meet up with Buddy in New York if his schedule matches mine.

I know you, Mama. I assume you are taking care of Baby Andy, as we both know that Andy is not exactly model father material. I hope you have plenty of help, as you do not have the energy you once had to tend to a new born infant.

Speaking of which, what would you like for Christmas for you, Papa, and the baby? I already have something for Darby and Stella, and for Buddy and Andy, but as usual, I am at a loss for what to get for two people who, in my experience, already have everything or if you want something you immediately send for it!

I am looking forward to being home. It has been a rigorous term and to be honest, I need the rest!

Your loving daughter,
Em

~

THURSDAY, DECEMBER 2, 1880

When Charlie and Rebecca entered the breakfast room that morning, Rex was dressed and clearly ready to head into town to conduct rounds at the small hospital that he and Elizabeth had established. The town was happy to have the hospital, but the staff made some blanch. A Chinese man and a female doctor were hard for the community to accept. The fact that Doctors Rex and Walker let Negroes in the front door for treatment made it more than some could tolerate.

"Good morning, my dears," Rex spoke, but distractedly as he perused a notebook. "I wonder, Rebecca, if you would do me the service of loaning me Miss Chris today? Elizabeth has a patient with a spinal injury and we would like her advice on appropriate physical therapy for him?"

"Of course, if she is willing. I often worry that she does not get to use her skills as much as she could or should staying here with me. I use her services as a secretary as much as I do her help as a therapist."

Rex went to the door to ask a footman to fetch Miss Baldwin, and then turned to Charlie. "You know that ambulance and team you gave us has been very useful. I want to thank you again."

"You are certainly welcome. Anything to help the community." Charlie smiled and shrugged.

"We used it to bring this man in from the brick yard and I think it saved his spine, since he still has feeling and some mobility in his feet. Not much, but some. That is why I think Miss Chris will be helpful."

As Miss Baldwin came down the hall, Otis met the postman at the front door. He carried the mail up to the breakfast room as Rex and Miss Chris went out.

Charlie sorted through the mail, tossing his work-related missives to one side. He was left with two envelopes, one from Buddy and one from Em. "Letters from our wandering children."

"Andy?" Rebecca asked hopefully.

"No, dear. Em and Buddy. By the way, I asked Richard to notify the sheriffs around the state to keep an eye out for Andy."

"I suppose that is something. I do hope he gets in touch. I miss my boy." Rebecca sighed. "So, shall I take Em's letter and you take Buddy's?"

"Certainly. Em's are easier to read. Will you please get glasses, dear?"

"Why should I get glasses when I only have one eye? The magnifying glass works perfectly well."

Charlie just shook his head and handed her Em's communiqué.

The two of them read silently for a few minutes, then Charlie looked up at the same time that Rebecca did.

"He is coming home on the seventeenth."

"She is coming home on the seventeenth."

They spoke at the same time, then laughed a little awkwardly at speaking over each other.

"And she suggested meeting Buddy in New York."

"And he suggested meeting Em in New York."

Charlie grinned at his wife. "Well, we raised at least four of them to be responsible adults."

"Yes, yes, we did, dear. Four out of five is not a bad record." She smiled, a wry look on her face.

JEREMIAH WOKE EARLY THAT MORNING. HE LOOKED AROUND, confused. Sue was not with him. Her side of the bed was cold to the touch. He pulled himself out of bed, grumbling at how cold the floor was on his bare feet, and fumbled for his slippers and robe.

His wife was not in their sitting room.

He walked across the hall to the nursery. There he found Sue, sitting in a rocker, holding Baby Andy to her shoulder and gently patting the whimpering child's back. Harriet was collapsed on her trundle bed, snoring gently. In the dim light of pre-dawn, Jeremiah could see that Sue looked like she had not yet slept.

Very gently, he asked, "Are you and Andy all right?"

Sue smiled ruefully. "I'm exhausted and Andy's had colic all night. I just want to get him to sleep so I can grab a nap before I have to meet with the new buyers Albert invited out today."

Jeremiah chewed his lower lip for a minute, and then bravely volunteered. "I can hold and rock him while you get some sleep. And I can get Harriet up in time for me to go to work."

"Oh, God, thank you, darling. I knew newborns were a lot of work, but I didn't know how much. Mama had two at the same time."

Jeremiah gathered his son in his arms and kissed his wife on the forehead as she stood. "Go, get some rest. Andy and I will cope."

The baby reached out and curled his hand around the lapel of Jeremiah's robe. "All right, little man, you and I will get that grumpy tummy under control." The novelty of someone new had stopped the whimpering as soon as his papa picked him up. Jeremiah walked up and down in front of the fireplace, making sure to stay in the warm part of the room, and gently bounced Andy while patting his back. Finally, Jeremiah managed to elicit an enormous burp from the little boy. The baby sighed, curled into his father's shoulder and was asleep in a matter of minutes.

Jeremiah settled him into his cradle, tucked the blankets around him, built the fire back up, and quietly slipped out of the room.

He returned to their bedroom, where he found Sue snoring gently. He quietly pulled his clothes and boots from the wardrobe and slipped out to the wash room to prepare for the day.

As he was finishing his second cup of coffee, Harriet entered the breakfast room. "I am so sorry, Mr. Jeremiah. The baby was colicky and when Miss Sue came in to check on him, she insisted…"

Jeremiah smiled at the nursemaid. "Harriet, I know my wife well. There is nothing you could have done to stop her. But in the future, you can come get me, too. We're new at this parenting thing, but we're willing to learn."

As she turned to leave, he added, "Oh, and can you get Miss Sue up around eight o'clock? She has a business meeting this morning."

"Yes, sir. And thank you."

~

FRIDAY, DECEMBER 10, 1880

Ro and Allison came into the back parlor. They had asked Rebecca if she would have time for them, and of course she said yes. For Ro and Allison, she would do anything they asked.

"Good morning, ladies. To what do I owe the pleasure of this visit?" Rebecca was smiling as she poured cups of tea for each of them.

Ro smiled at her friend and business mentor. "We haven't had a visit for a while, and we wanted to see how you were doing. With all that is going on with Eliza's death and Andy's disappearance, we thought you might want some moral support."

"Well, I admit it has been a difficult few week. Your care is appreciated, but what about you two?"

Allison laughed, a little ruefully. "Well, we have the two children at the house now, and I'm not sure how many dogs. I know a number of the dogs are going out as Christmas presents, though. And it is time for Esther to move in with us. Jamie is running the bar well, and he has hired Esther's niece to learn her aunt's recipes and way of running the kitchen. Between you and me, I think he has been courting one of the young women in town as well, so making the apartment above the bar available to him would not be a bad thing. And of course, Esther is no spring chicken any more. So she can come and be a grandmother to our two and have people to look after her."

"You two have done wonders with the old Sweet place. But why have you added so many extra bedrooms?"

A grin lit Ro's face. "We have a reason after your own heart. There are so many children wandering around without parents or a proper home, and with the space we have made, we have plenty of room. Allison and I have decided that we are going to adopt a small horde."

"Oh, my. How wonderful of you two!"

"And Ginny is looking for another couple of people to help out – ones that are good with children."

"How do you feel about this, Allison?"

Allison looked a little wistful. "I would like another girl or two. Ro and Jocko want boys, but even with Eleanor, I still miss little Esther Anne."

"Do you hear anything about her?"

Allison nodded. "Oh, yes. Katherine writes regularly. She and Nick are doing very well in Thunder Bay, with the shipping concerns on Lake Superior, the railroad, and the miners. Their store is doing very well! They are very well received and prosperous. There are a number of Indians there, and they have a very different standing than they did here. So, all in all, it's an environment that doesn't frown on their relationship. They have also had another child, so Esther Anne has a little brother to play with."

"Well, as long as she is well cared for and happy and loved, what more can one ask for?"

"I suppose you're right," Allison sighed. "But I still miss her."

"I know you do," said Rebecca gently, "but you will have your horde soon."

"Yes, we will! And a group of little hellions like you have never seen," laughed Ro. "We think we can take on as many as eight or ten children. Jocko is so excited about having brothers he cannot stand himself."

Allison joined in again. "Jocko is part of why we have come. Our boy needs a horse – he needs to learn to ride properly and our old nag is no good as a riding horse. At this point, she barely manages to pull the buggy or the buckboard. There is no one I trust more to find a decent horse for our son to learn on. Well trained, gentle, and able to tolerate the pranks of an eleven-year-old boy!"

Rebecca laughed. She remembered the messes that Andy and Buddy got into when they were learning to ride – and the number of times that they ended up sitting in the mud on their butts because they had tried to get a horse to do something that the animal had better sense than the children to attempt. "I will talk to Sue and we will find you something."

"Thank you so much. Jocko will be thrilled."

"If you are going to fill your house with children, you are going to need more than a new horse for Jocko. What about something more reliable than your old nag to pull? And a pony or two for the new children? How are you doing for furniture? And you will need toys, books, clothes – my goodness, the list just goes on! If you are going to create what will effectively be an orphanage, will you let the ladies of the community help get you fitted out for this effort?"

Ro and Allison looked at one another with a combination of shock and wonder on their faces. Allison finally responded. "We have never thought about it from that point of view. An orphanage? With help from the community? Oh, my!"

At that point, one of the footmen knocked on the door and brought in the luncheon that Rebecca had asked CeCe to prepare for them. The ladies talked and laughed, planned and argued about the idea of an orphanage, gossiped and traded stories about children and grandchildren throughout the meal.

SATURDAY, DECEMBER 11, 1880

Rebecca was pouring over the newspaper, using her magnifying glass to try and read the rather small type. Chris usually read the paper to her, but she was at the hospital today working with several of the cases that required a physical therapist.

"Rebecca, darling, why do you refuse to get glasses?" Charlie was genuinely curious.

Rebecca looked up and shrugged. "I only have one eye that works. Why should I spend the money on a pair of glasses when I only need one lens? The magnifying glass works perfectly well."

"As long as you know where it is and can find it when you need it." Charlie adjusted the glasses on his own nose, looking a bit frustrated with his sometimes absurdly frugal wife. She would spend money on him, the house, the farm, the children, and the grandchildren, but if she thought she was going to spend a penny on herself she bucked like a green horse.

Rex looked over at the two of them and just smiled. He had gotten Rebecca a gift for Christmas that would alleviate this ongoing discussion between them – a monocle with a black velvet ribbon so she could hang it around her neck.

Rebecca looked to change the subject, so she turned to Rex, who quickly wiped the tell-tale smile from his face.

"So, Rex, you have been keeping Chris busy lately. How is she doing at the hospital?"

"Ah, she is doing very well. Her skills as a physical therapist are outstanding, and she is very inventive in terms of finding ways for her patients to get the exercise they need, but because of their pain, they are unwilling to try." Rex chuckled. "She and Elizabeth have a particularly recalcitrant case – a man recovering from a dislocated knee who was afraid to try to walk. The solution was simple. They started putting his meal a little farther away each day, so if he wanted to eat, he had to walk."

Charlie and Rebecca both chuckled over that. In the early days of Rebecca's recovery, Chris had resorted to similar sneaky demands to help her regain her capabilities. She was still trying to find a way to get Rebecca back on a horse.

When Charlie and Rebecca had stopped chuckling, Rex hit them with an unexpected question. "Charlie, have you heard anything back from that alert you asked Richard to send around?"

Charlie shook his head. "Not a thing, but I keep hoping."

Rebecca sniffed and then excused herself from the table. "Well, gentlemen, I promised Sue I would look over the breeding books with her this morning. I will see you later."

As Rebecca retreated, Charlie looked at Rex. "I think I need to give her some time to herself."

"Yes, that would probably be a good idea. She will deal with the situation with Andy in her own way and her own time, but outright avoidance is probably not the best solution for anyone, so keeping us advised of the status is important, Charlie."

"Where did we go wrong? We were so careful to try and raise them to be responsible and honorable adults, and good citizens. We tried to not spoil them, but to be accountable and honest. Sue, Darby, Buddy, and Em all seem to have come out all right. What happened with Andy?"

Rex shook his head. "Every person is different. You know that from handling your troopers. And I think some people are just born missing something. In Andy's case, I think he is missing a sense of right and wrong except as it applies to him. He has no empathy for others and no ability to put himself into another's shoes. That makes a huge difference in how he sees the world. You have to understand, people like that are simply born that way. There is something in their brains that just does not work the way ours us do."

Charlie sighed and shook his head.

REBECCA HAD SPENT THE PREVIOUS HALF HOUR JUST SITTING IN the room downstairs that had once been her office but was now Sue's. Brooding over Andy was not doing any good, and she knew it, but she could not help herself. She loved him as much as she loved any of her children, but his behavior was past her understanding.

Eventually, Sue staggered in, cradling a large mug of coffee in her hands. "I am so sorry, Mama. You know I try to be prompt, but this morning, I just couldn't get up on time. Baby Andy was up all night with a sour stomach. I was up with him and didn't get to sleep until almost sunrise. How in Heaven's name did you manage when Buddy and Andy were both infants, and with me and Em terrorizing the house as toddlers!"

Rebecca managed to hide her smile. In her experience, every mother of a newborn suffered from severe lack of sleep, at least until the infant could sleep through the night without either having a nasty case of colic or having a demanding stomach that wanted to be fed every two or three hours. "I am so sorry, dear, but it is part of being a mother. I had good help and the ability to cat nap as I could."

"At least I didn't have to go through the misery of pregnancy and childbirth. I remember Aunt Elizabeth was miserable – and miserable to be around during her pregnancies, and poor Eliza had such difficult time and then died in childbirth. Is it a wonder that I do NOT want to be pregnant!"

"Fear is a great motivator, but you have to understand that carrying a child of your own, knowing it is developing under your heart, gives you an extraordinary feeling of wonder."

Sue looked at her mother, somewhat confused. Mama had spoken as if from experience, yet Sue was very aware that all of the Redmond children were adopted. "Were you ever pregnant?"

"Yes, dear. I was. Within a couple of months of my marriage to my first husband, Mr. Gaines, I became pregnant. When I was sure, I told him. He accused me of being unfaithful to him, and that the child was why I agreed to marry him. He beat me and I lost the baby. I never told anyone, not even your papa, but those few weeks of having a growing life inside me were very special."

"Why did you never tell Papa? I thought you shared everything."

"We do. We share everything that has an impact on our lives and our ability to be good parents to you, your brothers and sister, and friends to those around us. But you must understand, there would be no benefit to either of us for me to share this with him. He has always carried a bit of guilt that he could not offer me the same things a healthy man could. Why remind him that another man once had that privilege and threw it away?"

Sue sat, looking at her mother with awe at the simple, factual way she had delivered this long-held personal secret. Finally, she said, "Thank you for telling me. I will think about what you have said. With Uncle Rex and Aunt Elizabeth, I would get the best possible care. I know that."

FRIDAY, DECEMBER 17, 1880

Em had made arrangements for a hack to pick up her bags and herself and take them to the New York and New England Railroad train station. She was to meet Buddy at Grand Central Terminal, where they would find the private car that Miss Eloise had booked to bring them home.

She was downstairs a full half hour before the hack was due. She paced back and forth in the hall as she waited impatiently.

Mrs. Afton came in, curious as to what the stomping was about. "Em, please. You are shaking the house with your pacing. He will be here, I am sure. I have found Emmet to be very reliable."

"I am so sorry, Mrs. Afton. It is just that I haven't been home for Christmas in years and the idea of being with my family for a change is very exciting."

"I am sure it is, dear, but you are still a lady, and ladies do not rattle the china in the cabinet."

Em bowed her head, embarrassed at her own impatience. She then looked up and grinned at Mrs. Afton. "I left a little something for you under your tree. I hope you like it."

"Oh, my. You didn't have to do that."

"I wanted to. You have been so good to me."

"Should I open it now?"

"Oh, no. It's a Christmas present, so open it on Christmas."

"Well, thank you, dear." They heard a jingling of a harness outside. "Oh, here is Emmet. He is early. I told you he would be here."

The two women stepped out the front door as the carriage driver looped a lead over the hitching post outside the door, with Mrs. Afton hauling Em's carpet bag and Em pulling her trunk onto the front steps.

"Here I am, Mrs. Afton. I take it this young lady is my fare?"

"Yes, Emmet. She needs to get to the New York and New England station."

"Right you are." He came up the steps and hefted Em's trunk like it was a sack of feathers. "Come along, young miss."

Em hugged Mrs. Afton and then picked up her carpet bag. "I'll see you after twelfth night. Have a lovely holiday."

"Be well, Em. Safe travels."

BUDDY PACED UP AND DOWN THE CONCOURSE AT GRAND Central Terminal, waiting impatiently for his sister's train to arrive. He had caught a train in West Point and arrived early, but snow on the tracks had slowed the train from Boston. It was already a half hour late. He had already found their private car and loaded his gear into it, and then found a porter to haul his sister's inevitable load of luggage from one train to the next. Fortunately, he had enough money in his pocket to keep the porter waiting, so they could be on their way as soon as she got in.

Finally, the train pulled into the station, the engine sending up billows of smoke and steam in the air. Buddy motioned the porter to come with him and set off to find his sister and hustle her on to the next train.

Em jumped down from the car before the conductor had time to put the step stool in place and ran to her brother, throwing her arms around his broad shoulders. "Buddy, I finally made it."

He returned her embrace and said, "Yes, and the train home is waiting for us. Let me get your bags and we'll be on our way."

"Oh, there is only this carpet bag and my trunk back in the luggage car."

Buddy nodded to the porter. "A trunk for Miss Emily Redmond, please. And hurry."

The porter was prompt and the three of them pushed across the terminal to the private car as quickly as Buddy could get them moving. As they approached the train, Buddy waved to the conductor. "We're here. Give us a minute to get us loaded and we'll be ready to go."

The conductor nodded. He had an assistant waiting at the private car to load the lady's luggage. Meanwhile, he headed up to the head of the train to let the engineer know they were finally ready to go.

Buddy threw Em's carpet bag into her berth as she sank into one of the chairs. "Oh, my. Miss Eloise has gotten us a lovely car. This will be far more comfortable than the trains I rode on in England, and it's nice and warm!"

Buddy sat down opposite her and dropped a slightly greasy sack on the table between them. "It has a stove over in the corner. I stopped at one of the stands and picked up some lunch, as I knew you would not have time to stop at a restaurant, and the conductor told me that we have supper arranged for us."

"Ah, Miss Eloise thinks of everything."

Just then an older, gray-haired porter came shuffling into the car carrying a tray with tea, cups, and cookies. "As you requested, Mr. Redmond." He sat the tray on a table and latched it into place. "If you need anything else, just pull the bell cord and call for Old George." He motioned to a thin cable stretched above the windows and then quietly left.

The two siblings settled in for the trip, catching up on the goings on at their respective schools and grumbling about Andy managing to upset the entire family. The two agreed that as far as they were concerned, it was just as well that Andy would not be home for Christmas, even though they predicted that Mama would be a little weepy about her missing boy.

SATURDAY, DECEMBER 18, 1880

Rebecca had driven the house staff slightly crazy by urging them to get every Christmas decoration in place, then criticizing the placement of this candle or that wreath.

Finally, Charlie intervened. "Rebecca, it is perfectly lovely, and if you do not stop picking on each thing being done, the staff is going to rebel!"

"But Charlie, our children are going to be here and it has to be perfect."

"It is perfect. Now stop!"

"All right, dear. When are you leaving for the station?"

"The train is due in around three, so I will leave sometime after lunch."

Lunch was interesting, with Rebecca harassing CeCe about having plenty of butterscotch cookies and being sure to not overcook the venison for dinner. Rex and Charlie just looked at one another and rolled their eyes. The less Rebecca could do for herself, the more she drove the staff to distraction. Both men knew they needed to work on that.

At two o'clock, Rebecca came into Charlie's office, asking, "When are you leaving?"

"In fifteen minutes, dear. I figure I will have time for a quick drink at Jamie's before they arrive."

"Oh, Charlie, please do not be late."

"I will be on time, I promise. The train is more likely to be late."

At exactly a quarter after two, Rebecca was down in the front hall, waiting to see Charlie off to town. As she stood there, she heard an unfamiliar jingling out front. She looked out the window to see a sleigh, complete with sleigh bells, pulled by Sue's latest acquisition, a big chestnut gelding, pull up to the front steps.

"Good God, Charlie! When did you get a sleigh? And WHY!? If there is more than an inch of snow on the ground, I am an Amazon queen."

"Seemed appropriate to the season. You said you wanted the chestnut to be trained to drive, and there are those who think you are a warrior woman, darling," Charlie teased with a kiss to her nose as he walked out the door and pulled himself into the sleigh, taking the reins from the hostler who had brought it around.

Charlie was in Culpeper in less than a half hour, and thoroughly chilled by the brisk drive into town, so he did indeed stop in to see Jamie, and more importantly, to imbibe one of the barman's famous hot toddies. The bourbon, honey, lemon, and hot water mixture slid down his throat easily and warmed him from the inside.

He headed over to the train station and stood on the platform waiting for the train, which was running just a couple of minutes late. Given the weather, that was not unexpected.

"PAPA!" Buddy and Em chorused in perfect unison.

"Hello, children." Charlie called standing with his arms open as they both rushed up to him. They embraced their father, forming a huddle of happy Redmonds. The train staff unloaded their luggage, piling it on the platform, where one of the station men piled it onto a cart to haul it out to the sleigh.

Charlie escorted his children out to the road, where both children stopped dead in their tracks when they saw what their father had come to meet them in.

"Papa! What the hell is THAT?" Buddy knew his father had a love for carriages, but a sleigh?

"Buddy, do not use that kind of language with me." Charlie expected his son to be a gentleman at all times, especially around the ladies of the family. "A sleigh seemed appropriate to the season. Now, shall we head home? Your mother is waiting."

The ride home was quick, but to Em's discomfort, very chilly. An open sleigh, in weather cold enough that the snow on the ground showed no signs of melting, was not her idea of pleasant. By the time they got to Mountain View, her eyes were tearing, her nose was running, and her cheeks were reddened by the cold. At least Papa had brought carriage blankets and hot bricks for her feet and hands. Buddy, who rode up front, was in boyish heaven because Charlie let him drive.

Rebecca was waiting in the hall. Em got the first embrace, which was a little embarrassing since she did not have a chance to clear her eyes or nose before Mama enveloped her. Buddy babbled on about how wonderful the sleigh was.

Shedding outer wraps, Rebecca herded her returning prodigals to the back parlor, where Em was very grateful for the hot fire and pot of fresh tea, accompanied by a huge plate full of butterscotch cookies.

~

MONDAY, DECEMBER 20, 1880

Mama had monopolized Buddy's and Em's time all day Sunday, asking about every minute aspect of their lives at their respective schools. Papa had finally intervened well after supper, taking his wife off to bed.

Em had tried several times to get a few minutes alone with

WHITHER THOU GOEST

Uncle Rex, but it had not been possible. Today, Stella had arrived with LJ and Rachel in tow and little Ruthie bundled up like an Eskimo, an arrival that finally took Rebecca's attention away from Em and Buddy. Buddy took the opportunity to ride into town to talk with John Foxworth about the list of books that General Schofield had given him and to start creating a study plan for the West Point entrance exams.

Em slipped upstairs and knocked on Rex's door.

"Emily, come in. I was just about to make a cup of chai. Would you like some?"

"What is chai?"

"It's an Indian version of spiced tea. It's very good. I think you will like it."

"Thank you, Uncle Rex." She sat down in front of the fire and watched with interest as he mixed several herbs from his medicine kit with black tea in the tea pot, then poured hot water over the mix.

"So, to what do I owe what I assume is a surreptitious visit?" Rex asked as he handed her a cup of tea.

"I want to know what's really going on with Andy."

Rex nodded. He understood what Em was asking, having watched Rebecca attempt to whitewash the situation and Charlie become very tight jawed about it.

Rex told her the whole story; about Baby Andy's birth, Eliza's death, Darby yanking Andy out of a house of ill-repute that night, and Andy's disappearance the morning of Eliza's funeral, taking one of Sue's best horses with him. He finished by relating how both parents were wracking their brains to try to figure out how they went so wrong with Andy and his suspicion that the core problem was that Andy lacked a sense of right and wrong or any empathy and was probably born that way.

Em listened carefully and shook her head over her brother's

235

behavior. "I know, Uncle Rex. He has always been like that, avoiding unpleasant situations, walking away from responsibility, and trying to put the blame on others. I'm not surprised he ran."

"The real issue is to get your parents to understand that it isn't the result of anything they did wrong. Until they get past feeling guilty about his behavior and trying to convince themselves that somehow, they erred in how they raised him, they are going to go through life beating their heads against a very large brick wall."

"Thank you, Uncle Rex. I will do what I can. Maybe Mama will listen to me."

"I hope so. She isn't listening to anyone else right now."

~

SATURDAY, DECEMBER 25, 1880

The morning dawned clear, bright, and terribly cold. Charlie went down the hall, rousing everyone in the house. The rest of the family and friends who joined them for Christmas would be arriving soon, so Charlie wanted everyone up, dressed and ready to go.

The in-residence family assembled in the back parlor for coffee or tea, as they wished, while CeCe and her helpers set a buffet in the breakfast room for the soon to arrive guests. Cousin Albert made himself useful, handing out cups of coffee and tea to expedite the process. The family then adjourned to the hall, where people would come in, shed their coats, scarves, hats and gloves, and admire the huge Christmas tree. The hall was the only room with enough ceiling clearance to hold the monstrous evergreen.

The first to arrive were Sue and Jeremiah, with Baby Andy

bundled up like an Indian papoose. Rebecca laughed at how they had packaged the six-week-old to keep him warm, while Em commented on the value of using Indian methods. Darby and Stella arrived next, with Little Jerome whooping like a wild child, dancing around the Christmas tree. His three-year-old sister Rachel hung back, wisely avoiding the wild arm flapping of her big brother. Ruthie was in her travelling basket, hauled in by her other grandfather, as Jerome and Amelia had come down from Washington for the holiday.

LJ decided that dancing around the Christmas tree was not getting him what he wanted, which was to open presents, so he decided his MaBeh was the best target. He went to Rebecca, climbed into her lap and started frantically signing his wishes to her. Rebecca laughed and spoke and signed her response. "No, young man. You have to wait until everyone gets here. Now, be good." She handed him a butterscotch cookie to distract him.

Elizabeth and Richard arrived with Arial and Dickon in tow. Dickon, now fourteen, was trying very hard to look like a proper young gentleman, while eight-year-old Arial decided the babies were living dolls to play with. Little Andy was a bit too young, but little Ruthie, at almost a year, was tough enough to withstand her attentions.

The Nailers swept in with Ro, Allison, Esther and their brood right behind them. As soon as they shed their wrappings, Rex and Rebecca led them into the breakfast room for the day's first round of food.

Samantha Nailer managed to corner her daughter in law once they got into the breakfast room. "Oh, let me hold the baby, please." She took Baby Andy into her arms, cooing gently at the infant. "Oh, my. He looks like you, Sue." She ruffled the little tuft of reddish-blond hair straggling over the baby's scalp. "Pretty blue eyes, too!" Now that Samantha had hold of her first grandchild, she was not letting go.

Once everyone had gotten something to eat, although the process was somewhat rushed given the number of children of various ages in the group, the party trooped back out to the hall. Charlie stood in front of the tree and called Dickon and Sam to him. He handed each of them a red velvet elf hat. "Gentlemen, you are our Christmas elves this year. Your job is to deliver all of the gifts under the tree to the appropriate person. When all the gifts have been distributed, you may then open your own."

The two boys looked at each other, shrugged, and set about sorting gift packages as quickly as they could. They had seen Buddy and Andy handle this chore in previous years and decided that having one of them identify the recipient and the other deliver it was the quickest way to get the job done. They were quite efficient about it, as they knew what kind of gifts General Charlie got the children in his world, and were eager to see what this year brought.

As he always did, Charlie had sent to his friend Mr. Schwarz for gifts for the children. Within a few minutes, the hall was strewn with train sets, dolls and doll houses, fishing gear, and the always present lead soldiers and battle field charts, among other things. Every child had a new book appropriate to their age and interests, and several had puzzle games of various sorts. Buddy got a new military style saddle and his own hunting rifle. Most of the ladies had new jewelry, and Ro got a new wagon for the farm, refurbished from Charlie's ever-growing collection of wagons, carriages, and other conveyances. Ro and Allison had gotten Jocko a Morgan mare trained to the saddle, and Rebecca had provided a young, big, roan gelding to pull the new wagon.

CeCe slipped into the hall to let Rebecca and Charlie know that dinner had been laid in the dining room and she and her staff were ready to leave for their own celebrations. Charlie asked her to wait a moment and stepped to the back of the hall, where he pulled out a small keg of good brandy. "I thought you and your family and the folks at Redmond Grove would enjoy this after supper."

"Thank you, General Charlie. I promise not to let anyone have too much at one time! Merry Christmas, sir. Oh, Otis had all of the carriages and wagons hitched and ready. They are waiting down in the carriage house court yard, for when it is time for the guests to leave."

"Thank you, CeCe, and thank Otis and the staff for me. Miss Rebecca and I will see everyone tomorrow for Boxing Day."

The party moved to the dining room, for which Rebecca was grateful. It was warmer there than in the hall. Rex, Sue, and Em provided such services as were needed, though most of the guests served themselves from the platters and chafing dishes that CeCe had set out. Albert took on the role of bartender, though the most popular drink was Otis's milk punch, which he made following his father's famous recipe.

Finally, the day was over. CeCe and her staff would clear up the dining room tomorrow, and Tess and Otis's staff would straighten up the rest of the house. Albert excused himself to go and visit a friend, and the rest of the family retreated to the back parlor to relax, drink tea that Rex brewed up for them, and digest a huge meal. The younger children played on the floor with their new toys, while the adults broke into small groups to relax and chat.

Em managed to catch her mother sitting quietly beside the fire, looking at the assembled family members with a slightly wistful look on her face. "Missing Andy," she more stated than asked.

"Yes, yes, I am. I wish I could figure out what I did wrong."

"Mama, listen to me. Listen very carefully. Andy is my half-brother, and I suspect I know him better than anyone else, even you. Even when he was a little boy, he never could face up to difficult situations. He spent a lot of energy making sure that he was not blamed for anything he did – and let me tell you, he often managed to get you to blame Buddy for something he did. There is something Andy was born with, or more correctly born without, that makes him like he is. You and Papa did not do ANYTHING wrong – there is just something amiss in Andy. You gave him every opportunity to grow up a responsible, honorable man, but that is just not in him. Please, please, look at the four of us. We are all good people, whole people. Andy just isn't whole and it is not your fault."

Rebecca looked at her daughter, stunned by her impassioned speech. "You think he is as he is because he is somehow innately flawed?"

"I do. He doesn't have a sense of responsibility." Em patted her mother's hand. "Think on it, Mama. Talk to Papa and Uncle Rex. And stop feeling guilty, please."

LJ came up just then and asked MaBeh to help him play a puzzle game that Charlie had given him. Em had studied some sign in England so she could interact with her nephew. She intervened and offered to play with him.

As Em moved away with LJ, Rebecca looked at her thoughtfully. *Perhaps Andy has inherited something from that vile rapist who was his father. After all, like father, like son. At least Andy does not have the violent streak that Montgomery had.*

CHAPTER 9

Eᴍ ᴡᴀs sɪᴛᴛɪɴɢ ɪɴ ʜᴇʀ ᴘᴀʀᴇɴᴛs' office, curled up in her father's big, overstuffed wingback chair by the fire, reading a book when the mail was delivered to Charlie.

As Charlie flipped through the envelopes, he tossed one onto the corner of his desk. "Em, someone sent you a letter here."

"Thank you, Papa." Em got up to retrieve it. "Oh, it's from Professor Putnam. I wonder what he wants." She opened the missive, scanned through the message, and then grinned. "Papa, I will get to go out to the Serpent Mound dig this spring! He says to pack field clothes."

"Serpent Mound?" queried Charlie. "What and more importantly, where is that?"

"Oh, it's fascinating. It's a prehistoric effigy mound in southern Ohio – about fifteen hundred feet long, shaped like a snake eating an egg, a brilliant example of one of the Mississippi culture activities – the Adena group, we think, but no one knows for sure."

"So, you are off to do the same kind of work in Ohio that you did with the Bronze Age Britons? "

"That's about it. I think I'm being sent out there because I already have sound field experience, which is more than most of the others at the museum."

"Well, I can tell you are excited." Charlie grinned, remembering the look on the face of his daughter when she was five and found her first fish fossil. She had the same look on her face now.

"Oh, I am. This is the kind of work I was hoping to get involved with," Em squeaked.

"And you get to wear your britches and boots again," chuckled her father.

Em went off to find her dig clothes and tools, which she had left behind since she did not expect to be assigned to the field so quickly.

Charlie settled back to read his correspondence. Most of it was routine business information about the bank and his other investments, but one letter was decidedly annoying – the one from Fitzhugh Lee.

"Damn you, Fitz. I told you no and I meant it. I have no desire to run for governor, thank you, sir." If the man were actually present, Charlie would have turned the air blue and then escorted him out.

Just as he was cursing Fitz Lee in absentia, there was a tap on his door and Richard let himself in. "Someone got your ire up, Charlie?"

"Yes, Fitz Lee wants me to run for governor. I told him no, but he is being bloody persistent."

"Well, I have news to take your mind off him." Richard

reached into his breast pocket. "I got a telegram this morning and came right out here. Seems Andy got into some kind of fracas in Big Lick and is now sitting in jail down there."

"Oh, holy hell. He is in jail? Anybody get hurt?"

"Sheriff did not tell me. I assume so and he is trying to keep his cost down. All I got was this." Richard handed Charlie the telegram.

Have Andrew Redmond in custody for assault – Stop. Informing as requested – Stop.

"Well, I suppose it could have been worse. Richard, I need for you to do me a couple of favors, if you do not mind."

"Of course, Charlie. Anything you need."

"First, contact the sheriff and let him know that I will be down to collect my wayward son and settle his accounts in a day or two."

Richard nodded. "Going to let him stew in his own juices?"

"Precisely. He has never been in jail before. Maybe this will give him something to think about."

"I will take care of it. Anything else?"

"Once I have made travel arrangements, would you mind coming with me?"

"Absolutely. Let me go send this telegram and then I will let my wife know she is going to be on her own for a few days."

CHARLIE WENT LOOKING FOR REBECCA AND FOUND HER IN THE upstairs parlor, doing some knitting, with Chris Baldwin reading to her.

"Ah, ladies. I am sorry to intrude on you. What are you reading today?" Charlie was not looking forward to his discussion with Rebecca, so this gave him a good excuse to avoid the issue, a least for a moment.

"General Redmond, good afternoon. We are reading Mr. Henry James's latest work, called *Washington Square*, about a young woman who must learn some rather bitter lessons in life," Miss Baldwin spoke eagerly.

"Yes, a well written study of people who we have all met at some point in our lives," Rebecca added. "To what do we owe your visit, dear?"

Charlie turned to the nurse. "Miss Chris, could I have a moment with my wife, please?"

"Certainly, sir." She marked her place in the book, set it aside, and smiled. "I think I will go down and find some fruit. Would you like some, Miss Rebecca?"

"Thank you, no. I am fine for now." She dismissed her attendant with a smile. As the woman left the room, Rebecca frowned at her husband. "What is the problem, Charlie?"

"I have heard from the sheriff in Big Lick. He has Andy in jail down there for brawling."

"God, Charlie. I always thought it would be Buddy we would have to bail out of jail, not Andy."

"So did I, but Buddy seems to be on the road to an army career, and I hesitate to think what road Andy may be on."

"Ah, dear. It may be that he was just too young to deal with the whole situation – marriage, a child, a wife dead in childbirth. It may have just overwhelmed him. We will have to support him and get him back on the right track."

"I hope so. I truly do. Richard is going with me, so I will order an engine in the morning and take our car and one of our transport cars for his horses."

"If he still has the horses." Rebecca was disgusted at the thought.

"I am sure he does. He does understand the value of those."

"It is unfortunate that he does not seem to have the same empathy for the people around him."

"Perhaps cooling his heels in the Big Lick jail for a few days will enhance his ability."

"Charlie! You are not leaving him there!"

"I absolutely am." Charlie nodded as he poured himself a cup of coffee. "We know where he is. He is safe. There is not a lot to do in jail but think and pray. Either one of those would be of benefit to the boy."

"What if he decides we hate him because we left him there?"

"Darling, I am not talking about letting him see his next birthday in jail. I am talking about forty-eight hours. He is not going to grow gray whiskers in seventy-two hours."

"You said forty-eight."

"Did I?"

"Charlie! If you do not go get him, I will!"

"Now, Rebecca, it will take a day for the engine to get here. I will go get him as soon as it is possible. It is Monday now. I will be there Thursday." He grinned. "Monday at the latest."

"Charles Huger Redmond!"

He laughed outright as he leaned over and kissed the top of her head. "I will not leave him there any longer than need be, but I am leaving him there just long enough."

TUESDAY, JANUARY 4, 1881

Even on Rebecca's private car, the trip down to Big Lick was rather torturous. Stopped several times and made to wait for regularly scheduled trains, two rather significant accidents, four sheep, and a rather testy bull blocking the track, Richard and Charlie alternated between playing cards rather desultorily and smoking cigar after cigar while standing on the platform of the train car watching the landscape go by without really seeing it.

When they finally arrived in Big Lick, night had fallen. There were two bars open, one of which served food as well and offered sleeping accommodations for the freight men who came through the town. Richard and Charlie, both tired and hungry, settled for a meal of decidedly mediocre lamb stew washed down with some rot gut whiskey. They were forced to share a bed, and it was none to welcoming either, with loose ropes so that the whole thing sagged in the middle causing tight back to back quarters, and a general aroma of the unwashed bodies that had used the bed before them was nauseating to say the least. Charlie wished he had thought to bring one of Rebecca's perfumed handkerchiefs on this trip, as he did when he was normally away from her for long periods of time. It would have been a blessing that might have kept his eyes from watering. They hoped tomorrow morning would see them finding improved circumstances.

"MAMA, HOW CAN YOU THINK THAT ANDY IS INNOCENT IN THIS?" Sue paced up and down in front of her mother's chair, irate that Rebecca had been making excuses for her incredibly irritating brother all evening. "For God's sake! He stole one of our best saddle horses and has run from anything that even vaguely resembled being responsible. Did he even meet his son?"

Word had been sent to the family that Papa had left with Uncle Richard to retrieve the wandering brother, and they had all assembled to have supper with their mother.

Darby interceded, trying to calm his incensed sister. "Sue, you know that Mama and Papa will do what is needed with him."

Sue turned on her older brother. "I know nothing of the sort. Andy has always managed to wriggle out of trouble if he couldn't out right blame one or the other of us!"

Rebecca had been listening to her children rant since coffee had been served after supper. She was growing tired. "Now, children, Andy has had to face a number of severe challenges, what with fathering a child and having to marry so young, and then losing his wife. I think that it was probably just too much for one so young to handle, so he ran. Now we will have to support him so he can get back onto the right path."

That was a bit more than Darby could take. "I am not sure Andy knows what the right path is. He told me that he wanted to prove to Papa and you that he could find a way to make play pay."

Buddy, who had been silent thus far, added quietly as he checked the time on his pocket watch against the mantle clock which he had always known to be true, "And you have no idea how many times I had to pay for something Andy did. At least I'm not in trouble for this mess."

Em had been sitting quietly in the corner. Finally, in a rather thoughtful tone of voice, she joined in. "You and Papa raised the five of us the same way, with the same support and expectations and sense of right and wrong. The four of us in this room came out all right, and we do not run from problems. I agree with Uncle Rex. There is just something missing from Andy's makeup that can't let him be responsible."

Rebecca stood up and faced her brood. "We have all had our say on this, but the fact of the matter is that, until your father gets back with Andrew, we will not know what happened. Until we find out what made Andy run and what kind of trouble he got into, we cannot make assumptions. He is still my son and your brother, and I will NOT have you castigate him without knowing the facts. Now, if you do not mind, I am tired and it is time for you all to go to your rooms or your homes. We will have a more informed discussion when your father and Andy get home."

Duly chastened, the children gathered their things, mumbled apologies, wished their mother and Uncle Rex good night, and filed out of the parlor. Rebecca nodded to each of them, but never lost her stoic expression. Mama had spoken and her children obeyed.

As the door closed behind Darby, Rebecca sank back into her chair, burying her face in her hands. Through tears, she murmured to Rex, "Oh, God. What is wrong with my boy? How are we going to fix him?"

Rex slipped his arm around Rebecca's shoulders, urging her out of her chair to lead her upstairs to the private parlor and their rooms. "I honestly do not know, Rebecca. All I know is that we will all do our best to help him find his way."

~

WEDNESDAY, JANUARY 5, 1881

Richard and Charlie were outside of the sheriff's office at six that morning. They had to wait. Finally, a red-faced man wearing a Colt strapped to his waist and carrying a basket came strolling down the street.

Richard stepped forward. "Sheriff Green? I am Richard Polk. You sent me the telegraph about Andrew Redmond."

"Ah, yes, Colonel Polk. Come in, come in. I have young Redmond's breakfast here." The man turned to Charlie. "I assume you are the boy's father?"

"Yes, sir, I am. General Charles Redmond."

"Well, come in. I will put a pot of coffee on for us." They entered the small jail and took the seats that Sheriff Green waved them to as the man entered the cell area to deliver Andy his breakfast and then emerged to stoke the Franklin stove in the corner and set a coffee pot on it to brew.

Finally, the man came to sit at his desk, handing out cups of hot, very black coffee to Charlie and Richard. "I assume you want to bail your boy out."

"Yes, but first I need to find out what he did."

"Well, he's been hanging around town for a couple of months, mostly sitting in on the poker games over at Bailey's place during the evenings and doing whatever during the days. He's been staying at Mrs. Kelsey's boarding house, and I think he had a couple of horses at Jerry's stable, but I don't think he has them anymore. Anyway, there was a serious poker game on New Year's Eve at Bailey's. As I heard it, he got accused of cheating at the table, someone took a swing, and all hell broke loose. Now I have one guy with a broken jaw, another with a broken arm, and a third with broken ribs. And Bailey's got a hell of a repair bill for broken furniture and the mirror that was behind the bar. So, your boy's in for assault, disorderly conduct, and destruction of property, and he's not getting out until the repair bills and the medical bills are paid or he works them off." Sheriff Green gave Charlie a couple of minutes to absorb his story, then asked, "Do you want to see your son?"

"Not yet, Sheriff. First, I think I would like to talk with Mr. Bailey, the stable man, and Mrs. Kelsey, as well as the injured men. Then I shall have a better idea as to what to say to my reprobate son."

"Just as well, General Redmond. I will be around pretty much all day."

"Thank you, Sheriff."

Charlie and Richard started at Mr. Bailey's bar. As they walked in, it was clear that there was room for at least one more, and possibly two more, good sized tables and several chairs. Behind the bar was a large, empty frame that Charlie suspected had once held the reported mirror.

"Mr. Bailey?"

"That's me. What'll it be, gentlemen?"

"Coffee and some answers. Sir, I am Charles Redmond, and I understand my son Andy has done some damage to your establishment."

"I'll say. He got accused of cheating at the card game, and when confronted, he started to fight his way out of here. The whole thing turned into a brawl and he ended up breaking my expensive mirror, two tables, and seven chairs. Not to mention that I have three teamsters in my shed out back camping out because they are too broken up to work. If you're that brat's father, you need to pay up for the damages before I'll drop the charges."

Charlie sighed and reached into his pocket for his check book. "How much?"

"I think about three hundred will do it for me. The damned mirror alone cost me a hundred and I've been feeding the wounded men for the past few days."

"All right. To whom do I make the check?"

"Oh, no, Mister. I do not take checks. Cash only."

Charlie nodded. "Fine. I will go to the bank after I talk to the casualties."

"Sure. They're out back." He gestured to the back with his bar towel.

Charlie and Richard walked into the yard behind the bar. Charlie was stony faced, with his jaw clenched so hard Richard expected to hear the sound of cracking teeth. He knew better than to talk to his old commander when he was like this.

They walked into the shed, where they found three men in various states of recuperation. One had his arm splinted, one had his jaw tied closed, and the third one was reclining on a makeshift cot.

"Gentlemen, I am General Charles Redmond. I understand you three got into an altercation with my son, Andrew."

The one with the bound jaw just grunted, but the one with the splinted arm was very vocal. "Yeah, you could say that. The little shit cheated at the table, and when we called him on it, he started hitting and kicking like some kind of whirlwind. I'm out of work for six weeks at least and the other two are just as bad off."

Charlie looked at each of the men and asked, "Would fifty apiece be enough for you to take care of yourselves and drop the charges?"

The one on the cot spoke up. "Make it seventy-five – cash because we have to pay the doc – and you have a deal."

"I will be back shortly."

As Charlie and Richard trudged toward the stable, Richard gently asked, "What else do we have to do?"

"I need to find his horses, get his things from the boarding house, go to the bank, and stop by the telegraph office to get a decent engine so we can get home. I am still too furious to see Andy. I swear, if I go see him now, I might beat the hell out of him. How dare he use Rex's training to bust up a bar?"

"Then let's get to the telegraph office first to get the train situation handled, then find the stable manager and the horses, and do the boarding house last. Actually, we can probably stay in Andy's room tonight if we have to instead of that miserable excuse for a bed we had last night. That will give you until tomorrow to cool off and not kill your son."

"Humph. If I can get a train in here tonight, we will leave as soon as we can. I can do without spending any more time or money in Big Lick than I absolutely have to."

Charlie followed Richard's plan. By the time they finished making all the calls they needed to make, Charlie just barely had time to get to the bank before it closed. Every single person he had talked with wanted cash for what Andy owed, including the stable owner, who had taken the horses because Andy had not paid their board for two months. By the time he was done, he needed almost a thousand dollars cash to get Andy out of jail.

Charlie and Richard packed Andy's room at the boarding house and hauled his meager belongings along with their cases down to the train station.

"Richard, would you do me one more favor? While I go pay everyone off and have the horses brought down here, can you go collect Andy from the jail? I will wait on the train to see him."

"Certainly, Charlie. Can I at least warn him?"

"Oh, I think he will figure it out. If you go to get him, he will know I am waiting."

CHARLIE PAID ALL OF THE BILLS, AND WITH HELP FROM JERRY, the stable man, got the horses loaded onto the train, which sat in the station waiting for Richard and Andy. Charlie sat, sipping brandy and playing with the cold supper that had been sent from the inn. The sun was setting when Richard and Andy finally showed up.

Richard made a beeline for the brandy. "Sheriff Green is a decent guy when it comes to taking care of his people. He had to check with each one of them to confirm that all charges were dropped before he would release Andy to me."

"I suspected as much," grunted Charlie. He glanced at his son, who was standing at the entrance to the car with an expression on his face that was an interesting combination of embarrassment and dour sullenness. "You. Sit over there. Do not say a word until I tell you to."

Andy slouched in the chair against the wall that Charlie had indicated.

Charlie reached up and pulled the bell chord twice, indicating that they were ready to go, and then poured himself another brandy and a cup of coffee.

The three men sat silently, the only sound being the clack of the wheels on the rails.

THURSDAY, JANUARY 6, 1881

Charlie, Richard, and Andy arrived late in the evening, having had another difficult trip home. With so little notice, their private train had been made to sit and wait once again on sidetracks multiple times to allow scheduled trains to pass through safely. Travelling at night was slower as well. Charlie was tired and grumpy. Andy was tired and sullen. Richard was tired and staying very quiet. It was safer.

Louis had taken a buggy to wait for them. He had to wait for several hours at the Culpeper station. They unloaded the now very annoyed horses and tied them to the rear of the buggy, dropped Richard off at his house, and headed home.

Rebecca was waiting for them in the hall. After giving Charlie a cursory hug and kiss, she turned to her son, wrapping her arms around him. "Oh, Andy, we have missed you so. Please, come and tell me all about it."

"Mama, please. I'm dirty and tired and just need to get some sleep. I'd like to get a sandwich from CeCe, get a bath, and go to bed. Can we talk tomorrow?"

"Of course, dear. I am just so glad to have you home."

"Yeah, well... I'll see you in the morning, Mama."

Charlie, having shed his coat and hat, escorted his wife to the back parlor, where Rex was waiting for them. With a cup of hot tea in his hand, he settled in and related what he had found in Big Lick – and how much it had cost to get Andy and the horses back to Mountain View.

~

FRIDAY, JANUARY 7, 1881

Charlie was up and out of the house well before anyone else. He had tossed and turned most of the night; he was not sure how Rebecca had managed to sleep through it. Finally, when he could no longer stand it, he got up, dressed, slipped out of the house, and headed toward the barns.

He ambled slowly down the path between the house and what had become the business compound of Redmond Stables. He noticed a light on in the kitchen window of the farrier's cottage. A quick glance to the chimney told him he was probably correct in the assumption that someone must also be awake. He diverted his direction slightly, hoping perhaps there might be a pot of coffee to be shared.

As he approached, he could see through the front window. Brooks was at the stove cooking something in a cast iron pan. He rapped on the door before pushing it open.

The barn manager smiled and set his pan aside. "Good morning, General! You're up early. Care for a cup of mud?"

"I was hoping to find one, yes." Charlie nodded with a chuckle. He took the offered mug, taking a long drink. "That is terrible," he winced. "Army coffee if I ever tasted it."

"Glad to know Yankee coffee was just as bad." Brooks laughed as he went back to the pan. "Got some bacon and eggs here too, if you're interested. I was here a little early and couldn't resist a bite this morning since CeCe sent down the day-old baked goods yesterday. There's a loaf of her bread and blueberry muffins in there."

Charlie chuckled, knowing the farm staff loved it when the coveted dishes came out of the kitchen. "I could be persuaded."

"Have a seat. It'll be ready in just a few minutes."

As Charlie took a seat at the small table, Brooks glanced at his boss, who was enthralled by the coffee in his cup. "Anything I can help with, General?"

"What?" Charlie lifted his head.

"Seems like you have something on your mind. Anything I can help with?"

"Not unless you have a magic wand that will make Andy behave."

Brooks nodded as he moved the bacon around in the pan. "There are a few rumors going around."

"Wonderful." Charlie shook his head with disgust. "You may as well tell me so I can at least set the record straight."

"Well now, General, everybody knows they're only rumors. If Andy had done the things that are going around, you wouldn't have gotten him out of jail."

"He got into a fight over a card game down in Big Lick. Busted up a few teamsters and a bar. That is all."

"I told the fellas in town there was no way Andy murdered someone."

Charlie groaned, "Not yet."

"I used to think that I was missing something, only having girls, you know." Brooks shrugged one shoulder as he cracked the eggs into the pan. "But watching what you go through with your brood, I've been rethinking that."

"The girls are much easier." Charlie drained the coffee cup, standing to pour another from the pot on the stove. He leaned against a wooden counter as he continued, "I love all my children, but what Andy is doing to this family has me so frustrated I cannot even begin to think straight. And what he is doing to his mother has me in knots. Thought I would lend a hand in the barns this morning. Physical labor always helps me think."

"We're always happy to have you come down, General, you know that. We're doing some shoeing today. Got a new barn supervisor starting this morning in number one. Younger fella named Collins. Coming to us from Richmond. He's a little rough around the edges, but he knows what he's doing and he'll manage the boys alright. Miss Sue has a buyer arriving just before lunch, so we'll be needing to get those two big bay stallions ready for her to show. I've got a fence crew going out to the north pastures; that storm last week brought down some limbs and we've got several sections to fix. Roofing crews on barn two and the foaling barn are patching shingles. Miss Sue will have my backside in a sling if her mares get wet when their babies come."

Charlie laughed, knowing how protective Sue could be when it came to the horses. A lesson learned from her mama and well learned indeed. He had to keep his pride in check when it came to the abilities of the women in his life. Buttons for his vests were expensive.

Scooping the food from the pan into two tin plates, Brooks grabbed a basket of day-old breads from the counter and gestured for Charlie to take a seat at the little table. "It ain't fancy, General, but you can eat it without gagging."

As the two men ate and talked about random things, Charlie realized how nice it was to talk with someone who did not have a real interest in the situation. Brooks offered a willing ear to bend and a couple useful pieces of advice.

By the time breakfast was complete and the two men began walking toward the barns to begin a long day's work, Charlie was feeling a bit better.

"You are up early this morning," said Jeremiah as he poured hot water into the basin in front of his shaving mirror.

"Yes, well, I have an appointment with a buyer from New York later this morning and Mama has some sort of plan to try and bring Andy to his senses that involves introducing him to the baby."

"And you would like me to take our son to Mother Redmond on my way to work so you can focus on your business meeting."

Sue kissed her husband's neck. "Yes, please, dear, if you wouldn't mind. Have I mentioned recently that I adore you and think you are a wonderful husband and father?"

"Flattery will get you somewhere. What will we do if Andy decides he wants to raise his son?"

"Oh, Jerry, be realistic. My brother would no more want to raise a baby than he would want to walk into the lion's den like a modern-day Daniel. That is simply not who that brat is!"

Jeremiah scraped one side of his face clean, rinsing the razor in the bowl, as he thought about that comment. "You have a point there, dear. I have known Andy for all of his life, and to be honest, I do not think I have ever seen him be genuinely concerned about another human being."

"Yes. I think we are safe in letting him meet the baby. You might want to be careful. He may just throw little Andy in your arms and run screaming from the room." Sue continued to get dressed in her very practical riding habit as she spoke.

Jeremiah finished shaving and wiped his face clean of the bits of soap left afterwards. He turned to his wife, looked her up and down, reached over and straightened her collar, and kissed her gently. "You look the perfect horsewoman, love. Go, sell your horses and continue to enhance the reputation of Redmond Stables. I will be the good father. I think I will take Harriet with me. When Andy gets hungry or tired, he gets demanding and she knows how to get him to settle down and eat better than your mother does."

"Good idea, oh thou most excellent father."

CHARLIE WAS SHOVELING HORSE APPLES INTO A WHEELBARROW when an unfamiliar face popped up in the door.

"Hey, you! Old timer!"

Charlie's brows rose slightly when he looked at the younger man before him. "Yes?"

"Mr. Brooks says those two bay boys need to be washed up and readied to be shown later this morning. You need to go take care of it. Seems like an easy enough job for a fella of your limited skills."

"Excuse me?" Charlie tried to mask the look of surprise he was sure crossed his features. Clearly this young man had no idea who he was.

"Don't mean to offend ya, old fella, but hell, ya be missin' half your damn hand."

"Part of my leg and ass too," Charlie offered dryly as he leaned on the shovel. "Never interfered with my ability to shovel shit."

"I get it." The redheaded man nodded. "I think cleaning up the horses will be a bit easier on ya. Just go do it."

Suppressing the grin aching to break loose, Charlie tossed a casual salute and said earnestly, "Yes, sir, Mr.?"

"Collins." The man jerked his thumb over his shoulder. "New barn supervisor. Now get to it. I don't want to have to report you on my first day."

"Oh, yeah." Charlie nodded. "I can see how that would be bad. Mr. Collins, sir."

"Then let's make sure it doesn't happen. I'm easy enough to get along with. Just do what I tell you, when I tell you, and we won't have nary a problem. It's nice of the Redmonds' to give an old gent like you a job, I'll see what I can to do make it easy on ya. My own da is about your age; call me sentimental."

Charlie laughed to himself all the way down the long alley of the barn to the area where horses were washed. Without a word, he went about the business of drawing water before going to fetch the first horse.

SUE STOOD AT THE ARENA FENCE WITH MR. HARRINGTON Davies, a horse breeder from the great state of New York and therefore the New England horse territory, which Sue was desperate to break into. She hoped that the sale of these two studs would get her horses' hooves in the barn door.

"I think you will be truly pleased with these boys, Mr.

Davies. They are everything you are looking for. Stamina and outstanding speed, a rare combination."

The older man looked over the top rim of his glasses, then down his nose at the young woman. "I hope so, Mrs. Carter. I do hope so. I came down to look at these horses because my man, Joshua here," Davies gestured to the tall, colored man leaning on the fence to his right, "says he's seen your horses at some sales, and he thinks he can make something out of them or at least breed us something that will fly."

Sue looked past the buyer to the man indicated. She smiled and nodded in acknowledgment and thanks. He smiled and gave her a tiny wave with the hand resting across the fence as his attention was diverted by one of the horses being led from the barn.

Sue's head snapped around and she smiled when she saw her papa leading the horse out. After handing it off to one of Sue's trainers, who would put the horse through its paces for the buyer, Charlie headed straight for his daughter.

She was still laughing when he planted a kiss on her cheek. "Good morning to you, too, Papa! What are you doing bringing horses out?"

"I will explain later, daughter." He nodded slightly to the gentleman next to his child.

"Yes, of course." Sue regained her business composure right away. "Mr. Davies, may I introduce my father, General Charles Redmond."

The two men shook hands and exchanged pleasantries before Charlie climbed over the arena fence to join them on the other side.

As soon as the trainer began putting the horse through its paces, Sue and Davies were instantly engrossed in conversation about the beast. Charlie watched as the colored man leaned on the fence watching the horse.

Charlie joined him and gestured to the animal. "My daughter has mastered the art of the breed book."

The man nodded slowly. "It would appear so. I've been watching her horses for about three years now. Very impressive."

"I hope your employer thinks so."

"He thinks what I tell him to think when it comes to horses."

The men looked at each other for a moment, then back to the horse.

"Make him trot, please," Joshua called to the trainer, who immediately did as requested. The dark man nodded his approval. "If a horse doesn't have a decent trot, it's going to be useless for anything else."

After the first horse was shown, there was a short break before the second was brought out. Like an astute businesswoman and the hostess her mother had trained her to be, Sue saw to it that an alfresco brunch was served buffet style in the gazebo next to the arena.

As Charlie poured a cup of coffee from the service on the table, he glanced over at Joshua, who was filling his plate with eggs and bacon. "How long have you worked for Mr. Davies, if you don't mind my asking?"

"Oh no, General, it's fine." The man nodded. "Let's see, I think I'm about forty-five years old or so. I don't know for sure, you understand. I was born in South Carolina during the slave years."

Charlie grinned wide. "Really? I too am from South Carolina! Charleston. And you?"

"Charleston as well." Joshua set his plate down long enough to pour a cup of coffee, then both men adjourned to a small table. "I tried to make my own way there, but it was difficult."

"I understand. I left there when I was about fifteen."

"I would have been close to that, too, I think. A year of making my way north and I landed a job mucking stables in the barns that Mr. Davies's father owned. I've made my way up from there with hard work."

"Congratulations. It is nice to hear that the hard work of a colored man is being acknowledged and rewarded."

"It hasn't always been that way, for sure." Joshua wiped his mouth with the linen napkin, placed it in his lap, and looked Charlie right in the eye. "When I was a boy, I was accused of being a thief."

Charlie's heart rate doubled. He maintained eye contact, but he said nothing.

Joshua continued, "There was this girl. The daughter of a local merchant—Redmond was his name, too. One wet, windy, miserable day, she gave me some food. I was cold and..."

"Hungry..." Charlie offered softly.

"Hungry," Joshua said a second later. "I remember that day so clearly. How I was so grateful for that little bit of meat. How all I wanted to do was get home to my mama and sister so we could make some soup. I didn't even have a chance to thank her or say anything before her father arrived and went into a rage. I remember him screaming and the blood red color of his face."

Charlie closed his eyes and drew a deep, slow breath that he released just as slowly. He could still see that anger as well, even after all these years.

"I scrambled out of there, barely managing to hang onto that package of meat. I ran away like a coward. Leaving that poor girl to the rage of her father. I heard a couple days later he beat her. I tried once or twice to go back there, but never quite managed it. But I always wondered about her. If she was all right."

Charlie nodded, opening his eyes slowly and turning to his

companion. "You should not blame yourself. I will bet you good money that everything turned out just fine. I am sure your defender has had a wonderful life."

"I sure do hope so, General Redmond. I sure do hope so. That young woman saved my life. I hope hers turned out the way she wanted."

"I am sure it did, Joshua. I am very sure it did."

BUDDY'S HANDS WERE FULL. HE HAD TWO MUGS OF COFFEE IN one and a napkin wrapped around several ham biscuits in the other. So, he resorted to the most expeditious method of entering his brother's bedroom; one he had mastered several years ago. He kicked the door open.

Andy sat straight up in bed looking around for a weapon to defend himself with. "What the hell!" he yelled. He saw his brother standing there, holding coffee and breakfast, and calmed down a little. "What the hell are you doing getting me up at the damned crack of dawn, brother? You know I like to sleep in."

"I know perfectly well what YOU like, but you have to deal with the world, and that means taking into account what other people like, too. Get your ass out of bed, pull on some pants, and listen to me. The alternative to my trying to talk some sense into your thick head is me trying to beat it into you, and you know I can. I am much better at Uncle Rex's lessons than you are."

Grudgingly, Andy pulled himself out of bed, wandered over to the wardrobe, pulled a pair of britches and an old shirt out, and shrugged them on. "Thanks for the coffee," he mumbled as he threw himself into a chair. "What do you want to beat into my head?"

"Just this. You have shown yourself to be a right proper ass, a coward, and a lazy bum. You got a girl pregnant, and yet did you pay any attention to her? You have a son, but have you bothered to give him even a cursory glance? Then you steal from our family and run away. Finally, you got yourself in a mess, got thrown in jail and cost the family a small fortune to bail your sorry ass out. What the hell is your excuse? The rest of us work hard to be decent people, to make a place in the world, and to live up to the standards that Mama and Papa set for us. You have spent your whole damned life trying to do just enough to get by, blaming everyone else when you get caught, and running away instead of standing up like a man. Brother, it's time you start behaving. Figure out what you want to do with your life and do it. And stop bringing the rest of us down with your damned messes."

"God, you sound like him," Andy growled.

"Him who?"

"Papa. Self-righteous, critical, and unsympathetic. I just want to get by and enjoy life. We're a wealthy family. Why do I have to work? We have all the money we're ever gonna need. We both know other fellas whose families have money and they don't have to work. Why should we?" Andy leaned forward and asked as innocently as possible, "Tell me, big brother, how much did my mess cost you personally? Or are you just afraid there will be less to inherit?"

Buddy's fist balled and he had to let out a deep breath, opting to ignore his brother's attempt to bait him. "For starters, if Papa was unsympathetic, you would still be sitting in jail in Big Lick. Mama and Papa raised us to be responsible, independent, and honorable. So, we work."

"Well, they expect too damned much. Just let me be."

Buddy looked at his brother, an expression of absolute

disgust on his face. He set his coffee mug down, rose, and stomped out of the room, slamming the door behind him.

Em heard the thuds coming from the hall and cracked her door to see what was going on.

Buddy was stomping down the hall, headed for the stairs, mumbling to himself, "I'm just gonna have to beat his ass."

EM RETREATED BACK INTO HER ROOM, A THOUGHTFUL LOOK ON her face. She had heard Buddy's voice raised in anger, though she could not hear his exact words before he had stormed out of the house. Knowing her brothers, she assumed that Buddy had read Andy a riot act without any success.

"Well, there is one good side to this mess," she said to herself. "As long as Andy is the focus of Mama and Papa's attention, I won't have to cope with a major scene when I leave to go back to school."

Em rummaged through the cedar chest in the corner of her room. She lovingly removed her old field clothes; britches, linen shirts, and a specially designed vest with pockets all over it that she used to stow her tools, notebooks, labels, and findings when she was on a dig. At the bottom of the chest was a small leather case that contained the tools she had custom made while she was in England. There were small, fine picks, pries, scrapers, and brushes specifically designed to unearth small, delicate artifacts without harming them.

"Ah, I am so looking forward to getting back in the field. I hope I can find as many wonderful things as I did in England. That Professor Putnam would trust me in my first year is a great honor." Em smiled to herself. It was going to be a good year.

Charlie had returned to the house, gotten cleaned up, and was in the back parlor waiting for Rebecca, Rex, and Andy by ten o'clock, as promised. He poured himself a cup of coffee and settled in the corner after having greeted Jeremiah and kissed Baby Andy. Rex escorted Rebecca in as the clock was striking the hour and settled her in her usual chair by the fire.

When Rebecca arrived, Jeremiah lifted Baby Andy from Harriet's arms, laying him in his grandmother's lap, kissing Rebecca's cheek as he did so. After a few polite words were exchanged, he made his excuses and left for work, promising to return in a few hours to retrieve his son.

Rex got himself a cup of coffee and settled in the corner with Charlie. The two of them started a rather desultory game of chess. They had all agreed this was Rebecca's show. She had a plan and the two men were there to support her.

Andy eventually meandered into the room. His mother had sent him a note to meet her at ten o'clock. In Andy's mind, getting there within a half hour of the invitation was being on time.

"Good morning, son." While she did not say anything about him having kept everyone waiting for almost twenty minutes, her tone was not as warm and gracious as it usually was. "I trust you have recovered from your travels."

"Yes, thank you, Mama. Is there coffee?"

Rebecca nodded and pointed to the service on the side board. "It is in the same place it always is, or have you been gone so long you have forgotten?"

Andy shrugged, ignoring the sharp retort from his mother, and fetched himself a cup, then settled into the chair across from her. "I assume you are going to chastise me for my adventuring.

Buddy has already yelled at me and Papa would barely say a word to me on the trip back. So now it is your turn."

Rebecca smiled at her prodigal son. "I have no intention of chastising you. You were faced with a set of circumstances that I suspect were overwhelming for a young man of your age and instead of facing it, you ran. Now you are home and your family is here to help you find your way." She smiled gently at Andy, who was still slouched in the chair across from her. "Now, let me introduce you to your son." She lifted Baby Andy so he was sitting up in her lap, his little head resting against her breast.

Andy looked down at the infant, whom he had been carefully ignoring since he entered the room. "Well, you have another grandchild, and to be honest, I have no interest in caring for a baby, so you keep him. Do what you do best, Mama. Take on every wayward child that comes along."

Charlie clenched his jaw so tight Rex could hear his teeth grinding together. He reached out and placed a hand on his friend's closed fist beside the chess board. He whispered, "Easy, Charlie."

Rebecca looked at her son, shaking her head. "Andy Redmond. This is your son, the child of your body. How can you not care at least a little? He even looks like you did when you were a baby."

"He is the product of an afternoon of fun, nothing more. You and Papa made me marry Eliza, though I did not love her. I am sorry she died, but that is one of the risks that women face when they get pregnant. You love children. I do not. It is that simple."

The look of sorrow in Rebecca's face was enough to break most hearts. She lovingly cradled her grandson in her arms as he happily slept in their warmth and comfort.

Andy just shrugged.

"Well, son, Sue and Jeremiah have taken responsibility for

raising Baby Andy. Unless you object and are willing to take responsibility for him, Jeremiah wants him to have his last name."

"That is perfectly all right. If Jeremiah wants him, let him name him whatever he wants."

"So, what do you want to do with yourself? We can send you to school, or get you a position where you can learn a trade. Have you thought about it?"

Andy looked his mother straight in the face and spoke clearly. "I know what I want to do. I want to go west, see the country as it opens up, and make my living playing cards."

Charlie had had enough. He stood up and strode over to stand behind his wife. "No son of mine is going to be a two-bit card sharp. I warn you, young man, if this is the path you choose for yourself, I will not finance your so-called adventures, nor I will come and bail you out again. So, think on it very carefully."

"Thank you, Papa. I knew you would support me in being who I want to be – in doing what you have both always told me I should do with my life – be the man I want to be." With that, Andy pulled himself out of the chair, spilling his coffee as he did, and stomped out of the room.

"I love him," Charlie growled as he rubbed Rebecca's shoulders gently. "But I do not like him very much right now."

CHAPTER 10

MONDAY, JANUARY 31, 1881

BUDDY LIGHTLY TAPPED the door to the rear parlor, expecting his parents to be there enjoying their ritual of an after-supper game of chess. He was partially right in his expectations. His parents were sitting in front of the fire playing a game – they were playing mahjong with Uncle Rex. *Just as well*, he thought. *Uncle Rex will certainly understand.* The boys had always appreciated their adoptive uncle's calming ability to help them navigate the more treacherous waters with their parents, siblings, and peers.

Buddy stood at attention in front of the three adults looking at him questioningly. "Mama, Papa, Uncle Rex. I know we have always celebrated Andy's and my birthdays at the same time, but I would rather we didn't do that any longer. My birthday is in a week; Andy's is actually next month, and…"

"And you want to distance yourself from your brother," concluded Rex quietly as he placed a tile on the board, never looking up.

Buddy looked at Uncle Rex with gratitude. The month of January had been incredibly tense in the Redmond household, with Em packing and then heading back to school, and Andy stomping around like an angry stallion penned in a too-small stall while every mare in the herd was in season.

"Well, um, yes. He and I are so different. We have different interests, different friends. We even like different foods. So, well, it seems to me we would both probably prefer to have separate birthdays."

Rex looked up and smiled at the young man. "An excellent idea, Buddy." He looked at Charlie and Rebecca, an expression on his face that told them that he felt this was an important moment in the young man's life.

Rebecca looked at her son, a bemused expression crossing her features. "We have always celebrated your birthdays together. Even calling you twins. How did you find out?"

Buddy sighed and smiled at his mother, "Well, Mama, besides the fact that we look and act nothing alike, I was reading the *Memoirs of Lieutenant General Scott* and there was a quote from the Bible that I wanted to look up. I was thumbing through the big Bible in the family parlor and came across the family tree you have in it. There were your entries for both Andy and me, and I realized I am a full five weeks older than he is. Not to mention Andy is Em's half-brother. You marked them both down as Adams in the Bible. Darby and Sue are noted as Sweet. And I'm noted as Hobart."

Buddy neglected to mention he had also found the documents that had changed hands when he and the others were adopted. The papers provided by his birth mother that declared legally that Charles Redmond was indeed his father. He finally had confirmation of something he had believed since he was small;

he was indeed a Redmond. No matter what his brothers and sisters told him.

Rebecca nodded. "Yes, you are, but you have to understand, having two baby boys who were just five weeks apart presented, um, some challenges for us. It was just much easier to celebrate your birthdays together."

"I do understand." He nodded for emphasis. "I really do, but now that we are older, perhaps you can see fit to let us celebrate separately?"

Rebecca smiled, but it was Charlie who responded. "Of course, son. What would you like for your birthday supper?"

"Could we have chicken pirleau?" Buddy's efforts to emulate his dad extended to sharing the same favorite foods.

"I am sure we can, and who would you like to join you on this grand occasion?" Rebecca stepped back in to retake control of her party planning domain.

"Oh, I think the family, and Uncle Richard and Aunt Elizabeth, Ro and Allison, and Mr. John and Miss Annabelle, and maybe a couple of the fellows from school."

"That can be arranged. Shall we have it next Monday, which is your actual birthday, or on Sunday?"

"I don't want to mess up our traditions here. We always have the open house dinner after church, so perhaps on my actual birthday?"

"Absolutely, son." Rebecca smiled and patted her boy's hand.

TUESDAY, FEBRUARY 1, 1881

Em walked into the meeting room attached to Professor Putnam's office. She was early, so she took the opportunity to make a pot of tea for those who would be joining in the planning session. As she waited for the water to boil, she arranged her notebook and papers in the least conspicuous seat at the table, then poured the hot water into the tea pot and set out the mugs, sugar, honey, and a little pitcher of milk that were kept in the room for Professor Putnam's convenience.

She had poured her tea into a mug and settled at the table when the door opened and two young men came in, laughing and poking one another in the ribs. They ignored her as they went and collected mugs of tea for themselves and then wandered to the table, where they took seats on either side of Professor Putnam's seat at the head of the table.

Finally, Putnam came in and dropped a pile of notebooks on the table before he also got a mug of tea, draining the last drop from the pot Emily had made.

"Good morning. I trust you all had a pleasant holiday." It was a statement, not a polite question. "Now it is time to get back to work. Miss Redmond, I believe you met these two miscreants at my Thanksgiving party. Mr. Baer is a cartographer by training and does our illustrations. Mr. Hale is an ethnologist rather like Mrs. Smith and Miss Parker, who you met at the party." He was looking directly at Emily and smiled at her as he casually re-introduced the two men.

Baer interrupted the professor. "I didn't know you were getting a secretary, Professor."

Putnam glared at the cartographer. "I have not, Mr. Baer. Miss Emily Redmond is a doctoral candidate who studied with Professor Lane-Fox in England, is the protégé of **both** Mr. Huxley and Mr. Darwin, and is outstandingly proficient in the latest archeological techniques. You will treat her with the respect she is due as at least your equal and possibly better trained and with greater knowledge than either of you bring to this new discipline."

The two young men looked at each other, Baer with a raised eyebrow, Hale with a sideways nod toward Emily. The silent message between them was clear; there was no way a mere girl could know more or be better at this work than they were.

Putnam cleared his throat and opened one of the notebooks. "Southern Illinois has a number of sites of interest that we will be investigating over the course of the next few years. Across much of southern Ohio and down into Kentucky and West Virginia, there are a series of conical mounds, and one particularly interesting formation in Ohio is called the Serpent Mound. I have provided each of you with as much information as is currently available about these sites, starting with Ephraim Squire and Edwin Davis's *Monuments of the Mississippi Valley*, but at this point, we don't even know the age of these sites or which of the various cultures that have occupied this area built the funereal cone mounds or the effigy mounds. While the probability is that it was one of the Woodlands cultures, it could have been the Adena Culture, the Hopewell Culture, or the Fort Ancient Culture. Some even think it was the Mississippian culture, migrating east. Hell, the conical mounds and the serpent mound may be the work of two different cultures. So, we are going to see if we can figure some of these issues out."

"Professor, William and I have been out there, and you know it is a very rural, undeveloped part of the country. What location do you want to use as a base?"

"Well, students, that is one of the issues you will be addressing in your planning. There's Chillicothe, Hillsboro, and a number of other small towns and villages. The railroad is going through this year and I believe they are planning to establish a small town within a few miles of the Serpent Mound."

Putnam spoke on for almost an hour, providing each of them with their own notebooks that duplicated the one he was working from and going over the objectives he wanted them to meet in their planning, and then left them to get organized.

"I suppose we'd best get to work," said Baer, pulling the map out of the notebook and spreading it on the table. "Miss Redmond, would you mind fixing us another pot of tea?"

Emily looked at the man studying the map for a moment, then responded, "I will this time, Mr. Baer, if you will go get more water for the kettle."

Baer looked up and blinked a couple of times. He was accustomed to women who did his bidding, not those who gave him errands to run.

Hale jumped in. "I'll go get it. When I get back, I think I have a better map of the area we can use."

"Thank you, Mr. Hale. I have a copy of *Monuments of the Mississippi Valley* with me. We can start plotting the locations of the various mounds on your map to identify the closest town with decent facilities."

Em and Baer sat quietly, waiting for Hale to return with the water. Em thumbed through her book while Baer just impatiently tapped his fingers on the table.

Finally, Baer spoke up. "I presume you were some sort of note taker or artifact cleaner for Fox-Lane, Miss Redmond."

"No, Mr. Baer. When my family was in England, while my father served as the United States Minister to the Court of St. James's, I discovered a Neolithic site on a plateau above the Thames in Buckinghamshire, and excavated it myself, with the advice and oversight of Professor Lane-Fox, not Fox-Lane. I then served as a site leader for his excavations around Stonehenge. I have also had the honor to work with him on developing his standards for more effective and scientific excavation techniques." As she spoke, Em's tone evolved from polite conversation to her lecture voice that had been the bane of her siblings for her whole life.

"You are very young for such a level of responsibility, Miss Redmond. Most girls your age are trying to charm young men or plan their weddings."

"Mr. Baer, I have been studying archeology since I was a child, and have been conducting scientific excavations in the field for the past five years. I had the opportunity to work with some of the leaders in the field when I was quite young and have done my best to live up to their expectations. I hope you will be able to learn from my experience in our work with Professor Putnam."

Baer's face was taking on a rather unpleasant hue when they were interrupted by Hale's return. "Here's the water, Miss Redmond. Let me pour it into the kettle and get that started, then I'll get that map I promised." He realized that he had just interrupted what might have become an unpleasant scene.

"Thank you, Mr. Hale." Em managed to keep the terseness she had used with Baer out of her words to Hale.

"Of course, Miss Redmond. The three of us will need to work as a team, so this is a good start."

MONDAY, FEBRUARY 7, 1881

Charlie tried once again to get four-month-old Andrew Carter, known to the family as A.C., to lie down in the bed in the downstairs parlor that served as a nursery when their youngest grandchildren came to visit.

It was nap time, but the smallest member of the family was having none of it. Every time Charlie placed the boy down on his back in the center of the bed, it was only a matter of seconds before the little tyke had rolled on his side, kicking away any blanket or toy his grandfather offered. Then the screaming would start. Little Andy had lungs that would make a career army drill sergeant proud.

"Oh, little man," Charlie soothed his grandson as he lifted him from the bed, holding him close to his chest as he settled on the sofa by the fire. "You are not the only member of the family that dislikes that bed."

The elder Redmond chuckled as he pulled an afghan from the back of the sofa to cover his grandson. "I had that bed specially made by your other grandfather for Grandma Rebecca when we brought her back from Washington."

Charlie smiled when the baby gripped his finger, trying to bring it to his mouth for a suckle. "She was so sick. Everyone thought it would be easier to have her down here. So I had Duncan make that bed for her. The back lifts up, so we could sit her up. The rails are meant to keep you from falling out, just so you know." He smiled as the babe drew the tip of his finger into his mouth, happily chewing on it.

"Grandma 'Becca," Charlie continued quietly, more staring into the fire than paying attention to the child beginning to slumber in his arms, "was not faring well those first few weeks after coming home. Uncle Rex and Aunt Elizabeth were at their wits' end trying to keep her content. She barely ate; they had a terrible time getting her to sleep. She cried and carried on something fierce, but she could not talk." Charlie sighed as he looked into the sleeping face of his grandson. "And I was no use for the first few weeks. I had to clean up the mess left behind in Washington. I remember the day I came home."

Charlie entered Rebecca's recovery room within minutes of

returning home from Washington. He was startled to find Rex and Elizabeth in consultation over his wife's sick bed.

"Has something happened?" Charlie looked immediately to Rebecca.

She was in the bed, curled on one side, whimpering and crying. Her fists were drawn tight to her chest, her entire body was consumed with tremors, and the terrified look on her face broke his heart.

"What is wrong with her?" He asked as he stripped off his suitcoat and tossed it to the back of the davenport.

He began rolling up his shirtsleeves to the elbow as he pulled a chair next to his wife's bed. As he settled into the chair, he looked to his friends and physicians and asked again, "Well?"

Rex was the first to speak, stepping forward to the foot of the bed as he did. "Charlie, all we know is she is distressed. It is not uncommon in situations like this, but because she cannot fully articulate and communicate with us, it is difficult to know exactly what is wrong."

"What have you tried?" He asked even as he began running his fingers gently through her hair.

"Everything," Elizabeth sighed as she took a seat on the sofa. "We were just discussing giving her sedation so she will rest."

Charlie shook his head. "That is not what she needs. Just because you can drug her and make her quiet does not mean she is resting. I know from experience."

"I understand, Charlie, but honestly, this is the best course of action," his old army comrade offered sincerely. "We only want her to get some relief. She has been this way since you left."

He listened and nodded. Leaning over, he kissed Rebecca above the brow. "I will be right back," he whispered to her before removing his lips from her forehead.

Standing up, he kicked off his boots and began unbuttoning his vest. "I know what my wife needs. She needs me," he ground out as his suspenders dropped from his shoulders.

Charlie had no qualms about shedding his clothing in front of his doctors as he pulled his shirt off over his head. He stripped quickly down to his small clothes and turned back to the bed.

Rex and Elizabeth watched as he dropped the right rail and slowly began his approach. Even as he lifted the covers and carefully made his way under them, he spoke to her, reassuring her with every movement.

Once he was stretched out next to her, he gradually shifted and slipped his left arm under her, gently coaxing her close to his chest.

The physicians watched as their patient began to relax and calm down. Rebecca shifted into her place on Charlie's shoulder, his chin resting on the top of her head. It only took a few seconds for the two bodies to meld into one. Charlie tugged the blankets into place, tucking them tightly around Rebecca's back to make sure she was warm enough.

Elizabeth looked to Rex, who shrugged as Rebecca relaxed, falling into a deep and peaceful sleep, with Charlie's arms tucked securely around her. Elizabeth smiled when she saw Charlie, still kissing the top of Rebecca's head, and speaking words of comfort and reassurance to her. The fussing his wife had been doing, the whimpering and crying, had all but stopped, turning instead to a soft mewing sound as she settled in Charlie's embrace.

Rex grinned and gestured to the door for them to depart. "Seems Rebecca now has the best medicine possible. We are no longer needed, Doctor Walker."

Charlie shifted the baby's weight against his good shoulder and his own legs under him so they could both be more comfortable.

"I am so glad those days are over and you will never know your grandmother like that."

He adjusted the child again, giving the little brow a kiss, as ruby red lips blew bubbles. "I remember coming into the room and looking down at her. Knowing exactly what she needed. It was the first time in weeks I had held her in my arms. As soon as she settled against me, she went quietly to sleep. And honestly, so did I."

Charlie looked down at the child asleep against his shoulder. He was contemplating his ability to get up and put A.C. in the bed when Chris entered. She had been in search of a book that Rebecca had misplaced, but she was happy to help Grandpa Charlie settle his little bundle down in the bed. The nurse even offered to stay with the child so Charlie could take Rebecca the book she was seeking. Charlie smiled his appreciation as he tucked the tome under his arm and set out for his wife's parlor.

Buddy's sixteenth birthday supper that evening was rather formal. The guest of honor chose to wear the gray dress uniform that he had gotten while attending classes at The Point. Most of the participants were adult family friends, including Aunt Elizabeth and Uncle Richard, the Carters, Ro and Allison, and of course the Foxworths, who were tutoring him to prepare for the entrance examination. Andy's absence was decidedly notable.

It was Buddy's opportunity to use his sixteenth birthday as a declaration of his emergence into adulthood, though most of the actual adults' present were more than a little amused at his very earnest efforts, especially his carefully considered discussion of the current politics in Virginia. Hearing opinions on payment of war debts from a sixteen-year-old that had only been a month old at the end of the war was rather impressive. What was more impressive was when he chose to stand his ground and make valid counter arguments on points where he and his father disagreed.

After the dinner that featured CeCe's version of chicken pirleau and a beautiful lemon cake for dessert, Richard whispered to Charlie, "Well, he has obviously been listening to you, Charlie. If you decide to fold to Fitz Lee's persuasions and run for governor, it should be a good argument for the campaign trail." With that, Richard walked away, leaving Charlie sputtering.

Buddy had waited patiently after dinner. The guests had retired to the formal parlor, where coffee, brandy and cake were served. It finally was time for gifts.

Charlie sat Buddy down in the seat that Charlie himself usually took, in front of the fireplace, and at the center of the room.

"Charles Huger Redmond the Second, you have reached an age where you can assume the responsibilities and the privileges of a young man. I expect you will be going up to The Point in September. Even more, I expect you will become an officer, a gentleman, and a man of honor. I am proud of you, Buddy, and I am very pleased that you have chosen to follow me in your career choice. So, as a sign of my pride and my earnest belief that you will be as good or a better officer than I was, I want to present you with your first dress sword. You will need it when you go to school." Louis handed Charlie a long, thin wooden box, which Charlie laid across his son's knees.

Reverentially, Buddy flipped the clasps on the box, opened it, and lifted out a classic cavalry dress sword and scabbard. The scabbard was simple, but elegantly finished; the sword blade was inscribed with scroll work that included Buddy's full name. He looked up at his father, his eyes glowing, and choked out a simple, "Thank you, Dad. I will do my best, I swear."

The rest of the guests applauded as Charlie and Buddy just looked into one another's eyes for a few moments.

Then Rebecca broke their glaze. "And since you will need at least two mounts for your years at The Point, I have selected another horse for you. Go look out the window, son."

Buddy went to the French doors that opened onto the front lawn, then opened the door and stepped out. Several of the stable hands were holding torches, and one held the lead to a beautiful young stallion, his glossy black coat reflecting the torchlight, and the white star on his forehead shining brightly. "He is called Ebony, and his sire is Papa's Jack. I hope he will be as good a mount for you as Jack is for Papa."

Buddy tried to hide the fact that a tear was running down his cheek. Softly, he said, "Thank you, Mama."

Sue interjected just then. "And of course, what good is a horse without the proper equipment?" Jeremiah pulled a saddle rack out of a corner, where a proper military saddle, with all the rings, hooks and straps needed to carry gear was gleaming in the torch light.

Rebecca motioned for the staff to return Ebony to the stable and the guests returned to the warmth of the parlor.

Uncle Rex was next, and his gift took a totally different track. "A proper young man living so far away from home needs the resources to attend to his expenses without having to worry about being able to afford the little things that make the difference between a pleasant life and a difficult one. I have seen to it that you have sufficient resources to take care of all those little things." Rex handed Buddy a bank book.

As he opened it and looked at the initial balance posted in

the ledger, his eyes widened, and he stammered, "This is too much, Uncle Rex. Far too much. And I have money of my own."

"Yes, lad, I know you do, but you do not know what you will have to deal with in West Point, and I wanted to make sure you have enough to cover all contingencies."

The gifts continued, each of them providing Buddy with some piece of gear, books, or other item that would be useful for him as he started in his military career.

SATURDAY, FEBRUARY 12, 1881

Brooks compared his pay list to the envelopes bundled on his desk. After his third count he was satisfied that the bundle and the list matched. He set aside the paper and the envelopes and then poured himself a cup of coffee from the pot on the stove next to his desk.

He had barely taken his first drink when there was a knock on his office doorframe. He waved Collins in and gestured to the pot. "Help yourself."

The younger man poured a cup, then settled in the chair next to the stove. "Damn cold out there this morning. Wish the snow would make up its mind."

"Well, let the lads know that Miss Rebecca has ordered the kitchen to keep ham and bean soup and warm bread ready all day. They can come up and get it when they need it."

"Miss Rebecca is a good woman. She and Miss Sue take good care of us. Not another farm around like this one."

"That they are." Brooks reached for the bundle of envelopes and tossed them into Collins's lap. "Need you to make sure to pay everyone first thing, too. The regular paymaster is out this week so it falls to you."

Collins nodded as he thumbed through the envelopes, counting them in his head as he did. He glanced up with a puzzled look on his face. "There's one missing."

"Can't be. I checked it against the pay list three times."

Collins sighed. "Okay, well, I guess we'll see when I get them handed out."

"If there is a problem let me know and I'll get it sorted out with the general and Miss Rebecca. Can't imagine them missing someone. That would be a first. Of course, they are getting older."

Collins drained his coffee, saluting his boss with the empty mug as he dropped it to the counter by the stove. "Back in a few hours."

"I'll be here." Brooks poured another cup of coffee and settled down at his desk with the supply books.

BROOKS WAS PLACING SEVERAL INVOICES IN HIS FILING CABINET when Collins returned about three hours later. The supervisor did not even bother to knock before he entered, nodding his head.

"I was right. We were one short but the old fella wasn't here today, so it can be sorted."

"What old fella?" Brooks turned and crossed his arms as he considered it. He was actually the oldest man on the crew and he did not consider himself ready for a rocker on the front porch.

"That older fella that comes in occasionally. The part-timer who spends most of his time with that old black stallion in barn one. He's been around a lot recently and I figured he had a nice pay envelope coming."

Brooks wondered if he would be able to find his eyebrows after they launched off his head. "You mean with Jack? Who's been with Jack other than the regular staff? There will be hell to pay from the general if someone is messing with that horse."

Collins shook his head. "I don't know. That older fella with half his hand missing."

"Oh, shit," Brooks mumbled as the realization hit him. "What exactly have you said to him?"

"Nothing really." Collins shrugged. "He's a good worker. Takes about any task I put him on. I just never know when he's gonna be here. Figured he's one of the part-timers."

Brooks closed his eyes and sighed again, "Oh, shit."

"What?" Collins was truly dumbfounded. "I just want to make sure he gets paid."

"Son, when the good Lord passed out brains, you thought he said trains and you missed yours."

Before Brooks could explain Collins's mistake, there was a knock on the door frame. The barn manager nearly laughed out loud, but managed to offer in a professional tone, "General Charlie, come on in, sir. We were just talking about you."

The younger man whipped around to come face to face with the man he thought was another barn hand. Only now he was dressed in a fine business suit and great coat, holding a sliver knob topped cane in his right hand. Collins nearly swallowed his tongue as he took two steps back.

"I had no idea..." the young man stammered, looking for a corner in which to make himself as small as possible.

"Have I interrupted something important?" Charlie queried as he lifted his brow towards the coffee pot.

"Not at all, General." Brooks moved forward and poured his boss a cup of coffee as Charlie shed his coat, dropping it over the chair near the stove to help it dry out.

"Miserable day out there. The rain has started. I think I would prefer snow." Charlie nodded his thanks as he took the cup.

"What can we do for you, sir?" Brooks gestured to the padded chair at the desk before taking a seat on a bench by the wall.

"Oh, do not let me interrupt your business, gentlemen." He pulled an envelope from the breast pocket of his suit coat. "Miss Rebecca just reminded me I needed to drop off the funds for the petty cash reserves for the barns."

"Thank you, General. It seems Mr. Collins here didn't realize you were, well, you." Brooks could not help but smile. "He thought we were a pay envelope short."

"Is that so?" Charlie asked, his brows creeping up as he looked to the truly embarrassed barn supervisor. "Perhaps if Mr. Collins would learn to ask a man's name, rather than just giving him a moniker, this sort of thing would not happen. Yes?"

Collins nodded. "Yes, sir. I am very sorry, sir. I never meant any disrespect."

"Lesson learned, young man." Charlie nodded his assurances in return. "No harm done. Thank you for looking out for your men. I cannot fault you for that."

"Thank you, sir." Hesitantly, he offered his hand to Charlie, who smiled and took it without hesitation. "I really am sorry. If you will excuse me, sir? I should get back to the horses."

"Of course." Charlie nodded is approval. "Again, Mr. Collins, no harm done. This will not affect your position here at Redmond Stables. You are a fine barn supervisor, just young with a few things to learn."

Collins scrambled out of the office. Once Brooks was sure he was gone, his laughter erupted full force. "That was fun to watch!"

~

MONDAY, FEBRUARY 28, 1881

"Good God, Rex. If you give him the same amount of money you gave Buddy, you know damned well we will never see him again. He will do a flit and head west just as soon as he can sneak out. Do you want to break Rebecca's heart?"

"But Charlie, if I do not, he will see it as either punishment for what he has already done or retribution for not being 'a responsible, hardworking Redmond." And I had not planned to give it to him in a lump sum."

"Do you have a plan so that you can do it but limit his access to ready cash?" Charlie hung his head, shaking it. Andy was nothing if not a raging headache for him.

Rebecca had been sipping her morning tea as the men argued over Andy's birthday presents. She knew that Charlie had ordered new fishing gear for him, including the modern fly reel made by the new Pflueger Company. Rebecca had selected a beautiful mare, descended from Shannon and Jack, and paid Sue a pretty chunk of change for her saddle and gear, as Sue and Jeremiah were not willing to put out the money for the equipment since they were raising his son. She listened to the ongoing argument and finally broke in. "Gentlemen, what about an investment that will pay him the interest but will not allow him access to the principal?"

"Actually, Rebecca, since we all know he is going to strike out sooner or later, I was thinking that providing him with a monthly stipend that would be sufficient to cover his immediate expenses, with a stipulation that he had to contact you at least once a month to let you know he was well, might be a reasonable solution. I also thought that I would limit the stipend to four years, just as covering Buddy's expenses at The Point is for four years. This way, I maintain balance between the boys but hopefully still limit Andy's more impulsive actions."

Charlie and Rebecca looked at one another with slowly dawning appreciation for Rex's craftiness in offering an alternative. They both started nodding in agreement and looked at Rex with appreciation.

Rebecca spoke first. "Yes, yes, that might work very well. It would at least let us keep track of him and I would know he was all right."

"I am glad you approve. Trying to maintain balance between them while still recognizing Andy's weakness is an interesting challenge."

Charlie laughed weakly. "That is one way to put it, old man."

Just then there was a knock on the door, and before anyone could respond, the door opened and the subject of their discussions walked in. "Good morning, Mama, Papa, Uncle Rex. I assume you were planning on having some sort of party or something to celebrate my birthday and I just want to let you know you do not have to do anything. Rather than have some sort of stuffy family dinner, I am going down to Charlottesville that weekend for a poker tournament that some of my friends are holding and I will not be back until Tuesday or Wednesday at the earliest."

"Well then, son, we could have your birthday celebration when you return," Rebecca said sweetly. "Perhaps the weekend after your birthday?"

"No, thank you, Mama. You know I am not particularly fond of the family gatherings. Half the time, one or the other of my beloved siblings ends up lecturing me on what it is to be a Redmond and how I am not living up to the family standards. I think that as I approach some version of adulthood, I can choose to not subject myself to their haranguing. So, for now, I'm off to Granville's to demonstrate my servitude."

Rebecca was speechless, while Charlie's temper was rising rapidly at the cavalier treatment that Andy was giving them.

Rex spoke up. "Before you go stomping out, give me a moment. I have been talking with a friend at the East Tennessee, Virginia and Georgia Railway. They are planning to use Richmond as a major terminus for east-west traffic beginning this summer and will need someone to manage the livestock shipping. I think you might be interested in working for them if you can bring yourself to stay around here for a few more months."

"Would I live in Richmond?"

"Yes, you would have to."

"Would I be able to travel?"

"I do not know; you would have to talk with them. The best I can do is to provide you with an introduction to the manager. You will have to do the rest – including impressing them with your ability to manage a complex job and handle horses and cattle efficiently."

"Thank you, Uncle Rex. I will think about it."

"Let me know if you want that introduction."

With that, Andy waved a casual salute to all three adults in the room and departed as abruptly as he had entered.

Rebecca looked at Rex. "Do you really think you can get him a job with the railroad?"

"I can create an opportunity. He will have to follow through."

Charlie shook his head. "Follow through is not one of his strong suits. I just hope the attraction of living in Richmond will keep him in one place for a while."

TUESDAY, MARCH 8, 1881

It had been a relatively quiet month, with each member of the extended Redmond family occupied with their own interests. Em had returned to Boston. Sue and Jeremiah were busy with caring for Little Andy. Darby was going back and forth between Richmond and home, while Stella was dealing with little Ruthie, who was sneezing and coughing, and generally miserable, though she was not running a fever. Elizabeth called it allergies. Buddy was studying intensely, preparing for the official United States Military Academy entry examinations. Andy was keeping a very low profile and had returned to handling horses for Granville. Ro and Allison visited Rebecca frequently as they planned for expanding their family. Rex and Chris had several special needs patients at the hospital in town and spent a good bit of time away from the house.

The day was cold, gray, and rainy. Charlie and Rebecca had retreated to their upstairs sitting room, as it was the warmest, least damp room in the house. The arthritis in Charlie's hands was making writing impossible, and because of the misery in the rest of his body, he could not find a comfortable position, no matter what chair or sofa he sat on.

Rebecca watched him as he shifted, grumbled, moved, groused, and rearranged the lap robe over his knees, then generally twitched like a three-year-old with too much energy and no place to expend it. She has offered him a game of chess or cards, and then suggested he read to her, but nothing she could come up with caught his interest. She was about to order him to go to their office before he drove her crazy when Louis tapped at the door and brought in the mail. At least it was something to occupy Charlie's mind for a few minutes.

The general eagerly sorted through the mail, handing

Rebecca a letter from Em.

Rebecca resettled her lap robe, picked up the letter from Em, and stuck her new monocle in place.

They had talked about what life would be like when Charlie could retire. Certainly, he had been focused on his family, and especially on caring for Rebecca for the past five years, but as she had improved and had learned to adapt to the permanent changes in her physical capabilities, she had not needed him as much as she had in the first months after her incident on that terrible day. The only thing that she still needed, in his opinion, was to get back on a horse.

After a few very quiet minutes had passed, broken only by the crackling of the fire and the rustle of papers in Rebecca's hands, Rebecca finished reading Em's latest missive. She dropped her monocle on its velvet ribbon and gazed speculative at her moody husband. "So, Charlie, what have you decided about Fitz Lee's suggestion that you run for governor?"

Charlie looked at her like she had lost her mind. "How can you think I would consider it? Rebecca, darling, I think I have served my time as a public servant. I have paid with my body and my soul as a soldier. I helped put this town and county on a path to recovery and, I hope, prosperity. I uprooted our family to serve in England, which I suspect almost cost us your life. It is time for me to be a simple gentleman farmer and businessman. I want to spend time with you and to enjoy our beautiful grandchildren. So, yes, I have thought about it and I have decided that the answer is a clear no!"

"Are you sure, dear? You have been very restless lately. I suspect you may be getting bored with the life of the country gentleman. I would like to be able to do some travelling around the state this year, with the various suffrage speakers I am sponsoring. We could both go, if you like."

"My darling wife, I will go with you to support suffrage, but I have had more than enough of being a public servant. My answer is still no."

Rebecca smiled gently at her beloved. "Then you shall stay a private citizen, and we will travel and find something new to get into. I promise, together, we will figure out a way to not be bored."

~

WEDNESDAY, MARCH 9, 1881

Rebecca re-read the letter she had received from Em the day before. She looked thoughtful as she tapped her monocle against the chair arm and then pulled the bell that summoned Lizbet.

A moment later, Lizbet's head appeared around the door. "Yes, Miss Rebecca? What do you need, ma'am?"

"Lizbet, could you please see if Miss Chris is here this morning? If she is, would you ask her to join me?"

"Yes, Miss Rebecca. I believe she is here, since I saw Mr. Rex headed for the library just a few minutes ago."

"Thank you."

A few minutes later, Chris appeared in the sitting room door. "Good morning, Miss Rebecca. Are you feeling well? What can I do for you?"

"I was wondering if you would mind writing a letter for me. I know you joined us as a nurse and therapist, but you have somehow started to evolve into a secretary for me."

"I do not mind at all, Miss Rebecca. I have kept up with my work at the hospital with Dr. Rex and Dr. Elizabeth. In fact, I think I have learned a great deal of new techniques from them, and Culpeper Hospital is becoming an expert center for neurological injuries. You and General Charlie have given me a lovely home and a great opportunity to advance my career. I certainly do not mind giving you a few minutes of time providing other services."

Chris sat at Rebecca's desk and pulled a sheet of letterhead into place on the desk. She picked up a pen and dipped it into the ink well, then carefully began writing as Rebecca dictated.

Mr. George Pullman
Pullman Administration Building
Pullman, Illinois

DEAR MR. PULLMAN,

I am interested in acquiring a customized Pullman sleeping car for my daughter, Miss Emily Redmond. She is a field anthropology student working with Professor Putnam at Harvard University. She will be working in remote sites around the country and will need a train car that can serve as both living facilities and a working laboratory for her endeavors. I would be curious as to whether such a customized car would be possible and if so, how much would it cost to build?

Thank you for your immediate attention to this issue.

Cordially,
Mrs. Rebecca Redmond
Redmond Stables
Culpeper, Virginia

Chris slipped the letter into an envelope, addressed it, and placed it on the pile of correspondence to be placed in that day's outgoing mail.

MONDAY, MARCH 14, 1881

Rebecca sat at the dinner table, distractedly poking at the smothered pork chop on her plate.

"Rebecca, dear, you need to eat." Rex almost sounded like he was trying to wheedle her into eating, using almost the same tone he had used in those miserable early months after her stroke, when getting her to eat was difficult and communications were nearly impossible.

Charlie was also just poking at his dinner, when he usually consumed his share and more of CeCe's chops. They were better than Esther's, which was saying a great deal about CeCe's skill as a cook.

But tonight was special, and not in a pleasant way. It was Andy's sixteenth birthday. Rebecca, Charlie, and Rex had spent a great deal of time and effort, not to mention money, in making sure that Andy's birthday gifts were equivalent to his brother's, but instead of a lovely dinner and a house full of celebrating family, the three of them were the only people in the dining room that night.

Rebecca sighed and then laid down her knife and fork. "I cannot eat. I just have no appetite. I feel like I have lost Andy. It is one thing that we did not celebrate Em's birthday last month. She was at school and she has not been home for her birthday for years, but I have not missed even one of Andy's birthdays EVER." A tear crept down her cheek. She looked back and forth between Rex and Charlie, and then, in a wistful voice, asked, "He will never be my baby boy again, will he?"

CHAPTER 11

"NOT THAT I care in the least what your reasons are," Rebecca said as she burrowed deep down under the covers, into his side and then onto Charlie's shoulder where she was always warm, safe, and happiest. "But why are we going to Charleston?"

Charlie shifted so they were both comfortable as he pulled the sheets, blankets and the heavy winter quilt up to their necks. It was a cold night and even with the fire burning hot and low in the bedroom hearth and the winter dressing in place, there was a serious chill in the air. "There are a couple of reasons. First, we need a holiday. Even a short one." It also occurred to me that we would be there during the twentieth anniversary of the firing on Fort Sumter. I thought maybe we would pay our respects as well."

"That seems perfectly reasonable, as you all went through that horror together."

Charlie tightened his arms around his wife. "**We** went through it, my dear. You might find it interesting, too."

"I am sure I will." She nodded against his shoulder. "Is there anything else?" She asked quietly as the thumb of her left hand caressed his side, finding its way under his knitted shirt. "I know you got a letter from your cousin Edouard last week. Has something happened?"

Charlie drew a deep breath, letting it out slowly. "He, ah, he wrote to let Charlotte know that the family home is up for sale. Auction, actually. Seems the last of the Redmond's of my line have fallen on extremely hard times. A cousin who had inherited it has lost it to taxes. He thought Charlotte might want to know and this was the last place he knew of her residing."

"The house you were born in?"

He nodded somewhat stiffly. "Born and grew up in, until that fateful day."

"Are you thinking about buying it?" She asked quietly.

"Apparently." He could only chuckle. She knew him too well.

Rebecca shifted so she could look up at him. "And then what will you do with it?"

"I have no idea," he sighed. Tugging the blankets again, he turned toward her, holding her in his arms. "Maybe tear it down."

"Why?" Rebecca managed to push herself up, pulling from his embrace. Looking down at him, she smiled as she caressed his cheek. "You may buy it. I understand that need. You may not tear it down."

He started to protest, but soft fingers across his lips stopped it before the first syllable cleared them.

"You, Charles Huger Redmond, are better than that. You do not destroy. You nurture. You encourage. You build. You create. You care. When it has been in your power, I have never known you to knowingly or willingly destroy anything. I doubt you would be able to destroy the house where you remember the love of your mother, but I certainly will not stand by quietly and allow you to do it because you are trying to pull of some male bravado or bluster. Buy your house, Charlie."

She kissed his cheek and then, as she settled back down next to him, his neck. "We will find a way to use it, but you will not tear it down."

He smiled, a single tear rolling down his cheek. "Yes, dear."

THURSDAY, APRIL 7, 1881

The coachman pulled the carriage up to the rail shed. A wagon loaded with cases and bags for the group of friends pulled around them toward the loading dock where the luggage would be transferred to the private cars in the shed under the expert supervision of Louis and Lizbet.

The gentlemen assisted the ladies from the carriage, Charlie making sure Rebecca had a firm grip on his arm before they started for the platform leading to their entry. Rain the previous evening had made the path muddy and slippery. They did not need to start this trip with her taking a fall or twisting an ankle.

"Oh, yes." Elizabeth laughed as she lifted her skirts over a small puddle. "I forgot we would be taking the Redmond Stables Rail for this trip."

Rebecca threw her dearest friend and sister of her heart a withering glare. "You may hush now."

Richard snorted his amusement as he assisted his wife up the small set of stairs leading to the platform.

"And you can be quiet, too, Richard," Rebecca snapped playfully as she used both the rail to her left and Charlie's left forearm on her right to climb the steps. Richard then took her hand to steady her until Charlie joined them on the platform.

"I seem to remember," Elizabeth carried on, apparently impervious to the daggers Rebecca was currently hurling with her eyes, "a time when you were first married to our dear friend Charlie here and you used to give him just terrible grief for buying things…"

"Elizabeth," Rebecca said sweetly. "It will be a long walk to Charleston. We will be back home before you get there."

"I just find it terribly amusing that you were the one to start buying rail cars." The doctor smirked at her friend as they turned together and walked arm in arm toward the interior of the shed where the cars were parked and prepared for travel.

Rebecca shrugged. "After I did the arithmetic, with as much as we travel and with having to transport horses, it made sense."

As he watched them board the train, Charlie pulled his cigar case from his coat pocket and offered one to Richard. "Let us enjoy these now. Since Rebecca's stroke, the smoke annoys her so I have to leave the car if I want one."

Charlie let Richard stoke his cheroot first and then he followed suit.

"So, what is the real reason why we are off to Charleston? I do not believe your story about wanting to commemorate the beginning of a war you hated." Richard stood there, puffing on his cigar and waiting for an answer.

Charlie looked away from Richard, staring down the tracks, and spoke in a low voice. "I got a letter telling me that my family home was up for sheriff's auction for failure to pay taxes. I want to go learn what happened."

"The last time we learned something together we nearly ended up in a Rebel POW camp." Richard arched an eyebrow at him and quirked his lips into a small smirk. He was very aware that Charlie had extremely mixed feelings about his childhood home.

"Nearly being the operative word." Charlie laughed and chucked his friend on the shoulder. "I paid you back for that little fiasco. If I remember correctly, it cost me a room at the Willard, with a bath, dinner, a bottle of very expensive brandy, and the company of one of Lizzie's girls for the weekend."

Richard blushed at his youthful shenanigans. "You are an old man now. Clearly your memory is faulty."

"Perhaps." Charlie grinned and nodded. "There might have been two of Lizzie's girls."

"Charlie," Richard growled as he pulled his hand over his face. "You had better not dare…"

"Who, me?" The general flashed a smile that was all light and innocence. "Would I betray the confidence of my oldest and dearest friend?"

"I doubt it." Richard crossed his arms as he chewed on his cigar. "Your oldest and dearest is buried in the family cemetery. Since I am all that is left, I know you will ride me like a two-dollar mule."

"That much?" Charlie tried to chew his cheeks, but the smile crossed his face. "Thought maybe fifty cents for a mule that never made full colonel."

"Damn you, Charlie Redmond!" Richard pulled back lightheartedly as if he were about to take a swing as his old friend. His spirited attack was interrupted by the porter, sent to fetch them.

"Gentlemen, the ladies are waiting for you to board. Then we can be on our way." The elderly black man bowed and smiled. Then he looked to Charlie. "General Redmond, sir, Mrs. Redmond wishes me to inform you that 'You are mucking up the works.'"

"Of course, I am, George!" Charlie roared with laughter as he grabbed Richard by the shoulder. "Come on, man! Our women await!"

~

SATURDAY, APRIL 9, 1881

The trip to Charleston had been filled with reasonably decent food, fine liquors of every stripe, and excellent company. By the time the foursome arrived, they were in exceptionally good humor, having spent the last two days relaxing and enjoying the stress-free atmosphere of Rebecca's beautifully appointed private cars.

Charlie had booked them into the Mills House Hotel, the best Charleston had to offer. He made sure they were on the first floor, facing the street. He had taken all the rooms that had a balcony. The set of empty rooms between the married couples' boudoirs would serve nicely as a parlor and gathering spot.

Their train pulled into the station in Charleston shortly after lunch, where a carriage and a small dray were waiting to convey them to the hotel. Louis took responsibility for loading the luggage, while Lizbet collected Rebecca's and Elizabeth's personal effects, including reticules, parasols, fans and other miscellaneous items that no proper lady would be caught dead without when progressing through the streets of a grand southern city.

Once everything was gathered together, they headed out through the streets of Charleston. Charlie instructed the driver to take them down to the Battery before they went to the hotel, so his wife and friends could see at least some of the features of the city. As they went, Charlie kept a running dialogue of the places he remembered from his childhood. They passed the beautiful St. Philips Episcopalian Church, with its spire towering over all the other buildings in town.

As they proceeded down Meeting Street toward the Battery, they passed the Circular Church, under construction after it had been destroyed by a terrible fire in 1861 and then further diminished by the hardships of the war and the reconstruction period. Charlie smiled gently as they passed the building.

Richard asked what they all were wondering. "What kind of building is that?"

"That, dears, is probably the most inclusive, rebellious, innovative church in the United States. You see, Charles Towne was founded by a rather motley crew of mixed religious groups. There were the landgraves, the proper English Anglicans who held the charter for the Carolinas. They started the St. Philips congregation. The rest were a mix of Scottish Presbyterians, English Congregationalists and French Huguenots. The church has always been independent, with elements of all three groups bringing their own perspectives to the church. The congregation supported the Revolutionary War and helped to finance Francis Marion's troops. The only group here in Charleston that was more important to the Revolution was the Jewish community, who essentially financed the whole war! Then a group spun off to form the Unitarian Church. I am very pleased they are keeping the circular design and have managed to save the oldest cemetery in town."

As they drove further down the street, they kept looking at all of the beautiful wrought iron work, the gardens, and the lush foliage.

Elizabeth was charmed by all of the lovely architecture that was unique to the city. "Charlie, why are the houses all sideways to the street?"

Charlie grinned. "Well, it gets damned hot and humid here in the summer, so most folks live on their porches and balconies to take advantage of the breeze coming off the harbor. In the summer, we even slept on the porches. Granted, sometimes the aroma leaves something to be desired, but being able to cool off a bit is much better than sweltering inside. Setting the houses sideways to the street not only catches the breeze more effectively, but it also offers some degree of privacy for the porches and balconies."

Rebecca smiled. "It is very like the lovely gardens and patios that the houses in New Orleans are built around."

Richard looked around. "So why all the pastel colors? Driving through here is like driving through a pastry shop with an overabundance of colored icing!"

The other occupants of the carriage could not help but laugh at Richard's rather disgruntled opinion of the colors of the houses they passed. Charlie caught his breath and responded to the rather grumpy gentleman. "Most of the houses are made of stucco. In its natural state, it is a dull, ugly light gray, and stucco does not take well to being painted. So we color the stucco before it is applied to the walls. Light colors are better in this climate – they absorb less heat from the sun, so Charleston ends up with a lot of pastel-colored buildings. My father's house is pink."

Richard groaned. His sense of housing propriety – red brick and white trim – was deeply offended.

Their driver took them around Battery Park, where the Ashley and Cooper Rivers came together to form Charleston Harbor. In the distance, they could see the hulk of Fort Sumter and the ongoing reconstruction of the fortifications at Fort Moultrie on Sullivan's Island.

They returned up Meeting Street to the Mills House. They

were met in the entry atrium by the hotel keeper, who was eager to make his clearly affluent guests welcome and comfortable. Charlie had reserved two corner rooms on the first floor, with their balconies looking over Queen Street, and the parlors between the rooms to provide them with space for private breakfasts, meetings, and just relaxing as they explored the old city. The rooms were all light and airy, with extremely high ceilings and large windows. The décor was done in light blues and creams, simply decorated with tasteful paintings of flowers and local scenes on the walls. It was lovely.

Louis and Lizbet had preceded them and were already busy unpacking for the old friends. After all the years they had spent together, sharing their valet and lady's maid was easy for everyone and offered Elizabeth and Richard the rare treat of living like a truly wealthy couple. Richard still refused Louis's offer of shaving him in the morning. He said after so many years of using his own hand, it would be hard to trust anyone else's.

They spent what was left of the afternoon relaxing, enjoying long baths to rid themselves of the dust, sweat, and detritus of travelling, and enjoyed a very elegant dinner that evening in the hotel's white and crystal dining room on the ground floor.

The first course took everyone but Charlie by surprise. They were served a rather rich, sherry spiked soup redolent with the aroma of crab. It was one of Charleston's signature dishes – she-crab soup, and the Mills House cook had mastered this unusual dish.

Rebecca looked askance at the bowl set before her. "She-crab soup? Charlie, you know I do not care for seafood."

"My love, you like lobster bisque. This is very similar, but more delicate in flavor. I think you will enjoy it."

"All right. I will try it, but be warned…"

Charlie just smiled as his dinner partners picked up their

spoons and took tentative spoonfuls of the creamy golden substance. After the first taste, silence reigned over the table as the four old friends tried to scrape the finish off the porcelain bowls.

The next course was a huge platter placed in the middle of the table with a number of different small cold treats, including an interesting cheese spread accompanied with cheese straws, pickled okra, pickled shrimp, a light shrimp paste and crackers, and an assortment of locally made charcuterie. Charlie also got a plate of fresh oysters on the half shell, but did not impose his particular taste for these not particularly appealing-looking treats on the others.

Rebecca watched him consume the oysters with a somewhat disgusted look on her face. "Dear, if you want to share a bed with me after slurping down those repellent pieces of oceanic snot, you had best brush your teeth – multiple times."

Charlie looked sideways to his beloved and smirked, "After all these years, do you not think I know that? I pack two toothbrushes when sea food is on the travel agenda," he added just before slurping down one of the slimy shell-bound bites.

Rebecca could only laugh and shake her head at him as she sipped her wine. More than fifteen years of marriage had clued her into when her biggest boy was simply being silly. She loved him most when he was at his silliest.

Each of them had their own entrees. Charlie relished a duck pirleau, while Rebecca enjoyed a roast marsh chicken. Richard opted for what he considered the safest dish, roast pork, while Elizabeth continued to indulge her taste for shrimp with a shrimp pie. Dessert was a light, creamy, alcoholic concoction called syllabub, which was about all they could down after the rich and varied meal they had enjoyed.

SUNDAY, APRIL 10, 1881

The four of them had breakfast in their parlor and then headed to St. Philip's Episcopalian Church for morning services. Richard and Charlie were startled to discover that they knew the rector, Reverend John Johnson. He had been trained as an engineer at West Point at the same time Charlie had been there.

The service was very traditional, adhering to the *Book of Common Prayer* to the letter. The building was beautiful, the organ player was good, and the sermon was mercifully short though not particularly inspiring, all of which made the morning tolerable.

As they filed out of the building, Reverend Johnson pulled them aside. "Charlie Redmond, as I live and breathe! Please, wait until I have finished the parting blessings and we can catch up, at least for a few minutes."

The four of them stepped to the side under the beautifully columned portico of the church and waited patiently.

Once the minister had finished seeing the congregation on their way, he bustled over to where Charlie and Richard were chatting quietly with their wives.

"Charlie! Richard! What brings you two to Charleston? And who are these lovely ladies?"

"Johnny, please let me introduce my wife, Rebecca. Rebecca, this is Major John Johnson, or at least he was when I knew him. He trained as an engineer with me at The Point," said Charlie, rather formally.

"Mrs. Redmond, it is my pleasure." Reverend Johnson bowed over Rebecca's hand.

"And Johnny, you probably heard of Richard's wife, Dr.

Elizabeth Walker Polk. She was one of our field surgeons at the end of the war."

"Dr. Polk, I do wish you had chosen to stay with the South. You could have done so much good for the cause."

"I am a physician, Reverend Johnson. I try to do good for whosoever needs it."

"And a good Christian attitude that is, ma'am." Johnson turned to Charlie. "So, what brings you to Charleston, Colonel?"

Before Charlie could answer, Richard jumped in. "It is General now, Johnny." He comically threw up two fingers, wiggling them to indicate two stars.

"Why am I not surprised," grinned Johnson.

Charlie smoothly picked up the thread. "As you may or may not have known, I am originally from here, and I have some old family business to deal with, so I thought I would show my wife and Richard and Elizabeth the town, and I wanted to join in the twenty-year remembrance."

"Well, that is lovely. Ladies, I hope you enjoy our beautiful city. I would invite you to luncheon with me, but I have a meeting with the council of elders in a few minutes and cannot join you. Perhaps I will see you on Tuesday." He turned to Charlie and Richard. "Fellows, it is good to see you after all this time. Have a lovely day. Ladies." He bowed slightly to them, then returned to the bowels of the church.

They settled into the carriage and Charlie told the driver to take them to Poinsett Tavern, which served a Sunday ordinary that Charlie remembered as having been excellent. Richard sat with a strange look on his face, partially angry and partially bewildered.

"What is bothering you?" Charlie asked, giving Richard's booted foot a bit of a shove with his own.

"What did Johnny mean by 'The Cause?' The war has been

over for years; the Southern Cause, such as it was, has been dead for a long time!"

Rebecca spoke softly. "For many southerners, the Cause will never die. They think of themselves more as Confederates than as Americans, and to be honest, you can still see how much damage was done during the war. They long for things to be the way they used to be and can never be again."

Elizabeth chimed in. "Why do you think we still have these idiots in white robes and red shirts and whatever else still skulking around and trying to intimidate the Negroes and the whites who support them, dear? You had to deal with them more than any other problem when you were the sheriff." She gave her husband that 'do what your wife tells you to do' look. "So darling, you will just have to swallow your pride and your sense of being the victor on Tuesday and accept it that you are here where the whole mess started. Twenty years is not enough time for that passion to die, dear."

They pulled up in front of the tavern just in time to end what could have become a rather intense conversation and headed into the dining room. A huge buffet was set against one wall, with a mélange of smells filling the room.

The four of them were seated at a large round oak table with four other guests. In the middle of the table was a lazy Susan loaded with items such as salt, pepper, a cruet of hot sauce, and a pot of pepper relish. There was a large plate of neatly trimmed raw vegetables with a crock of cheese dip in the middle, and bowls with lightly pickled cucumber slices and onions and another of pickled finger okras.

A host came to their table, greeted them, offered them an assortment of beverages, and announced the offerings of the day. Bowls of steaming vegetables were brought to the table and set on the lazy Susan while the host asked what the guests wanted for their entrees. Today, there was Frogmore stew, shrimp pirleau, fried chicken, garlic crabs with crab rice, country captain, deviled crabs, and a sugar-cured ham.

As the entrees were being recited, Richard leaned over and whispered to Elizabeth, "Damn, no beef. Do you think we will find a decent steak or joint while we are here?"

"Sweetheart, look around. Where in this swampy mess would you graze a herd of cows?"

Richard thought for a moment then said, "Oh. Seafood and the odd pig, right?"

"Right, honey."

After lunch, Charlie directed the carriage driver to take them toward the wharfs, and specifically to East Elliott Street, where his father's ship chandlery had been located. As they slowly drove down the street, Charlie could not find the shop. He had the carriage travel back up, then tapped on the driver's shoulder and asked, "Do you know where Redmond's Ships Chandlery is located?"

"Oh, sir, I am sorry, but this whole area was burned out in the fire of sixty-one. Redmond's was destroyed. Burned to the ground. Never rebuilt. Old man Redmond had died a few years before. From what I understand, there were no immediate heirs and it fell to distant family who opted for the insurance money rather than to rebuild."

Charlie nodded, thought for a moment and then asked the driver to take them up Tradd Street to the block between King Street and Meeting Street.

Rebecca asked softly, "Where are we going, Charlie?"

"My father's house. It goes up for sheriff's auction tomorrow at noon. My cousin has not paid the taxes in quite some time from what I understand." Charlie's answer was rather terse, his tone of voice very flat.

As they drove up the street, they noted a pink stucco Charleston style house with a sheriff's notice attached to the gate. Charlie tapped the driver to stop, then got out and scanned the notice. Finally, he looked over the house for several minutes while his companions waited in the carriage.

Even from the street and behind the locked gates, it was possible to see that the house was in bad shape. Some of the iron balcony rails were rusted out and broken away, several windows were boarded over, the azalea bushes had not been trimmed in years, grass was growing between the slates that formed the entrance path, and one could see bird nests on top of two of the chimneys. There were also several poorly done patches on the roof. Charlie shook his head as he climbed back in the carriage.

"I appreciate you all accompanying me on this trip through my childhood memories. This is not a trip I would have liked to make alone."

Rebecca took his hand, Elizabeth patted him on the knee, and Richard reached into his coat pocket and pulled out a flask, which he offered to his friend.

Charlie looked at him, a question in his eyes. Richard's response was one word. "Brandy."

Charlie nodded, took a swig, and then asked the carriage driver to take them up the street to the First Scots Presbyterian Grave Yard, park and wait for them.

They drove around the block and the driver took them into a small alley leading toward the back of the church. He found a tree shaded area just outside the back gate to the grave yard with a water trough for the horse, so he pulled up, settled the horse in for a good drink, and smiled at Charlie. "We can wait here, sir."

As they walked toward the gates of the cemetery, they noticed several groups of people scattered about around various graves. Most of them had blankets and picnic baskets, clearly enjoying a quiet Sunday with lost loved ones.

Just inside the gate, a small girl of about seven straightened to her full three-and-a-half-foot height and offered a small bunch of spring flowers gripped in her fist. "Just a penny, sir. If you need them for someone you love."

Charlie looked to the child, her long dark hair braided down her back. Hazel eyes that seemed so sad while trying to be happy and brave. Her dress had seen better days but was patched, clean, and as well-kept as could be expected. Her little feet were bare and dirty and her face slightly smudged with what Charlie suspected was coal ash from helping start morning fires before leaving to pick and sell her flowers.

"Just a penny?" Charlie smiled at the child as he fished in his trouser pocket. "Those are terribly pretty flowers. I am sure that my mama would like them and they are worth more than a penny. Would you let me buy them for say, a dollar?"

Little eyes went wide as Charlie pulled the shiny coin from his pocket. "A real dollar?" She asked, not really believing him.

"A real dollar." Charlie nodded and handed her the coin for her inspection. "For those very lovely flowers."

The child nodded, clutching her fist tight around the coin as she handed Charlie the flowers with the other hand. "Thank you, sir! I ain't never made a whole dollar before! Even when I sold all my flowers!"

"Well, now you have." He winked as he gave her a pat on the head and then the cheek. "Thank you for reminding me I should take these to my mama."

Rebecca smiled, opened her reticule, and before they departed, purchased the three remaining bunches of flowers for the same price of one dollar a bunch. She was rewarded with a hug and a kiss. The girl squealed with delight as she began her dash home to show her own mama what good fortune she had selling flowers at the church on this Sunday.

The four friends strolled around the graveyard until they came to a small plot with two gravestones. One was relatively new; the other had started to show signs of weathering.

Charlie ignored the newer one and knelt down beside the one that read, "Emelia Huger DuBosque Redmond. October 8, 1812 to April 18, 1834. Rest softly, beloved wife and mother."

Elizabeth put her hand on Rebecca's shoulder and drew her and Richard away, leaving Charlie to commune with his mother.

Charlie leaned over and pressed his lips to the stone as he placed the flowers at its base. "Salut, Maman," he whispered his hello in the soft French she had always sung in his ear. Then he sighed and settled down a bit more on the ground.

"It has been a long time. I am so sorry I have not been back before now, but it just was not possible. I know this is probably not how you expected to see me."

He looked into the clear blue sky and then back to the stone. "Maybe if we had been able to stay together, things, things might have been different, but I doubt it. It has taken me a very long time to understand it, but this is me. Charlie Redmond.

"I am married to a wonderful woman. You would love her. The daughter you never had. She is so much like you. Such a good mother. A wonderful woman who loves me without question. I could not ask for more or better. We have adopted and raised five children. They are good children and have become everything I could expect. Except for Andy, but I hope he will find his way, too. You are a great grandmother, four times over. Though if Darby and Stella have their way, there will be many more. I think they are part rabbit. Rebecca and I love our grandbabies. You should see the way she dotes over them."

He leaned in close, chuckling as he whispered, "She is a very different grandmother than she was a mother. LJ, our oldest grandson, can get away with things that his father would have been striped three ways to Sunday for."

"I have tried to make a good life for them, Maman. I have always taken care of them. I have not always given them what they wanted, but I have always provided what they needed. I love them like you love me, with everything I am.

"I am happy with my life. It has been a good one."

Leaning over, he pressed his lips to the stone again and whispered, "Je t'aime, Maman."

As he rose to rejoin his wife and friends, Charlie looked at his father's grave. It was stark, simply reading Russell Redmond, 1807 to 1859. Charlie leaned down and gathered up a handful of dirt, sprinkling it over the grave.

Rebecca looked at her husband's face, then turned to Elizabeth and Richard. "I think we have had a rather trying day. Shall we return to the hotel and rest a while before supper?"

"Excellent idea, Rebecca. Although I think supper will be a light meal. I am still stuffed from that dinner at the tavern!"

"And I can have a steak for supper. I checked the menu at the hotel."

Charlie, with some effort, boosted himself into the carriage and they set off up Meeting Street to rest, though Charlie was a bit fidgety.

As they arrived at the hotel, the host came into the atrium to meet them, asking how their day was going and if they needed anything.

Rebecca looked at her husband and concluded that something cool and refreshing would be good. "Perhaps some iced tea with mint? And then a light tea, some fruit?"

"Certainly, madam. Anything else?"

Charlie got a slightly evil grin on his face. "Yes, please. Some boiled peanuts, if you do not mind. About two pounds?"

The host blinked and hemmed for a moment, then said, "Certainly, sir, though it will take a few minutes to get them. Shall I send the other items up first?"

"Thank you. That will be fine." Rebecca was back in full force, the Mrs. Redmond who had her hand on every aspect of their lives. She turned to Charlie and raised a single brow. "Boiled peanuts?"

"A childhood memory come home to roost." He smiled somewhat sadly.

A waiter arrived at the parlor door within minutes of the four friends having made it upstairs, divested themselves of the various items needed to be out and about, and splashed their faces with cool water to rid themselves of the dust stirred up as they meandered through town. Rebecca's order was complete and the cool fruit and tea was welcome. Though it was early April, afternoon in Charleston was still warm and humid.

Charlie was decidedly restless, but not particularly communicative. He wandered from window to window, glanced at the newspaper on the side table, opened his briefcase and flipped through some papers, stuffed the papers back in the case, wandered back to the window, and generally made himself perfectly annoying as Richard, Elizabeth, and Rebecca chatted softly about the things they had seen and the new flavors they had experienced.

Finally, Rebecca had enough. "Charles Redmond, damn it. Light, man. You are going to wear their beautiful carpet bare and drive me insane."

Just then there was a soft tap on the door. A waiter came in with a tray in one hand. On it was a good-sized silver dish with a domed cover and a large, empty bowl. "Your peanuts, General Redmond, sir."

A slow grin spread over Charlie's face. He was fairly certain that the hotel's manager had sent a runner over to the market to one of the sidewalk vendors selling peanuts from big pots to get his treat. "You have to try these peanuts. They are perfectly delicious."

Richard looked askance at the pile of slightly soggy, steamy brown pods. Peanuts had been desperation food during the war and were not high on his list of favorite substances, but he stepped over to try one. Very tentatively, he pressed the pod along its seam. The shell popped open and he pried the meat out, then dropped it into his mouth. It was warm, soft, almost buttery, and slightly salty from the brine it had been boiled in. It was delicious.

$\sim$

MONDAY, APRIL 11, 1881

Rex was sitting in the breakfast room, drinking his black tea laced with a splash of milk and reading yesterday's paper. It was very early; the light coming in the window was still tinged pink with the light of dawn. The only sounds were the rustle of the house servants just starting to begin their day's chores and the early birds chirping to one another as they attacked the worms that had emerged during the night and had yet to return to the safety that burrowing in the dirt offered. It was a time of blissful solitude.

So, when Andy burst through the door, saw that the coffee pot was not yet filled, and impatiently rang the bell, Rex was more than a little startled. Seeing Andy before eight o'clock was unusual, and seeing him at sun up was unheard of.

Rex spoke quietly from his preferred corner by the window. "What has you up and about at this early hour, Andrew? And dressed to the nines as well!"

Andy spun around, startled to have anyone in the room with him. "Oh." He paused. "Good, good morning, Uncle Rex."

"Good morning." Rex peered at him over the rims of his reading glasses, a questioning look on his face, waiting for answers to his query.

Andy spoke quickly, anxious to get his coffee and get out the door. He already had his horse waiting for him outside to make quick work of the trip to the railway station. "That railroad fellow you told me about is in Richmond and I have an appointment to see him this afternoon. So I need to catch the first train to Richmond and I need to look good for the interview. Oh, and thank you for the introduction, Uncle Rex."

Just then one of the kitchen boys came into the room with a steaming pot of coffee. Andy quickly poured himself a cup, sweetened it with sugar, stirred in a splash of milk, and gulped it down, scalding his mouth as he did so, and fled out the door. The East Tennessee, Virginia and Georgia Railway offered him a way out of the clutches of the family at Mountain View, and eventually, out of Virginia and over to the Mississippi River at Memphis. He saw it as his route to the life he really wanted.

CHARLIE WAS UP EARLY. HE HAD ASKED LOUIS TO LAY OUT HIS best business garb for that morning, so with Louis's assistance, he was washed, shaved and dressed in plenty of time to wend his way to the local branch of one of the New York-based banks he used in order to make arrangements to buy the house at the auction that day.

He had been on the steps of the bank when the doors were unlocked, and had been graciously received by the bank manager. It took only a few minutes to ensure that Charlie had the letters of credit he needed for the auction safely tucked in his breast pocket.

As he walked into their parlor at the hotel, Rebecca looked up from her second cup of coffee and asked, "Where have you been, my wandering man?"

Charlie walked over and kissed his beloved on the forehead. "Oh, I went to the bank to make arrangements about the house." He poured himself a cup of coffee as he turned to Richard and asked, "Would you mind accompanying me to the auction this morning?" He turned back to Rebecca and then glanced over to Elizabeth. "Ladies, I hope you will not mind being left to your own devices for a short time while I try to acquire the house."

Rebecca smiled, taking his free hand. "We will be just fine, dear. There is a lovely little hat shop around the corner that Elizabeth and I will be patronizing after luncheon. After that, I am sure we will find something to plot."

Charlie and Richard looked at one another. Leaving Rebecca and Elizabeth to plot usually meant that something would happen that would complicate their lives.

A few minutes later, Charlie and Richard pulled on their coats and gloves and strolled the three blocks to the old Redmond house on Tradd Street.

They were a little early, but there was no one else standing in front of the house waiting for the sheriff.

Charlie and Richard looked at one another, a little confused by the absence of anyone else. Charlie went up and re-read the auction notification posted on the gate. "Yes, this is where the auction is to be held. We are in the right place."

Just then a pair of men on horseback rode up. One unlocked the gate and led his horse in, followed by the other man on horseback. They tied their horses to the hitching post that Charlie remembered with such dislike, then looked at Charlie and Richard. "Have you gentlemen come to bid on this property?"

Charlie nodded while Richard spoke up. "He has. I am just moral support."

"Uh huh. Well, we will wait a few minutes to see if anyone else shows up. Would you like to look around while we wait?"

Charlie thought for a moment. "Yes, if you do not mind."

"I don't mind. If you are going to buy this mess, you should know what you are getting into."

Richard said, "I will wait here. I would rather not dirty this suit with dust and cobwebs, thank you. I do not have the wardrobe you do."

Charlie shook his head as the sheriff's assistant went and unlocked the door to the house. Richard watched him make his way to the front door, making a large and purposeful arc past the hitching post.

Charlie walked through the house quickly. All of the paintings and decorations were gone, either stolen or sold, but most of the furniture remained – moth eaten, moldy, and beset with wood rot. He could smell mouse droppings and could hear the rodents scurrying around in the wood work above, below, and all around him. It was going to take a lot of work to return this house to being livable, much less the comfortable and well-appointed home it had once been.

Charlie did not dare go up to the first floor, as he did not think the stairs were reliable enough to bear his weight. He returned to the courtyard, where the three other men waited.

"We have waited ten minutes and no other bidders have arrived. What is your bid, sir?" the sheriff asked briskly.

"What is the minimum you will accept, sir?"

"Well, the sum of back taxes due is six hundred twenty-seven dollars. I will accept that."

"You have it. Here are my letters of credit from the bank. Shall we go over and finalize the deal?"

"By all means, sir. Oh, I did not get your name."

"It is Redmond. General Charles Redmond, US Army, Retired."

"Oh! Keeping the old place in the family, are you, sir?"

"You could say that."

"Would you be the Redmond who was at Appomattox Station?"

"I would, sir."

"You put up a hell of a good fight. I was on that train."

"It was a hellacious battle. We are all fortunate to have survived."

"So," Rebecca started as she poured them both a nightcap of very good brandy, "you bought the house?"

Charlie nodded, taking the glass from her. He took a sip and offered, "I did. I was the only bidder. Took it for the minimum. Not quite six hundred and thirty dollars in back taxes."

"And now what will you do?"

"No idea. The place is a mess. It needs a lot of work. It might just be better to tear it down."

"Charlie," Rebecca growled as she took a seat next to him. Her right hand came to rest on his thigh. "There is no way it is in such bad shape it needs to be torn down. Why do you keep mentioning it?"

"Darling, it is a disaster. It needs new windows. Probably a new roof. It is hard telling what damage mice and other creatures have caused. I am sure I paid far too much for it..."

"I am sure you did." She nodded knowingly. "Because you needed this. You needed to reclaim this lost part of your life. To gain some sort of control over your past. You have done that. Now let us decide how best to utilize it."

TUESDAY, APRIL 12, 1881

Charlie rose early that morning, anxious to rouse his travelling companions and stake a claim to a good position on the Battery where they could see and hear the speakers and the activities out on the water. Fort Sumter was situated approximately two and a half miles out from the Battery, at the entrance to Charleston Harbor, and was clearly visible from the waterfront park. After the speechifying, he had hired a boat to convey them to Sullivan's Island for dinner with the lieutenant colonel who was expanding the shore defenses at Fort Moultrie.

The hotel staff had packed them a large picnic basket, filled with the mandatory fried chicken, a number of fresh raw vegetables and hard fruits trimmed to provide convenient dipping in the spicy cheese spread that seemed to be ubiquitous in all Charleston restaurants and taverns. Bottles of sweet tea, cider, and white wine were included as well, along with biscuits, hard cheese, ham slices, and Charleston's famous benne seed crackers. Charlie had specifically asked for more boiled peanuts, and they were packed separately to keep the brine from spilling into the other foods. Louis and Lizbet came with them to provide service and tend to the foursome's needs.

All four dressed modestly in clothing that would have been appropriate at a funeral, as this was less a celebration than it was a remembrance event. Charlie and Richard both wore morning coats, subdued vests, and soft ascots in subtle shades of grey to nearly black. Elizabeth chose to wear a two-piece day dress in a medium gray with off-white lace, while Rebecca's choice was lavender and dove gray with grosgrain facings. Both women chose modest bustles – large enough to be fashionable, but small enough to be discrete.

Their coachman drove them to the park that mostly fronted onto the Ashley River where it joined Charleston Harbor. He found a large oak tree near the intersection of South Battery and East Battery with a well-tended lawn beneath it where they could clearly see the presentation stand on Oyster Point, and that had a lovely view of the harbor and the remains of Fort Sumter.

The driver helped Louis unload their gear – folding chairs, tables, a good-sized portable cabinet with linens, plates, glasses, and silverware, the picnic basket, a case of wine, and assorted other accoutrements to a proper outdoor reception. "General Redmond, I cannot keep the carriage here. With your permission, I will return to the hotel and come back to collect you at around 2 o'clock?"

"Going back to the hotel is fine, and Louis and Lizbet will need you this afternoon, but I have a launch coming over to take us to Fort Moultrie for an early supper. So, we can either walk to the hotel when we return or I will hail a cab."

"Very good, sir. Have a pleasant time," the driver said as he tipped his cap and turned to the carriage.

"Shall we walk down to the river while Lizbet and Louis

finish setting things up?" Richard was a little twitchy and wanted to be moving.

"I take it you do not feel like standing here feeling a bit out of place?" Elizabeth chuckled at her husband.

Richard smiled ruefully as he offered his wife his arm.

They strolled toward the river, Charlie and Rebecca following and looking around as they went. Charleston was in prime color, with azaleas providing the primary colors, and all sorts of other flowers in full bloom.

As they stood at the railing looking out over the water and enjoying the breeze coming in off the ocean, a cheerful voice greeted them from behind.

"Charlie, Richard, and your lovely ladies!" Reverend John Johnson came bustling up to them, grinning. "I have so many people I would like you to meet."

"Good day, Reverend Johnson. I would enjoy meeting your friends, but I fear that my condition…" Rebecca raised her cane, "makes it difficult for me to mingle. Please, feel free to bring them over to our little enclave. We have some lovely nibbles to share, and I promise some nice cool wine, too."

The minister bowed politely to Rebecca. "It would be my honor to bring my friends – and I believe at least one of your friends – around on this day of remembrance, ma'am."

They strolled back to their site, with Reverend Johnson pointing out the houses that faced the park on South Battery Street, the Bath House off Murray Boulevard in the middle of the Ashley River, and the lovely pavilion in the middle of the park. "However, Mrs. Redmond, I think that they are planning to tear down the bath house. Every time we get a big storm through, it gets damaged and has to be rebuilt. I think they are just going to surrender to mother nature."

After delivering the little party to their picnic site, Reverend

Johnson went trotting off into the crowd to find some people to help entertain these representatives of the Yankee forces during the War of Northern Aggression.

Lizbet had been waiting for them, and placed a tray with four tall glasses of minted iced tea on a table. "Seems it's getting warm, Miss 'Becca. Thought some nice tea would be welcome."

Rebecca laughed. "Welcome indeed, Lizbet. Sometimes I think I should just surrender and let you order me around. God knows you try hard enough."

Within a few minutes, Reverend Johnson came bustling up with two gentlemen in tow.

"May I introduce Mr. Milledge Bonham, who served as our governor during the war, and Mr. Charles Pinckney, a planter in the area? Gentlemen, this is General Charles Redmond, Mrs. Redmond, Colonel Richard Polk and his wife, Dr. Elizabeth Walker Polk. I was in the Mexican War with General Redmond."

The two gentlemen made appropriate introductory noises and then Bonham said, "Redmond? You wouldn't happen to be related to the Redmond's who had a large chandlery before the war?"

Charlie nodded. "Yes, distantly, though."

"And you are certainly the Redmond who served as our representative to England. You managed to negotiate some excellent trade agreements, sir."

"Thank you. It was something of a challenge, what with the East India Company being dissolved and all."

"Not to mention the scandal you had to clean up."

The two men continued discussing international trade agreements while the younger man cornered the women. "Yes, yes, my great aunt created the first indigo plantation here. It is such a lovely blue; do you not agree?"

"Yes, it is. Just beautiful. Have you had any problems with

the new chemical dyes cutting into your market?" asked Rebecca as she brought her glass to her lips.

"Alas, yes, but no one has created a blue that will replace the indigo dyes, thank God." He took a sip of the tea that Lizbet had brought him. "Say, do either of you two ladies have daughters of marriageable age? I am looking for a wife and . . ."

Elizabeth and Rebecca both laughed. "I am sorry, Mr. Pinckney, but neither of us has an 'available' daughter. Mine is too young and Mrs. Redmond's are already spoken for, one way or another." Elizabeth was finding this third-generation scion of an old family of revolutionary leaders to be horrifically boring and boorish.

Just then, an old friend strolled up and rescued the ladies. It was James Longstreet, a gentleman that both Charlie and Rebecca had come to know well during the days they had spent in the fall of eighteen seventy, supporting Mary and the Lee family when General Lee had passed. Longstreet bowed over Rebecca's hand, then Elizabeth's. "How charming to see you here. It has been too long, Rebecca. Though I must confess, I wish we had met under more pleasant circumstances."

Bonham had joined the group when Longstreet arrived, and Kirby Smith slid into the group as well, nodding to Richard and Charlie, whom he knew from their time together in the Mexican War.

Longstreet looked to Rebecca for permission, then turned to the gentlemen. "We met at General Lee's funeral in eighteen seventy. Mrs. Redmond is cousin to both Robert and Mary, and Charlie served under Lee several times during his career. Mrs. Walker-Polk's family were old friends of Robert's, so this group of kith and kin went down to Lexington to support Mary when Robert died."

Elizabeth smiled gently. "It was the least we could do. After all, Robert gave me away at our wedding."

Rebecca nodded and added, "It is what family does for one another, James. You know that as well as anyone."

The talk turned to Lee's funeral and the arguments that had almost destroyed the stateliness of the occasion, with the political faction wanting him buried in Richmond as a southern hero and the family wanting to honor his desire to support Washington College. James, Charlie, and Richard dealt with the politicians, and Rebecca served as Mary's spokesperson, while Elizabeth worked quietly to hold everyone together during a very stressful time. The general was buried as he wished on the college grounds.

The day proceeded with a rather windy set of speeches delivered from the podium and subtly mourning for the failure of "The Great Cause." Fortunately, as boring as the speeches were, the food that had been provided by the Mills House chef was excellent – and more than ample enough to provide something to everyone who visited with them.

The launch picked them up from the Battery pier and they were taken out to Sullivan's Island for a traditional low-country supper on the lawn facing the entrance to the Atlantic Ocean. They returned to town just as the sun was setting, with Richard whining about wanting some good, proper beef at some point.

The four old friends staggered into the hotel, tired, sweaty, and a bit overwhelmed by the number of people they had been required to be polite to during the course of the day.

Richard summed it up. "When are they going to get it through their heads that 'The Cause' is a lost one? So what that the first shot here twenty years ago started the war? The war was ended sixteen years ago, for Heaven's sake. We are NOT going back to the bad old days."

CHAPTER 12

Rex walked into Andy's room that evening to find the young man sorting and packing his things.

"I was going to ask how the interview went, but since you are packing, I see it went well."

"Of course, it went well. You know I can be charming when I want to. And who in Richmond wouldn't want a Redmond working for them? Big brother Darby has set the standard being a partner in his firm there and with Papa's name having been bandied about for governor, they were quick and seemingly happy to offer me a position. I will get to travel and can stay based out of Richmond."

"Well, I am happy I was able to give you an entrée into their hallowed executive offices."

"Yeah, well, thank you, Uncle Rex." Andy continued to pack.

The elder man crossed his arms, "If you think you are leaving as soon as you are packed, think again, young man. You will wait until you parents return from Charleston."

"I need to get over to Richmond. I have to find a place to stay, get settled, and start work next Monday."

"You can manage to wait until Thursday. They should be back in time for a late lunch. You can be in Richmond first thing Friday morning, and I am sure Darby can suggest places for you to stay."

"Darby – he's such a stick in the mud. Such a right proper Redmond, he'll probably recommend some place run by a little old lady whose idea of a fun time is to have tea with the church ladies on Wednesday. I want to find a place for young men."

"Fine – but in the meantime, you can have a place to sleep and eat while you look for something that is, shall we say, more to your taste. If you try to leave before your parents return, you will have to deal with me – and I have no intention of giving you any leeway. You will give your parents a proper good-bye. Your days of sneaking out and running away are over. Do I make myself clear?"

Andy glared at Rex, who responded with a steely stare that the young man had only seen when his adoptive uncle gave demonstrations of his Asian combat skills. It did not take long for Andy to lower his eyes and mumble, "Yes, sir."

EM WAS SITTING IN THE LARGE MEETING ROOM THAT CONNECTED her small office with that of Dr. Putnam, pouring through the collection of papers that Dr. Erminnie Smith had written on Algonquin mythologies, trying to find some link between the imagery in the Algonquin stories to what little had been found in the Mississippi cultures. It was a rather fruitless effort.

There was a knock on the door and she called, "Enter," rather distractedly.

Two nicely dressed gentlemen that she had never seen before in her life entered and stepped to the other side of the table she was working at. "Miss Redmond? Miss Emily Redmond?"

"Yes?" she said, looking puzzled.

"Good afternoon, Miss Redmond. I am James Craven. This is my associate, Mr. Arthur Wilson. Mr. Pullman asked us to call on you to discuss the customization of your research support train car. Have you thought about the facilities you will need?"

Mr. Wilson added eagerly, "We can fit a great many amenities in the new seventy-foot car, miss."

Em looked at the two men, blinking in bewilderment. *Research support train car? Facilities? Seventy-foot car? Oh, my God, Papa. What have you done this time?*

She managed to gather her wits and invited the men to be seated across the table from her. "Would you gentlemen like some tea?" Without waiting for a response, she rose and put the kettle on the hob. Over her shoulder, she admitted to the two men, "I assume my father has commissioned this, um, specialized train car? I have to confess, I was unaware of it, and so am unprepared."

"Actually, Miss Redmond, your mother placed the order. According to my paperwork, that is. You should know Mr. Pullman is very excited about creating a specialized vehicle to support scientific endeavors and your researchers."

"My mother?" Em blinked, not having considered the possibility that her mother would spend money like this had to cost to support her science. Usually, Mama was busy haranguing her to come home. "If you do not mind, gentlemen? Let me see if my advisor, Professor Putnam, has time to join us."

"Certainly. Perhaps you will not mind if we set the tea to steep when the water boils."

Nodding her permission, Em slipped into Professor Putnam's office. "Do you have a few minutes, sir?"

"Of course, Em. What can I do for you?"

"It seems my mother has decided we need a customized train car to support the dig out in Ohio. The gentlemen from the Pullman Company are here to find out what we need. I would very much like your help."

Putnam blinked. "A customized train car? What in the world?" He was as flummoxed as Em.

Em was looking rather abashed. "Yes, sir. My parents have always been very supportive of my scientific interests, and I suspect this is my mother's way of apologizing for how she acted when I left for school this winter."

Putnam pulled on his coat, straightened his tie, and said, "Well then, let us go see how much advantage we can take of your mother's guil..." His eyebrow went up, "um, generosity."

Em chuckled, nodding as she did. "Yes, let's do." The young woman continued to snicker as she followed her mentor.

The two went back into the meeting room, where they found Mr. Wilson pouring water into the large tea pot, while Mr. Craven was setting the mugs, sugar, lemon, and milk on the table.

"Gentlemen, let me introduce my thesis advisor, Dr. Frederick Putnam. Professor Putnam, Mr. Craven and Mr. Wilson are from the Pullman Company and are here to discuss the design of the research car."

"Shall we start by laying out the basic dimensions of the vehicle, gentlemen?" Putnam pulled a large sheet of paper from one of the cubbies along the wall and started sketching.

The foursome spent the rest of the afternoon drawing

sketches and laying out the design for the car. By the time they had finished, there was a preliminary design that included private sleeping rooms with commodes and sinks for four, small cabins for a couple of servants, a well-designed pantry with the ability to prepare simple meals, and a decent-sized work room with lots of light, plenty of storage, several work tables, and a drawing board. There were multiple chairs and bunks that could be pulled down from the ceiling if necessary.

Mr. Wilson folded the sketches and promised to get actual designs back to them for review within the week.

Dr. Putnam and Em escorted the gentlemen out of the building, chatting about this and that, with Putnam shaking his head and repeating under his breath, "Amazing what you can fit into 70 feet,".

When they returned to Putnam's office, they both slumped into comfortable chairs, with Em grinning like the Cheshire cat and Putnam looking sly. Em glanced at her advisor. "I wonder if Mama has any idea how much money she's just spent?"

"From what I've seen and heard of your family, I rather suspect she is perfectly aware of what she is doing." He thought for a moment and then added, "I wouldn't let Baer in on the source of this largess. He will simply accuse you of buying your way into the school, and you and I both know that is not the case. I will simply note it as an anonymous gift."

WEDNESDAY, APRIL 13, 1881

"Ah, it was a lovely trip, Charlie, but it is certainly good to be home again."

Rebecca shed her cloak and headed directly to the family

parlor at the back of the house, with Charlie following along. He stopped for a moment to ask Otis to let Dr. Rex know they were home and to ring the kitchen for a light lunch.

Louis and Lizbet coordinated the luggage being collected and carried in, and then went upstairs to oversee unpacking.

Charlie finally made it to the family parlor, where he found Rebecca standing on the porch looking out over the stables and pastures, while Rex was sitting quietly beside the unlit fireplace.

CeCe had anticipated their return and had already laid a light lunch of finger sandwiches, fruit, minted iced tea, and butterscotch cookies for them.

"Welcome back, Charlie." Rex grinned at his friend. "I take it the trip was pleasant and successful?"

"Well, I bought the old house for back taxes, I ran into some old acquaintances, I showed Rebecca and my friends around Charleston, and I visited my mother's grave. So yes, I suppose it was successful."

"Excellent. We had a bit of a breakthrough here, as well. Andy has secured a position with the railroad and will be going to Richmond. I feel confident that my old friends at their office will keep an eye on him, and Darby has found a place for him to stay. It is a boarding house for young men, run by a retired soldier."

"Well, at least it is a job. Though to be honest, I am less than thrilled with him not being under my roof." Charlie grumbled as he lit a cigar, flicking the lucifer into the fireplace.

"Charlie, my friend, if you do not loosen the reins on that boy, he will run again. And this time, I doubt you will be able to bring him back."

"You are probably right, Rex, and between the three of us, we should be able to keep an eye on him." Charlie sighed. "Where is he now?"

"He is finishing his packing. I would not let him leave before you and Rebecca got back. He is due in the shipping office at eight o'clock Monday morning."

"So he will be leaving on tomorrow's train?" Rebecca finally spoke.

Rex nodded to his dearest friend. "Yes."

AT SUPPER THAT NIGHT, ANDY OFFICIALLY TOLD HIS PARENTS about his job with the East Tennessee Virginia and Georgia Railway and his need to be in Richmond on Monday morning. He explained that Darby had found him a men's boarding house, so he had a place to stay, and if he got to Richmond tomorrow, it would give him time to unpack and get settled before he started to work, so he would be leaving in the morning. Of course, all of this was said in a rush, and he then excused himself, promising to say goodbye before he left for the train station in the morning.

Charlie watched the expression on his wife's face change from anger, to frustration, to profound sadness, and then to resignation. It broke his heart.

Charlie stood from his place at the table, tugging his ruby red vest down as he addressed both his companions. "How about we adjourn to our private sitting room and have a strong drink and a game of three handed whist?"

"Lovely idea, darling." Rebecca nodded, trying not to sound as despondent as she felt. She knew Charlie and Rex were simply trying to occupy her thoughts from her troublesome boy. "I think Rex is due for a winning streak."

"I certainly hope so," Rex added as he began following them from the room. "I have already run through my gambling budget with you two this month and you've been gone for most of it."

AFTER SUPPER, ANDY WALKED OUT TO THE BARN TO INSPECT HIS horses and make sure they were in shape for the trip to Richmond tomorrow. As he approached the barn, he saw Buddy bearing down on him, moving with all of the purpose of a battleship in full sail.

Sue came out of the farrier's shop, and thankfully intercepted his determined looking brother. Andy shrugged and stomped into the barn, intent on his own errand.

Sue wrapped her hands around Buddy's upper arm. "Little brother, from the look in your eyes, I suspect you were on your way to teach our brother a lesson. You cannot go beat the shit out of Andy. And for him, and honestly, for the whole family, it is better that he go and find his own way in the world rather than be forced to stay here, where he is obviously miserable."

"Yes, but did you see the look on Mama's face at supper? She is STILL blaming herself for how he acts, trying to figure out what she did wrong. I saw that look and all I want to do is beat some sense into his head."

Sue sighed. "I know. We have all tried to convince her that there is nothing wrong with her, that she didn't do anything wrong. It is just that Andy is… different. But Buddy, beating the snot out of him is NOT going to change him; it's just going to make Mama want to defend her wayward child even more."

Buddy's whole body sagged. "I know, Sue, but he just makes me so mad!"

"No, little brother; he makes you want to keep Mama and Papa from hurting any more than they already have."

"Well, at least we can maybe talk him into telling them it isn't anything they did wrong."

"Maybe we can. The best we can do is go try."

Sue and Buddy walked side by side into the barn, determined to try and talk, if not a little sense into their brother, at least some compassion for their parents.

ANDY CAME DOWN TO BREAKFAST WITH THE ADULTS THE NEXT morning, a huge smile on his face. He leaned over and kissed his mother on the cheek wishing her a very good morning before taking his seat at the table and snapping open the napkin to be placed in his lap.

"I assume," Charlie began as he placed his coffee cup back in the saucer, "that your good mood is brought on by the fact that the train to Richmond leaves in two hours?"

"Why, yes, Papa. You are always very astute."

"Andrew..." Charlie growled, leaning forward.

"Please!" Rebecca interrupted before Charlie could start an argument. "Do not squabble. Andy is leaving. That is his choice. I do not want him leaving home after a quarrel. Please?"

Looking at the tears welling in Rebecca's eyes, Charlie nodded and sat back. "I am sorry, Andy. I apologize."

Andy nodded, trying to smile. "It's okay."

There was a moment or two of uncomfortable silence as more coffee was poured and a few bites were taken. Andy finally glanced up, catching the raised-brow look Uncle Rex was giving him.

The young man cleared his throat gently. "I'd like to say some things before I leave. I'm not good with words like Buddy, I'm not clever like Em, I'm not as honorable as Darby, and I'm not dedicated like Sue."

"Andy..." Rebecca tried.

Andy shook his head and reached over to take his mama's

hand. Looking into her eyes, he continued. "It's okay. I've never fit in here. We all know that. I do love you, Mama." He smiled and gripped her hand tighter. "I'm just not a Redmond and we all know it. I need to find my own way."

He turned his head to Charlie. "Papa, I do appreciate everything you have done. I know I would not be alive if it were not for you and Mama. I know I have made mistakes and I am sorry. Seems I bring you both more grief than I am worth. I do not want to do that anymore."

"Andy." Charlie stood from his place at the head of the table and joined his wife and boy at the other end, taking the seat on the other side of his son. He dropped his hand to Andy's back, rubbing it in small, soothing circles. "Son, we all make mistakes. It is how we respond to them that matters."

"Yes, sir." Andy nodded. "I agree and until now, I have not responded well. Let me try to fix that. I can't change what happened to Liza and A.C. is doing just fine with Sue and Jeremiah. But I can change for the better; I just can't do it here. Set aside the fact everyone knows what happened, half the town already thinks I'm worthless. They only tolerate me because I'm a member of this family. I will go to Richmond and make a home and a life for myself. I will not run away. I will take responsibility, but I must leave to do that."

Charlie nodded. "I understand. Even though you did not come to us in the traditional manner, we are still your family, son. We want what is best for you. You are God awful young to be striking out on your own."

"No younger than you when you left Charleston. I am more than a year older, and I am also leaving with more than the clothes on my back, a knapsack with cheese, bread, and dried meat, and seven dollars in my pocket. You have told me those stories yourself. This is best, Papa." Andy turned back to his mother, who had unshed tears in her eyes. "I promise you, Mama, it was never you or Papa. You have always loved me the best you knew how. You gave me every chance, every opportunity, and everything I needed. You are my mama, even if I'm not a true Redmond. I promise to stay in touch with you. I promise to let you know every boring little thing that is happening in my life until you tell me, enough." He smiled as tears pooled in his own eyes. "Agreed?"

"Yes, agreed." Rebecca nodded and smiled a watery smile, dabbing her tears with the corner of her napkin. Then she turned and gripped his hand tight, making sure she held his eyes. "But Andy, you are a true Redmond. Please, do not ever doubt that. We love you. You will always have a home here."

"Thank you, Mama." He leaned over and kissed her cheek, whispering in her ear, "I will remember that and I will come home. I promise. I love you."

THURSDAY, MAY 19, 1881

Charlie, Rebecca, and Rex were sitting in the family parlor with all of the French doors open enjoying the gentle breeze coming in and the beautiful late spring day when one of the footmen brought in the morning mail.

Charlie flipped through it, tossing the dutiful weekly missive from Andy over to Rebecca, as well as a rather thick envelope from Charlotte. Rex's mail looked rather official, bearing the insignia of the Chinese embassy. He also had a thick missive from Charlotte. Charlie's mail was rather different. Other than the usual business reports, one was from his friend Filipp Brunnow and the other was from Fitz Lee. He opened Filipp's letter first.

Dear Charlie;

First let me tell you that Arabella sends her love. She is as much a leader of society here in St. Petersburg as she was in London and is thriving in the social scene. She has become a patroness of the Imperial Russian Ballet, which, to be honest with you, is worse than the bloody opera. I have NEVER found a way to become bored more quickly. Your flask solution only goes so far to buffer the pain.

Charlie chuckled, remembering how many bottles of vodka and bourbon he and Fillip had consumed when Bella and Rebecca just had to see the newest opera. He was grateful Culpeper offered no such venue. The traveling theater troupes were tolerable, giving them just enough of a cultural repast that Rebecca did not seem to pine for the opera. He adjusted his glasses and continued reading;

I want to thank you for your kind letter of condolence on Czar Alexander's assassination. While Alexander II was very fond of you, and Czarina Marie was very appreciative of your letter, I fear our new emperor is not as warm toward you, or to be honest any Americans in general. After his father "The Liberator" was blown up in front of him by one of the very class of people he liberated, Czar Alexovich has withdrawn from his father's progressive position. The movement toward creating a constitutional monarchy has been squashed and not too kindly. The Ohkrana has been arresting people all across the country and political suppression is blatant. I fear that the atmosphere in Moscow is very tense, and I am glad that we chose to live here in St. Petersburg when I retired.

Alas, retirement is decidedly boring. I stay at home, tend to my library and gardens, and escort my wife to events as required. Perhaps it is time to return to London.

Filipp went on to convey news of various friends and acquaintances, and ended by sending his love to Rebecca and regards to Rex and the children.

Charlie smiled ruefully. The situation in Russia was obviously worse that the politics of the red shirts and Ku Klux Klan in the States. He tossed the letter over to Rex, shaking his head as he did so. "My friend, if you have any Russian investments, I would suggest you shed them. I will be doing so with mine."

Rebecca flipped Andy's letter over to his father.

Charlie looked at her questioningly. "Does he actually have any news?"

Rebecca shook her head. "No, it is more of the usual. His 'how are you, I am fine, work is boring, but at least I am making money.' That is about the limit of it. At least there has not been a 'Please send me money' message."

"Well, I guess that is something. My sources in Richmond say he seems to be doing well. Yes, he is gambling, and yes, he has found a group of ladies to keep company with on Friday and Saturday nights, but at least it is a reasonably reputable house of ill repute."

"Oh, like Lizzie's!" Rebecca laughed. It seemed that Andy was settling down, sort of.

Rex and Rebecca both dove into their letters from Charlotte. The Transvaal Rebellion had ended in March and Freddy had returned from the front mostly intact. He had risen to the rank of regimental sergeant major, and had not seen as much actual fighting as many, but instead had been responsible for maintaining morale and caring for the battered and injured boys who did not even have the glory of having won the war. All in all, it was a disheartening experience.

Charlotte's children were rapidly approaching their teens, and she was looking to Rebecca for advice on how to give them enough freedom to be responsible, but not so much to become wild. Given the situation with Andy, Rebecca was not sure she could give any useful advice.

Rex's other letter, the one from the Chinese embassy, was enough to have his usually calm features draw into a frown of annoyance. The old empress, Empress Dowager Ci'an had died, leaving the Empress Dowager Cixi in full control of the court. Rex's rather nebulous relationship as a member of the family but an unwelcome member of the court was further re-enforced. Cixi did not want him anywhere in Asia, let alone to return to China. The letter was a short, rather forcible reminder of his status as an unofficial exile.

~

MONDAY MAY 23, 1881

Mr. Craven and Mr. Wilson were standing outside Professor Putnam's door that morning when Em arrived.

"Gentlemen, what can I do for you?" She was stunned to see the two gentlemen just five weeks after their first meeting.

"Miss Redmond, we were hoping you and Professor Putnam would have some time to come and review the current version of the research car. It still needs some finishing touches, but if you want any changes made, now is the time to ask for them."

"I don't know what Professor Putnam's schedule is today, but I suspect he will rearrange it for you, gentlemen. Would you like some tea while we wait?"

As the three of them strolled down toward the conference room and the tea pot, Professor Putnam arrived. He looked surprised. "Gentlemen, to what do we owe the pleasure of your company?"

"Ah, Professor. Good morning." Craven smiled. "It is time to review the car and make any adjustments you want before we finish up."

"Oh, my! Excellent. Shall we have a cup of tea and then head over to the rail yard?"

After a pleasant cup of tea with polite but insubstantial chat, they made the short trip over to the train yard in Craven's carriage. The new car was standing on a side rail, with various scaffolding and ramps still attached.

"Please, be careful. There may still be some saw dust around, but we wanted you to see it at this point so if you wanted to make any changes, it would be less complicated."

The four of them filed into the car. At the front were two small sleeping compartments, large enough to be comfortable, but not wasting any available space either. The hallway opened into a large area fitted with racks of storage chests, work tables, and with large windows on both sides and in the ceiling. Beyond that were a compact galley and larder, two more sleeping compartments, and a toilet and bathing room at the end of the car. Wilson pointed out that there were additional bunks that could be let down in the work room area.

"What do you think, Professor? Miss Redmond?" Craven and Wilson were both beaming with pride in their company's craftsmanship.

Em deferred to Professor Putnam as they walked back out of the car. "I believe this has the flexibility and capacity to support a wide range of research efforts. It is well thought out and beautifully constructed, gentlemen. The university is very grateful for your hard work."

"Oh, no, Professor. See," he said pointing to a neat brass plate on the door of the car, "we have acknowledged this as the gift of Mrs. Rebecca Redmond."

Em cleared her throat. "Gentlemen, my mother is very

discrete about her gifts and would prefer this one remain anonymous, please."

Both men looked a little surprised. In this day and age, magnanimous gifts like this were usually labeled with the contributor's name in large letters. Competition among the wealthy about their philanthropy was common; a request for anonymity was unusual to say the least. "Well, of course, Miss Redmond. We will have the plaque removed."

"Then perhaps the car should be called the Peabody Museum Mobile Research Laboratory," Putnam suggested with a shrug in Em's direction.

"An excellent idea, Professor." Em grinned. "Thank you, gentlemen."

"Of course, ma'am." Wilson cleared his throat and formally announced, "The Peabody Museum Mobile Research Laboratory will be ready for use within three weeks, and in the spirit of support for the university, the George Pullman Company will provide storage here in Cambridge at no charge when the car is not in use."

"My mother will be very pleased."

"So will the university."

Craven and Wilson beamed as they returned Em and the Professor to their offices.

Em went through the rest of the day with a small, satisfied smile on her face. Even Baer's digs did not shake her good mood. That evening after dinner, she wrote her mother, describing the Peabody Museum Mobile Research Laboratory in great and appreciative detail.

~

SATURDAY, JUNE 11, 1881

Andy and his gambling buddy Jamie Witt strolled out of the Richmond Theatre, having seen the Texas Jack Combination perform their play *Life on the Border*.

"Well, at least that was cheaper than an evening at O'Grady's playing poker." Witt was trying to make light of the less than thrilling stage performance.

"Yeah," grumbled Andy. "Lousy rope tricks, fake shooting, and not a horse or real Indian in sight. Who do they think they're fooling?"

"Andy, every one of us has read the dime novels about folks like Bill Cody and Wild Bill Hickok. How could something like that be put on a stage?"

"Stage, my ass. Put it in a tent, like the circus. Have real people, real horses, and real guns. Show us what it was really like!"

"You think the stuff in those books is real?"

"Well, it's more real that the horseshit we just spent two dollars each on!" Andy stomped down the street, Jamie racing to catch up.

"Where are you going?"

"I'm going to go find a drink, a game, and a woman. There's still time to have at least a little fun tonight."

TUESDAY, JUNE 14, 1881

Charlie had been pacing the floor since yesterday morning. The proctor for Buddy's entrance examination to West Point was due to arrive sometime this week. The exact date had not been conveyed, just that he would arrive between June 13th and June 17th.

Surprisingly, Buddy appeared to be as cool as a cucumber. As he explained to his mother, he had done everything he could, read every book, worked every problem in mathematics, physics and engineering he could. John had quizzed him until they were both blue in the face. His father had asked Senator Mahone to nominate him officially to West Point, and General Schofield had endorsed the nomination. In addition, Buddy was a legacy, and that always was an advantage, even if it was not officially acknowledged. There was nothing more to be done – it just had to be enough.

Otis was downstairs working in the wine cellar when the two officers knocked at the front door. One of the junior footmen, Seth Jones, welcomed them in.

"Good morning, gentlemen. How can I help you?"

"Good morning. I am Major Hauptmann. This is Captain Leyland. We are here to see Mr. Redmond."

"Yes, gentlemen. Please follow me. I will take you to his office."

The two officers looked at one another, a little confused. They were expecting to be taken to see a sixteen-year-old boy. Most young men of that age did not have an office.

The young footmen led them up the stairs to Charlie's office and knocked on the door, then entered. "General, there are two officers here to see you." He then stepped aside.

Hauptmann stepped into the room followed by Leyland. Both men looked at the tall, graying gentleman standing behind the desk. They glanced around and saw Charlie's swords, insignia and medals displayed above the fireplace. Both of them snapped to attention and saluted.

Leyland, as the actual proctor, should have spoken up, but

somehow his tongue seemed to have adhered to the roof of his mouth when faced with this cavalry legend. Hauptmann stepped in. "General, please excuse us. We are here to see your son."

"Yes, gentlemen. We have been expecting you. Buddy is downstairs in the library. Shall I take you to him?"

Hauptmann nudged Leyland, who finally found his voice. "No, sir. Could you just have your man take us down? We are not supposed to interact with the family. I am the proctor, and the major has come along as a courtesy to you so that the examination can be graded immediately."

Charlie called Seth back and the two officers were escorted to the correct Mr. Redmond.

Seth left the officers in the room with Mr. Buddy, then scurried downstairs to collect coffee for them.

"Well, Aunt Beulah, the big day has arrived. The officers are up there with Mr. Buddy and giving him the test," Seth panted to Beulah and CeCe. "I took them up to Gen'l Charlie first. Guess I shouldn't have, since they only wanted to see Mr. Buddy. Hope I don't get yelled at for that. Can I take the tray up for them?"

Beulah could not keep her young nephew from babbling, so she looked at CeCe, who just quietly thrust the tray with the coffee service into his hands and shooed him back out the door.

Seth knocked very softly, then let himself into the library. Buddy was seated at the big table. There was nothing on it. Leyland was standing across from him with a stop watch in one hand and a rather thick booklet in the other. The major had settled into one of the deep leather chairs on the other side of the room and was thumbing through a book he had obviously plucked from the shelves.

Buddy looked up. "Thank you, Seth. Please, set the coffee on the sideboard." He turned to Leyland. "Captain, what time would you like to break for lunch?"

"I'm sorry, Mr. Redmond. This is an examination. There will be no breaks until the test is completed."

"Oh." Buddy swallowed hard. "Then, sir, shall we begin?"

With that, Seth discretely put down the coffee service and slipped out the door.

~

CHARLIE RAN INTO THE SITTING ROOM, WHERE REBECCA AND Rex were playing chess, and announced, rather dramatically, "Buddy is being tested."

Rebecca moved a piece on the board and quietly said, "Check." She then looked at her husband, who was yanking on the pull that would summon Seth. "We were expecting them. I am sure Buddy is prepared."

Charlie continued to yank on the bell pull. "Yes, but he is being tested. What if he..."

Rex looked up. "Charlie, he will not fail."

"But what if he does?"

"He will not fail."

Seth came through the door without bothering to knock first. The urgency of the clanging downstairs sent a clear message to the young man. He was just hoping he still had a job, based on how the bell had been ringing.

Charlie turned to him. "Ah, Seth. What took you so long? When are they going to break for lunch?"

"They are not going to break, sir. They said the test will go until it is completed."

Charlie just looked at him, blinking like an owl.

Softly, Rebecca said, "Seth, would you ask CeCe to prepare for two guests for supper? And warn her that they will be hungry."

Seth excused himself and escaped.

Charlie began to pace.

Rebecca and Rex went back to their game.

"Checkmate."

Rebecca and Rex reset the chessmen and started another game.

Charlie continued to pace.

Rebecca won another game.

"Charles Redmond, would you please light somewhere? This is a new carpet!" Rebecca snapped at him.

"But Rebecca..." Charlie whined.

"All right. That is enough." She stood and rang for Seth – again.

The boy came running in. "Seth, please, have my carriage brought around as quickly as possible. We are going into town."

"Yes, ma'am."

"Now, gentlemen, if the two of you would please prepare yourselves, I expect us to leave as soon as possible."

Charlie looked a little confused. "But dear, how can we leave while Buddy is—"

Rebecca interrupted him. "We are leaving. Now. Before you drive me insane."

"Yes, ma'am."

Rex looked at his friend and started chuckling. "Charlie, if I did not know better, I would say you are acting like a first-time expecting father who was locked out of the birthing room."

They drove into Culpeper, stopping at the iron works to order some new railings for the gazebo, then went to Jocko's for lunch. Rebecca and Ro found several players for an afternoon of cards, and at four o'clock, she finally relented and let Charlie return home.

Major Hauptmann, Captain Leyland, and Buddy were just emerging from the library as they came into the front hall.

Immediately, Charlie looked to the senior officer. "Well, how did he do?"

Hauptmann turned to Buddy, ignoring the angst-ridden father. "Congratulations, Mr. Redmond. I am sure General Schofield will be happy to see you this fall."

Before Charlie could ask anything, Rebecca smoothly cut in. "That is wonderful, Buddy. Gentlemen, would you care to join us for supper?"

"Thank you, Mrs. Redmond, but we need to get back to the train station."

"Very well, gentlemen. Let me send for your mounts," Rebecca said as she motioned to Seth.

As they waited for the horses, Charlie could not resist the urge to question Leyland and Hauptmann. "So how did my boy do?"

"He passed." Hauptmann was not going to be swayed.

"Gentlemen, your horses are here." Seth interrupted Charlie's futile efforts.

"Thank you." Hauptmann turned to Rex and the assembled Redmonds. "I hate to test and run, but I really must get back to DC this evening."

And with that, they left.

~

TUESDAY, JUNE 21, 1881

Darby sorted through the mail his secretary had sent from his office in Richmond. Even during his supposed time off, there was always something coming in from the office that needed his attention.

Most of it was mundane communications concerning various clients and cases his firm was handling. A request for an opinion or guidance on a matter or two. Nothing earth shaking.

The thick envelope from a law firm in Lexington, Kentucky caught his attention. Retrieving his letter opener from his desk set, he sliced cleanly into the parcel and removed a substantial set of documents.

After reading through the first few pages, he gathered them up, slid them back into the envelope and stood, grabbing his coat from the back of his chair. He slipped his suitcoat on as he made his way to his wife's parlor.

Stella was seated near a window that brought a gentle breeze into the room. She had in her hands some mending, her sewing basket open on the floor next to her chair. He smiled as he realized she was mending something for one of the children.

Darby whispered in his wife's delicate ear before placing a playful kiss on her neck, "You can buy new clothes for the children. We are not destitute."

Stella laughed and nodded, caressing his cheek before he pulled away completely. "Yes, I know that, but why in the world have the expense of new clothes when these are still perfectly fine? I only need to mend a tear or two. Perhaps we should spend some time hammering down loose nails. It will be easier on their clothing."

"My beautiful, practical wife. I love you madly." He smiled at her, his mirth showing in his eyes. "I have to step out for a bit and go see my sister. Some family business has come up and I need to let her know."

"What is it, Darby?"

"Our aunt Victoria Landau has passed away and apparently, Sue and I are her heirs."

Stella looked up, surprised. "I didn't even know you had an Aunt Victoria."

"My blood mother's sister. We only met her once. As a matter of fact, I think you were there. She appeared unannounced at the house a couple of days before Thanksgiving when you and I were twelve. It was not a pleasant visit. She tried to take Sue and me with her. That is when Papa and Mama officially adopted us. Your father handled the legal adoption right then. I need to go see Sue."

"Ah, yes, I do remember that vaguely. We had two Thanksgiving dinners that year. By all means, sweetheart. I shall be here mending."

Darby kissed his wife on the forehead and then made his way to the barn to saddle his horse. Tucking the papers in his saddlebags, he headed in a meandering way towards Mountain View. He suspected Sue would be there at this time of day.

He was correct; she was at Mountain View, but not in her office as he expected. Sue was in the arena lunging a horse. He smiled and shook his head. "Just like Mama," he mumbled as he retrieved the papers from his bags.

Making his way to the small gazebo at the south end of the arena fence, he tossed the papers on a bench before pouring himself a glass of lemonade from the pitcher on the table in the center of the structure.

Taking a seat, he sipped his drink and watched his sister work. He saw several of the men who worked at the stables standing around the far side of the fence watching Sue as well.

He sighed, knowing that most men did not take well to a woman trying to interfere in a man's world. Especially one as tough and competitive as the world of horse breeding and training.

Men who worked at Redmond Stables knew when they were hired that it was a business owned and run by women. They either had to adjust their attitudes or keep their opinions to themselves. Giving any guff at all over that fact alone would earn them a hard boot right back out the gate, usually delivered by an irate Charlie. The patriarch of the family had no tolerance for those who did not respect the authority of the Redmond women.

Darby's mama and sister where both very astute businesswomen and their knowledge of horses was encyclopedic, and most of the men they worked with respected them for that fact if nothing else.

Now Sue, like Rebecca before her stroke, could handle any horse God saw fit to put on His good, green Earth. Darby had seen her tame stallions' others had deemed dangerous and in need of a bullet.

One of Sue's finest studs was the result of his sister betting she could gentle him in three days.

She did it in two.

Now the horse threw some of the finest foals that Redmond Stables could offer, second only to foals sired by Blackjack.

Darby waited patiently for her to complete her time with the horse. He was in no real hurry to have this discussion anyhow. He knew what was about to happen and he was dreading it. He had time for a second glass of lemonade before she finally handed the gelding off to another trainer and made her way to him.

"Well, hello, big brother!" She leaned over and kissed his cheek. "What brings you out? I figured you were home making another little Redmond."

"Very funny, little sister." He chuckled with a nod. "Stella is quite happy not to be expecting this year. We are trying to control Grandpa Redmond's bunny population on the other side of the property."

Sue laughed, pouring herself a glass from the pitcher as she settled down at the table. "So, what does bring you over? Papa is not home and I know you do not need a horse or carriage."

He nodded and retrieved the papers. "I know. This is about us." He sighed as he pulled the documents from their confinement. "Aunt Victoria passed away and we have inherited her estate."

Sue blanched, and it was not the lemonade. "Aunt Victoria? That horrible woman from Tennessee, was it?"

"Kentucky. I can see you have the same wonderful memory of our visit from her as I do."

"Darby, to be honest, I don't really. I was young and she scared me witless. All I remember clearly about her visit is how Mama held onto us and cried when she left."

"Well, here is the situation. There is an estate and we are the only heirs."

"What does that mean? What is the estate made of?"

"Property."

"Property is always nice."

"In Kentucky."

"That could be a bit of a headache."

"I'm glad you see it that way. Perhaps we should just sell it and split the money?"

"What kind of property is it? A house? A business?"

"It's a…, um," he hedged. "A horse farm."

"A horse farm? How could we possibly think of selling a horse farm without going to see it first?"

"Sue…"

"Darby, in case you missed it while you were in school, horses are the family business."

"Horses are your business."

"Yes, and now I own a horse farm in Kentucky too," she chirped happily.

"Half a horse farm."

"We need to go see this property."

He sighed deeply, his chin dropping to his chest. "You are right, of course. I could go next week. Would that work for you?"

"I can make sure that Jerry is squared with Little Andy." She nodded. "Yes, next week will be fine."

"I will make the arrangements and let you know."

"Thank you. Do we know anything else at this point?"

With another sigh, he began filtering through the papers. "A farm in Harrodsburg, Kentucky. Just southwest of Lexington. Apparently, it is about one hundred acres with the buildings you would expect. A house built in," he paused, scanning the page. "eighteen thirty-nine. Barns. Outbuildings. Sheds. Hay storage and the like."

"How many horses? Does it say?"

He thumbed through a few pages and offered, "Looks like about twenty to twenty-five."

Sue looked thoughtful as she sipped her lemonade. "About half the size we have here. I bet they are all thoroughbreds."

"And probably worth a tenth."

"Darby, don't be such a snot. We have no way of knowing what is there until we see it with our own eyes."

"You sound just like Mama."

"Thank you. I take that as quite the compliment."

⟳

WEDNESDAY, JUNE 22, 1881

"You ARE joking!" Sue was in complete disbelief. She glanced at the map he had tossed across her desk.

Darby shook his head. "I'm sorry, Sue, but I'm not. The trip to Kentucky will be time consuming. It will take a week. One way! Let's just sell the place! It's going to cost a month minimum to just go look at it. Aunt Victoria's attorney is prepared to sell it and the money is not insubstantial. You could do a million new improvements here and buy yourself a whole herd of new horses. I will have to take an extended leave from the office."

"Well, since your name is on the door, I doubt there will be a problem. I know you were planning on taking most of the summer off anyhow."

"Yes! But not to go chasing after some damn horses in Kentucky."

"Then I will go by myself."

"God! You are stubborn!"

"Not at all. I am being practical from a business perspective. I have now had a chance to read through those documents and Aunt Victoria has some fine horses over there. Horses I may want to add to my program. We own them; I need to go see them."

"Why not just have them shipped here?"

"Do you have any idea how much it costs to move horses around? Brother dear, you only ship a horse when you have no other options. We have a built-in facility there. Not to mention that the Kentucky horse world is very different from the Virginia horse world. They do flats racing like we saw in England. As a matter of fact, the premier event in in the state, the Kentucky Derby, has been running for six years now and is strictly based on three races in England, including Epsom. Aunt Victoria's horses are probably racers, not jumpers and hunters like we do here for cross country. Our horses are built for stamina. Her horses are probably built for speed. This is an opportunity to open up Redmond Stables in other areas. Mama and Papa say the role of the horse is going to change. I believe them, and when it does, I want to make sure we are ready to change with it."

"Fine!" Darby's hands went up impatiently. "I will make our travel arrangements and you should be prepared to leave on Friday."

"Fine! I will be." Sue mimicked his gesture and tone. "Make sure we have a sleeping car!"

"I'm going to borrow Mama's," he yelled as he turned and stomped out the office door. "I hate you, little sister!"

"No, you don't, big brother!" Sue laughed as she listened to his boots hammer against the kitchen floor on his way out. "Oh, CeCe will be on you about slamming the back door," she muttered as she folded up his map and laid it aside. "How long have you lived here that you don't know that?"

"Miss Sue!" CeCe yelled from the kitchen. "I'm gonna tan your brother! Slammin' my kitchen door like that!"

"Tell him!" Sue shook her head and laughed as she yelled to the cook. "You know we ain't got no control of these Redmond men!"

One of the cook's assistances appeared at the door a moment later with a coffee tray for Sue, and the cook herself soon followed with a laugh and a huge grin. "I know that's right! Miss Rebecca, God bless her, has an ornery bunch of men. I remember some of the things General Charlie has gotten up to in my time growing up in this kitchen."

Sue stopped working on her ledger. She sat back in her chair, an evil grin crossing her lips. "Really?" She gestured to the armchair next to her desk. "Do tell."

The cook laughed as the tray was placed down between them. She poured two cups of coffee, winking as she did. "Just like my mama and yours. They spent more than a few hours sitting in here doing just this."

"Then let us carry-on time-honored traditions." Sue nodded, pulling a cookie tin from her desk drawer and opening it. She sat the cookies on the corner of her desk and grinned shamelessly at the cook. "I believe you know stories about my papa."

CHAPTER 13

"WE NEED A FAVOR," Sue and Darby chorused.

Charlie rolled his eyes. Rebecca sighed. They might now be adults, married and with children of their own, but they were still children when it came to dealing with their own parents. And one thing about being their parents was that, no matter what else was going on, when the children needed them, they were always available.

"Hello, children." Charlie was cautious. The older they got, the more expensive it got when they needed something. Rebecca just lifted her face for the mandatory kisses on the cheek from each of her progeny.

"What is so urgently needed that we are not allowed to relax, enjoy our lunch, and have a glass or two of lemonade to cool down in this miserable heat?" Charlie poured a glass of the cooling fluid for Rebecca as he spoke, handing her both the lemonade and the ratafia. He knew she would alternate between them all afternoon.

"Well, actually, we need to ask you, Mama." Darby turned his most charming smile, the one she loved so much, on his mother. "You see, Aunt Victoria passed away and left us her property in Kentucky."

Sue broke in over her brother. "It's a horse farm, Mama! Just outside of Lexington, with about twenty-five head, and since there are several Kentucky Derby winners who have been bred in the area, I am hoping Aunt Victoria had the good sense to have bred some of her stock to the winners. But I'll have to see the books first and..."

Darby took over again. "There is property and a variety of estate issues to deal with, as well as the herd, and I would like to attend to it as quickly as possible."

Sue continued filling Mama in on the blasted horses. "Not to mention that it is where James Ben Ali Haggin is from! You know about his breeding farm in California. I am hoping perhaps some of his family influence remains in the area. Maybe there is a cousin in the breeding business."

Rebecca just nodded while Darby looked angry and frustrated, and poor Charlie just looked bewildered. Rebecca took pity on her confused husband. "Darling, Ben Ali Haggin is a major breeder of race horses. Sue is right; we do need to diversify our stock." She looked at her children. "I assume you want the train car to get you to Kentucky." She chuckled, sipped her lemonade and asked, "When do you plan to leave?"

Darby answered, never taking his eyes from the face of his determined sister. "In the morning. I already have the connections booked."

Charlie looked at his oldest son. "Confident, were you?"

Finally, Darby broke eye contact with Sue and looked to his

father. "Well, Papa, it's Mama and Sue and there are horses involved, and sometimes I suspect they love horses more than they love people."

Rebecca nodded. "Sometimes we do, son. Sometimes we do."

~

JUST AS THE SUN WAS SETTING, EM CLIMBED OFF THE REGULAR passenger train from Washington. She left her trunk with the station master and trudged over to Jocko's Pub. Jamie Benson was behind the bar, cleaning up from the pre-dinner crowd and getting ready for the after-dinner regulars.

"Why Miss Emily, what are you doing here?"

"Good evening, Mr. Benson. My train was late and I was hoping I could find someone over here who could give me a ride out to Mountain View."

Ro Jackson heard Em's voice from the kitchen and came tromping out. "Emily Redmond, what are you doing in this tavern? And why didn't your father send a carriage?"

"Good evening, Miss Ro. I am looking for a ride home actually because my father and mother don't know I'm coming. I'm a bit of a surprise."

Ro looked at Em with an expression that was hard for the younger woman to read; half amusement, half annoyance. "A most welcomed one, I would think." She stripped off the apron covering her clothes. "Get your stuff and meet me out back."

"Um, my trunk is at the station."

"Fine. We will stop on the way."

"Yes, ma'am."

It was almost completely dark by the time Ro pulled up in front of Mountain View, but there was a heavenly, comforting glow from the lights in the windows that told the young Redmond woman she was finally home.

Em slid down from the wagon, almost running up the steps to push open the front door, ringing for Otis or one of the footmen to come get her trunk.

"Thank you for the ride, Miss Ro," she called as two boys bowed and nodded past her to grab the bags from the porch.

"That's all right, Em. Tell your mother that Allison and I will be over in a couple of days."

"Yes, ma'am."

With that, Ro whistled to her horse, who loped off down the driveway.

Em trudged back in to see her trunk and carpet bag making their way up the stairs propelled by a pair of long legs. She could not tell who was carrying her baggage, but was very grateful it wasn't her. A light appeared at the end of the hall as the door to the family parlor opened and Charlie peered out to see what the commotion was.

"IMP! What the he...er...heck are you doing here?"

"Oh, Papa." Em dashed down the hall and threw herself into his chest, relishing the feeling of his arms wrapping around her. "I have been nice, and patient, and proper, and lady-like for weeks, no, months! I needed a little while to just be me!"

Charlie's arms tightened around his first child. He laughed in her ear. "Come in and say hello to your mother."

He ushered Em into the parlor, where Rebecca and Rex were waiting with curious looks on their faces.

Charlie opened the heavy door with a flourish. "Look what I found!"

"EM!" Rebecca extended open arms to her wandering daughter.

Rex showed a rare grin as Em dashed across the room, falling at her mother's knees while Rebecca embraced her scholar.

"Are you hungry?" Rebecca was first and always a mother, and food was the currency of motherhood.

Em nodded gratefully, sitting back on the floor, her heels tucked under her rump. At Mama's knees was always the best and safest place to be if Papa's arms were otherwise occupied. "Starving. Exhausted and starving."

Rex rang for the kitchen while Em picked herself up from the floor and then promptly collapsed in a chair, happily consuming a full glass of Papa's minted iced tea in one long draught.

He asked gently, but with quirked brow, as he watched her imbibe, damn glad it was not liquor. "So, what brought you home? And why no message to let us know you were coming? I would have made arrangements for you."

"I just needed to get out of there for a few weeks before we begin the dig. We finished planning early, thanks to you, Mama, and we are not supposed to start until September. I just grabbed my things and headed home."

Rebecca grinned at her daughter. "I am so glad my little contribution got you home early. What is your plan for this trip?"

"I have no plan except to sleep, relax, and try to stay cool. Boston turns into this miserable, hot, muggy, smelly place in the summer. Very much like London. It is a blessing our home is already in the country."

Charlie looked at his wife. "So, my dear, what did you do to improve our daughter's life?"

Rebecca waved him off. "Oh, just a little something to make field work a bit easier. We can talk about it later."

Em laughed. "A little something, huh? Papa, she bought us the most magnifi—"

Rebecca interrupted, and rather sternly pronounced, "I said we will talk about it later."

Charlie looked at his daughter. She was clearly tired, and dusty and sweaty from the train ride home. Regular train cars were nowhere near as comfortable as the family was used to. "I would say there was something else that ran you out of town, Imp. Do you want to talk about it?"

"Not tonight, Papa. Can we discuss it later?"

CeCe entered just then, carrying a tray with a delicious cold cantaloupe soup, biscuits with shaved ham, and fresh strawberries and cream. A new pitcher of iced tea and another of lemonade with sweat from the ice already gathering on the pitchers were brought in by the fireboy who was following behind her. There was a small plate covered with a napkin as well. When CeCe removed the napkin, beautiful butterscotch cookies were waiting.

"Welcome home, Miss Em. Your father has me keep the cookies on hand all the time. He uses them to bribe the grandchildren now."

Em laughed as she picked up a cookie before she even touched any of the other treats on the tray. Around a mouthful of crumbs, she mumbled, "Bless you, CeCe. I'm not really home till I have one of your mama's butterscotch cookies."

"Tell us about your plans, dear," Rebecca inquired as reasonably as possible.

"Oh, Mama, can we do this tomorrow? I am so tired. I just need food, a bath, and my bed."

"Of course, dear." Rebecca was disappointed. Her girl was home and she wanted every scrap of information and time she could get, but looking into Em's tired eyes was enough to have Rebecca curb her curiosity. There was a reason for this unexpected appearance, but she would wait until Em was ready.

FRIDAY, JUNE 24, 1881

Rebecca sat in her chair beside the empty fireplace in the family parlor. She was fidgeting, first playing with her knitting but barely finishing one row of stitches, then leafing through the newspaper, flipping pages of a fashion magazine, polishing her monocle using a fine linen cloth, then back to the magazine, then polishing her monocle again. Charlie poured himself another cup of mid-morning coffee and strolled out the French doors to stand on the veranda and scan the horses working in the near paddocks. Two of Jack's newest progeny were being trained and he could not resist seeing how the offspring of his old friend worked when asked.

He also knew why his wife was a ball of nerves. Sue and Darby had come by early that morning to pick up Sue's breed books on their way to the train station and Kentucky. Buddy had grabbed a quick breakfast and headed out to do some fishing with some of the boys from town. Rex and Chris had eaten early and left to make rounds at the hospital before eight.

Em had not yet appeared. For a member of her family to not be up and eating breakfast by seven was unusual, but as far as Rebecca was concerned, failure to come down for breakfast by eight usually meant someone was deathly ill. Ten o'clock meant someone had died.

Rebecca hauled herself to her feet. "I am going to go check on her. Something must be wrong."

"Rebecca, dear." Charlie turned to his wife and sighed. "The only thing that is wrong is that she has been working very hard, made a quick and tiring trip home at the last minute, and is probably still sleeping. Leave her be. Let her rest."

"But Charlie..." Rebecca started to protest, a whine that was interrupted by the door opening and a still sleepy looking Em staggering in.

"Please, tell me there is still some coffee. I need some coffee, even if it is cold and greasy." She slogged over to the sideboard, grabbed a cup, poured coffee and drank it all down in one draught, then poured another cup.

Rebecca eyed her daughter, her eyebrows crawling up her forehead. "Emily Adams Redmond, what is wrong with you?" Her tone was stern. Her disapproval of Em appearing after ten o'clock wearing her slippers and robe instead of a proper morning dress was manifest.

"Mother, please. Before I got home last night, I had been up for thirty-six hours straight. I have been a perfect, proper southern lady every day and night for months, even though I sometimes had to grit my teeth to do it. I THOUGHT that being home would allow me the indulgence of being a bit informal and relaxed."

Charlie stepped in from the veranda, where he had listened to this charming exchange between his fidgety wife and his tired daughter with more than a little amused annoyance. "Ladies, may I suggest you two start the morning over? And Em, I do like your morning dishabille."

"Good morning, Mama, Papa. I do apologize for my lateness this morning, but it has been a few exhausting days."

"Good morning, daughter. Please, get some coffee and come tell me about it. Would you like me to ring for some breakfast?" Rebecca took Charlie's rebuke as well as Em had, though she still looked a little annoyed.

"Much better, ladies," Charlie commented as he strolled over to join them.

"About breakfast, no, thank you. It is not that long until CeCe will have luncheon ready. I can wait until then."

"Why are you so tired and obviously frustrated?" Papa had no compunction about cutting to the heart of the matter.

"Oh, well, we have been working like mad to get everything in order for the site survey this fall in Ohio. There are between twenty-five and thirty sites across the state and we are going to attempt to conduct preliminary surveys of all of them in a matter of about ninety to a hundred and twenty days. It has been insane."

Rebecca interjected, "I thought you were going to go and dig at the Serpent Mound."

"We were, but your beautiful gift made this survey possible. This way, we can take a more careful look at the cultures involved, since there are at least three different cultural groups associated with the mounds in Ohio."

Charlie's eyebrows went up. *Rebecca's beautiful gift?* "So, tell me about this gift." He bit his bottom lip as he looked down at his wife and smiled; he was truly amused.

Em's face lit up. "Oh, Papa. Mama asked Mr. Pullman's company to make this wonderful combination of rolling research laboratory and field camp in one of his new cars. It is beautiful. It has sleeping quarters, wash rooms, a galley kitchen, and a huge, well-lit lab with lots of storage to clean, catalog, and store artifacts. It is wonderful. It will make our work so much easier."

"Really?" Charlie scratched his chin and looked at his wife. "Sounds like an extravagant gift."

Rebecca lowered her head. "It was, but Em and her colleagues needed it and I had the funds so..."

"So, you went and ordered it. Well, dear, this is your response to my home for war widows and orphans."

"Oh, Charlie, is that what you are doing with the Charleston property?"

"I think so, but let us focus on Em's issues." Charlie turned to his daughter. "So, Imp, what has you so frustrated? And do not try to white wash it. I can always tell when you are angry, and I think you are plenty angry at someone."

"It's that Horatio Hale. I swear, Papa, that man takes every opportunity he can to irritate or insult me. Somehow, he thinks that women are simply not smart enough to be scientists. He thinks I should be quiet, sit in the corner, make tea, and take notes for the MEN."

Rebecca nodded as she sipped her coffee. "My dear daughter, I have spent my whole life dealing with men like him. All you can do is smile sweetly and beat the tar out of him at his own game."

Charlie looked thoughtful. "What kinds of things does he say to you? I have found that when someone is unjustifiably denigrating, they are usually accusing you of something they themselves are guilty of."

"Hummm. He does keep coming back to the idea that you bought my way into graduate school."

"Let me suggest we check into his academic background. It may give you some ammunition with which to counter his arguments."

Rebecca grinned at her daughter. "I can tell you from experience, it is a great deal of fun to thoroughly whup those annoying men."

Later that day, Rebecca handed Em a slip of paper. On it was written the address of the Pinkerton Agency and the name of the person they kept on retainer for minor issues.

~

FRIDAY, JULY 1, 1881

Darby cursed under his breath for what had to be the hundredth time as he tried to yank his mud-caked boot loose from the earth that seemed to be aching to suck him down.

"Does it do anything in Kentucky besides rain?" The lawyer grumbled as he tried to follow his sister to the next area everyone wanted to call a pasture. All Darby could see was swamp.

"It rains in Virginia too, brother dear," Sue called over her shoulder as she led the group toward the next gate.

"Not every DAMN day!" Darby yelled back.

Sue turned on her heel and squared her shoulders. Darby only had a few seconds to realize that everything Mama had ever taught Sue about business, horses, and especially the horse business was about to hit him square in the chest.

"Then go back to the house and have a cup of coffee. Go back to Virginia for all I care, Mr. Redmond!" Sue's fists fell to her hips as she took a deep breath, and the four barn hands who had been following her all took a half step back. "I have to look at and evaluate these horses. I do NOT need YOUR help to do it. As a matter of fact, brother dear," she took a full step forward, coming nose to nose with him, "we might get it all done a little bit faster if we didn't have to listen to YOU whine and complain about the whole process every step of the way!"

"I think I'll go back to the house."

"What a grand idea," Sue said slowly, twitching her brows as she finished. Darby recognized it as another of Mama's traits. She did it when she was done talking and it was time for you to go.

He nodded quickly, without a word, and turned for the house.

⚬

DARBY WAS ON HIS FOURTH CUP OF COFFEE AND THIRD BUSINESS ledger for their aunt's farm by the time Sue came back an hour later. She was wet, muddy, and happy as a clam. She had a towel around her neck and patted the dampness from her face and hair as she made her way to the coffee.

"How are the horses?" Darby asked without looking up from the ledger.

"There is some very fine horseflesh here. Victoria also had the good sense to breed to the last five Derby winners. That's very big for us. It will take me some time to get the books in order. Apparently, when Victoria got sick, the books were passed around and no one took proper care of them. That's going to be a bit of a headache, but with a month or so of effort..."

"A month!" Darby shook his head vigorously. "There is no way we are staying here for a month."

Sue sighed, placed her coffee cup in its saucer, and laced her fingers together, placing her hands very lady like in her lap, before smiling sweetly and saying, "I told you earlier today, brother dear, go back to Virginia any time you like."

"And face Papa and your husband because I left you here alone?" He shook his head and laughed. "I don't think so, sister dear. You are simply going to have to figure out how to handle it more expediently."

"Darby! I am perfectly capable of handling myself and this farm. I do run Redmond Stables and the entire staff there is made up of men. I know that is what you are concerned about."

"And those men damn well know not to give you guff or Papa will bury them in three adjacent counties. These men already have a bad smell under their nose because you came here to take over."

"Victoria ran the place; why should my presence be a problem?"

Darby sat back and sighed as he tapped the financial ledgers. "That's the thing. Victoria didn't run this farm. Her farm manager, a Mr. Braxton, ran every detail and he expected he would be remembered in the will. He wasn't. He's not happy. He was at least hoping for a male heir to arrive."

"Looking to keep the place to himself? Has he at least done a decent job of managing the place?"

"For the most part. You've seen the place. It could use some work, but it's certainly a solid property with a good history."

"What is the property worth? I have a general idea of the horses, but I really need to get those books squared away to have a real number."

"Well, seventy-five acres of improved land at the top dollar in the area right now would be twenty-two hundred, just for the land. Figure in the buildings, barns, and this house and we're probably looking at closer to say, six thousand. Once we add the value of the horses, we can then determine the best course of action."

"The best course of action is to make this part of Redmond Stables."

"Are you planning on moving to Kentucky? What does Jeremiah think of that?"

"Of course, I'm not planning on moving to Kentucky, but Victoria did have Mr. Braxton. You said he was managing the property alright. Perhaps we could come to an agreement."

"You are intent on this particular plan, aren't you?"

"Yes."

"Remember, I own half of it and I am not intent on it. I know you and Jeremiah are doing well, but with a new baby, I doubt you have the money to buy me out."

"Darby, be reasonable…"

"I am being reasonable. I have no desire to own a horse farm. Especially not a horse farm in Kentucky."

SATURDAY, JULY 2, 1881

Rebecca looked at the yellow telegraph envelope, eager to open it, but knowing reading it might be a task. She was just about to break the seal when Chris entered the parlor with Rebecca's tea tray.

"Ah, my dear." Rebecca smiled as she gave the paper in her hand a shake. "I have received a telegram from Sue. Would you mind? You know how difficult small type is for me."

"Of course, Miss Rebecca." the nurse smiled and nodded as she set the tea tray down. She gestured to the serving. "Should I read the telegram before I pour your tea?"

"Please. I am anxious for news of their trip to Kentucky."

Taking the paper from the lady's hand, the nurse moved toward the window, where the morning light was best. Opening the envelope quickly with her nail, Chris unfolded the telegram and cleared her throat before beginning.

Dear Mama stop
Kentucky property beautiful stop
Many excellent horses stop
Well bred stop
Potential Derby winners stop
Books a mess stop
Need time stop
May need loan stop
Darby being a prat stop
Love Sue stop"

Rebecca chuckled and gestured for the telegram. Chris handed it back and returned to the tea tray as Rebecca placed her monocle in her left eye and made her own attempt to peruse the missive.

"Seems Sue has her heart set on this Kentucky property," Rebecca mused as Chris placed the tea to the elder woman's left.

"It would appear so. Are you keen on diversifying Redmond Stables?" Chris asked in a matter of fact way as she settled in a chair with her own cup.

"It is certainly worth considering. Charlie and I both feel that the horse world is changing. I have trusted Sue's judgment for years. Even as a girl, she has been able to identify the best of horseflesh. I am not sure I should doubt her now."

"Kentucky is a long way away. Would it be possible for you to effectively manage another farm from Virginia?"

This question gave Rebecca pause. She tapped her monocle light against her chin as she considered the idea. "You know, I do think so. Would you mind ringing for a footman, please?"

"How could I resist when you have that look in your eye?" Chris chuckled and reached for the pull near the wall.

"Good thing I still have one good one," Rebecca quipped as she glanced over Sue's telegram one more time. "Yes, I think I know how to solve Sue's most immediate problem."

ALBERT NODDED, SMILING AS HE SIPPED HIS TEA. "WELL, IF THAT is what you need, Rebecca, of course I will go to Kentucky to support Sue."

"It would be a great load off my mind if you were there. I am sure my eldest children are acting just like little brats right now. I am their mother; I know how they can bicker and argue. When they get going, if no one is there to make them get away from each other, they go at it constantly. Darby barely wanted to make the trip at all and I am sure he is anxious to get home. It seems," she handed her cousin the telegram, "Sue needs more time than her brother is willing to grant her."

"As if she needs his permission." Albert laughed as he read the telegram. "I can leave tomorrow. Assuming we can get the proper connections."

"I actually asked Mrs. Haliburton to look into it for me when she went back into town today. Your tickets will be waiting at the stationmaster's office. You leave at two o'clock. I got you the best cars possible. I think one of them may be a sleeper."

Albert smiled and handed the telegram back to his cousin. "Thank you, Rebecca. Is there a message for the troublesome duo?"

"I will have a letter tomorrow that I would like you to take, but I think your unannounced arrival will carry the message I intend to send."

"So, we are expanding into race horses?"

"It would appear so." Rebecca smiled and nodded toward the tantalus. "Pour us a brandy so we can toast our future in race horses."

ANDY LAUGHED AT THE STUPID JOKE HIS FOREMAN TOLD AS HE signed the pay book. "That's a good one, Joe!" He managed another laugh as he took the pay envelope from the paymaster seated behind the table. "Thank you, sir." Andy nodded to the man as he stepped away, opening the envelope.

He was pleased; there was more money than he had actually figured on. His willingness to pick up shifts from his coworkers had definitely worked to his benefit this week. He had an extra five dollars to do with as he pleased.

Tonight, it would be a nice steak dinner and a few drinks over at the new tavern that opened up around the corner from his boarding house. He liked the place. It was new and clean. The food was good. After the supper crowd came through there was usually at least one little card game to get in on. And because of his last name, he was a bit of a bigshot in the place. Folks called him Mr. Redmond and he had decided recently he rather liked that.

He made his way up the street to the boarding house where he kept a room on the ground floor in the back, allowing him to come and go via the alley, rather than the front door. He knew the old soldier that ran the place was sending reports to his family. The little bit of privacy the extra fifty cents for the back room afforded him was, in his opinion, well worth the money.

Andy hung up his work jacket on the hook near the door. Slipping his suspenders over his shoulders, he poured water from the jug to the bowl so he could have a quick wash. He had arranged his schedule so he had most evenings off, and on this particular evening, he wanted to not only look good, but smell mostly clean.

Stripping to the waist, he was quick to wash his face, neck and ears, washing biceps, forearms and chest with his hands last. Glancing in the mirror, he decided it was good enough as he reached for the bottle of Bay Rum. Pouring the liquid into the palm of his hand, he rolled it between his palms before applying it to his cheeks. He examined his face closely in the mirror, wishing his beard were just a bit thicker. It took him three days of trying to even come close to a five o'clock shadow. He ran the tip of his finger over a bright pink scar, about a half inch long and an inch wide, near the corner of his left eye at the top of his cheek. A permanent reminder of his last bar fight.

He decided that he was going to have to be more diplomatic and less combative. His first real scar had soured him on getting the hell beaten out of him. He knew he was handsome and he couldn't afford to look old before his time. He understood from growing up with his papa that scars were nothing to be ashamed of, but Andy had no desire to be covered in them. He knew this one would fade over time, though right now, it was just a blazing reminder of his 'youthful indiscretions,' as Papa would call them.

He acquired a clean shirt from a small wardrobe, slipping it over his head and buttoning it quickly. Next, he chose a tie he liked and then looked for a vest. He fingered the paisley vest his mama had given him for his birthday before sliding it off the hanger.

There were times like this when he missed home. He missed Mama most of all. She was always there to put her arms around him and tell him it would be alright. No matter what he did, Mama always made sure it was alright.

Looking in the mirror, he realized he was looking at an idiot. With a sigh, he stepped away from his preparations for an evening out and took a seat at the small desk by the window. Withdrawing a sheet of paper from the drawer, he then pulled his pen and inkwell from their cubby.

He fingered the pen for a moment, feeling truly homesick as he dipped the nib. The pen had been a gift from Papa when he and Buddy had finished school in Culpeper. Buddy would be taking his to West Point. Andy tried to push that thought from his head as he put pen to paper.

He remembered to print as clearly as possible so the recipient would be able to read it.

Dearest Mama,

Things are going well in Richmond. I am working hard and doing very well. My supervisor, Mr. Carlson, says I should expect to see a promotion next month. That would make me a supervisor of a small work force of about six men. Mr. Carlson says that would make me one of the youngest supervisors in the company.

I know it is not what you and Papa wanted or expected, but I am happy and doing well.

I have been going to church on Wednesday evening, because honestly, I do not like getting up on Sunday morning.

Actually, I do not like getting up early any morning, but I do the other six days of the week, because you and Papa taught me to be honest in my work and business. Thank you. I am sure that has what has led to my doing so well with the railroad. I think God may forgive me for not making Sunday morning.

Well, I will let you go now. I am off to have some supper.

I love you, Mama.

Give my love to Papa and all the others.

Andy

MONDAY, JULY 4, 1881

Rebecca stood on the veranda outside of her sitting room looking down on the remains of the Fourth of July party. There were bits of bunting still hanging from the gazebo rails and over the passageway between the house and the summer kitchen. The long tables that had supported the bowls and platters were still there, and even from a distance, she could see the stains on the table cloths where food and drink had been spilled by boisterous guests.

Charlie walked up behind his wife and wrapped his arms around her still slender waist. "Did you have a good time, my love?"

"Oh, yes. I always do. I think one of the best things we ever did was make this a daytime party. That way, no fireworks, but everyone has time to get to town before it's dark."

"I appreciate it. I have learned to deal with most things, but the sound of the mortars going off and the smell of gun powder still bothers me."

"I know, dear." Rebecca smiled. "That first Fourth of July, you tried so hard not to show how much it bothered you, but I think it did some good for the town. Every one of you soldiers, regardless of which side you fought on, had trouble with the fireworks that night. I think somehow it created a sense of being brothers in arms in a strange way."

"A very strange way, particularly when they tried me for murder. But enough of the past. How do you think Darby and Sue are doing?"

Rebecca snorted. "Personally, I wish I was a fly on the wall to see their faces when Cousin Albert walks in, and again when they see the cheque to buy Darby out."

Charlie grinned. "Want some fireworks? I should have taken you into town."

"My love, the fireworks in town are nothing compared with what Sue and Darby can generate when they are defending their respective professions."

"Law versus horses. I predict that horses win."

Rebecca slapped Charlie's arm. "You know they will. They always do with us Redmonds."

~

THURSDAY, JULY 7, 1881

Charlie propped his feet up on a log, watching with an amused grin as Buddy finished setting up their camp. Setting up was not exactly accurate, as putting away supplies from the back of the wagon was more like it. Charlie had procured his padded folding chair and put his feet up, and that was the extent of his exertions for this trip.

Many years ago, Charlie, Richard, Duncan, and Jocko had built a permanent, large half-timbered tent on the farthest side of the Redmond property, near a small pond and at the foothills of the Blue Ridge, where game was plentiful. The canvas roof had been replaced several times, and with repeated little additions and updates, the place had become more like a rustic cabin than just a timbered tent. The last major addition had been a woodstove about two years before when Charlie's arthritis would no longer stand chilly damp nights on a bunk under wool blankets.

Over the years, all the men had camped here, together and separately. They brought their children or just spent time alone in an environment well known to them when they needed time to think.

Charlie and the children spent a lot of time at this place as the kids were growing up. It was here he taught them many of the skills they would apparently need for all their adult endeavors. All of his children could shoot, fish, trap game, and make a livable environment out of the things around them.

Skills he had spent a lifetime crafting and honing were well passed to his children. He watched with an indulgent smile as Buddy started the small campfire with impressive speed.

"Coffee?" the young man asked as he ladled water from a rain barrel into an old, crusty coffeepot.

"Thank you, son."

Buddy worked quickly and had the pot on the fire in a few seconds. "I think Mama had CeCe pack us food."

"Of course she did." Charlie chuckled. "She is afraid we will starve out here if she does not see to it."

"She knows we hunt and fish." Buddy shook his head, laughing as he did. "That's just Mama."

"Well, she knows that fish and deer are not always available at midnight when you are up and famished. I also think she planned it that way for us on purpose this time. She intends for us to relax and enjoy our time together."

Buddy really laughed now, remembering many times when he and his siblings would be sitting out with their dad in the wee hours of the morning eating apples, cheese, hardtack, and jerky, watching the moon and the stars, singing songs, telling stories. Papa was the master of the scary stories that always made the girls squeal and the boys look behind them all night. After he told the one about the snipes in the forest, with the sharp little teeth, claws, and a tail made of fire, Andy refused to go into the woods for a pee for six months.

Buddy made the coffee, pouring them each a cup. He handed his dad the beverage and then settled down on the ground next to the log Charlie had propped his feet on. "I'm glad we had time to do this before I leave for The Point."

"I agree. This is your opportunity to ask me anything you might want to know about."

Buddy laughed heartily, nearly spilling his coffee down his chest. "You mean the million questions I've already asked you did not cover everything?"

"Probably so, but this is our chance to have any conversation you might want to have, man to man. You are after all, by all standards a man now."

Buddy blushed, nodding a bit. "Yeah, well, if you're talking about women, Andy gave me a pretty complete education there. Remember I had to share a room with him."

"I am not sure Andy's tutelage is something that should be relied on, Son."

"Fair point. Though he did serve as a wonderful example of what not to do."

"There is that." Charlie nodded before sipping his coffee.

"And you have been the perfect example of what to do. If I manage a marriage half as happy as you and Mama, I will consider myself very successful."

"The big difference is you will be a military officer moving from post to post. I was at the end of my military career. Our marriage was made easier by my coming back here. Your mama is not the army's biggest admirer."

"I'm not planning on getting married any time soon. I have army brass to earn first."

"Focusing on school would be the wisest course of action." Charlie nodded. "You will have plenty of time for a family after your career path is more assured. Have you given any thought to your preference?"

"I'm drawn towards engineering." Buddy chuckled. "No pun intended. I'm good with numbers and I like solving problems. Though the calvary offers a certain mystique."

"You think that until you get the first callous on your ass. What about artillery?"

"No, sir." Buddy shook his head. "I'm either building or riding. I have no desire to shoot cannon balls at things."

"There is always the infantry."

"Dad, don't even joke."

EM WAS BURIED IN HER TRUNK, HER HEAD AND SHOULDERS scrabbling somewhere in the heavy box, her feet planted to help her keep her balance as she sorted through the detritus that inevitably ended up at the bottom of the case. Muttered curses emerged periodically, though exactly what she was muttering was indistinct.

Rebecca watched her daughter, a look of bemusement hidden behind the hand that covered her mouth. *She is no longer my little girl. Well, actually, she is. I doubt she will ever get any taller, but she is clearly a woman grown. I wonder if I will ever get to host her wedding or if she is wedded to her career. Some women are, I know. Where did the time go?*

"Em, dear, what are you looking for?"

"I had a small sewing kit in here somewhere and I need to restock it."

"You mean this kit?" Rebecca picked up a leather case that was sitting on the table beside her chair.

Em emitted a long sigh. "Yes, Mama. That kit."

"Tell me about this project you are working on."

"It is fascinating. All through the area there is evidence of a tribe or tribes that we call the Mississippian Culture. They were mound builders, which gives us some interesting possibilities for researching their culture. To add to the challenge, several ethnologists like Erminnie Smith think there was an older culture that predates the Mississippians. We are starting the mapping and planning to see if we can add to what we know of them. And given that, at this point, what we know is damned little, it's an interesting challenge."

Rebecca shook her head at her daughter's excitement. "You find this kind of thing compelling. I love watching you come alive when you talk about it. To be honest, I do not understand it, but I admire it."

"Mama, you've seen the look on Sue's face when she sees a horse she particularly likes or when her favorite mare foals. You get the same look, you know. For me, this is as good as a great new foal."

Rebecca laughed. She knew the look Em described; now that she thought about it, Em had the same sort of look when she was describing her research. She nodded. "I think I do understand. It is about having a passion in life. Sue and I have it with horses. Darby with business and finance. Your father with service to his country. Yes, I do think I understand."

As Em continued to sort her belongings and set aside those things she needed for the upcoming field research in the Ohio Valley, they talked of various inconsequential things. Finally, Rebecca's curiosity got the best of her.

"So, daughter, is there any man that has attracted your attention?"

Em looked at her mother with an expression that was a cross between bemusement and disbelief. "After what I've told you about my experiences with the male students at Harvard, I am rather surprised you asked that. Frankly, I'd rather be fated to herd cats than become involved with any of these sorry excuses for gentlemen."

Rebecca laughed. "And most of the young men around here are intimidated down to the soles of their boots by your intellect. Not to mention the fact that you are a Redmond and your father scares the hell out of them."

Em laughed, being fully aware of the position her father and her family held in the Culpeper community. "I'm afraid that a small-town boy with little education would not be my choice in a partner, Mama."

"I never thought that a Yankee army officer would be mine, but…"

T. NOVAN & TAYLOR RICKARD

"That's the thing, Mama. Watching you and Papa, Darby and Stella, Aunt Elizabeth and Uncle Richard, Sue and Jeremiah, and even Ro and Alison, has taught me what a relationship can be. I'd rather do without than settle for less than what you've taught me it can be. Until then, you know that the life of the intellect makes me happy."

Rebecca smiled ruefully. "I hope you find what you are hoping for, dear."

MONDAY, AUGUST 1, 1881

"Imp, I still do not understand why you chose to travel in a commercial car. You could have had our car if you wanted it."

"Papa, I told you, I am only going to Philadelphia, where I am meeting the rest of the team. Then we will have the new research car. Anyway, aren't you and Mama going somewhere for a little break?"

Just then, Rebecca strolled up to join her daughter and husband on the platform at the Culpeper station. "Charlie, dear, you were the one telling me that our daughter was a grown woman and that we had to let her make her own decisions." *Much as I hate it,* Rebecca added to herself.

"Thank you, Mama. I do appreciate it." Em turned to her father. "Papa, if Sue can go off to Kentucky to take over another horse farm, I can certainly get myself to Philadelphia in one piece."

"Yes, dear." Charlie had learned long ago from Rebecca that sometimes that was the only available answer.

"Now, Em, you ARE going to be home for Thanksgiving this year."

"Of course, Mama. I promised, so I will be here."

"Thank you, dear. It will seem so strange to not have Buddy home, but they only give him a day off for Thanksgiving, and he obviously cannot get home and back. I just hope that Andy will come home from Richmond. I do so love to have all my children home."

"Yes, Mama."

Fortunately for Em, the conductor, standing beside the entrance to the passenger car, bellowed.

"I have to go now." She embraced her mother, noticing that not only was Rebecca several inches shorter than her, but she felt so frail under her hands. It was startling to the girl, who had always seen her mother as big and strong and vital. She kissed Rebecca gently on each cheek, then released her and turned to her father. Charlie's bear hug was just as satisfying as it had always been. *Papa's like an oak tree,* she thought.

Papa handed her carpet bag of books and papers to the conductor. Em mounted the little foot stool, then onto the train step. She turned to her parents, smiling gently, and said as clearly as she could over the lump that had suddenly formed in her throat, "I love you. See you soon."

Rebecca smiled through the tears that were finally running down her cheeks, waved, and mouthed, "I love you, too."

Charlie stood there, biting his lower lip to keep from joining his wife in tears, and waved.

Em entered the parlor car and chose a seat on the left side so she would not be sitting in the direct sun. Even in the early morning, train cars were hot, rather like sun ovens. The window was open, so inevitably smoke and ashes would blow in and get in her hair and clothes, but at least there was something of a breeze to give a little relief from the unremitting heat.

She pulled a book out of her carpet bag and settled in to read.

BRIDGET SAT IN BEULAH'S OFFICE, HER HEAD IN HER HANDS, crying helplessly. The elderly housekeeper came in with a tray with tea, cookies, and cups in her hands. She poured the tea and set a cup in front of the sobbing girl.

"Tell Aunt Beulah what the trouble is, child."

For a few more minutes, nothing was heard from the young woman but sobs. Finally, in a tiny voice, Bridget said, "I canna do it. She wants a new dress every time, and I canna do it."

Beulah thought for a minute. "Well, make a list of every dress for every day. Add all the other do-dads. Then you can pack what you need and know what to get out when its needed."

The sobbing got worse. "Oh, Aunt Beulah, I canna." More sobs ensued. "I canna read or write," Bridget hiccupped out.

Beulah took a deep breath and let it out with a sigh. "Let me think on it, child. I will find you some help. And you can ask Louis for help, too. He can read and write and knows Miz 'Becca's style."

"Yes, ma'am. Thank you." Mournfully, Bridget sipped her tea, got herself back together, and wandered out to try and find Louis.

Beulah immediately sent for one of the boys she used as runners. While she waited for him to arrive, she went about writing a message. Help was on the way.

EM IGNORED THE STARTS AND STOPS OF THE TRAIN AS IT MADE its way from Culpeper to Warrenton to Manassas to Falls Church to Alexandria, picking up and dropping off passengers as they went. Finally, they pulled into the station in Washington proper.

The conductor came by and asked Em if she wanted to debark and get some luncheon and a cold drink. He said there was a pleasant little tea room inside the station, and told her she had approximately an hour and a half before they were to resume their travels. He also offered to watch her carpet bag if she wished.

"Oh, yes, please. I could drink about a gallon of lemonade! If you would be so kind to watch my case, I would appreciate it, though why anyone would want to take it, as it only has books and stuffy old scholarly papers." She laughed. "Well, then, onward to luncheon and a cold drink."

Em pulled herself together, slipped on her gloves, since no proper lady would ever be seen in a public place like a train station without them, and strolled down the ramp to the main station building. Looking around, she spotted the little tea shop off to one side of the large lobby of the station, stopped for a moment to buy a newspaper, and entered the restaurant.

Within a few minutes, she had been seated at a small table for two, had gotten her first lemonade, and was reading the paper while she waited for her chicken salad with walnuts and grapes and another lemonade to appear.

"Excuse me, Miss Redmond?" A soft voice inquired, as if the speaker was not quite sure that Em was Em.

She looked up from the paper she was reading with a curious look on her face. The woman standing before her, with dark hair, dark eyes, interestingly tanned skin, and wearing a quiet, tasteful travelling suit, looked familiar.

"I am sure I know you, but to be honest, I cannot place you."

Camille laughed, a low-pitched chuckle. "I am not surprised. I wasn't sure you were you either. I'm Camille Parker. We met at Professor Putnam's last year. He telegraphed me day before yesterday and asked if I wanted to accompany the team going to

Ohio. Seems it occurred to him that an ethnologist with first nation experience might be useful."

"Oh, of course. I remember. You were with Mrs. Smith." Em smiled. "Please, have a seat. I was just about to have a quick bite of lunch. Would you like something?"

"Thank you. Some tea would be nice."

Em waved the server over, asked for tea for her companion, and the two settled into a pleasant hour of small talk before their train was due to leave for Philadelphia."

LATE THAT NIGHT, A YOUNG WOMAN KNOCKED ON THE DOOR OF Beulah's house in Redmond Grove. When she opened the door, she pulled the young woman into the house and wrapped her in a loving embrace. "Thank God you are here, dear. You are desperately needed!"

CHAPTER 14

TUESDAY, AUGUST 2, 1881

EARLY THAT MORNING, Bridget came down to the kitchen to get a cup of coffee and an early breakfast before she started in on the daunting process of packing Rebecca's clothes and accessories for the upcoming trip. Sitting at the kitchen table was a welcome figure. Lizbet, clad in a simple dress, quietly sipping a cup of coffee, was waiting for the young woman.

"I understand we have a challenge ahead of us. Getting Miz Rebecca ready for a week of formal events is, um, interesting, to say the least. Get yourself some breakfast and then we will start in on it." Lizbet smiled gently at Bridget.

"Oh, Lizbet, thank you, thank you, thank you. How did you know?"

"You have a champion, Bridget."

"Oh, thank you so much, Beulah. Thank you both so much."

After finishing eating, the two women trudged up to Rebecca's dressing room – a room that had been added to accommodate the mistress's rather extensive wardrobe. She had long ago outgrown the chests, bureaus, and armoires.

Lizbet pulled a large clothes rack out into the middle of the floor. "Here is what we are going to do. Miz Rebecca is going to need a morning dress, an afternoon receiving dress, and a dinner dress every day. She may need two or three ball gowns as well, but we will deal with those later."

"How can I keep all of this straight?"

"I'm going to teach you a little trick I learned years ago. I color code things, then use tags to keep track of what goes with what."

"But... but... I canna read."

"Not a problem. You know colors, so all the morning dresses will have one color tissue, the day dresses another, dinner dresses a third, and for accessories, I will use symbols. Match the symbol and you have it."

"Symbols? Like stars or crosses?"

"Letters. I will write out your letters. Each one has a unique shape. That way, you can start learning them while you work."

"Oh. How smart."

The two women worked throughout the day sorting Rebecca's clothes. They selected seven morning dresses, seven day dresses, seven dinner dresses, and three ball gowns. For each dress, they carefully selected accessories, including shawls or scarves, reticules, parasols, slippers or shoes, and jewelry. For some of the outfits, they decided that some of the accessories could be shared, and Lizbet duly noted the exceptions. Finally, when all was sorted to Lizbet and Bridget's satisfaction, they carefully labelled each item so that Bridget could match the right elements together into a stylish whole. Underwear, bustle frames, and sleeping clothes were selected and set aside as well.

By the end of the day, both women were tired, but satisfied

with their progress. Lizbet smiled to herself as they parted for the night. Not only was Miss Rebecca prepared, but Bridget had learned to recognize her letters. Tomorrow, they would pack the trunks, again using Lizbet's code to sort things so that dressing Miss Rebecca would not require unpacking all of the trunks at the same time.

THURSDAY, AUGUST 4, 1881

Rebecca and Charlie stood on the steps of Mountain View, watching as Otis and his staff finished loading the luggage on Charlie's second-best travelling coach. Four well-matched horses were hitched to each coach. Alfred sat on the box of the big one, looking pleased with himself.

Behind him, driving a smaller coach, Seth Jones looked a little nervous, though just as proud as Alfred. He had most of the luggage, as well as carrying Louis and Bridget in his coach.

Louis and Bridget were seated in the smaller coach, looking excited, though a little cramped with the bulk of the luggage loaded with them. They, too, were anticipating the upcoming adventure. Indeed, Bridget had never been on a trip with her mistress – she had never been on any trip other than the frightening trip to America in steerage, then a sooty train ride from New York to Culpeper. Now she was going with Miz Rebecca to some place called The Homestead where all the ladies were fancy and the gentlemen were elegant. She just hoped she wouldn't embarrass Miz Rebecca or General Charlie.

Louis was looking forward to the food.

THEY HEADED SOUTH AND WEST OF CULPEPER, STOPPING IN Charlottesville for lunch before the horses pulled them up into the Blue Ridge mountains and through Rockfish Gap. The descent down into the Shenandoah Valley was a little touchy, as Alfred and Seth had to ride the brakes to keep the coaches from overtaking the horses.

As they rose up into the mountains, the temperature started to drop and a cooling breeze blew off the peaks, making the trip far more pleasant that the first miles down into Charlottesville.

In the late afternoon, they pulled into a lovely inn that had obviously once been a private home in Staunton. Charlie had arranged for dinner to be brought to their suite, and the two of them simply relaxed, cooled off, and made an early night of it. The longest leg of their trip was over.

～

FRIDAY, AUGUST 5, 1881

The drive through the Shenandoah Valley was beautiful. This area was lush with wheat, corn, sorghum, and large truck gardens, with tomatoes, squash, beans, collards, and a host of other vegetables and fruits that were commonly found on people's tables. Apple orchards were common, and occasionally one could smell the telltale aromas of corn mash or boiling cider that indicated a home distillery was busy making moonshine or applejack.

Charlie and Rebecca spent time discussing a number of issues before them, including Andy's wayward ways, the complexity of adding the Kentucky farm to the family's holdings, and several investment opportunities they were both considering. However, for most of the time, they just relaxed and chatted about the changing landscape they passed through as they started into the foothills of the Allegheny mountains.

They arrived at The Homestead in mid-afternoon, in time for a late luncheon, but too early to check into their suite. The innkeeper came to meet them personally while Louis and Bridget worked to unload their luggage. He escorted them to a garden seating area behind the three-story brick building that looked west into the mountains.

"Can I get you some luncheon? Our kitchen is still open, as they are preparing for afternoon tea."

Rebecca smiled and Charlie answered. "Yes, please. Just something light, and some mint iced tea, if you could."

"Certainly, sir. It will just take a few moments."

"And if you could, sir," Rebecca added. "Please join us and tell us something of this lovely facility."

"It would be my pleasure. Let me get your lunch started and I will be right with you."

Within a few minutes, there were cold glasses of tea on the table and the innkeeper had rejoined them. "I'm Thomas Goode. My family owns The Homestead. This beautiful place has housed an inn since 1766, when it was just a wooden building with eighteen bedrooms, a kitchen, and a common room. Even then, people came here as a resort and to rest because of the hot springs. Even before then, the Indians came to the springs as a place of healing."

Rebecca smiled. "Even without the springs, I can see why. It is a lovely escape from the heat of summer, and so peaceful."

"That is what my grandfather, Dr. Thomas Goode, thought when he bought the land in 1832. He wanted to build a spa like those in Europe – you know, Vichy, Baden, Malvern, and Bath. So, he built this hotel, got a good chef from New York, and created a place where people could relax, take the mineral waters, and enjoy the comfort of the springs in a beautiful setting."

"It certainly is beautiful," Charlie said. "Tell me, is there any way one can enjoy the waters with some privacy? I was badly wounded in the war and most people do not like to look upon the scars."

"Why, of course. We have several cabanas with tubs cut into the rock and we pipe the waters into them for those who would rather not expose themselves to strangers."

"Excellent. Most excellent." Charlie turned to Rebecca. "Perhaps you would join me, my love?"

"Of course, dear. I would love to."

Just then, their luncheon arrived. Mr. Goode excused himself after telling them that tea would be served here in the garden at four and dinner would be served at eight in the main dining room. He added that a cotillion was planned for Saturday evening, with an early dinner, dancing, and a supper served at eleven.

Once in their room, Rebecca threw herself down on the bed. "Charlie, I love you more than I can tell you, but a two-day carriage trip in August is just plain exhausting!"

Charlie stripped off his coat, tie and waistcoat, while kicking off his boots. "I understand. At least you can wear cotton and linen." He sat down and pulled off his socks. "Shall I call Bridget for you?"

"No, dear. I think you can manage to unbutton me."

Charlie smiled and leaned down to kiss Rebecca's shoulders. "I am very sure I can."

～

DINNER THAT EVENING WAS SERVED AT SHARED TABLES, MUCH like they had experienced on the ship to England. They were seated at the table with an interesting gentleman named M.E. Ingalls and his wife Louisa. Ingalls was looking into bringing the rail lines for the Chesapeake and Ohio Railroad Company into western Virginia and over into West Virginia.

At the table was a gentleman and his wife that Rebecca and Charlie had met in New York at a political event, Mr. John Pierpont Morgan and his wife Frances. Also, there was another banker, Anthony Drexel, and his wife Ellen.

Drexel looked at Charlie with a question in his eyes. "General Redmond? You wouldn't be the Redmond that served as our ambassador to Great Britain during Grant's administration, would you?"

"Yes, sir. I had that honor."

"You worked some excellent deals, General Redmond. Surviving the maneuverings of the East India Company as they tried to survive was quite an accomplishment. Certainly, neither your predecessor nor your replacement did as well."

"Thank you, Mr. Drexel. I had some outstanding assistance."

Ingalls spoke up. "Ah, well, obviously we have assembled some successful businessmen at the table. I have a proposal for you, gentlemen."

Charlie looked at Rebecca with a raised eyebrow, but did not disabuse the gentlemen of his belief that the only business people at the table were men. He expected Rebecca to handle that attitude adjustment if and when it was appropriate.

Ingalls went on with the enthusiasm of a fanatic. "Well, I believe Dr. Goode had a great idea with this site, but unless people can get here more easily, I doubt it will grow beyond what it is today." He grinned. "Fortunately, I know that the Chesapeake and Ohio company is planning to run track into this area. Since we know where they are going, it will not take too much more to bring a spur into Warm Springs. With that, The Homestead could become the pre-eminent spa in the country."

Rebecca raised an eyebrow. "Suppose the railroad does come near. This facility would still have to be expanded and modernized to support such a goal."

Drexel took the opportunity to wipe his lips with his napkin. It also hid his smirk. "Mr. Ingalls, you might want to know that Mrs. Redmond owns the most successful horse breeding farm in Virginia, and is, I believe, worth more than her husband, whose personal wealth is not inconsiderable."

J.P. Morgan smiled. "Indeed, Mrs. Redmond has used our banking services for a number of years. I would listen to her if I were you."

Rebecca smiled softly. "Of course, it is easy to become entranced by a place as lovely as this one."

"One day, I hope to have my vision become reality."

"I wish you luck, Mr. Ingalls."

Charlie leaned over and whispered in his wife's ear, "Morgan's bank? Really? I own a bank, you know?"

She whispered back, teasingly, "He has a bigger interest rate."

AS THEY PREPARED FOR BED THAT NIGHT, CHARLIE CHUCKLED AT his wife. "You rather gave Mr. Ingalls a little dose of reality. I thought he was going to swallow his tongue when both Morgan and Drexel stood up for you."

"And you wonder why our daughters are generally seen as feisty and pushy – they have to be."

"They learned it from the best, my love." Charlie finished

stripping down to his underwear. "Would you like to soak in some smelly water tomorrow morning, dear?"

"Certainly, if we can get one of those cabanas. Somehow I would like a little water play with my husband – and no witnesses!"

SATURDAY, AUGUST 6, 1881

Charlie and Rebecca, dressed in morning dress, walked into the cabana that had been made available to them. The young woman who escorted them to the small building asked if she could assist them, but was excused. Charlie walked to the door and shot the bolt home to lock it. Privacy was his concern, not only to protect his long-held secret, but also to give the two of them a bit of privacy.

"So, darling, can you get my buttons?" Rebecca asked with a sultry smile on her face. They may have been well into middle-age, with gray in their hair and lines around their eyes, but the fire between them still burned. It was just a little slower to burst into flames, due to age and injury.

"Of course, my love." Charlie gently worked his way through the row of small buttons down Rebecca's back. As her shoulders became exposed to the warm moist air in the cabana, they were met by Charlie's warm, moist lips as well. Rebecca smiled. Charlie was still and always the gentle lover of her soul.

He helped her slip out of the rest of her clothes, then started to strip his own away, until her hands gently moved his aside. One of Rebecca's favorite activities was to slowly reveal her beloved spouse's beautiful combination of strength and softness. Even though scarred and worn, to Rebecca, Charlie's unique blend of male and female characteristics always touched her' heart and ignited her passion.

Once they had both disrobed, Charlie spent a few minutes just holding Rebecca in his arms, always relishing the feel of skin to skin and the warmth and unity that holding her in his arms always gave both of them. Then slowly, they moved to the natural depression in the rocks that had been augmented carefully by the builders of this spa. Slipping into the water together, they sighed at the feel of the naturally heated water against their skin.

The heat on Charlie's arthritic limbs felt glorious. Even their big tub at home did not offer the almost instant relief of his constant, low-grade aches that this pool did. For Rebecca, the pool eased the strain on her leg that was permanently weakened from her stroke. The two of them lay, wrapped together, floating in the gently bubbling water, savoring the sense of peace that the solitude and the healing waters brought them.

Slowly, Rebecca started tracing random patterns on Charlie's chest, playing with his nipples and stroking along his ribs down to his belly. Charlie ran his fingers up and down Rebecca's spine. While both had acquired a bit of padding over the years, that just added softness to their forms. Yes, Charlie's stomach was no longer the washboard it once had been, but he was still fairly lean for a man of his age. Rebecca's once flat belly was now sporting a small pooch, but the skin was still silky smooth.

The mutual caresses slowly became more intimate as the two joined into one. It was bliss.

~

SUNDAY, AUGUST 14, 1881

The coaches were packed. Rebecca and Charlie were having a last glass of tea on the porch with Mr. Goode. Bridget was settling in the second coach, gratefully slumped in her seat after an exhausting week, with at least three changes for Miz Rebecca daily, and four on Wednesday and Saturday. Louis was standing beside the first coach, waiting to help Miz Rebecca and Gen'l Charlie up.

Finally, they were on their way home.

Charlie settled Rebecca, then relaxed back into his own seat. He reached out with his left hand, took Rebecca's hand in his own, and tapped on the ceiling of the coach with his walking stick to signal to Alfred it was time to start.

They were quiet for a while as they headed back toward Staunton. Then Rebecca spoke quietly. "Thank you, Charlie. We both needed the break – from the heat, from the stress. It was a good week."

Charlie smiled gently. "I must say, I enjoyed your lesson for Mr. Ingalls. Having Drexel and Morgan there did not hurt one little bit."

"And you wonder why the girls and I have to lesson the odd gentleman on occasion."

"I do not wonder. I have seen how some men treat their women like ornaments on their arms or baby machines. I am simply fortunate enough to have a wife who is smarter than most men and stronger than almost anyone I have EVER known." He squeezed her hand. "I love you, my 'Becca."

"And I you, Charlie." Rebecca paused for a moment. "You know, you dance very well, even with the leg. It was so lovely to be able to dance together again."

Charlie nodded, waiting for Rebecca to say more. Sometimes it was better to let her just have her head.

"You know, I always thought that one of the things that happened as a result of 'the change' was that I would no longer have any need for intimacy nor would I have any further attractiveness to the gentlemen. Seems I was wrong." She giggled as Charlie reached over with his right hand and softly caressed her cheek, down to her neck and ending his stroke at her decolletage.

He leaned down and whispered in her ear, "My dear, when you love someone like we love each other, desire and passion never die." He sat back up. "Just sometimes they have to limp along like our bodies do."

Rebecca laughed at him, slapped him with her folded fan, and kissed him on his cheek, in that order.

"So, husband, what are we going to do when all of the children are out on their own?"

The rest of the trip home was spent on planning for the future, sharing fantasies of the possibilities, and mourning the fact that their children were growing up and they were growing older.

~

THURSDAY, SEPTEMBER 1, 1881

Buddy threw the last of his luggage onto the back of the carriage that held his mother, father, and Uncle Rex, and then mounted his favorite horse. Seth was already up on Buddy's second favorite horse. He had volunteered to go to West Point as Buddy's batman, and was quickly hired by General Charlie for the job.

"Is that it, son?" Charlie was not anxious, exactly, but he was concerned that Rebecca would not be able to hold up as her last child left home.

"Yes, Papa. I am more than ready." Excitement was rolling off the young man. He was going back to The Point, this time as a cadet. Even though Rex was coming with him, it was his first step out into the world as his own man rather than as one of the Redmond children.

The trip to the train station went too quickly for Rebecca.

Buddy and Seth quickly stripped the horses of their tack, brushed them down and loaded them into their car, while Rex supervised loading the humans' luggage into the parlor car that would take them to New York.

The conductor called out.

Charlie gave Buddy a hug and a firm pat on the back, then the young man turned to his mother.

Rebecca cradled his face in her hands, looking up into the tall young man's eyes. "Charles Huger Redmond the Younger, go with all my love and faith in you, that you will be as good a man and as good a soldier as your father. And know that we will always love you." She pulled his head down to her level, kissing his forehead, both cheeks, and his lips in a motherly blessing. "Now, go." She could say no more.

He turned, grinned at his father, and jumped up the steps to joined Rex and Seth on the small platform that was the entrance to the parlor car. The engineer sounded the train's whistle and the cars jerked as they started to move down the track.

Rebecca and Charlie stood on the platform at the station, waving until the train disappeared around the curve, headed north.

Charlie put his arm around his wife. Silently, they walked back to the carriage. For the entire trip home, Charlie simply held

Rebecca. Not a word was said. Not a tear was shed, a condition that had Charlie more than a little concerned.

They walked into the house. Rebecca stopped in the middle of the hall, turning around and looking a little lost. Em had left a month before, Sue was back from Kentucky but had her own home, her own husband, her own child. Darby and Stella were in Richmond more than they were at home. Andy was established with the train company and had written that he might be transferred to the terminus in Memphis. Now Buddy was gone.

"It is too quiet." Rebecca gave Charlie a lost look. "They are all gone." Tears finally threatened to fall.

Charlie wrapped his arms around his beloved wife. "We had planned to spend time together, just the two of us, when the war ended. Now we can, my love."

Rebecca buried her face in Charlie's shoulder. A watery chuckle drifted up. "Things never go the way we plan. Why should that change now that the children are off on their own?"

"Why, indeed, my love. But I would not trade a moment."

Rebecca took Charlie's right hand in her own and gently kissed the scars where the last two fingers should have been. "Oh, I can think of some moments I would rather trade, but never the children and never you, my love."

T. Novan and Taylor Rickard

The Redmond Civil War Era Romance Series

Book 1: Words Heard in Silence

Book 2: Paths of Peace

Book 3: Enemies in the Gates

Book 4: Honor Thy Father

Book 5: Love Beareth All Things

Blayne Cooper and T. Novan

Madam President

First Lady

Susanne M. Beck and T. Novan

Driven

ABOUT AUSXIP PUBLISHING

AUSXIP Publishing opened its doors in 2015 and came about as a natural evolution to the expansion of the AUSXIP Network. We publish quality stories with strong female characters that inspire, strengthen and enrich the soul. To build up, to create a sense of achievement and most importantly to entertain. We love reading about strong women who change their world. Come with us on our journey and lose yourself in our books and grow with us.

Official Site
https://ausxippublishing.com

AUSXIP Publishing Store
https://store.ausxippublishing.com

Facebook:
https://facebook.com/ausxippublishing

Twitter:
https://twitter.com/ausxippublish

Instagram:
https://instagram.com/ausxippublishing

Made in the USA
Monee, IL
17 April 2021

64840502R00233